Praise for Anna Schmidt

"Readers wanting a good old-fashioned Western romance need look no further than this one."

—*Dear Author* for *The Drifter*

"A satisfying read and one that has me excited for more. Schmidt definitely wowed!"

—*Historical Romance Reviews* for *The Drifter*

"The perfect read."

—*RT Book Reviews* for *The Lawman*

"A fast-paced story with well-developed characters, a sneaky antagonist, and a plot twist that will leave readers speechless."

—*Fresh Fiction* for *The Lawman*

"With its lovingly crafted narrative, spirited heroine, dark hero, and realistic backdrop, readers will truly enjoy the third of Schmidt's Last Chance Cowboys series."

—*RT Book Reviews* for *The Outlaw*

"A warm, satisfying, gently sexy Western historical romance."

—*Kirkus Reviews* for *The Outlaw*

A

Also by Anna Schmidt

LAST CHANCE COWBOYS
THE
RANCHER

ANNA SCHMIDT

sourcebooks
casablanca

Published by Sourcebooks Casablanca, an imprint of Sourcebooks,
Inc.
P.O. Box 4410, Naperville, Illinois 60567-4410
(630) 961-3900
Fax: (630) 961-2168
sourcebooks.com

Printed and bound in the United States of America.
OPM 10 9 8 7 6 5 4 3 2 1

One

Arizona Territory, Early Spring 1891

TREY PORTERFIELD STOOD IN THE OPEN DOORWAY OF THE outbuilding that served as the ranch's office. From there, he could see Juanita Mendez moving around the kitchen of the main house, a large rambling adobe structure that spoke well of the prosperity of the ranch and its owners. As usual, Juanita, who had been with the family for as long as Trey could remember, was gesturing to someone out of his view—her husband, Eduardo, no doubt. The evening was mild with a lingering hint of this year's unusually cold winter. But a good deal more than the weather had brought hard times over the last several months. The trouble was not between man and nature, but between man and man—neighbor against neighbor.

"*Hola, Jefe.*" Javier, Trey's best friend and Juanita's younger son, crossed the yard, the smoke from his cigarette trailing after him.

"Better not let Nita catch you smoking," Trey said.

Javier smiled. "I'm twenty-three, and *Jefa* still treats me like a kid."

"I dare you to call your mother 'boss woman' to her face," Trey teased, but then he sobered. "'Course Nita's that way with me too—babying me and bossing me in turn. Especially since Mama died."

The two men were quiet for a long moment. "I miss her—your mama," Javier said as he blew out a long stream of smoke. "I miss them all—Maria and Chet, Amanda too. Seems awful quiet around here these days."

Trey nodded. It was true. The family had scattered after his mother's death. His sister Maria and her husband now lived in California with their three children. His sister Amanda had married an undercover Wells Fargo detective; he'd since left that job to become sheriff of the entire region. They lived in Tucson—close, but not close enough to Trey's way of thinking.

"I miss Helen too," Javier said quietly.

Helen Johnson had caught Javier's eye a few years earlier when his older brother, Rico, had been courting Helen's sister. But after her father died, Helen and her mother had gone back east where they had family.

"You still have Rico—and Louisa."

Javier grunted. "It's Rico's fault that I never got my chance with Helen. Running off the way he did with Louisa? How was Mr. Johnson ever supposed to trust me to do the right thing by Helen?"

Old Man Johnson had disowned Louisa after she and Rico had eloped and announced if he so much as thought he saw Javier coming around his youngest daughter, he would shoot to kill.

"Rico and Mr. Johnson made their peace," Trey reminded his friend.

"And then the old man up and dies, and Rico's got his business to run, so he can't take on running the ranch for Mrs. Johnson."

"You could go east, find work closer to Helen there," Trey reminded him, wanting to shift his friend's focus to something more positive.

"I guess." It was a grudging admission and one he would probably never act on. "Rico says I dodged a bullet. He never much cared for Helen, the way she didn't stand with Louisa."

"Tell you what. Let Addie know you're looking for a wife, and my guess is she'll have you matched up in no time."

Trey's older brother, Jess, was the marshal in the nearby town of Whitman Falls, and his wife, Addie, had taken over her father's medical practice.

Javier snorted. "I doubt Jess would want her to get involved with the likes of me. I'm not exactly your brother's favorite cowboy these days."

When a sheep rancher bought the Johnson place after the old man's death, Javier had turned all his frustration on herders in general, picking fights whenever he and any sheep rancher crossed paths. Trey had had to get him out of jail more than once, and Jess had warned them both that next time, Javier would be bound over for trial and sit in jail until the circuit judge reached town.

"But he's my foreman—*our* foreman," Trey had argued, reminding his brother that the ranch still belonged to the entire family. "We're short-handed as it is."

"You wouldn't be if this cowpoke could keep his mouth shut. You should get Rico to come back."

"Rico has no interest in working for us now that he's taken over the livery and moved his family into town. Besides, Javier is family," he had reminded Jess. "What we need is to find a way for herders and cattlemen to share the land."

Jess had laughed. "Not likely in our lifetime."

Arizona Territory still had a good deal of open range, acreage that now needed to accommodate both cattle and sheep. In the fight over land and water rights, the "herders," as the sheep ranchers were known, were at a distinct disadvantage. It took only two or three men and some well-trained dogs to manage a couple thousand sheep, while the same number of cattle required a dozen or more cowhands. So right away, the herders were outnumbered four to one, and lately, that disparity had cost them dearly. Just six months earlier, a herder named Calvin Stokes and his shepherds had been murdered. Trey hadn't known Calvin, but as a peace-loving man who treasured the land, Trey wanted no part of violence.

As if to underscore his thoughts, Trey heard the distant bleating of sheep.

Javier threw down his cigarette and ground it into the dirt with heel of his boot. "Them woolies sound closer than they ought to be, Trey. I'll just get a couple of the boys from the bunkhouse and ride out there and..."

"You get some sleep. We need to get started on branding early tomorrow so we can move the herd to higher ground for the summer. I'll take care of this."

"But—"

Trey rested his hand on Javier's shoulder. "Last thing we need around here is more trouble, Javier, and you know how some of the hands feel about the sheep ranchers." He chose his words carefully, even though it was Javier's constant harping on the damage sheep did to the land that had gotten the other hands riled up in the first place.

Javier snorted. "You've always been a dreamer, Trey. You still think we can all live in peace? After what's happened these last months? There's a war comin', *amigo*."

"A war with a price that's too dear to pay, Javier. When neighbor turns on neighbor, it's time to find another way." Trey headed for the corral, lifting his saddle from the fence as he passed. "I'll be back directly. You and the others get some sleep."

Javier wasn't easily dismissed. "Calvin Stokes was not our neighbor or friend," he argued.

"He was a good man," Trey said as he pulled the cinch tight on the saddle and patted his horse's flanks. "A good man with a wife and a youngster. A good man who was the first of our neighbors to die because of this ruckus. We need to be sure nothing goes that far ever again, or he will surely not be the last."

"If Stokes's wife had the sense God gave her, she'd pack up and head back where she came from." Javier stroked the horse's muzzle while Trey mounted.

"Now there's a thought. She just abandons that flock of woolies, leaves them to roam free and deliver the lambs they're carrying all on their own while she hightails it back east or wherever she might have people. That's your plan for her?"

"She's got family here. Word is she's no longer in charge. From what I hear, her brother and her husband's cousin have been running things since the funeral."

Trey frowned. "You think she signed everything over to them?"

"Don't know details." Javier shrugged. "There's been some talk about her and the cousin marrying. Seems to me if the cousin is willing to take on the debt plus her and the boy, that might be her best choice."

"That's one option, I suppose." Trey had noticed the family in passing when they started coming to his church. He had been vaguely aware of the woman and boy. She usually wore a sunbonnet that covered her features and did not stay after to visit with the other women, even wives of other herders. Calvin Stokes had made sure of that, hustling his wife and son away as soon as Reverend Moore spoke the benediction and took his place by the door to greet his congregation.

Once, Trey had found himself standing in the aisle next to Stokes. He had smiled and extended his hand in greeting. "I'm Trey Porterfield," he'd said.

Stokes had stared at Trey's outstretched hand for a moment, then ducked his head and ushered his family up the aisle. By the time Trey had reached the exit, they were walking briskly down the road. Herders rarely used horses. They traveled by burro or on foot. The Stokes woman had matched her husband stride for stride while the boy rode a burro.

Javier lit another cigarette. "You got something else in mind for the widow Stokes?"

"What if I was to buy her out, leaving her free to go back to her family? If that's what she wants."

"You're saying you'd make the Double J part of this place and bring it back to cattle?"

"I'm saying maybe it's time to explore what might happen if cows and sheep shared one ranch." Trey was as surprised as Javier was to hear himself say this. But the more he considered the idea, the more he thought it was well worth contemplating. "Seems to me if we could make it work for the animals, we could make it work for the people," he added as he gathered the reins.

"You're joshing me, right?"

Trey shrugged. "Maybe." He grinned down at his friend. "Maybe not."

As he rode away, he heard Javier laughing and was pretty sure he heard the word *loco* echoing through the silence of the night.

Of course, Javier was right to ridicule him. The idea was absurd, and the truth was, he hadn't been thinking anything beyond finding some way the sheepherders and cattlemen might work together. Still tonight, as he left the boundaries of his property and heard the distant bleats, he had to wonder: What if both sheep and cattle could share the land? There would have to be separate pastures to accommodate the differences in grazing, but with all this land, why wouldn't it work?

As he crossed the open range where the sheep were settling in for the night, Trey tipped his hat when one of the shepherds keeping watch glanced his way. Joining forces might just work if he could persuade Mrs. Stokes to hear him out.

His best approach might be to take Addie's advice. The Stokes boy was sickly, as Trey had been as a boy. Addie had been after him to stop by and visit.

"Especially now," Addie had argued, "with his father dead and no siblings to lean on, Trey. Seeing you and all you've accomplished in spite of being so sick would maybe help them both see possibilities for the boy's future."

She made a good case. Maybe tomorrow, he would ride over there and pay a neighborly call on Mrs. Stokes and her son. For now, he would just enjoy the night ride over the range that lay between the two properties, the free range that was fast disappearing as more and more people discovered this land Trey loved so deeply.

❧

Juanita saw Trey ride away and shook her head. He was the youngest of the four Porterfield children she and her husband had helped raise and, to her way of thinking, the least prepared to deal with the realities of life.

"There he goes, riding off to who knows where when he needs his rest," she fussed, setting a plate of fresh churros on the kitchen table. The pastry was Trey's favorite. "That *niño* has about as much business trying to run a ranch as I do."

"That *niño* is a grown man, Nita," Eduardo reminded her. "He is doing a fine job."

"Pushes himself and he'll pay a price." Juanita poured herself a cup of coffee and sat down heavily in the chair next to her husband. She rubbed her swollen knees with one hand, held her cup in the other. "That boy is an artist more than a rancher or businessman. He needs to get back to that."

"Trey is no longer a boy, Juanita, and thankfully, his health is no longer a question. If you insist on worrying about someone, I suggest it be our Javier."

They sat in silence for a long moment, both knowing that Eduardo had a point. Their youngest son had changed a good deal over the last several months. These days, the boy Juanita remembered as so good-natured had become impatient and sullen, taking the most innocent question or comment as criticism. She frowned and sighed as she stared at the dark liquid in her cup. "He spends too much time at the Collins ranch," she said.

Eduardo nodded. Pete Collins was not only antagonistic toward the herders, but as the area's second-largest landowner, he had the power to persuade others to join in his fight. "Perhaps Trey could speak with Javier."

Juanita shrugged and sipped her coffee. After a moment, she said, "I miss the old days. So much is changing."

Eduardo covered his wife's hand with his. "Remember the first day we came here?"

The memory could always pull Juanita out of a sour mood. They had driven their rickety wagon up the trail toward the small adobe house that now served as the ranch's business office. Juanita had been pregnant with Javier. Their older son, Rico, had been nine. The sun was setting, and that thin line of smoke rising from the chimney was like a star they had been following for the last half hour.

Isaac Porterfield, Trey's father, had stepped outside, and when he saw them, insisted they stay the night. Eduardo had accepted and offered to sleep in the barn. He would repair their wagon, and they would be on their way at dawn.

And that was when a woman with hair the color of a sunset burst through the door. She'd carried a frail-looking boy of about three or four—Trey. Three older children pushed forward as well.

"Absolutely not," Trey's mother, Constance, announced.

Juanita recalled how she had assumed the woman was objecting to the offer of hospitality, but how wrong she had been. Constance Porterfield had ushered them inside the small house, sent her children to fetch a wooden bench from outside to add sitting space at the table, dished up a meal, and started planning the rest of their lives. By dawn, Juanita and Eduardo had work at the ranch, she as housekeeper and cook and her husband in charge of the chuck wagon that traveled with the cowboys as they followed the herd.

And when the Porterfields completed the larger adobe house that became the hub of the ranch's vast acreage, there were rooms for Juanita and Eduardo and their children. From that first night, the Porterfields had treated them as family, making it clear to their own children that if Juanita gave them a chore to do or reprimanded them, she was to be obeyed without question. When young Trey's health had caused endless nights of worry for his mother, Juanita had prepared special broths to ease his breathing and poultices to treat his racking cough. She had sung him Spanish lullabies and, when he showed a talent for sketching, posted his work in the kitchen for all to admire. And no one had ever doubted—or objected—that of the four Porterfield children, he was her favorite.

That had been over twenty years earlier. Both Isaac and Constance were gone now. Juanita and Eduardo were not that young anymore. All either couple had wanted in life was to see their children well settled. Now only Trey and Javier had yet to find their ways. Trey would be all right, but her baby? Her Javier? Juanita had her doubts.

∽

Nell Stokes was exhausted, but sleep was not a luxury she could afford. Calvin's death—his *murder*—had left her with a bank note to pay off, a couple thousand sheep to manage, a large house, and acres of land surrounded mostly by cattle ranchers who hated sheep—and by association, her. There were lambs coming any day now, and most distressing of all, she had a ten-year-old son who had lost his father at a time when he spent a good many of his days sick in bed and needed constant care.

When some soldiers from nearby Fort Lowell had discovered her husband's body and brought him home to her, Nell had at first been so consumed by grief and panic that she'd ignored the rage building within her. But as the months passed with no progress in catching Calvin's killers, she felt a hardness growing at her very core. It was formed of anger at the unfairness of it all, how they'd been treated since Calvin had bought the ranch from the Johnson family, who had been cattle ranchers like many of her other neighbors.

After being assured that at least a couple of the cowboys who had worked for the Johnsons would stay on to help, she and Calvin had awoken one morning to find the bunkhouse in flames and no sign of the men who had once lived there. That was the first indication that life was not going to be easy. But Calvin had reminded her that there were other sheep ranches in the area, including one owned by her half brother, Henry Galway. Calvin had promised her that, in time, folks would come around.

He was wrong.

Three weeks after the fire in the bunkhouse, Calvin had been out with the sheep and she'd been hanging laundry when a band of masked men had galloped into the yard, whooping like savages. They had torn down her wash lines, trampled the clothes, and circled her with their horses, brandishing their guns and firing into the air. Her son, Joshua, had stumbled from the house, his thin body dodging the hooves of the horses as he made his way to her. She had reached for him and folded him in the safety of her embrace, bowing her head and praying that the men would leave. They had finally ridden away, after what seemed an eternity, but not before shooting out the windows of the house. And they'd shouted a warning—either she persuade her husband to leave, or they would return.

Even if she'd intended to follow their orders, she had no chance. After her husband and the two shepherds were found brutally murdered, the soldiers had completed the drive to bring the sheep back to the lower grazing land. Because the winter had been so cold and harsh, there had been no further incidents.

Following Calvin's funeral, Henry had told her he would manage both places until she could decide what she wanted to do. He was ten years older than Nell, the child of their mother's first marriage. They were not close, but there was no other family she could rely upon.

In the meantime, Calvin's family had gone back to Nebraska—all except his cousin, Ernest. It was Henry who had persuaded Ernest to stay. At first, Nell had been relieved. Allowing the two men to assume responsibility left her free to attend to Joshua and the house. Sheep ranchers were still something of a rarity in this part of Arizona, and those that had settled there were widely scattered—circumstances that left Nell with few women beyond Henry's wife, Lottie, to rely on for support. When Henry and Ernest were away tending the combined flocks from the two ranches, often for weeks at a time, Henry insisted that Lottie and at least one of their twins, Ira and Spud, stay with Nell to be sure she and Joshua were safe.

In spite of everything, Nell had made one friend whom she trusted to listen and offer advice. The local doctor, Addie Porterfield, called on her a couple of times each month. She came to examine Joshua and told stories of her husband's younger brother, who had also been ill as a boy. "Now he is a big, strong, healthy man, and one day, you will be as well," the doctor assured Joshua.

But on the nights when the menfolk were away, Ira or Spud slipping off to town instead of sticking around on watch, Nell sat alone and held Joshua as he coughed and gagged. She wondered what the future

might hold for them. Was she doing her best by staying? Would Joshua be better off if they moved back to
Nebraska, closer to Calvin's family? Her own family
was scattered—her parents had died just before she and
Calvin had headed West, and her siblings had hardships
of their own. She had been discussing her options with
Lottie when her sister-in-law had suggested perhaps it
was time she consider a union with Ernest.

"It's not yet six months since Cal died," Nell had
protested.

"Henry says you need to think past normal grieving." Lottie had bitten off a thread on the shirt she was
mending for her husband. "Henry says, come spring,
with the lambing and all, we'll have all we can do just
managing our place, and you're gonna need someone
to take over here. Ernest is a good man and a hard
worker. You could do worse."

Nell had tried to convince herself that Lottie had a
point, but the truth was that she barely knew her husband's cousin. Ernest was nothing like Calvin, and it
bothered her the way he had taken her late husband's
place at the table right away without asking her. He
had taken liberties from the day he arrived, in fact—
smoking Calvin's tobacco, going through the papers
in Calvin's desk with Henry, even wearing Calvin's
yellow slicker when the weather turned cold and wet.

But none of that compared to the liberty Ernest had
taken one bitterly cold winter night. Henry, Lottie,
and the boys had gone back to their own ranch,
leaving Ernest to keep watch. Someone had made an
attempt to rimrock or stampede Henry's flock over a
cliff. Her brother had insisted that Ernest set up his

bedroll downstairs in the kitchen and spend the night inside the house. "If there's a gang out looking for trouble, they'll not miss the opportunity to strike here if they think it's a woman alone."

Nell had agreed, recalling how frightened she had been when those men had attacked in broad daylight. But sometime during the night after she had finally gotten Joshua settled, she had heard the soft click of her bedroom door, a door she always left open so she would not miss Joshua calling out for her. Before she could come awake enough to react, Ernest had crawled into her bed. Without saying a word, he had pressed himself against her, and beneath the covers, he had run his hand up and under her nightgown. Tears had filled her eyes as she stiffened against his touch.

Blessedly, Joshua had started to choke, his racking coughs penetrating the closed door. Somehow, she had found the strength to push Ernest away and run to tend her child. Once she had gotten Joshua settled again and returned, she had found Ernest sound asleep and snoring in her bed. She had spent the remainder of the night sitting in the corner of the room in the rocking chair her husband had built for her. On her lap was Calvin's loaded shotgun.

Just before dawn when Ernest began to stir, she had walked to the side of the bed and placed the barrel of the gun just even with his nose. "If you ever try something like that again," she had said in a low, husky whisper to keep Joshua from possibly overhearing, "I will blow your brains out. Are we clear?"

He had pushed the barrel of the gun aside and stood. "You might want to check with your brother on that, you ungrateful bitch," he had muttered. He had picked up his clothes and walked downstairs. Still carrying the shotgun, she had followed him and seen him go out to the porch, break the ice that had formed on the wash basin, and then splash water on his face. She had set the gun within reach while she stirred the embers of the fire in the cook stove. Moments later, Ernest had returned, snapping his suspenders over his shoulders. He had poured himself a cup of coffee and taken Calvin's place at the table as if nothing had happened.

For weeks, she'd kept the incident to herself even as she served up meals for whoever was in residence with her. In the evenings, after she'd put Joshua to bed, she sat darning socks while whichever nephew was there for the night flipped playing cards into a hat. On the day before the men were to drive the flock to a ranch fifty miles away for a communal shearing and lambing, Lottie had fallen ill. Ira would stay with his mother, Henry had told Nell, but he needed at least one son to come with him. Therefore, Ernest would stay behind to make sure she and Joshua were safe.

"No. Take Ernest with you and let Spud stay here, or I'll stay alone," she had said. It was an order rather than a request.

"Not a chance. Leave you and your boy here on your own?"

"The soldiers will come by, and Doc Porterfield, and—"

"Ernest stays."

She had seen no choice but to tell him what had happened. Fighting back tears at the memory of Ernest putting his hands on her and pressing himself against her, she had given her half brother the details. But instead of being outraged as she had expected, he had sighed heavily and said, "Calm down. If you're so all fired determined to make more of this than it warrants, he'll come with me. Maybe a few weeks on your own will bring you to your senses—if the cattlemen don't get to you first."

"He was in my bed, Henry."

"We'll sort this out after him and me get back. But, Nell, you need to come around to seeing Ernest as your best hope if you're determined to stay on here. He may have gotten ahead of things, but a man has needs."

She had stared up at him openmouthed with shock while he had instructed his sons to stay behind—Ira with Lottie and Spud with Nell—then climbed aboard the wagon and shouted for Ernest to grab his gear. "Change of plans," he said before turning his attention back to her. "Do not fight me on this, Nell. You need a man to run things around here, and Ernest wants the job."

Now, a few days later, Nell saw a single rider in the distance. Having sent Spud off with a basket of food she'd made for Lottie and Ira, she was alone in the yard with Joshua, and for the first time since pleading with Henry to take Ernest with him, she felt a shiver of fear.

"Go in the house, Son," she said softly.

"Should I bring you Pa's gun?" Joshua asked.

"No. Just go inside."

Joshua did not argue.

Nell continued the repair work she'd begun on the chicken coop the raiders had destroyed.

As the man came closer, she saw that he was tall—taller than Calvin had been. He wore brown trousers, a faded blue shirt, a tan suede vest, and a battered Stetson that looked as if it had seen its fair share of bad weather and hard use. She thought of the hat she had saved up to buy for Calvin last Christmas, the hat she had placed on account at Miss McNew's dry goods store in Whitman Falls, paying it off a little each time she went into town. The hat she had never gone back to pay off and collect. There seemed little reason to do so now.

She tightened her grip on the ax she was using to hammer the chicken wire into place, her mind racing. She needed to come up with a plan for protecting herself and Joshua should the man not be alone. She glanced around, searching for any sign of other riders who might plan to come at her from all directions.

This was a cowboy—that much was evident. He rode a large stallion, and there was a coil of rope fastened to the horn of his saddle and a holstered gun strapped onto his waist. The man was taking his time, and that frightened her more than if he had come riding into the yard at a full gallop.

"Can I help you, mister?" she shouted, shielding her eyes with one hand even as she kept a tight hold on the short-handled ax with the other.

He reined his horse to a stop and dismounted. To her surprise, he removed his hat as he approached her. "Mrs. Stokes?"

She planted her feet and faced him. "Who's asking?"

His lips quirked into the beginning of a smile, but he squelched that by squinting into the sun behind her. "Name's Trey Porterfield. My sister-in-law Addie's the doctor in Whitman Falls."

This was the man Addie had told Joshua about?

This tall, robust cowboy who looked like he'd never been sick a day in his life?

"Doc Addie has been good to us," she said. "Did she send you?"

He rolled his hat in his hands. "Not exactly. She has talked a good deal about your boy. Seems to think we might have something in common. I was pretty sickly as a kid myself."

"So we've heard." She waited.

"Then there's the fact that my pa died when I wasn't much older than your son."

"Joshua's father was murdered," she replied in a low growl that did nothing to disguise her rage.

"So was mine," he said softly.

She realized he was focusing all his attention on her.

"I'm sorry for your loss," she said and glanced toward the coop. "I've got work to do here, Mr. Porterfield. Thank you for stopping by. It was kind of you."

"How 'bout I finish that coop for you?" He waited a beat, then grinned. "I don't charge much—just a tall glass of water. That sun's already hot enough for it to be July, and here it is not even May."

Nell wrestled with the urge that came over her to return his smile, to lower her guard after months of always expecting the worst. But she had been through enough to know trusting a cattleman—trusting *any* man—was a dangerous business. "You can fill your canteen in the stream over there before you head back," she said. "I can manage the coop."

From the corner of her eye, she saw Joshua had eased out onto the front stoop and was watching the exchange.

"That your boy there?" Instead of being insulted at the rejection and stalking off as she had expected, Trey Porterfield remained standing a few feet from her. He even raised his hand in greeting to Joshua.

A lump of fear hardened in her throat, and for the first time ever, she wished that Henry or one of his sons—or even Ernest—was around. "What is it you want, mister?" The words came out in a whisper. She could make no sense of his presence and therefore could only think that his taking notice of Joshua was somehow a threat.

Something in her expression must have revealed her distress, because he took a step back, holding up his hands as if to calm her, then he put on his hat and mounted his horse. "I mean you and your son no harm, Mrs. Stokes. Addie has… I was in the area and…"

"Thank you for coming by," she managed as she forced herself to turn away and give the appearance of working to repair the coop again. But in reality, she gripped the ax handle and listened for his horse to retreat. If he rode toward her or the house, she would sling the ax at the horse. She imagined the horse injured and perhaps rolling over the rider, giving her time to make it to the house and Joshua—and Calvin's shotgun.

When she heard the horse walk away, then break into a trot that faded with the distance between them, she let out a breath and with it some of the knot of fear that had threatened to paralyze her. Her eyes filled with tears, and for the thousandth time since Calvin's death, she wondered what kind of future lay ahead for her and Joshua. Was she being foolhardy by insisting they stay and carry on Calvin's dream? The ax fell from her trembling fingers, and she knew that her thought of throwing it at the horse had been nothing more than the fantasy of a desperate woman.

❧

After leaving the Stokes place, Trey stopped at the top of a ridge overlooking that property. He sat for a moment, staring down at the sheep farm. He knew this place almost as well as his own ranch. The Johnsons and the Porterfields had been close—his sisters and Louisa Johnson had been the best of friends, and he had once sat at the big cypress table in that house sharing many a meal with his father and older brother and George Johnson while the men talked business.

Below him now, he could see the Stokes woman working to complete the repair of the coop. He dismounted, pulled out the sketchbook and pencil box he carried everywhere he went and hadn't found the time to open in months. He'd picked up the habit as a boy, a way to help him think through any situation. Through the years, his art had continued to be a refuge for him, a place he retreated to when he needed to work out the challenges that came with being in charge of the largest spread in the region.

With a few quick strokes, he drew the outline of the house, the outbuildings, and the fenced pastures that surrounded the property—all subjects he had drawn many times in the past. He added the boy standing just outside the door of the house, and he drew the woman with her sunbonnet hanging down her back. The bonnet was of little use to her if she didn't wear it properly. He recalled the way she had squinted up at him and shielded her eyes with one hand, even as she clung to the ax with the other.

He did not sketch the ax.

Nell Stokes had surprised him. He'd paid her little attention the few times he'd seen the family in church, more interested in her husband and how they might be able to relieve the tension between cow men and herders. Now he realized that she was young— younger than his twenty-seven years, to be sure. She was slender, almost fragile-looking. And yet he recalled the way she had walked alongside her husband as they left church services, and just now, when she had faced him, he had seen such strength in her. He'd also seen something else. Fear of him. It was the fear that had made him back away and leave.

He had hesitated before approaching the house when he saw a husky older boy walk away with a picnic basket tied to his burro's saddle. It had occurred to him that it might be best to return when her brother was there to advise her. But he hadn't been able to resist getting a closer look at a woman who had decided to stay in spite of her horrific loss and the hardships she must have known lay ahead.

If he were to be completely honest with himself, the single thing that had kept him from even hinting at the idea of buying her out was the fact that business was the last thing on his mind once he saw her. No, what he felt on meeting her was an attraction so unexpected and intense that the feeling had taken hold of him and muddled his thinking.

He turned the page of his sketchbook and began a

more detailed drawing of Nell Stokes, beginning with her oval-shaped face. With quick, sure strokes, he added eyes—large and filled with questions, thin lines radiating from the corners hinting at a time when she had laughed freely and often. He moved on to her cheeks and the sprinkling of freckles that danced across them and the bridge of her nose. As he prepared to sketch her mouth, he hesitated. He closed his eyes to recapture the details—her lower lip full and a little chapped from the dry heat. Her upper lip a perfect bow. Her teeth when she spoke surprisingly straight and even.

Trey worked quickly, his mind a blur of detail as it always was when he sketched. Art and reading were the two activities he had used as a child to fight off the boredom that came with spending weeks in bed. He'd challenged himself to remember tiny details, minor facts. At the moment, it was the details of the widow Stokes's lovely face that found their way onto the page.

He paused in midstroke and stared at the image he'd created. Something was missing. This was not the face that had set his heart racing. Trey frowned. He was known for his ability to capture the very essence of a person. Family and friends had come alive on paper because of his gift. But this was different— she was different.

Of course, he didn't know her. Maybe that was the problem. He stood at the edge of the mesa so that he had a better view of the ranch below. She was just walking back to the house. By her gestures, he figured she was saying something to the boy. He continued to watch and saw her glance back, raise her hand to shield her eyes once again as she focused her gaze on him before hurrying into the house with her son.

The last thing he wanted was for her to be afraid of him, to consider him just another cattleman determined to run her off her land. What if, instead of buying her out, he proposed a merger of their properties? Under such an arrangement, they could pool their resources and work together. More to the point, they could set an example for others and perhaps stop this madness that had changed the region from a bucolic, peace-loving community to one where mischief and vandalism had escalated to outright murder and mayhem.

As he packed up his sketchbook, he realized she'd been repairing a chicken coop—but there were no chickens. He wondered why, but then another thought pushed that from his mind. Maybe if he sent Nell Stokes a peace offering—some new residents for that coop—she would understand she had nothing to fear from him.

❧

The fact that Trey Porterfield had stopped at the top of the mesa and stood there for some time worried Nell. She could feel him watching her as surely as she felt the hot noonday sun beating into her back. She continued working on the coop, banging her thumb twice for her trouble. What could he be planning?

His polite—almost courtly—manners had unnerved her. His half smile and the way he had made sure to keep his distance were not what she might expect from a cowboy. In her experience, such men were more likely to bully and threaten. Their smiles, offered at church or in town, were derisive and mocking. The truth was that she feared Trey Porterfield a good deal more than she did any cowboy she had met, precisely because he was well-spoken and clearly intelligent. In her experience, men like that could be awfully cunning when it came to getting what they wanted.

So the following morning, after a night spent lying awake listening for sounds that would alert her to any danger, she was relieved to see Dr. Addie Porterfield driving a buckboard wagon up the lane. At Nell's insistence, Spud had ridden to town to get Doc Addie to check in on Lottie.

"I just sent my nephew to get you," Nell said.

"Saw him on the road. Told him I'd just stop here and make this delivery, then be along directly. I sent him off to let his mother know I was coming." She hopped down from the buggy and went around to its rear. "Got a present for you."

Joshua came running at the sound of her voice. "A present?"

"Mind your manners, young man," Nell said, although she doubted her son could hear her above the squawking of half a dozen hens and the crow of a rooster coming from the back of Addie's cart. "What on earth?" she asked as Addie wrestled a cage filled with chickens to the ground next to the mostly repaired coop and opened the latch.

"A gift from my brother-in-law," Addie replied, grinning as hens and the lone rooster shook themselves off and strutted across the yard.

"I don't…I can't…"

"Trey said he stopped by yesterday and you were working on the coop, but he didn't see any sign of chickens, so…" She shrugged and grinned. Then she glanced toward the empty coop and frowned. "What happened to your hens, anyway?"

Before Nell could think what to say, Joshua blurted out the truth. "They got killed one night when my cousin snuck off to town and we was alone here. A bunch of bad cowboys came riding through our land, and you shoulda seen how Ma…"

"That's enough, Joshua. Dr. Porterfield doesn't need to concern herself with something that's over and done with."

Addie placed her hand on Nell's forearm. "I'm truly sorry for the troubles you've had to endure, Nell. Hopefully now that your brother and…"

"Half brother." Nell's correction came automatically. Henry had never truly felt like family even when Nell was growing up. The age difference was certainly a factor, and these days, the way he had reacted to Ernest's unwanted advances only added to her reluctance to claim him as her kin.

Addie started to say something but then seemed to think better of it as she turned her attention to Joshua. "You're looking a little flushed, young man. How about we go inside and let me take a listen to that heart of yours?" She wrapped her arm around Joshua's shoulders as they headed for the house. "There's a sack of feed in the back there for the chickens," she called out when they reached the porch.

"There's coffee on the stove," Nell replied, giving Addie a wave.

"Was hoping there might be."

Addie's voice trailed off as she and Joshua entered the house, but her comment made Nell smile. She always felt so much better whenever Addie came to visit.

As she scattered feed for the new arrivals, Nell realized that smiling was not something that came naturally to her these days. Most of the time, she was so tied up in knots of worry and nerves that it was all she could do to put three words together. But Addie had a way of making things seem like they could work out. Nell stood for a long moment, watching the hens peck at the feed and squawk at each other. They seemed content, and that meant perhaps by morning, she'd have eggs. And that meant she could make something special for Joshua.

She brushed the chaff of the feed from her hands and walked toward the house. Of course she would insist on paying Addie's brother-in-law. They might be neighbors, but they really didn't know each other, and besides, there was the matter of the range war. They were on opposite sides of that issue, and she could not afford to be beholden to the man.

When she entered the house, Addie was leaning close to Joshua, her stethoscope pressed to his bony chest. "Deep breath," she said softly. "And again…"

Nell clenched her hands as her son followed the doctor's instructions. There was no reason to believe anything had changed. There was no magic potion that Joshua could take. Addie had told her time and rest were the only possible remedies.

"Sounds to me like maybe somebody has been

overdoing things a bit," Addie said as she put away her stethoscope.

"Uncle Henry don't believe in coddling," Joshua said, glancing at his mother.

"Well, unless your uncle can show me a medical degree, I think it best he stick to tending sheep and let me do the doctoring."

"He won't like that. He says I need regular chores."

Addie smiled. "Then maybe he can tend the sheep while you care for those hens I brought today."

"Ma?"

"I think that sounds like a very good compromise." Nell pulled Joshua's shirt closed and ruffled his hair. "But for now, I want you to go to your room and write Mr. Porterfield a note of thanks." She took down a tin can she kept hidden among the crockery on the shelf and opened it. She pulled out a single coin and handed it to him. "And tell him that this is the first payment and you intend to pay for the hens and rooster over time by selling eggs at the market in town if that's agreeable."

Joshua stared at the money. Addie took a sip of her coffee.

"Trey sent you a *gift*, Nell. Don't insult him by turning it into some kind of business deal."

"I just want to make sure he knows we appreciate his kindness."

"Then use some of the eggs you'll be getting and bake him a cake. You can bring it when you and Joshua come to the church social next Friday."

Joshua's eyes went wide with surprise. "We're going to the social?"

"Yes," Addie said at the same time that Nell said, "No."

While she and Calvin had attended church whenever possible along with other sheep ranchers and their families, she had not been back since Calvin's funeral. Nell sighed. "Joshua, go write that note, then lie down until lunch. We'll sort this out later."

"Yes, ma'am."

Addie wandered outside, taking her coffee with her. Nell filled a tin cup and followed her.

"Addie, I appreciate everything you do for Joshua— and for me. Your friendship means more to us than I can say."

"Here's the thing, Nell. This business between the cattlemen and you and your kind has got to stop sometime. Either the two sides are going to find some way to work together, or more good people are going to die. On the other hand, if you and some of the other wives come to the social…"

"I haven't even been back to church since last fall. Seeing me there, everyone will be whispering about Calvin and how he died and—"

"Exactly. The thing that needs to happen here, in my opinion, is to get folks talking instead of shooting."

"I don't want pity."

"Why on earth not? Seeing you there is gonna make people squirm a little, and it's gonna make them think, and I reckon that's a big first step toward maybe finding ways to talk this thing out."

"I just want to be left alone, Addie."

"No, you want to be left to live in peace. There's a difference."

The two of them sipped their coffee in silence. Nell watched the chickens. Addie stared at the horizon. After a moment, she dumped the dregs of her coffee on the ground and handed Nell the cup. "Sorry for pushing you. Joshua needs to take things easy with the hot weather coming on. Keep him inside during the middle of the day, and no heavy lifting or exerting himself at any hour."

"Is he worse?"

"No. He's just not better." She went inside and emerged seconds later with her black leather bag. "I hope to see you both next Friday, but it's your choice. So if you decide to stay holed up here, I'll see you the following week. But in the meantime, if there's any more trouble, just send word."

Nell followed her friend out to the wagon and watched as Addie settled herself and picked up the reins. "Thank you," she said.

"We're friends, Nell. Heaven knows, out here, that's a blessing. You take care now." She snapped the reins, and the horse started forward.

"Hey, Addie? About that cake…"

Addie's laugh was like a burst of welcome rain on a tin roof. "His mama used to make a cake flavored with vanilla and a hint of cinnamon," she called out as she rode away. "Bring it to the church social Friday."

Two

THE FOLLOWING FRIDAY WHEN TREY CAME IN FROM
the range, Juanita was standing in the kitchen door,
hands on her ample hips. "You're going to be late,"
she grumbled after he'd handed his horse off to
Eduardo and walked toward her.

"There's no set time for this thing," he replied as
he bent to kiss her cheek before squeezing past her.

"No, but the cake auction comes early on, and
that's what you promised Addie you'd be there for."
She watched him down a glass of water and then pour
himself a refill.

Trey wasn't much for socializing, especially not
since his mother had died and his siblings had gone
their separate ways. He'd never really had a serious
courtship, and if he had considered marriage at all, it
had been something he might do "someday."

Addie and Jess had tried to match him up with a
friend of theirs once. Ginny Matthews was the daughter of the pharmacist in Tucson and worked for the
newspaper there. After he'd returned from spending
several months in the wild area called Yellowstone

in Wyoming, he'd worked with Ginny to illustrate a series of articles she had written for the paper.

Like Addie, she was lively and outspoken, and he could understand why his sister-in-law thought they might make a good match. "Opposites attract," she liked to say, pointing out the obvious contrast of his quiet, live-and-let-live ways to Ginny's determination to save the world. And he liked Ginny. She made him laugh, and she made him think, but she didn't make his heart race, and not once had he thought about what it might be like to kiss her. On the other hand, after that day he'd called on Nell Stokes, he'd repeatedly experienced both feelings—feelings he had rejected as disrespectful of her grief.

He finished the second glass of water. "I'll go get cleaned up," he said, knowing Juanita would not allow him to beg off attending. "But save me some supper, 'cause I plan to go bid on Addie's cake and then come right back here. I left Javier out there mending those cut fences and—"

"Javier can handle the fences. You never take any time for yourself. Why can't you go and just enjoy the social?" She stroked his cheek. "You might meet someone," she said with a twinkle in her eye.

Trey grinned. "You and Addie think any single woman in the territory might make a good wife for me."

"It's time. A man needs a wife—a partner." Juanita patted his cheek and relieved him of the water glass. "Go get washed up."

Sometimes when Juanita—and Addie—got something in mind, it was just easier to go along than it was to try and come up with excuses for refusing.

So he washed up, changed his shirt, decided he didn't have time to shave, and headed out. He knew that Addie and Juanita wanted the best for him. It was just that what they thought he needed to be happy differed from his plans. Running the ranch was his job. His passion was sketching the land, the animals, and the people he loved. At best, courtship would be a distant third.

When he arrived at the church hall, it was clear his sister-in-law had found some new match for him, given the way she fussed over the fact that he hadn't shaved.

"You look like a grumpy old bear," she said, scowling up at him as she touched his whiskered jaw.

"Had some trouble. Somebody cut through the fences in a bunch of places. I had to have the boys—"

"Well, at least you smell nice enough," she interrupted.

"I've gotta get back, so I'm not staying for the supper," he announced. It was high time Addie saw him as a grown man capable of making his own choices.

She muttered something that sounded like, "Wanna bet?" but he chose to ignore it.

"Now tell me what your cake looks like so I can bid on that and head on home," he said.

She looked alarmed. "You plan on bidding during the cake auction?"

"It's for charity, right? I thought that was the point."

"Right." Addie drew out the word, and he could practically see her plotting something. "Excuse me a minute. I have to see about…in the kitchen… Be right back," she said and hurried away.

"Your wife is up to no good," he told Jess when his brother came to stand next to him.

"She's trying to find you a wife. Get used to it, or go find your own." Jess scanned the growing crowd and frowned. "You think there'll be any trouble today?" He nodded toward a large wagon just arriving, driven by the Galway boys. "Looks like the sheep ranchers' wives and their young'uns decided to show up."

Trey followed his brother's gaze. "Their men have all gone over to the Booker place near Tucson for the shearing and lambing. I expect they told their wives to put in an appearance, a reminder they live here too. I doubt there will be any trouble from a bunch of women and children." But then he remembered his fences. He had no doubt the wire had been cut by herders—payback or a warning. "Have you heard something?"

"Just a gut feeling, one I've learned the hard way not to ignore," Jess replied.

"It's a church social, Jess. Even if some of the womenfolk and children are here, it's neutral ground. There's no reason to—"

Jess snorted and jerked his head toward the door where Nell Stokes and her son were just stepping into the hall, followed by her sister-in-law, Lottie Galway, and her boys, as well as several other wives and their children. It was the largest gathering of sheep folk that the town had seen outside of Sunday services. The crowd parted, making a wide berth for them. The hall, which had been filled with chatter and laughter just seconds before, was now deadly quiet. And then Trey heard the beginnings of a low murmur. It sounded like bees and grew to the rumble of distant thunder. Wives tried to quiet their husbands, who were now openly asking what *those* women were doing here. Children glanced from one adult to the next, aware that something had changed but unsure what to do about it.

Trey saw Addie spot Nell Stokes and hurry across the hall to usher the widow and her son into the kitchen. He noticed that Addie nodded to the Galway woman but didn't include her.

The drone of protest grew louder.

"Some people just never seem to learn their place," Pete Collins bellowed, making sure he was heard by all assembled. "And what's that stench? Oh, I got it—sheep manure. Them people must roll around in the stuff."

"That's enough, Peter," his wife said softly, trying to shush him by placing her hand on his arm.

He shoved her hand away. "I'm only saying what everybody's thinking."

Trey saw one of the Galway sons start toward Pete, but Jess stepped in front of Pete, blocking the boy's way. His tin star caught the sun as he did so. "Just settle down, Collins," he said, "and stop shooting off your mouth before you've got all the facts."

"The fact is—"

Jess held up his hand. "The fact is these women and their families have every right to attend a church function. The fact is, in this particular case, they were invited."

"By who?" Pete glanced around the room.

"By my wife," Jess said, and this news set everyone to chattering again.

Most everybody in Whitman Falls respected Jess

and Addie. Each of them had had a chance at bigger
things. There had been some talk of Jess going into
politics one day, and for sure he could have been the
regional sheriff, living in Tucson and making a lot
more money than he ever could in Whitman Falls. As
for Addie, once she earned her medical degree, she
could have set up practice anywhere. But after her
father died and the community lost the only doctor it
had known, Addie and Jess gave up any dreams they
might have had about moving to Tucson and stayed
on. Folks didn't forget loyalty like that.

So when it became known that Nell Stokes and her
kind were there at Addie's invitation, most of those
attending the social turned a deaf ear to Pete and his
rantings, and went back to the business of enjoying
the event. There was a clear division in the room,
though, with sheep folks to one side and cow folks
to the other, just like during Sunday services where
cattle ranchers and their families crowded into pews
on one side of the aisle while the few sheep ranchers
filled only a few pews opposite them. No one dared
cross over. For his part, Pete stormed out of the hall,
his wife close on his heels, still trying to calm him.

Minutes later several women emerged from the
kitchen, each carrying a cake. They lined their offer-
ings up on a row of tables set up for that purpose.
Trey paid close attention to the cake Addie carried
and grinned when he saw the white frosting. Addie
wasn't much of a cook, but it was hard to spoil the
simple cake his mother used to make. He was prepared
to bid high so that he could leave. It occurred to him
that Nell Stokes might have brought a cake as well,

one hidden under the cover of tea towels in the large basket she'd been carrying when she arrived. But there was no sign of her among the women setting up the cake display. If he bid on her cake, maybe—

"Made your choice, little brother?" Jess had returned to stand next to him now that the ruckus seemed to have died down.

"Addie's."

Jess clapped him on the shoulder and grinned. "Good. That means I can save my money. Bid high, okay?"

"If you're not bidding against me, why should I?"

Jess grinned. "Well now, there's two reasons. One, I happen to know that Addie was out delivering a baby when that cake was made, meaning Addie's mother made it. And two, do you really want to disappoint Addie by having her cake raise considerably less than any other for the church?"

Trey frowned. Jess had him cornered. "I'll bid high, but then since you'll be eating at least as much of that cake as I will, we'll split the cost." He clapped his older brother on the shoulder in return and walked away.

✎

Nell could not understand why Addie had insisted on placing Nell's cake on the table instead of letting her simply give it to Trey. It had taken her hours to make it. Her first thought was that if she presented the cake to Trey, others would start to whisper and point, causing Nell embarrassment. Addie had shown herself to be a good friend, one who was very protective of the feelings of others.

"But how will he know the cake is for him?" Nell argued. "I mean what if someone else bids and—"

"He already knows, but this way, it will raise some money for the church."

Nell glanced around the hall, well aware that others were whispering about her and the other sheep ranchers' wives. "I'm not sure it was the wisest idea for Lottie and me and the others to come here today," Nell said. "It seems like we've upset some folks."

"Pete Collins was born upset. Pay him no mind at all." Addie motioned toward the churchyard where the children were gathered, and Joshua was there with them. He was talking intently to a boy about his age. "That's my oldest, Isaac," she said proudly.

"He's got his father's red hair," Nell said.

Addie let out a hoot of laughter. "He's also got his father's temper. But just look at them, Nell. They don't give one whit if one's family raises cattle and the other sheep. They just know they like each other. We could all take a lesson."

Nell nodded. She had to admit that it was nice to see Joshua with someone his own age. "Yes, I wish there were some way we could all get along," she said wistfully.

"Trey has some thoughts on that," Addie replied. "You two should talk." She turned away then, hurrying off to oversee the cake auction.

Left to herself, Nell found a place near a window where she could watch Joshua. There were other boys around him now, and at least one of them—a heavyset kid carrying a stick—seemed intent on causing trouble. Nell walked quickly to the exit, ready to protect her son. But by the time she stepped out into the yard, Trey Porterfield was already there. As she watched, he spoke quietly to all the boys and relieved the bully of his stick, using it instead as a kind of bat like the boys used when they played baseball.

"What we need is a ball," she heard him say as he glanced around the yard. "Jess!" His shout caught his brother's attention. "We need a ball."

She watched as Joshua shyly reached into the satchel he carried pretty much everywhere and produced a ball.

"Here, Mr. Porterfield."

The ball was the one his father had given him for his birthday two years earlier, along with a promise to teach him the game as soon as he was well enough to play. She had often seen him lying in his bed and tossing the ball in the air. He lobbed the ball to Trey.

"You've got the makings of a player, kid."

Joshua grinned and ducked his head. It had been a long time since Nell had seen her son looking quite so pleased with himself. Behind her, she heard the minister calling for quiet, and even the boys forgot about the possibility of a ballgame as they crowded inside to hear the announcement.

"It is time for our annual cake auction, and as you can see, we have a fine selection for you gents to bid on. Of course, you also are buying the privilege of dining with the lady who made that delicious confection!" He swept his hand in the general direction of the tables holding the cakes. "I need not remind you the church relies heavily on the monies raised today, so be generous, my friends, and bless you for your largess."

The ladies tittered with excitement as the men

moved closer to examine the wares. The youngsters rolled their eyes and went back outside to play.

Reverend Moore walked the length of the display and back again. "Let's begin with this luscious-looking entry, shall we?"

As the minister held up her cake, Nell blushed and edged her way to the back where Lottie sat in a corner, her hands clenched and her eyes darting nervously around the room. She heard Trey make the opening offer; Addie must have put him up to bidding. It was bound to ruin everyone's fun when others realized he'd just bought the cake made by a sheep rancher's wife. She tried to think how to stop the bidding and persuade Addie to just give Trey the cake without all this fanfare.

But Addie was standing next to the minister, grinning broadly at her husband and brother-in-law, who had worked their way to the front of the crowd. "Two bits," Trey Porterfield called out.

"Four," his brother shouted.

"Two dollars," someone in the back of the room added.

"Three," Jess countered.

Nell saw Addie frown at her husband and shake her head. Nell searched the crowd for the third bidder and saw that it was the Collins man. *Please don't bid.* Of all the ranchers and cowhands she had encountered, Pete Collins was the one she feared most. He was one of those men who smiled with his mouth, while his eyes remained cold and threatening. And while she would prefer no one spend their money on a cake that was supposed to be a thank-you gift for Trey Porterfield, at least if Addie's husband ended up the winner, he wouldn't make a scene.

"Three dollars, going once," Reverend Moore intoned. "Twice—"

"Five dollars," Trey said quietly, glaring at his brother in the process.

"The bid is five dollars, gentlemen. Any takers?"

"Too rich for my blood," Collins huffed.

"Going once, twice, and sold." Reverend Moore hit the podium with a gavel. "Congratulations, Trey. Now if you'll just pay what you owe to my wife there, we'll go on to the next cake—this beautiful apple slab entry."

"Wait a minute," a cowboy shouted. "Who made the cake? Who's Trey having his supper with?"

"My brother and his wife," Trey said as he prepared to pay Mrs. Moore and grinned at Addie. "And by rights, Addie's mother, since I suspect she's the true baker."

Everyone laughed.

Nell was confused. Why would he think that? She watched as Addie stood on tiptoe to relay a message to Trey. Whatever she said to him had him looking around the room, scanning each face until his gaze settled on her.

"Well, that's fine, Addie. Just fine," he said, his eyes never leaving Nell's flushed face. He handed over the money and then made his way through the crowd.

She wanted to run and hide. She wanted to explain that she hadn't known what Addie was doing. She wanted Addie to stop him. But it was too late. He was within three steps of her, a grin on his face as he held out his hand to her. "Mrs. Stokes, I believe I have the pleasure of your company—and your son's—for supper." He glanced at Addie. "Looks like I'll be staying after all."

Lottie stepped forward. "Really, Nell…"

Trey moved aside to include Lottie in the circle with Addie and himself. "Perhaps you'll join us as well, Mrs. Galway?"

Lottie looked like she might faint from being the center of attention. Her lip trembled, and her face flushed bright red. "I…my husband would…"

One of the boys shoved his way between Nell and Lottie. "Ma ain't sitting down to supper or anything else with the likes of you, mister."

"Now, Ira—" his mother began but bit off the word as her son glared at her.

"You heard my brother, mister," Ira's twin, Spud, said, his voice shifting between the croak of youth and the grumble of manhood. "And that goes for our aunt as well. We don't eat with your kind, do we, Aunt Nell?"

What was she going to say? A hush had fallen over the hall as if everyone had drawn in and held a collective breath.

"You could just leave," Nell heard someone mutter—a rancher's wife. "That would be best for all concerned, dear."

Maybe it was the assumption that others knew better than she did what was right. Maybe it was that it had been so very long, well before Calvin's untimely death, since she'd had the pleasure of adult conversation and company for a meal.

And maybe, just maybe, her decision was born of the fact that she saw something in Trey Porterfield's eyes and the way he waited patiently for her answer.

What she saw was a man who looked at her not as an enemy, but as if he truly wanted her to say yes. Trey Porterfield was a quiet man, a man who seemed to have none of the rage she had seen in other ranchers and even in her own husband. A man who appeared genuinely interested in spending time with her and Joshua. And that was more than enough to make her smile at him and say, "Doctor Porterfield has been suggesting you and my son might have something in common, Mr. Porterfield. If there is anything you might say to help him, I would be most grateful."

The release of held breaths surged into whispers as well as outright protests and murmurs of disgust. Her nephews clearly did not like her response, but she realized that although they had the height and bulk of grown men, they were too immature to make more of a protest. They took their mother by the arm instead and led her to a far corner of the hall. All the other sheep-ranching wives followed. After that, some in the large room turned their attention away from Trey and Nell and back to the auction, but others—Trey's brother, Jess, among them—scowled at her. She realized she had thought she would have his support since, clearly, Addie had arranged this entire business.

"I'm afraid I have placed you and your brother in an awkward position, Mr. Porterfield," she said in a voice meant for Trey's ears only. "Perhaps it would be best if—"

"Stand your ground, Mrs. Stokes," Trey replied. "If we are to have any chance of peace in this community, this is an important first step."

She hesitated briefly, reflecting on how badly she

had misread the way he had looked at her a moment earlier. It had not been beauty he saw, but opportunity. Like many men she had known, Trey Porterfield had an agenda, and while she wholeheartedly agreed with his hope to bring peace, she had no desire to be the pawn he used to achieve that goal.

When he turned to pick up the cake he'd left on the table while he paid the minister's wife, Nell touched his forearm. "Mr. Porterfield?"

His smile when he faced her almost made her lose her resolve. There was such kindness in that smile and a sense of expectation that everything was just fine—or would be. How she wanted to believe in that promise, believe in him. But before she could steel herself to say what she knew must be said and follow Lottie and the others to that corner, Jess stepped between them.

"Trey, we need to talk."

The marshal's back was like a solid wall separating her from his brother.

"No, we don't. Have you met Mrs. Stokes?" Trey stepped around Jess to take his place next to her.

Jess glanced at her. "Ma'am," he muttered by way of acknowledgment. "I'm sorry for the trouble you've had to deal with since…" He searched for the proper words.

"Since my husband was murdered?" She would not allow the truth to go unsaid. She owed Calvin that much. "Have you come any closer to identifying his killers, Marshal Porterfield?"

"It's really not my jurisdiction, ma'am. Until they close down the fort for good, open territory is still patrolled by the militia, and frankly, there's not much I could do."

She did not miss the way his face flushed at the admission. *But it's been months. Have you even tried?* The depth of her anger surprised her, and for the second time in less than ten minutes, she changed her mind about accepting the invitation to share her supper. She had an agenda of her own.

"Mr. Porterfield?"

Both men looked at her and then at each other. Trey smiled. "Maybe if you'd be all right with it, we could eliminate any confusion if you called me by my given name?"

She hesitated. "I suppose it would be all right."

"And may I do the same—call you by your given name?"

Maybe it was because she heard Jess let out a huff of disapproval and saw him roll his eyes that she agreed. And just maybe it was because she was curious to hear the sound of her name coming from Trey Porterfield's mouth. She nodded.

"It's Nell, isn't it?"

"Yes." She had always disliked her name—it had no charm. But when he said it, somehow it was like hearing it for the very first time.

"I'll go get Joshua, and we can have our supper," she said and fled the hall.

❧

Nell.

Her name had strength, not unlike the woman herself. She might be petite in stature, but the tenacity Trey saw in her could not be denied. When she had questioned Jess about his progress, she had spoken without hesitation and looked Jess directly in the eye. Jess was the one who had refused to meet her gaze, looking instead at some point over her head. It also occurred to Trey there was a dignity about her name, a single syllable with no need for embellishment. When he repeated it in his mind, he could not help but smile and forget all about his plan to leave early. Trey chuckled when he realized he'd been right about one thing—his sister-in-law was matchmaking.

"What's so funny?" Jess grumbled.

Trey had long ago learned to read his brother's moods. "Nothing," he said.

"Then wipe that grin off your face. I can't believe you don't understand what you and my wife have started here."

"I'm having supper with the widow and her son. I haven't started anything—yet. It's you as much as Addie that's been after me to think about finding a wife and starting a family."

The look on his brother's face would have been comical if Trey hadn't known how truly upset Jess was. "Tell me you only bought a cake that Addie tricked you into buying, and once you've lived up to your end of that bargain, there will be an end to it."

Trey was tired of Jess always treating him like a kid brother. He was a grown man, old enough to know his own mind and make his own decisions. "Maybe it's Addie you need to be lecturing, Jess. I've had my fill of it."

The day didn't get much better after that. The auction continued, and the bidding was high, but Trey was distracted when he saw Javier arrive.

"Fencing's all taken care of, boss," Javier assured him.

"That's good. Glad you have a chance to enjoy yourself."

But a moment later, he saw Javier and Pete Collins huddled together in a corner. He didn't like the way they kept glancing at Nell, who was speaking quietly with her sister-in-law. Lottie Galway was a timid woman, which stood in sharp contrast to her height and large-boned body. Her sons were big for their age as well, which Trey judged to be somewhere around fifteen. Those two young men looked as if they were spoiling for a fight, and Trey thought Jess would do well to keep an eye on them. But Jess had started working his way through the crowded room toward Javier, and he looked anything but happy. Trey circled around to intercept him, a tactic he used often when herding stray cows, a tactic he'd learned could serve him equally well in intercepting people.

"Javier's not doing anything wrong," he said when he reached Jess's side. "Leave him be."

Jess released a sigh of exasperation, but he stayed where he was. "One of these days, you're gonna realize that Javier has changed—and not for the better. I know he's been like a brother to you, but—" Jess broke off the thought and stared hard at Javier and Pete.

Trey wondered if with the mention of *brother*, they were both thinking the same thing. There had been a time when Trey had needed his brother's support and guidance, but Jess had left home and stayed away for months. It had been right after their father died, and by the time Jess returned, Trey had found other sources for the comfort and guidance he needed.

"Just keep your head when it comes to Javier," Jess said as he turned and walked away.

The minister clapped his hands loudly, and someone whistled to silence the crowd. "Suppertime, folks. Gents, it's time to find the lady who baked you that cake and enjoy a fine meal with her." He pointed to the tables outside where the women were busy setting out a variety of platters and bowls filled to almost overflowing with an assortment of food.

There was a general shuffling and shifting as lines formed. To his surprise, Trey saw Nell's sister-in-law leading her toward the exit. The other wives followed, keeping their children close by.

He saw Nell stop and stand her ground as she had words with Lottie Galway. She glanced at him, said something to her sister-in-law, who kept walking to a place in the yard near the wagons. Nell remained where she was, her son in front of her, her gaze on Trey.

Pretty much everyone in the hall turned their attention to Trey. Knowing that it was unlikely anyone would be so bold as to start a fight in the church, he locked eyes with Nell Stokes and crossed the room to her.

He offered her his arm, which she took. "It's a fine day, Mrs. Stokes. How about we enjoy our supper outside under the cottonwoods?" He could feel her trembling, but she nodded and followed his lead.

"Trey?" Addie smoothed the front of her apron as she took hold of her husband's arm. "May Jess and I join you?"

He glanced at his brother, whose jaw was so tightly clenched, Trey couldn't see how the man would be able to take a bite of his food.

"Yes, please," he heard Nell say.

Addie hurried to the food line and filled two plates that she handed to Jess, then served up two more. Trey understood the extra plates were for Nell and him, making it unnecessary for Nell to go through the line.

"Go on and sit," he said to Nell. "I'll just get some food for young Joshua here."

"He can share mine," Nell was quick to offer. "Really, this is more than enough for us. Thank you."

From the corner of his eye, Trey saw Javier and Pete step into the churchyard, but then Javier placed a restraining hand on the rancher. The Galway boys, on the other hand, seemed determined to make a stand, their wide bodies blocking the way to the shade of the trees.

"Now, Aunt Nell," one of the boys said, "you know Pa would want you to stay with Ma and us."

Trey waited.

To his surprise, Nell turned to her sister-in-law, who hurried over, no doubt to try and control her sons. "Lottie, won't you and the boys join us?" she said quietly.

Lottie Galway shrank away, clearly wanting to dissolve into those surrounding her. Her eyes were wide with fear, and she picked nervously at the collar on her dress. Words failed her, but she finally managed to shake her head. She turned away from Nell then, and Trey saw another of the herder women reach over and pat her hand in solidarity.

Jess handed the plates he carried to Trey before edging his way between the Galway twins. "Pardon us, boys." Having breached the barrier, he stood aside and waited for Addie, Nell, and Joshua to find their way to the cluster of trees. But before they arrived, Jess stepped closer and murmured, "I hope you know what you're doing, little brother. Chances are you just made this whole deal a lot worse than it was."

∼

Nell was shaking so badly by the time they reached the grove of cottonwoods, she had to lean against one of the rough solid trunks to settle her nerves.

"You all right, Ma?" Joshua's worried inquiry made the others turn to her.

"Fine," she assured them, forcing a smile and pushing herself away from the tree. "Just a little overheated."

Addie handed Jess the plates she carried and took hold of Nell's hand. She found her pulse, which Nell knew was racing. "Sit down," Addie ordered, pointing to a seat on the rough, wooden bench. "Trey, stay with her while Jess gets some water."

"Addie, please don't fuss. I'm fine."

"You're scaring the boy, Addie," Trey added, but Nell noticed that he did as Addie had instructed and sat next to her on the bench. He nodded to the space between himself and her. "Come sit, Joshua, and tell me what you've been reading lately." He handed the boy one of the plates of food.

His kindness—and nearness—did nothing to calm her racing heart. Joshua's shy smile told her that he too found the cowboy appealing.

"We don't have too many books," he said, "and I've had to miss a lot of school."

"Well, now, it happens that I've got a whole room

filled with books," Trey said. "Maybe one day you and your mother could come by my ranch, and you could borrow a few of them." His eyes shifted from Joshua to her, and she felt as if she might drown in their dark-blue pools.

"You mean like a library?" Joshua asked.

"Exactly like that." His gaze did not waver, and it seemed to Nell that they were engaged in some private, secret conversation that had nothing to do with books or reading—or Joshua for that matter. "Will you come?"

It also did not escape her notice that Addie had made herself scarce, standing a little away as if waiting for Jess to return with the water.

"Ma? Can we?"

"We'll see."

"You think Uncle Henry will let us?" Joshua asked.

Instinctively, Nell pressed her lips together. "It is not for Uncle Henry to decide," she said softly.

"Maybe your brother could come as well," Trey said, addressing her now as Jess returned and handed her the water. "I'd like to meet him."

"Half brother," she murmured automatically. "We should eat," she added, turning to Addie.

"Of course," Addie replied. She took a seat on the bench and shared her food with Nell.

They ate in silence, broken only occasionally by Trey's gentle questioning of Joshua. Jess kept glancing back toward the entrance to the church hall as if expecting trouble, while Addie kept pushing more of the chicken and black bean empanadas at everyone, urging them to eat.

Nell felt the awkwardness of the situation and wondered what had possessed her to agree to Trey's invitation. She should have refused, stayed with her own people. There would be more trouble, not all of it from the cattlemen. Henry would be furious once he learned what she had done. She considered asking Lottie not to tell him, but even if her sister-in-law agreed—which she never would—someone was bound to tell. Whitman Falls was a small community.

No, she had brought this on herself.

"It looks like your brother's wife and sons are leaving," Trey said. "If you and Joshua want to stay, I could—"

Nell was on her feet before he could finish that thought. "Come on, Joshua. We need to go." She glanced at the picnic basket she'd brought to carry her cake in. The cake sat uncut on a flat rock. Addie's husband and children were still eating, although everyone paused midbite when she made her sudden announcement.

Beyond them, Nell could see all the sheep-ranching families were climbing aboard the large wagon they'd traveled in for the occasion. Lottie kept glancing her way even as her sons hustled her toward the buckboard. "Joshua, we need to go now."

Addie seemed to understand the situation. "You and Joshua go on," she said. "I'll pack up some leftovers in your basket once we've finished here and bring it to you tomorrow. Would that be all right?"

"Please don't bother. I can get the basket some other time, and we have plenty to eat at home. Thank you."

"But I thought we were supposed to have cake with Mr. Porterfield," Joshua protested.

"Another time," Trey said, ruffling Joshua's hair even as he watched Nell.

"But Ma makes the best cake."

Nell had never heard her son be quite so outspoken—or disobedient. "Joshua, where are your manners? Now come along." She pressed Addie's hand in a gesture of gratitude, then led Joshua toward the wagon where her nephews were ready to drive away.

"Wait," she heard Lottie shout. "Here they come." Lottie pointed toward Nell and Joshua.

They had to run the last few steps as Lottie's sons pretended to try and control a restless team but in fact were deliberately stopping and starting the movement of the wagon. Lottie and another herder wife pulled Joshua aboard as the team plunged forward, leaving Nell still trying to catch up. Suddenly, she felt herself lifted, and in seconds, she had been deposited on the wagon bed. She tottered to gain her balance before looking back to see Trey Porterfield standing just a few feet away. He tipped his hat to her and Lottie and raised a hand in farewell to Joshua.

❦

When he rode the range, Trey's thoughts were more often than not on the scenery around him—that lone tree by the creek or the sunset over the mountains. He supposed he looked at the world with an artist's eye, considering how he might capture the color and beauty of it all. Lately when he envisioned these scenes as paintings, he saw Nell as part of them. She was the figure seated under the tree by the creek, her hand trailing through the water. She was the woman watching the sun rise, her back straight, her arm around her son, as they faced what might come. She filled his thoughts, waking or sleeping, and he wasn't at all sure what to do about that.

He let the next full day and night pass before he headed back to town for a visit with Addie. It was Sunday afternoon, and he saw people leaving the church after services. He stood for a minute scanning those departing, but Nell was not among them. Nor, for that matter, were any of the sheepherders or their families. Not a good sign.

Knowing he would likely find Addie in her office, he crossed the street and knocked lightly on the office door before opening it and going inside.

"Did you take the basket back yet?" He was pretty sure he didn't need to explain what basket he meant.

"A bunch of folks from the picnic came down with food poisoning overnight—Sybil Sinclair's chicken salad, I expect. I'll go tomorrow with some canned peaches and two pieces of her cake." She put down her pen and stared at him over the rim of her glasses. "Why?"

Trey shrugged. "No reason. Thought I might save you the trip. I've got some business at Fort Lowell and—"

Addie burst out laughing.

"What's so funny?"

"You are. 'Got some business at Fort Lowell,'" she mimicked. "You are a worse fibber than your brother, and that's saying something."

"Don't know what you mean," Trey grumbled. "Just thought I could save you a trip." He slammed his hat on his head and started for the door. "Sorry to have bothered you."

"Oh, for heaven's sake. Get back in here and talk to me."

Trey had never been able to stay mad at Addie for long. He sat in the chair opposite where she sat at her father's old rolltop desk and leaned forward, his elbows resting on his knees. "I can't seem to get her out of my head, Addie. I've never felt like this before about any woman."

"And why do you think that is?"

"I don't know. At first, I thought it was because of the way her husband died or the way she's been raising that boy and managing the ranch almost alone, but that's not really it."

"What does it feel like?"

"How the hell should I know?" He stood and began to pace. "I can't seem to get through chores or anything else without her being there on my mind. And it's dumb stuff like the way she chewed her food, for heaven's sake. Who pays attention to something like that?"

"Let me think," Addie said, pretending to take his rant seriously. "Got it. A man blindsided by love."

"Love? I don't have patience for your teasing, Addie. I have work to do, and there's a range war brewing, and—"

"And just when you least expected it, along came a woman who might turn out to be a perfect match."

"Look, all I was thinking was that if Mrs. Stokes

and I joined forces, maybe we could change some minds around here. Strictly business."

"Uh-huh," Addie said. She got up and pulled a wicker basket from under her desk. "Well, as long as you need to talk about business with Nell, you may as well be the one to take her this. You can let her know I'll stop by later in the week." She held the basket out to him, and it dangled there between them. "Well?"

"Maybe this is a bad idea." Trey might have been talking to himself.

Addie blew out a huff of exasperation, grabbed his hand, and hooked the handle of the basket over his wrist. "Go on and git. I have work to do." She walked to the door and held it open.

"Best not mention this to Jess," he said.

"You let me worry about Jess. What's important here is that you be happy. If, in the bargain, you can do something about this feud, so much the better."

"I barely know her," Trey protested.

Addie grinned. "Well, take my word as a doctor. There's a remedy for that. It takes time and conversation, but it's a surefire cure for the problem."

Trey smiled. There was something about Addie that reminded him of his mother. He was glad his brother had finally gotten around to marrying her. "Have I told you lately how good it is to have you in the family?"

"Not often enough," she said and pushed him the rest of the way out the door before shutting it behind him.

⁂

It was midafternoon when he reached the Stokes place. No one was out in the yard, although clothes hung on a line stretched between a large saguaro cactus and one of the posts that supported the porch roof. A thin stream of smoke rose from the chimney at the back of the house, and the front door stood open. The way Trey's horse was snorting and whinnying, it was hard to believe nobody had heard him ride up to the house.

Trey dismounted and approached the two steps up to the porch, removing his hat and sweeping his fingers through his thick hair. "Nell? Joshua? Hello?" He reached the open door and knocked on the frame as he peered inside.

The two front rooms were unoccupied, but he could smell something cooking—make that burning. He followed the smell and found the kitchen empty as well, while the contents of an iron skillet on the cookstove sizzled and hissed. He pulled the pan from the hot surface and set it aside. "Hello?" he called again as he peered through a small open window that looked out the back of the house.

Suddenly, he found himself staring down the double barrels of a shotgun, and he leaped away from the window.

"Get off my property," he heard Nell hiss. "I'll shoot. Don't think I won't."

"It's me, Nell. Trey Porterfield." He raised his hands.

The barrel of the gun wavered as she backed up a step to better see into the house. "What do you want?"

He reached for the basket that he'd set on the table when he entered the kitchen. "Addie asked me to return this. And I wanted to tell you in person how much I enjoyed that cake you made." He moved closer to the window to show her the basket and was shocked at her appearance. Her hair was tangled and hung in long strands over her shoulders and back. There were dark circles like bruises under her eyes, telling him that it had been some time since she'd slept. "Where is your son, Nell?"

"Joshua?" She said the boy's name as if she weren't quite sure who or where he was. "I sent him over to stay with my sister-in-law. He's not safe here."

Trey's heart hammered as he realized there must have been more trouble. Nell Stokes was not just scared—she was wild-eyed and terrified. "Nell, whatever you're cooking in here seems to be done. If you were of a mind to invite me to share your meal, I would be most obliged."

He waited while she lowered the shotgun, letting it hang loosely at her side as she surveyed the surrounding area. "Did you come alone?"

"Yeah. Addie said she'd be stopping by later in the week."

She glared at him. "I am not asking after Addie," she said. "I am asking if there are others out there waiting."

"Waiting?"

"For dark. That's when they come. Two nights now, they've come, riding hard toward the house and barn, carrying torches and swinging them around. The chickens you sent are dead," she added. "Burned alive. They set fire to the coop last night. I figure they plan to work their way through the property, burning the outbuildings and making me watch from the house."

She was talking more to herself than to him, rambling on as she described her ordeal. "They came right up to the door and banged on it so hard, it shook. Told me to get ready, 'cause they'd be back, and if I was still here, they'd make me wish I hadn't stayed."

Slowly, she set the gun aside and sank onto the ground, folding her arms around herself and rocking slowly back and forth. "So at first light, I sent Joshua away. He'll be all right. He got started before the heat rose, and he knows the way and..." She started to sob as she pounded the dry earth with her fist.

Trey, who had been standing by the window, disbelieving, dropped the basket and ran out the back door to her. He sank to his knees and gathered her into his arms. "Shhh," he whispered as she clung to him, her tears wetting the front of his shirt. He kissed the top of her head. "I'm not going to let anything more happen here," he promised. "I'll take you to your brother's place, and we'll get Joshua and then go into town where you can stay with Addie and Jess. They've got plenty of room. And then—"

"No! If I leave the ranch unguarded, they'll surely destroy whatever is left. This is Calvin's legacy for our son. I have to protect that. There's nobody but me to do that. My nephews are angry with me, and the rest of the men are away and..." She was looking up at him, her face streaked with dirt and tears, her eyes pleading with him to understand.

He stood and held out his hand to her. "Come inside out of this heat," he said. "We can talk about what's best for you and Joshua."

She only hesitated a moment before she got to her

feet, and they walked around the side of the house to the back stoop, but when she stumbled, Trey picked her up and carried her the rest of the way. She did not resist, resting her head against his shoulder. She didn't say anything more even once they were inside, as he helped her to a chair. At the sink, he pumped water to fill a canning jar that was as close to a glass as he could find. When he handed it to her, she cupped both hands around it as if warming them before drinking the contents down without hesitation.

He noticed sweat trickling down her neck and temples. Gently, he removed the glass from her fingers and refilled it, then soaked a towel made from a flour sack in the trickle of tepid water running from the pump. "Here," he said, giving her the water. "Take it slow this time." He stood by while she sipped at the water, her eyes fixed on the open window, her hands shaking.

"They came from that direction," she mumbled. "We were asleep. I first woke when I heard the horses and saw the flash of the torches they carried."

"Your nephew?"

"Both boys were so upset about that business at the church that they refused to stay."

"How many men?" Trey asked as he lifted her hair and lay the wet cloth across the back of her neck. Her skin felt like it was on fire.

"Six…maybe eight?" She shook her head. "It seemed like dozens. They rode in circles around the house, hooting and hollering. Some of them waving those torches and others firing their guns in the air."

"Did you recognize any of them? Maybe from the church social?" He was thinking of Pete—and Javier.

"They had their faces covered with bandanas and wore hats." She pulled the cloth away from her neck and began wiping her face. "They could have killed Joshua firing their guns that way," she said, and this time, her voice was filled with rage.

He had to keep her calm so that she would remember as many details as possible. He lifted a thick strand of her hair and began to comb through the tangles with his fingers. He remembered his mother doing something like that whenever one of his sisters was overwrought. "How were you able to get Joshua away?"

"Just before dawn, they set fire to some brush near the barn, and they all rode over that way to watch. They were laughing and cheering for the barn to catch fire, but thank God, it didn't. Anyway, that's when I told Joshua to go. Henry and Ernest had left one of the mules behind for me. The mule was in that corral there behind the coop. Joshua—bless him—was able to make it to the corral, climb on the mule's back. Once he loosened the gate, that mule bolted for the hills, taking Joshua with him."

She surprised him by reaching back and grasping his hand. "Will you go see that he made it? That he's safe with Lottie and the boys?" And when he hesitated, she stood and clutched at his shoulders. "Please. I have to know that he's safe. If anything were to happen to Joshua…"

It seemed the most natural thing in the world to fold his arms around her, pull her close, and rest his chin on top of her head. "I'll go," he promised. "But I won't leave you here alone, Nell. Either come with me and stay with your sister-in-law, or agree to get your son and go into town. If we start out now, we can have you settled one way or the other before dusk, and I can be back here to watch over the place until your brother returns."

She hesitated, then stepped away, just out of reach, and began hastily twisting her hair into a knot. "I can't ask you to do that."

"It's me asking you, Nell. Let me do this for you."

"Why? Why do you care what happens to somebody like me?"

It was a fair question and one he thought he was prepared to answer—he could do it so it wasn't personal, in terms of trying to find some way for the sheep and cattle ranchers to live together in peace. But as he looked at her tear-stained face, her skin tanned to a golden sheen, as he recalled how perfectly she had fit against him, he realized his offer had nothing to do with range wars or politics. This was about her and this unfamiliar urge to protect and watch over her. And realizing that, words failed him.

"It's not important why. Are you coming or not?"

She nodded.

"Get dressed then. I'll be outside." He knew he sounded gruff and short-tempered, but the woman confused him—what he felt for her baffled him and made him uneasy. Trey wasn't one who liked change, and there was something about Nell Stokes that promised to change his life in ways he hadn't considered.

Three

Nell had no idea why she trusted Trey Porterfield, but she did—so much so that when he mounted his horse and then offered her his hand to pull her up to sit in front of him, she did not hesitate. His kindness in sending them the chickens and in the way he had included Joshua and her at the church social certainly were factors. But the truth was that his was the only offer of help she was likely to get before darkness came and with it, perhaps, the return of the marauders.

The fact that he was the kind of man to offer help when others simply turned away spoke volumes.

Although her land and Henry's combined covered nowhere near the territory the Porterfield ranch did, the ride would still take over an hour. Conversation between them was limited to Trey making some observation or comment about their surroundings or the effect of the weather on crops and animals. Long periods of silence filled the rest. Nell felt her head bob and her eyelids flutter as the exhaustion of the last two nights of little sleep claimed her.

"Almost there," she heard Trey murmur.

She glanced around. "Surely not," she protested. "We haven't—"

She could feel the rumble of Trey's chuckle under her hand, which was resting on his chest. Quickly, she withdrew it.

"You've been sleeping for a while," he said. "Your brother's place is just over that rise."

"Half brother," she replied.

"You don't care for him?"

"I don't know him. He was grown and gone before I was ten," she replied as she straightened so she was not leaning on him and glanced around. She was glad there was no one to see them. What a sight they must make. If Lottie—and especially the boys—saw her come riding up practically in the arms of a cattle rancher, they were going to have more questions than she was prepared to answer. "Let me walk," she said as she made a futile effort to dismount the still-walking horse.

"Whoa!" She wasn't sure if Trey was speaking to the horse or to her, since at the same time as he pulled at the reins, his strong forearm encircled her waist and held her firm against his body. "I'll walk," he said. "You stay put."

He climbed down, made sure she was secure, and then clicked his tongue against his cheek as he led the horse up and over the rise. He paused for just a moment, surveying the scene below. Lottie was in the yard, gesturing to her son, Ira. Joshua was nowhere to be seen.

"Hurry," Nell urged. "I don't see my son. What if he didn't make it here? What if we passed him on our way and he's hurt or—"

"There's somebody looking out that upstairs window there." Trey pointed, and relief took the place of panic when Nell saw Joshua lean out the open window and point in their direction.

"He's there," she whispered around the lump in her throat. "He's safe."

"Good." Trey led the horse down the hillside, and when Lottie looked their way, he waved.

Neither Lottie nor Ira made any move toward meeting them. They just stood where they were and watched. But Joshua came running from the house and across the yard. When he reached them, he was so out of breath and coughing so hard, he had no voice for speaking. Trey immediately lifted him onto the horse to straddle the animal behind Nell. He unstrapped a canteen, removed the cap, and handed it to Joshua. He was, she decided in that moment, a genuinely kind man.

"Thank you, Trey." She liked saying his name. She liked the way he ducked his head to hide a shy smile at her gratitude. She liked the way he patted Joshua's knee before picking up the reins again. The truth was, she liked a good deal about Trey Porterfield, and in these times and this part of the country, that was not a wise choice.

"You all right, Nell?" Lottie called as Trey tied the horse to a hitching post outside the wrought-iron gate of the yard that was surrounded by a high adobe wall.

"Yes. Thanks to Mr. Porterfield."

Ira scowled at her and refused to even look at Trey. "What happened, Auntie Nell?"

"I told you," Joshua interrupted, having found his

voice. "We got home from the church social, and some men came real late after we was asleep and scared Ma real bad, and then they came back last night."

Ira waited for Trey to help Joshua and Nell down and then stepped between him and them. "You wouldn't know anything about that, would you, cowboy?"

"Ira, mind your manners," Nell said. She didn't miss the fact that Lottie had said nothing to reprimand her son's rudeness. "Mr. Porterfield has been very kind to go out of his way to bring me here."

"Sort of a coincidence then that he just happened to show up?"

She noticed that Trey was saying nothing in his own defense. "Well, thank heavens he did. Lottie, can Joshua and I stay with you just until the men get back from the shearing?"

"Of course." Lottie seemed relieved to be able to agree to something. "But what about your place? If those men come back and find it deserted?"

Trey cleared his throat. "I told Mrs. Stokes that I would keep watch."

Ira laughed. "Talk about a fox and a henhouse. Come to think of it, you've got some similarities to the fox—beady eyes and a shifty way about you."

This time, he'd gone too far, for it was Lottie who spoke up. "That's enough, Son." She turned her attention to Trey. "As soon as Joshua showed up this morning, I sent my other son to carry the news of these attacks to my husband and the other men. I expect he and the others will be back by morning at the latest. Ira here can watch over Nell's place until then. We do appreciate you looking in on her, but she's fine."

Trey turned his attention to Nell. "What do you want me to do, Mrs. Stokes? I can leave you here and go back to watch over your place. I can take you and Joshua into town to stay with Doc Addie and send soldiers from the fort to make sure things stay safe at your ranch. Or I can just go."

The news that Henry and Ernest would be returning soon, coupled with the way Lottie kept nervously wringing her hands and Ira stood with boots firmly planted and his muscled arms folded over his chest, made Nell's decision for her. "Just go," she said softly, deliberately repeating his words so there could be no mistake.

She watched as a shadow passed over his normally genial face and his lips twitched as if he wanted to say something more. He nodded, replaced his hat, and unhitched the reins as he climbed back in the saddle in one fluid motion. "Ladies," he said, tipping his hat before riding away.

As soon as he was gone, Ira confronted her. "Don't know what you've got in mind, Aunt Nell, but you'd best think again if you're planning on getting friendly with that cowboy—any cowboy."

He towered over her, but he was still a child to her adult, and their relationship alone should have required respect. She ignored him and turned her attention to Lottie. "Thank you for taking us in. If it's all right with you, Lottie, Joshua and I will stay here until the men return."

"Of course," Lottie replied after glancing at her son to get his approval. He shrugged and grunted. "I'll just go see about making up the spare room for you." She hurried back to the house.

Nell turned to her nephew. "Do not ever speak to me in that tone again, Ira. What I do and who I involve in my business is just that—my business."

"We'll see about that once Pa gets back." He stalked off toward the barn.

"Why's everybody so mad?" Joshua asked.

Nell had been so caught up in the standoff with Ira that she had momentarily forgotten her son was witnessing it all. She forced a smile and ruffled his hair. "No need for you to worry. Families sometimes fight, but it's more out of love than anger."

Joshua looked doubtful. "Ira was pretty mad. You shoulda heard him right before you got here."

She saw her nephew emerge from the barn leading the one horse Henry owned and carrying a rifle. "Go on up to the house, Joshua, and see if you can help your Aunt Lottie. I'll be right there."

As usual, Joshua didn't question her but trudged away as if the weight of the world were on his shoulders. Nell turned in the opposite direction, reaching Ira just after he had mounted up.

"Where are you going, Ira?" Her heart hammered with fear that he planned to go after Trey.

"Not that it's any of your business, but I'm headed to your place to stand watch till Pa and Ernest and Spud get there."

He started to turn the horse's head, but Nell reached up and held the bridle firm. "I meant what I said, Ira. That ranch belongs to me, and I expect you and everyone else to respect that, understood?"

Ira leaned down so that his face was close to hers. "You don't deserve no respect, woman. I saw the way you looked at that rancher. I saw the way he looked at you. Your husband ain't been dead a year before you go cozying up to some cowboy? You that desperate for a man in your bed?"

She knew he had to be repeating talk he had heard from the older men, but she was so shocked at his venom that she loosened her grip on the bridle. Ira saw his chance and kicked the sides of the horse so suddenly and viciously that the animal took off, leaving her standing in a cloud of dust. And as she walked slowly back to the house, she was shaking. Her fury was tempered only by the realization that there was a kernel of truth in what Ira said. After all, the two nights of terror she had endured had come at the hands of cowboys. Trey may not have ridden with them, but he was one of them. Those men were his friends. Some of them might even work for him. Ira had no right to chastise her, but could she blame him? Could she blame Henry or Ernest when Calvin, their cousin and friend, had most likely died at the hands of these men or others like them?

"Lottie, would it be all right if I lie down for a bit? It's been—I've not slept."

Lottie set aside the towels she'd been placing on the washstand. "Of course. It must have been so awful, and I expect it's just now catching up with you." She wrapped her arm around Nell's waist and walked with her to the narrow bed. "You sleep as long as you like."

"No, wake me when Henry and the others…"

Lottie knelt and unlaced Nell's shoes. "Anything Henry might have to say can wait until you've had a chance to regain your strength."

It occurred to Nell that this was the first time she had ever heard Lottie say a word that might be seen as in conflict with what her husband might think or want. "Thank you, Lottie," she murmured.

"That cowboy, Nell, well. Anybody can see he's a good man, but he'll have to choose who he's gonna stand with at some point—and it won't be you."

Nell heard the soft click of the door closing and turned onto her side, facing the window. A few minutes later, she saw Joshua and Lottie walk to a bench under the shade of a cottonwood tree. Lottie handed Joshua a dishpan filled with early peas to shuck. Nell's eyes fluttered shut, and the last thing she heard before sleep claimed her was her son's laughter.

༺༻

When Trey reached home, it was after dark, and he rode straight to the bunkhouse. Javier sat on the *banco* outside the door, his arms folded across his chest, his legs outstretched, and his hat covering his face.

"Javier!"

Trey reined in his horse and dismounted. By the time he had covered the distance between the horse and his friend, Javier was standing, watching closely as he clearly tried to judge Trey's mood.

"*¿Qué más, Jefe?*"

Trey grabbed his friend by his shirtfront and backed him up to the wall of the bunkhouse. Never before had he laid his hands on Javier in anger, but this time, the man had crossed a line that friendship couldn't forgive. "You tell me." He stared at Javier, who met his gaze briefly, then glanced away.

"Not sure what you're—"

Trey shook him. "The Stokes place last night, and the night before. You have anything to do with that?"

He had his answer before he finished the question.

Javier scowled up at him, meeting his eyes directly. "You gotta choose a side, Trey."

Trey felt an anger unlike any he had ever experienced in his life. It was born of frustration and exasperation—and fear. The fear that after the decades that his parents, his sister Maria, and her husband had managed the ranch successfully, despite all kinds of human and natural disasters, he might be the one who failed. He gave Javier one more shove and then released him.

"Why do there have to be sides? Why can't we all just live here and work the land and—"

While Trey might be quick to anger and quicker to let things go, Javier had no trouble showing his rage. He stepped closer to Trey and, with no pretense of modulating his voice, shouted, "You know why, Trey, and stop pretending you don't. Them damned woolies chew the grass down to the nub, all while their sharp hooves finish the job by digging up whatever's left by the roots. This used to be open range—cattle range— and now we're supposed to share it? You got any idea how far we've had to drive the herd to find decent pasture for the summer? That's because of them."

"And that makes it all right to terrorize a widow and her sick son for two nights running?" Trey roared in return.

Javier studied him hard for a long moment. They were both flushed, their fists clenched, their bodies poised for a fight. Javier was the first to step away. He stared down at the ground, waiting for his breathing to calm, then looked up at Trey. "You falling for that sheepherder's woman, my friend?" His tone was sympathetic.

Trey pulled off his hat and ran his fingers through his sweat-slicked hair. "She's an innocent in this fight, and I just don't want to see anybody else get hurt, Javier. There's got to be a way we can work this out. They aren't going away—and neither are we."

"We were here first," Javier said, his voice petulant.

Trey allowed himself a wry smile. "Technically, the Indians were here first, and look what we did to them. After that, it was the Spaniards—your ancestors. And they raised sheep, my friend, long before cattlemen showed up."

The two of them leaned on the corral fence and gazed out into the black night for a long moment. "This isn't just about sheep versus cattle, Javier. The truth is things are changing—everything about the life our parents knew is different. Every year, another new town springs up or spreads out. We either learn to live with that or we spend the rest of our time on this earth fighting against progress that'll surely beat us in the end."

"So what's your plan?" Javier asked.

Trey shrugged. "Don't have one. Just the notion that we need to make this more about how we're gonna live in peace and less about needin' to be right."

"Let me ask you something, Trey. If that woman and her boy weren't part of this, would that change the way you look at it?"

"I hope not, but yeah, maybe."

Javier pushed away from the split-rail fence. "Got

to give you one thing—she's awfully pretty, and from what I saw of her at the church social, she's not afraid to stand her ground. She's got conviction. You need somebody like that, Trey. Too bad she's on the wrong side of things."

Trey bristled. "*Need* someone like her? Is that how you see me? As a man who needs somebody to speak for him because I'm too weak to do it myself?"

"You're strong in ways I'll never be able to understand, Trey. But you've got this way of thinking that everybody's as good as you are. Few are. Most folks are a blend of good and bad. Nell Stokes appears to know that."

"I know that."

Javier shook his head. "Trouble is you have this idea you can change those other folks to come around to your way of seeing things."

"It's called hope," Trey argued.

"It's called impossible." Javier glanced back at a couple of the other cowboys coming out of the bunkhouse, stretching and yawning. "We got the night shift," he said as he pulled on his hat.

Trey turned to the other hands. "You boys head on out. I need Javier here to help me."

"With what?" Javier's eyebrows lifted with suspicion.

"Come morning, we're gonna pay a call on Henry Galway and see if we can work something out, a council or something to start decidin' what's fair. And then you are going to apologize to Mrs. Stokes for scaring the bejesus out of her and her son. But before we do any of that, we're gonna head for the Stokes place and see if we can repair any of the damage done there before she and her boy get home. Get some rest, Javier. We leave at daybreak."

⤏

But next morning when they reached the Stokes place, they were greeted by four men, each carrying a double-barreled shotgun. Trey recognized Henry Galway and Nell's nephews. He assumed the other man must be her late husband's cousin.

"Gentlemen," he said, raising two fingers to the brim of his hat by way of greeting. He noticed the burned-out chicken coop and the remains of the small fires that had been set close to the barn.

"Nell, get out here," Galway shouted without taking his eyes off Trey and Javier.

She came to the door and waited.

"You recognize either of these men?"

Trey watched as she slowly walked across the yard. She looked first at him and then for a longer moment at Javier. Trey noticed how Javier ducked his head and pulled his hat lower over his eyes.

"I do," Nell said, and all four men raised the guns an inch higher and took half a step forward.

"That man is Doc Addie's brother-in-law, and both of them were at the church social I attended last Friday. You know who he is, Henry. Our families sit across the aisle from each other in church." To Trey's amazement, she walked directly to Javier and held out her hand. "I don't believe we've been formally introduced, sir. I am Nell Stokes, and you are?"

Trey saw how Javier's hand shook as he returned her greeting and mumbled his name.

She turned around but did not move away from them, positioning herself in such a way that if anyone fired his weapon, she might be the victim. "Gentlemen, I believe you know my half brother, Henry Galway. This is my late husband's cousin, Ernest Stokes."

"Go in the house, Sister," Henry growled, ignoring her attempt at civility.

"Not until you put down those guns," she replied and continued to stand her ground.

"Nell." The man called Ernest simply stated her name, but Trey heard the warning in his tone.

She ignored him. "Was there something you needed to discuss with me, Mr. Porterfield?"

"For God's sake, Nell," her brother hissed.

"I'll thank you not to take our Lord's name in vain, Henry, and furthermore, I would remind you that this is still my land and home. Therefore, I assume that whatever business these gentlemen have here, it is with me, not you." She turned her back on her relatives and looked up at Trey. "If you had second thoughts about the need to keep watch over my property, Mr. Porterfield, I appreciate that. But my brother made good time and made sure it was safe for me to come home. As you can plainly see, everything is under control."

She might be speaking to him, but Trey was well aware her little lecture was really directed at her brother.

"Holy…" Trey heard Javier mutter under his breath and knew he was impressed.

"Just wanted to be sure everything was quiet and see if we might be able to help repair some of the damage," Trey replied. "Glad to see you have all the protection you might need."

"More than enough," she said. "But thank you for coming."

Trey turned his attention back to the four men. Henry and Ernest had lowered their guns, but the two younger men kept theirs at the ready. "Mr. Galway, I'm glad we had this chance to meet. I was wondering if perhaps you might organize a few of the sheep ranchers to become part of a council with me and some of the other cattle ranchers."

"And just why would I do that?"

Trey removed his hat so the man could see his face clearly. "Because, sir, your brother-in-law has been killed, and if things continue on that kind of a path, there's bound to be more bloodshed."

Ernest raised his gun again. "You threatenin' us, mister?"

"He's trying to find a way to peace," Nell said before Trey could respond. "Now lower your guns and keep them lowered."

Henry Galway studied Trey closely. "I'll see what I can do," he said after a long moment had passed in silence.

Trey noticed that Henry's sons and Ernest looked at Henry as if the man had gone loco.

"Good. I'll set up a time and place and—"

"I'll set the time and place," Henry replied. "You worry about getting your kind to go along with this meeting."

"Fair enough," Trey replied as he pulled his hat back on.

"Neutral territory," Javier insisted, and Henry nodded. "And we bring Reverend Moore just to make sure things are fair."

"Agreed," Henry said.

Nell started back toward the house, but paused after passing her brother and the others. "Thank you for your concern, Mr. Porterfield. Good day to you both."

"Ma'am." Trey and Javier spoke in unison as they watched her enter the house.

Her brother and the others seemed less impressed. "Just so we understand each other, Porterfield," Henry said, "my sister don't need you checking in on her property—or her."

"Half sister," Trey couldn't resist saying. Knowing he was on the verge of undoing the little progress he'd managed to make, he nodded to Javier, and the two of them rode away.

❧

Henry wasted no time making his feelings about the whole encounter clear. He stormed into the house, followed by Ernest. "If you ever do something like that again, Nell, I swear I will make you regret the day you crossed me."

Nell marked the passage in her Bible she'd been pretending to read, set it aside, and looked up at him. "Do not threaten me, Henry." She stood and brushed past both men. She opened the front door. "You should get home. You've left Lottie there on her own, and you know how she worries."

"That cowboy has got to you, woman," Ernest

grumbled. "His fancy talk and all has you thinking maybe you can do better than the likes of me."

Nell felt a bubble of laughter rising in her chest at the sheer lunacy of that statement. She swallowed hard to keep it at bay and faced Ernest. She wanted to say, *I could set my sights on just about any man in the territory and do better than the likes of you, Ernest Stokes.* But all she said was, "Good day, Ernest."

"Ernest stays," Henry grumbled.

"No. He doesn't. And if I have to explain why to either of you, then I am in more danger from members of my own family than I ever was from those renegade cowboys. Now go home." She fixed her eyes on her half brother's weathered face until both men moved past her and out the door.

"I'll have Ira stay the night," Henry said softly.

"Thank you. Give Lottie my love." She closed the door and, a few minutes later, saw both men and Spud walk up the trail and over the rise. She lifted the lace curtain and saw Ira feeding her burro and his father's horse near the corral.

The day passed as she and Ira cleaned up the aftermath of the attacks, ate a silent supper together with Joshua, and then mumbled their good nights. As she walked through the house extinguishing the lamps, she saw a lantern burning dimly in the barn and knew Ira had bedded down there for the night. She thought of going out and telling him to come inside where he could sleep in one of the extra bedrooms, but if trouble did come, he would be more likely to hear it if he was out there. She banked the fire in the kitchen stove and headed up the stairs.

For once, Joshua was sleeping soundly. He was curled onto his side, the blankets thrown back.

She covered Joshua and ran her fingers lightly through his hair before crossing the hall to the room she and Calvin had shared, to the double bed where they had once whispered their dreams and hopes for the future to each other. The bed that Calvin had abandoned in those last months of their marriage. Calvin had shown little interest in their son once he realized Joshua was not likely to develop into the strong boy he needed to take over the sheep ranch one day. Instead, Calvin had pushed her to produce more babies, and after she had miscarried three times, Calvin seemed to have given up. The last few months before he'd been killed had been hard ones for their marriage. They barely spoke. She was preoccupied with Joshua, and Calvin spent more time than usual out in the field or barn, coming to bed after she had already lain down for the night. The bed where she had lain awake these last several nights, listening for the trouble that seemed destined to come.

She sat on the side of the bed, the wire springs creaking under her weight. She unlaced her shoes and removed them, then walked to the window, taking down her hair and brushing through the strands with her fingers. Outside, a nearly full moon cast a stream of light from the house onto the trail that led away from the ranch, the trail Trey Porterfield had followed to rescue her. Just after the raids, she had been too terrified to register details. But now as she stood at the window in the moonlight, it all came back to her.

The strength of his arms enfolding her.

The warmth that emanated from his body as he held her close and consoled her.

The ease with which he had carried her into the house.

The way she curled into him so naturally as he rode with her to Henry's ranch.

The steady beat of his heart against her cheek during the ride.

The way his large hands practically encircled her waist when he lifted her down from the horse.

The way his chuckle rumbled deep in his chest and his eyes crinkled with interest and concern.

The scent of him—pine soap mingling with the worn leather of his vest and the unique fragrance of his skin.

She ran her fingers over her throat and cheeks and thought of his hands, those long fingers that had combed through the tangles of her hair. She lifted her hair and inclined her head as if to receive his touch, his kiss on her neck. A shudder of desire coursed through her body like a waterfall freed from winter's grip, and she instinctively stiffened to hold on to it.

How long had it been?

Too long.

Never.

Never like this.

❧

"You don't really think Galway will show up for this meeting, do you?" Javier said the following day as he and Trey rode slowly across the Porterfield land, checking for more vandalism.

"Why wouldn't he want to end this as much as I do—as *we* do?"

"Because they think they can beat us, starve out our cattle and poison the water with that stuff that oozes from them woolies' split hooves."

"That's a myth, Javier. Don't go believing everything Pete Collins tells you." Trey had heard it before, the story that the gelatin secreted from the hooves of the sheep poisoned the water and grass so cattle would refuse to drink or graze. The truth was that while the strange scent stopped the cattle momentarily, in time, they ate or drank anyway with no harm. But he also knew this was a debate he would not win. "Nell Stokes recognized you, didn't she?"

"I guess. She saw me at the church social."

Trey clenched his fists, determined to hold his temper. "She saw you at her ranch as well. You and Collins and his men." It was not a question, and Javier's refusal to comment told him he was right. "Collins is going to end up shot one of these days. I'd just as soon you not be in the line of fire when it happens."

"We just thought to scare her a little. Just thought if we could run her off, then maybe—"

"That ranch is all she and the boy have left in the world, Javier. Would you put them out with nothin'?"

"Things got out of hand," Javier admitted. "The others wouldn't hear reason, so I left."

"Not soon enough," Trey muttered. Neither man spoke for the rest of the ride back to the Porterfield ranch.

They reached the corral and dismounted, and Trey could only hope he had given Javier something to think about. "Come on up to the house for your supper," he said. Turning his back on Javier wouldn't help his oldest friend find his way from all this needless violence and hatred. "Your ma claims it's been too long since you sat down with her and your pa instead of with the other hands."

"I'll just see to the horses first."

Trey nodded and hefted his saddle to rest on the split-log fence.

"She's something, that Stokes woman," Javier said. "The way she stood there facing down her own brother."

Trey heard a grudging hint of respect in his friend's words and smiled. "Yep. She's quite a lady."

As usual, Trey couldn't seem to stop thinking about Nell, long after he'd had his supper, checked on the herd, said good night to Juanita, and gone to the library where he opened his sketchbook. He drew a man and a woman on a horse, all the while reliving the rescue of Nell Stokes. There had been something so right about the way she had rested her head against his chest, her breath coming in even little puffs, her fist curled against the base of his throat. And before that, there had been the rage he'd felt on her behalf when he saw her collapse in tears in the dirt, energy spent, fear draining whatever strength she might have left.

As he worked, he thought about Javier admitting he had been party to the raids. He knew if this were Addie who had been terrorized, Jess would have beat the living daylights out of Javier, friend or not. But that was not Trey's way. The months he had spent sketching the wonders of Yellowstone had strength-ened his natural bent toward finding the way to harmony—in nature and in life. Javier was his lifelong friend, as close to being a second brother as one could be without actual blood. Trey would no more strike Javier than he would Jess.

But the way his friend had changed worried him—worried Juanita and Eduardo as well—and this twisting of the man he'd always seen as a brother was something Trey could not stand by and let happen. He thought about the way Javier had spoken with admiration for Nell. Maybe he was finally coming around. The thing about Javier was that the other cowboys respected him. Maybe asking Javier to go with him as his foreman and a man who held influence over other cowhands for the meeting with the sheep ranchers would turn his friend away from Pete Collins and back to the man Trey knew him to be.

He had no intention of trying to recruit other ranchers at this point. He couldn't think of a single one he might persuade to attend such a meeting. Once he'd had a chance to talk calmly with Henry Galway and whoever he brought along, then he would have the information he needed to talk to his fellow cattlemen.

As he continued to work on the sketch, Trey smiled, imagining how grateful Nell Stokes would be if he could work something out so that the two factions could live in peace. It occurred to him she might even be inspired to give him a kiss, or at the very least, she might wrap her arms around his neck and hold him close. Of course, that led to the more carnal thoughts of lying with her. And just when he thought he'd settled his worries enough to finally get some sleep, he realized he had something else on his mind—his body entwined with hers, their appetite for each other insatiable.

He forced himself to put those thoughts aside for now.

Convinced he would get no sleep, he started another picture of Nell, this time out on the range, her hair wild around her. The long hours of thinking about holding her had made him realize his feelings for her had little to do with finding a way for herders and ranchers to live in peace. No, he wanted her, wanted to spend his days—and nights—with her, hear her laughter, listen to her talk.

Hadn't everybody been saying it was high time he found himself a good woman and settled down? Well, the way he looked at it, Nell Stokes was about as close to a perfect match as he was likely to find. She certainly was the first woman who had him losing sleep. He considered his original idea—the one about joining forces with her in business. That might be the best way to start getting better acquainted. And if she got to know him and didn't want more from him, well, he'd respect that.

Besides, if they did join forces, it might help pave the way for this meeting between the herders and the cattlemen. It might show everyone there was another way to cut through all their differences.

He stretched and closed his sketchbook. Morning was hours away, and he knew he would get no sleep. Restlessly, he wandered the rooms of the house. What if he went to see her? He'd have to make sure her brother wasn't around if he hoped to talk to her about joining forces. She might turn him down flat, but he had to try. He grabbed his hat and headed for the corral. If he rode hard, he could be at her place well before dawn.

❧

Juanita was standing at the window of her bedroom when she saw Trey go riding off in the middle of the night. Earlier, she had watched Javier do the same thing, although he'd been headed in the opposite direction.

When Trey's mother was dying, Constance had gripped Juanita's hand and exacted a promise.

"Trey lives in a world of his own creation," she had said. "He believes the world is fair and just. My fear is someday that belief will be tested, and he will be destroyed. Promise me you'll keep watching over him."

Juanita had assured her friend and employer she had no reason to worry. "You raised all your children to be strong and do what's right," she had reminded Constance. "Trey will find his way as they all have."

"He's a dreamer, Nita."

And because she couldn't argue with that, Juanita had promised. Now, as she watched Trey go riding off to who knew where, she wondered if she had the strength to keep her vow.

Behind her, she heard Eduardo sigh. "*Querida*, what is it?"

"The boys have ridden off," she said. "Not together."

"You have to trust that they will find their way, Nita."

She went back to the bed and sat, leaning against her husband for the strength she no longer had. "I do trust them," she said softly. "It's others I don't trust—this range war. Everyone is so bitter and angry, everyone taking sides. 'Them,' 'those people'—it used to be that was for us, those with a different color of skin. But now those are names they call one another. Our boys are in the middle of that, Eduardo, and I am afraid for both of them."

And when Eduardo did not reply but simply wrapped his arms around her and held her close, she understood that he too was afraid.

⁓

Nell had just checked on Joshua and returned to the kitchen to warm herself a cup of milk when a soft tapping sounded at the back door. She inched the lace curtain aside and saw the figure of a man—a cowboy, judging by the wide-brimmed hat he wore. She reached for the rifle.

"Nell?"

The voice was deep, husky, and familiar. It was the voice she'd heard in her dreams in the nights that had passed since Trey Porterfield had rescued her.

"It's me, Trey. Put the gun down and let me in," he said, and there was a hint of humor in his tone.

She loosened her grip on the gun but did not put it away. "What do you want?"

"To talk."

"Why? It's the middle of the night."

She thought she heard an audible release of his breath, but it could have been the wind.

"Because I… Come on, Nellie, let me in."

No one ever called her "Nellie." Coming from his mouth, it sounded like an endearment.

She opened the door enough so that he was able to sidle into the kitchen. "You can't stay," she said, suddenly nervous being alone with him in the deep shadows of a room lit only by the lantern on the table near the stairs. "My nephew is in the barn and…"

"That's part of why we need to talk. He's sound asleep—hardly the watchman you need these days."

She didn't know what to do. He was standing so near and yet not near enough. She could hear his even breathing. "I can't expect him to stay awake through the night," she said.

"That's exactly what you should expect. What good is having someone on guard otherwise? If he were out watching over the sheep, would his father put up with him sleeping?"

He had a point. "Did you come to check up on me?" she asked.

"Partially. I also want to talk about how we might prevent this range war that's about to destroy us all. I've got an idea about how you and I might work together to head things off before somebody else ends up dead. I'd like your opinion."

No man had ever sought her opinion on anything more serious than whether to put another log on the fire. "Why me?"

Trey let out a long breath and placed his hat on the table. "Can we sit?"

She nodded. "Do you want coffee? It's cold but—"

"No, thanks." He pulled out a chair at the kitchen table and waited for her to be seated before taking the chair next to her. He leaned forward, his elbows resting on his knees. "It occurs to me that of all the people around here who raise sheep, you are the only one who has made any connection with those outside of your own community."

"You're talking about Addie?"

"Yeah."

"She reached out to me, just stopped by one day after Calvin died. Said she was in the neighborhood and thought she'd see how Joshua and I were doing."

"And you let her in—into your house and into your life," Trey pointed out. "You did the same with me. And the other day, even though you knew Javier had ridden with those cowboys, you didn't give him away to your brother."

"There was no point. Henry would have—"

"That's my contention. You kept the situation from escalating." He took hold of her hand. "Nell, if we work together, I think there might be a way we can broker some form of a peace."

She was sure the passion of his words lay behind the spontaneous physical contact, and yet she couldn't ignore how intimate it felt with his hand covering hers, more so because they were sitting in the near-darkness. Slowly, she withdrew her hand. "I thought when you mentioned working together you were speaking of sheep and cattle ranchers—the men. I can't think how I might make any difference at all."

"What if we joined up?"

She pushed back her chair and stood. She walked to the dry sink and stared out the window at the darkness. "I don't understand. What are you suggesting?"

"We could work together, make your ranch and mine one big operation that raises cattle *and* sheep."

"Henry would never stand for that."

"It's your land, your place, Nell."

"My late husband left instructions that put Henry in

charge." She continued staring out the window, and he remained seated.

"But this place belongs to you—and Joshua. If we became partners, then—"

"Your intentions are admirable, Trey, but you have to be realistic. It's not going to be that simple, working things out," she said. "I mean, the feud has deep roots and—"

She heard the scrape of his chair on the wooden floor and seconds later felt him standing behind her. "There's another way," he said softly. "It's gonna sound crazy, but hear me out."

Her curiosity piqued, she faced him.

He took a deep breath. "If you and me got married, then neither Henry nor any other man would have a say in what you do with this place."

She was so shocked by his suggestion that words failed her. Suddenly, she realized the position she had allowed him to place her in—alone, middle of the night, no one to hear should he try to…

"I have to go check on my son," she said, brushing past him, barely noting that he stepped aside and made no move to detain her. But instead of heading for the stairs, she picked up the rifle she'd left by the door and aimed it at him. "You should go, Mr. Porterfield."

He raised his hands to shoulder height, retrieved his hat from the table, and walked to the door. "I mean you no harm, Nell. Just please think about what I've said. Joining forces, whether as a business arrangement or through matrimony, would—"

She lowered the gun and her head. "Just go," she whispered and waited for the click of the door.

Four

WHAT COULD HE HAVE BEEN THINKING? HE WAS NOT an impulsive man—that was Jess's role. But blurting out a proposal like that without thinking it through? Not that he hadn't thought about the two of them as more than just business partners, but acting on such thoughts? All of a sudden, he found himself proposing, probably destroying any chance he might have of persuading her to join with him in a dual ranching venture. No, it wasn't his finest hour. On the other hand, the more he thought about it, the more he realized marriage was the only answer. It took her half brother and his cronies out of the mix altogether.

But on the ride back to his ranch, Trey was forced to admit that seeing her tonight, the two of them alone like that, set him to thinking about what it might be like to spend every day—and night—with Nell. And that possibility had overpowered whatever common sense he had. It wasn't like Trey to think of what he might want. He tended toward letting life come to him. But all of that went straight out the window when it came to Nell Stokes.

Of course, maybe she didn't feel what he felt. She liked him all right—he was pretty sure about that. But maybe she was still grieving her late husband. Maybe she had somebody else in mind if she was to remarry.

And that brought him around to thinking about Javier and George Johnson's daughter, Helen. Her parents had tolerated Javier mainly because of his close association to the Porterfield family, but they would never have allowed a union between those two. Especially not after Javier's brother, Rico, and Helen's older sister, Louisa, ignored her father's threats to disown her and eloped. Not even after George Johnson died. Everyone knew Javier could have run that ranch as well as any white man, but Mrs. Johnson had been adamant. She'd had enough of ranch life. She and Helen were going home to Ohio. Helen hadn't exactly put up a fight to stay, and that told Trey her feelings for his friend did not run as deep as Javier thought.

The differences between Nell and him might be less obvious, but they were just as ironclad in the eyes of some—on either side. Trey had to acknowledge that Henry Galway would not be the only one against such a union. The other ranchers wouldn't like it either, and that didn't begin to consider what Jess might think of the idea. At least he could count on Addie to be on his side.

Of course, the whole topic was moot now. Once she grabbed the gun, he hadn't for one minute thought she would intentionally pull the trigger. But the way her hands were shaking, there was every possibility she might have shot him by accident. The repercussions of that could have been disturbing to say the least. While

Calvin Stokes's death had not caused a total range war, the death of a Porterfield at the hands of a herder certainly would.

The sun was just coming up when Trey dismounted and walked his horse the rest of the way to the barn. Javier was giving instructions to a group of hands leaving for the day shift. Trey acknowledged the group with a tip of his hat but kept on walking, leading his horse to a stall in the back of the barn.

"Want me to brush her down for you, Trey?" Eduardo stepped out of an adjoining stall.

"I'd appreciate that."

Normally, Eduardo would be out with the others. He drove the cook wagon and served the meals the men ate when out on the trail. But this was branding season, and the day's work was closer to home.

"Juanita's got your breakfast waitin'," Eduardo added. "She was worried."

No more needed to be said. The older man did not like seeing his wife upset. "I'll apologize," Trey said as he pulled the saddle from his horse and rested it on a sawhorse nearby.

But once he reached the house, it was obvious that a simple apology was not going to satisfy Juanita. She greeted him with a snort of derision before turning her back on him and dishing up breakfast. "You determined to get yourself killed or what, Trey Porterfield? If your Mama—God rest her soul—were still alive, she would not tolerate you running around all night, and if I'm to keep my promise to her to take care of you, neither will I. Now where were you and why?"

"I went to see Nell Stokes."

"In the middle of the night?"

"It seemed like a good idea at the time." He grinned sheepishly at the housekeeper but realized he was not going to charm her out of her tirade.

"And not for a minute did you consider that her brother might be there and you might get yourself shot. And furthermore, not for one minute do you seem to have considered the damage you might have done to her reputation if anyone saw you there. She's a good woman from what Addie tells me, and I won't have you adding to her troubles."

"I just went to talk to her, Nita. I thought—"

"That's just the point—you did not think. Jess was the one always going off half-cocked. Come to that, your sisters are just as bad. I don't know how the three of them lived through childhood. But you? This isn't like you, Trey." She refilled his coffee and pushed a dish of peach preserves closer to his plate. "Want me to warm up those biscuits?"

"They're fine." He took a tentative sip of the steaming coffee. "I asked her to marry me."

If charm had failed him, shock did the trick. Juanita stared at him for a long moment, her hand still clutching the coffeepot. Then she set the pot back on the stove, pulled out the chair next to his, and sat down as if her arthritic knees would no longer hold her upright.

"You have lost your mind."

He did not miss the fact that she posed this thought as a statement—not a question and definitely not up for debate.

"Maybe," he agreed.

"Tell me she didn't say yes."

"She threw me out."

Juanita breathed a long sigh of relief. "Well, at least one of you has the good sense God gave you. What were you thinking?"

"Nita, we have to find some way around this feud."

"And you think marrying up with one of them is the way to do that?"

"That's just it. There's no 'them' that's all that different from 'us.' You and Mama taught us that way back when we were just kids. Then, it was a question of skin color. Now, it's sheep versus cows and the men who raise them."

Juanita shook her head. "You have always been a romantic, *mi'jito*. I blame your mama for that—filling your head with all those stories and praising you every time you drew the world the way we wanted it to be instead of the way it was. But that's the past. You need to face facts and deal with what's real, and this fight between cattlemen and sheepherders won't be solved by you marrying the widow."

"I never thought it would solve it. I just thought it would be a first step."

"A step that could end up getting you both killed, so just get such nonsense straight out of your head. You've got a ranch to run, and I've got laundry to do." And with that, certain she'd had the last word as usual, Juanita left the kitchen.

But the more Trey thought about it, the more he was convinced joining forces with Nell Stokes was exactly what was needed. He just had to find a way to plead his case so that Nell might someday come to agree.

❧

The more Nell thought about it, the more she had to admit Trey might have a point. If a cattleman and a sheep rancher were to become partners, surely that would at least start a proper conversation. Of course, marriage was out of the question.

Or was it?

Certainly, people married for convenience, especially out here on the frontier. She knew of at least one mail-order bride living in the area. Of course, Trey might not be so interested now that she had threatened to shoot him. But even if she were willing to go along with his original idea of becoming business partners, Henry would never stand for that. Calvin had given her half brother power when he'd named him executor to his will. And in that will, he had stated that while Nell was free to sell the ranch and live elsewhere, under no circumstances was she to sell their property to a cattle rancher.

Well, he hadn't said anything about *marrying* a cattleman, had he? And with Trey managing her property as well as his own, she and Joshua were bound to be safe. The more she thought about it, the more sense Trey's proposal seemed to make. But how to be sure she had considered the matter from every possible angle? She wished she could discuss it with Addie, but as Trey's sister-in-law, Addie was bound to be biased—that much was obvious by that business with the cake auction. She couldn't speak to Lottie either, but perhaps Reverend Moore would listen and offer the counsel she needed.

So on Sunday, just before services, she left a note

for the minister with his wife. "If he has time after services, perhaps we could meet in the church?"

"Of course, my dear. I'll see that he gets your message."

"The matter is…private, Mrs. Moore. I would rather no one know of my request."

"I understand. What about your son? Would you like me to watch him while you and my husband talk?"

"Dr. Porterfield has been asking me to allow him to stay overnight with her and her husband so she can observe him over a longer period of time and run some tests that might help improve his health. Joshua is very excited to have an opportunity to spend time with her son, Isaac. I'll need to get home to be sure everything is all right, and the marshal will bring Joshua back tomorrow."

"I see you've thought this out." The preacher's wife smiled as she squeezed Nell's hand. "I hope my husband will be able to offer you the guidance you need."

"Thank you."

It occurred to Nell as she walked across the yard to the church that if the women were in charge of things, this feud might have worked itself out some time ago. Women—at least the ones she had gotten to know since coming to Whitman Falls—seemed to have less of a need to come out the victor in such matters. All they wanted was a chance to live in peace and have their children do the same. Women understood the necessity of compromise.

As services started, Nell slipped into an aisle seat next to Joshua and Lottie. Henry stared hard at her, his expression questioning her tardiness. She ignored him. Ernest and her nephews did not attend services, staying behind to watch over both properties. She saw Henry shift his gaze to someone entering the back of the church. Lottie placed her hand on his knee as if to calm him. Why? Then she saw Trey Porterfield pass on his way to the pew opposite where she sat. He took his place and nodded to Addie, Jess, and their children who were already seated in the pew, then glanced her way.

Nell focused all her attention on finding the page for the first hymn and turned a little away from him as she stood and shared the hymnal with Joshua. But she could not keep Joshua from peering around her, his curiosity piqued. Joshua had talked a lot about Trey ever since the day he had come to the ranch, asking Nell all sorts of questions and bugging "Doc Addie" for more answers.

How come Trey'd been able to get over his sickness when Joshua couldn't?

Did he run that big ranch all by himself?

How come he didn't seem to be mad at them the way the other cowboys were?

And on and on until Nell ran out of answers. Clearly, the fact that Addie had assured him Trey had been every bit as puny and unwell as Joshua was had made the rancher into a hero for her son. At the church social, his kindness to Joshua had only added to his status in the boy's eyes. And she couldn't deny that Trey Porterfield was a very appealing man—on many levels.

Nell barely registered the minister's sermon, and before she knew it, he was calling for the congregation to stand for the final hymn and benediction. The organist pounded out the prelude, overpowering the rustle of people fumbling to find the right page and getting to their feet. Nell noticed that Lottie had to gently shake Henry's shoulder because he had fallen asleep. He shrugged her off even as color crept up his neck, and he glanced around to see if anyone had noticed.

In the crush of others filling the narrow aisle once the benediction had been delivered, Nell found herself next to Trey.

"Good morning, Mrs. Stokes," he said politely. Then he looked beyond her. "Mr. and Mrs. Galway. Fine morning, wouldn't you say?"

Henry let out a grumble, and Lottie smiled nervously, but neither returned his greeting as Henry guided his wife up the aisle. Joshua had already pushed ahead to walk with Addie and her son, Isaac. And that left Nell little choice but to walk with Trey. She heard the whispers following them, but Trey kept walking, his hands clasped behind his back, his eyes on the wood floor.

When they reached the doorway and paused to take their turn speaking to Reverend Moore, Nell deliberately stepped back, allowing Trey to go ahead and hopefully squelching any rumors that they were together. Trey thanked the minister for a message that surely spoke to the need for unity. As he went down the steps to the street, he glanced back at Nell but walked directly to his horse, mounted, and rode away.

In the meantime, Henry, who had paused to talk to another sheep rancher, pushed his way between Nell and Lottie and shook hands with the minister. "Good sermon," he said pumping the preacher's hand up and down as if trying to get water. Without giving Lottie a chance to say a word, he took her by the arm and headed for the street. When Nell didn't follow, he looked back and scowled. "Come along, Nell."

Before Nell could say anything, Reverend Moore turned to Henry. "I've asked Mrs. Stokes to stay for a bit and discuss a church matter, Mr. Galway," he said. "I'll make arrangements to see that she gets home safely and in due time," he added, then indicated that Nell should wait for him inside as he returned to greeting the rest of the congregants.

Henry hesitated, then steered Lottie up the street.

Back inside the empty sanctuary, Nell took a seat in a pew near the front and stared up at the small stained-glass window behind the pulpit. The sun streamed through the colored pieces separated by lead solder, creating a rainbow on the worn wooden floor.

"Forgive me for keeping you, Mrs. Stokes." Reverend Moore hurried down the aisle, sat next to her, and took hold of her hand. "How can I be of help?"

It took less than five minutes for her to lay out the business proposal Trey had made and to tick off the problems she saw with it.

"Perhaps there is another way to approach this," the minister said, although his expression suggested he could not come up with anything. "Why don't we pray together on the matter and seek God's guidance?"

Without waiting for Nell to agree, he bowed his head. She followed suit, and they sat like that for what seemed a long time before Reverend Moore said, "Amen."

"Mr. Porterfield did have one alternate suggestion," Nell said. She had not planned to share that bit of news with the preacher, but now thought she may as well give him the whole story. "He thought if he and I were to marry…"

A range of reactions flitted across the minister's face in the span of a few seconds—shock, delight, concern. He cleared his throat and glanced up at the stained-glass window before looking at her. "Trey is a good man, Mrs. Stokes, and he will make someone a fine husband one day, but to marry under these circumstances? You barely know him, nor he you."

"Clearly, it would not be a match of romance or true love," Nell hurried to reassure him. "But out here, people have married for all sorts of reasons, and surely joining our two ranches would be a first step toward setting this feud to rest." She could not believe she had moved from seeking the preacher's guidance to trying to convince him to support this idea.

For the first time since sitting down, Reverend Moore released her hand, sat back, and stared up at the window again. "Trey's family gave that window in memory of his father," he said. "There was trouble then as well—of a different nature, to be sure, but without the Porterfields working to make sure the community survived…" He continued to stare up at the window for a moment, then turned his attention back to her. "You say this idea of the two of you marrying was his?" He was frowning as if trying to find a reason why Trey would do such a thing.

"Yes. It is hard to say if he was serious. I mean, only a moment later, I was pointing a gun at him." She had meant to lighten his mood but immediately saw she had only given strength to the minister's doubts.

"Of course, you would benefit greatly from such a union," he said. "You and your son."

"I cannot deny that, but I believe Mr. Porterfield's intent is for the community to benefit."

"Of all the Porterfields," he continued as if she had not spoken, "Trey has always been the most trusting, the most naive when it comes to his interactions with others. He is first and foremost an artist—a man who sees beauty and goodness wherever he looks. He has taken on a monumental task in managing that ranch. If he were to add yours to the mix—"

"I would be there to help, as would my son."

The minister smiled. "Forgive me, Mrs. Stokes, but it is your brother and late husband's cousin who manage the true work of the ranch, is it not?"

She saw his point. If she and Trey were to join forces in any way, there would be no further help from Henry or her nephews or Ernest. And when she considered the reality of the situation, she had to question how Trey's hired hands might feel about working sheep—the "woolies" they so despised.

"Yes, you raise a good question," she said as she smoothed the fingers of her gloves and then pressed her hands over the skirt of her dress. "Thank you for seeing me and for your discretion, Reverend. Please understand my purpose in coming to you was to seek a way that I might do something to ease tensions."

She stood, and the minister scrambled to his feet. "You're giving up?"

"Even I can see the idea is ludicrous." She smiled and offered him her hand.

He took it between both of his. "No. You have

misunderstood me, Mrs. Stokes. It is my duty to look at things like this from every possible angle. I believe what you and Trey are proposing is risky, but promising. It is quite likely that you and he will suffer greatly. On the other hand, it is also possible that in time, others will come around, and this terrible conflict can be brought to a peaceful conclusion. If the two of you are willing to take that initial step, then you have my support and my blessing."

"You are saying we should be married?" Nell was nearly speechless with surprise.

"I am saying that having spoken to you, I would like to speak with Trey and make certain you are both in agreement as to how best to proceed. Once that has been accomplished, I see no reason we shouldn't move forward if the two of you are resolved."

In spite of the stuffiness of the church, Nell felt a shiver run through her—whether of excitement or anxiety, she could not have said. "Thank you," she managed.

"No, thank *you*, my dear. Now let's make arrangements for getting you home." He led the way up the aisle. "It's been some time since my wife and I had a chance to take a ride in the country, Mrs. Stokes, and I know she has wanted to get better acquainted with you as well as some of the other sheep-ranching women. She has some idea about a spinning and knitting group using some of the wool from your sheep."

Indeed, on the ride from town to her ranch, Mrs. Moore talked of little else than her idea for the craft group. By the time they had accepted Nell's invitation to share an early supper before returning to town, Nell had agreed to talk over the idea with Lottie and some of the other women.

❧

At breakfast the next day, Trey sat long after finishing his meal, talking to Juanita about his parents and his siblings and their marriages. Juanita was not fooled.

"This conversation is not about your parents or siblings, Trey. As I've told you before, it's time you settled yourself, but choose carefully and wisely. Your heart may not be your best guide. Not in times such as this."

"And yet there is a family history of following our hearts," he said, smiling as he stood, bent to kiss her weathered cheek, and headed out to his office.

The last person Trey expected to see pulling his buggy into the courtyard of the ranch that afternoon was Reverend Moore.

"Trey," he called by way of greeting as he climbed down.

"Reverend. What brings you out this way?"

"I need to speak with you about a matter of some confidence."

"Come inside out of the sun. I'll ask Juanita to bring us some lemonade." Trey led the way to the house and then paused to allow the minister to go ahead of him. He closed the carved double front doors to hold the cool air from the night in the house. With a gesture, he invited Reverend Moore to enter the large sitting room while he went on to the kitchen to ask Juanita to serve them.

When he returned, the minister was still standing,

his hat removed, his hands resting on the deep window well. He stared out over the landscape that stretched to the horizon like a vast ocean of shrubs and grass, interrupted only by distant mesas.

Trey took the tray from the housekeeper as she approached the door and set it on the sideboard. "Thank you, Nita," he said, and she left—reluctantly.

"Has something happened?" he asked, fearing there had been more trouble.

"I had a most interesting meeting with Mrs. Stokes yesterday."

Trey handed the man a filled glass and noticed that he drained it almost immediately, a combination of being parched from the long ride from town and wanting to get to the business he'd come about.

"And how does that concern me?"

"With her permission, I will tell you the content of our conversation. I have come here to verify that you and she are of one mind in the matter." Without embellishment, he laid out what he had been told. "Mrs. Stokes believes her brother and husband's family would oppose a business union." He paused to refill his glass and took a sip.

Trey's pulse raced. From the moment he had suggested he and Nell wed, he had hardly thought of anything else. All Sunday evening as he paced restlessly through the rooms of the large ranch house his father had built, he imagined her there.

Reverend Moore cleared his throat.

"And she is opposed to the idea of marriage," Trey guessed.

"Not entirely. In fact, I had the sense she had

thought a good deal about the two options—dismissed the one as not feasible given her brother but not entirely rejected the other."

Trey felt a flush crawling up his neck. "And what is your opinion?" he asked.

"I have prayed on the matter through the night and on the ride out here. Yours will not be an easy union. Not only do you know little about each other, you have the added obstacle of upsetting both sides in this disagreement. While your intent is laudable, it's possible that a marriage between you could make matters much worse."

The minister had a point.

"And what if I have feelings for this woman that go beyond the idea of settling this feud?" Trey asked.

Reverend Moore said nothing, so Trey continued.

"Of course, I have no way of knowing if she has similar thoughts. But in time, I would hope that we might find our way to…companionship."

The minister sighed deeply. "The fact that she came to me and then agreed to have me speak with you would indicate to me that at the very least, she respects and trusts you." He placed his hand on Trey's shoulder. "But the matter of utmost importance is whether you are placing her—and yourself—in danger if you pursue this plan."

"I have asked to meet with a group of the herders led by Nell's half brother."

"I see. You would seek his blessing for the union?"

"Nell doesn't need his blessing," Trey replied and heard the edge in his tone. "I would meet with Henry Galway to try and form a sort of council where both sides are represented."

"And Mr. Galway has agreed to this idea?"

Trey moved so that he could face the minister directly. "Not entirely, but he said he would speak to you about attending this meeting and set up a time and place." He was annoyed that several days had passed since he'd discussed the matter with Galway and obviously nothing had been done.

Reverend Moore rubbed his hand over his whiskered jaw. "But, Trey, if a council comes together, is there a need for you and Mrs. Stokes to go forward with this union of yours?"

"By combining our ranches, Nell and I would be able to prove that sheep and cattle can coexist, then eventually—"

"You say you have feelings for Mrs. Stokes, Trey. Are you certain your true purpose here lies in healing wounds in the community? Or, as my dear wife might say, is your heart ruling your head?"

Moore had a point. Ever since Trey had suggested the idea of marriage, he had pictured Nell and Juanita laughing together in the kitchen. He had imagined hosting a large party as his parents always had after the stock had been taken to market. He had envisioned holidays and children and coming home to her at the end of a long day's work.

"Either way, will you give us your blessing?"

"You have that already. Just be very sure of your decision and the timing, Trey. Go to her and talk this through, and if both of you come to the same answer, I would be honored to perform the ceremony." He set his glass on the tray and picked up his hat. "Now I must get back to town. Should Henry Galway come to me to set a time to meet, I will let you know."

"In the meantime, I'll call on Nell and get her answer."

"Make sure she understands the risks, Trey." They walked together to the front door and out to the preacher's buggy. "Make sure *you* understand them as well."

Trey nodded and watched the man drive away, and for the first time in months, he felt as if perhaps things could get better. Together with Nell and with the support of Jess and Addie and others in the community who prayed for a solution to the discord, he knew that change was possible. He only hoped Nell Stokes would feel the same way.

Five

TALKING THINGS OVER WITH NELL SOUNDED EASIER than Trey knew it would be. Since the raids, her brother, her late husband's cousin, or one of her nephews was always around. Of course, he could go back after dark again, but he'd already upset her once by calling so late. On the other hand, he had to see her.

For several days, he made it a habit to ride the fence line that connected their ranches. One day at sunset, he stopped at the creek to rest his horse and refill his canteen, and she stepped out from the shadows.

"You need to stop this," she said, her voice unsteady and nervous. "Ira's seen you coming by day after day and is sure you're planning another raid. You are going to get yourself shot."

"I've been trying to find a time when we could talk. I hate that I can't just come calling like any normal person." He glanced at her, feeling suddenly shy. He saw how the evening wind played with tendrils of her hair. "You've taken a risk coming here." He hoped that was a good sign.

"Reverend Moore spoke with you?" She kept

glancing back over her shoulder as if expecting any minute to be discovered.

"Yes. We have his blessing if you—"

"And you are convinced this is best?"

He stepped forward and placed his hands gently on her shoulders, which made her look directly at him. "Nellie, who knows what's best or not? This feels like something that will change things—certainly for the two of us, and perhaps for the entire territory. It's a gamble, but one I am willing to take. The question is, are you?"

"We're really just strangers," she said softly, speaking more to herself than to him.

"I can't argue with you there."

"You can't be sure this is the right thing," she persisted.

He chuckled and bent his head so that their foreheads were touching over the barbed wire fencing that separated them. "Oh, Nellie, if there is one thing you and I both know, it's that it's impossible to know what's right." He stroked her cheek with his knuckles. "But it feels like something that we could make work if you're willing."

She closed her eyes but did not move away. "I wish…"

He felt a tear slide down her cheek, and although he wanted more than anything to take her in his arms and assure her everything would work out, the sharp prongs of the wire fencing made such closeness impossible, so he stepped away. Her tears confused him. Was she grieving her late husband, wishing he was the one standing before her?

Trey cleared his throat. "Tell you what. I'll make

the plan with Reverend Moore and get word to you once it's in place. It'll take a few days at least, so you'll have time to think about the idea."

"I should get back," she said, neither agreeing nor disagreeing. "Stop coming here, Trey. It's far too dangerous." She gathered her skirt and turned away.

"Nellie?"

She paused but did not look back at him.

"I'll set everything up and get word to you, but even then, it's your choice. If you come, we'll be married and figure things out together from there."

"And if I don't come?"

"Then I won't bother you again."

She nodded and walked determinedly up the path. Trey watched her go and tried to recall the last time in his life something had seemed as important to him as winning the hand of Nell Stokes did now.

❧

Later that week when Addie arrived for her biweekly visit to check in on Joshua, she handed Nell a sealed envelope. "Read this in private," she muttered, her body turned away from Lottie and Henry, who were both seated on the porch. *It's from Trey*, she mouthed.

"What are you two whispering about?" Henry demanded.

Addie faced him with a smile. "Matters of the female sort. Nothing that would interest you, Mr. Galway."

Nell saw the scowl that crossed Henry's face. He did not like being dismissed, and he did not like

Addie. She crumpled the envelope and shoved it into the pocket of her dress.

"Lottie, it's good to see you looking so much better," Addie said. "Perhaps I could check you over as long as I'm here? Just to be certain there are no lingering effects from your recent illness."

"She's fine," Henry grumbled as he stood, glanced briefly at his wife, then stalked off toward the barn.

Addie raised her eyebrows at Nell before entering the house and calling out for Joshua.

Lottie sighed. "He's got a lot on his mind," she said to no one in particular as she watched her husband enter the barn.

"Has he made the arrangements for the meeting with the cattlemen?" Nell asked.

"Ernest and him have been talking about it. Ernest thinks it may be a trap."

"But Trey…Mr. Porterfield agreed to let the herders set the time and place and include Reverend Moore. Surely, they would not do anything with the minister there." She was well aware that Lottie had not heard anything she'd said from the moment Nell had uttered Trey's given name.

"This Porterfield man seems to have caught your fancy, Nell. You'll want to be careful. People are talking, and Henry says you're in danger of losing everything if that man gets his way. Henry went to the bank just the other day to see how he might secure your property. It's the reason why we came calling today. Henry wants to discuss something the banker suggested about him taking over for you as a kind of protector." Nell mused that though Lottie was always demure when her husband was nearby, she did have one quirk—whenever Henry wasn't around, she was almost bursting to tell whatever news she might have been privy to hearing. And today, that news was all about Nell.

"But surely, I would have to agree to anything—"

"I don't know. I heard Henry tell Ernest there are ways around that. You know he wants you to marry Ernest, and if you ask me, where would be the harm?"

Nell was practically speechless. Lottie knew what Ernest had done, and she was still defending the idea of a union between them? "You can't mean that," she finally managed.

Lottie frowned. "Henry says you have this way of thinking you're better than others. It's not an attractive trait, Nell. I don't see eligible men lining up here to take on you and Joshua or the debt of this place. Ernest is ready and willing to do that."

"And it doesn't matter that I don't love the man—really don't even like him?"

Lottie waved a dismissive hand. "Love? You had love with Calvin. You're too old to play those schoolgirl games, Nell. You need to be practical and do what's best for you and the boy."

Fortunately for Lottie, Nell had no chance to express her outrage. Joshua came running down the inside stairs and slammed open the screen door of the house. "Ma! Doc Addie says I'm better." He was breathless but beaming by the time he covered the short distance from the front hall to where Nell sat in the wooden swing. He sat next to her and kicked the swing into motion.

"That's wonderful news, Joshua." She looked up as Addie joined them on the porch. "Has there really been some change for the better?"

Addie grinned. "Well, this young man is not exactly going to be running races anytime soon, but yes, the signs are there. Reminds me of when Trey started to improve—little by little—and just look at him today."

Lottie coughed, and Addie turned to her. "How about let's have a listen to those lungs of yours, Mrs. Galway? Just to make sure they've cleared up."

"No, thank you."

Nell did not miss the way Lottie glanced toward the barn as if expecting her husband to overhear.

"No charge," Addie said.

"I am fine, really." Each word was bitten off.

Addie shrugged and turned her attention back to Nell. "I'd like to get Joshua back into my office for another round of those breathing treatments," she said. "And I might have promised Isaac that Joshua could be coming to spend another night or two with us," she added with a grin. "I'm headed back to town when I leave here, and it being Saturday, he could stay over and you could collect him tomorrow after church. How does that sound?"

Nell could feel Joshua's body twitch with excitement. She placed a hand on her son's knee and looked up at Addie. "You really think the breathing treatments are making a difference?"

"They are, Ma. I can tell," Joshua said.

"I don't see why these so-called treatments can't be handled right here," Lottie interjected. "After all, it's nothing but steam."

Maybe it was the earlier conversation about Henry's plans for her future left unfinished, but suddenly Nell had had quite enough of her brother and his wife making decisions for her. "Go pack your Sunday clothes and your nightshirt," she told Joshua, who was off the swing and through the door before she finished speaking. "And don't forget your comb and toothbrush," she called after him.

Addie took Joshua's place on the swing, and for a moment, it felt like the two of them against Lottie. Lottie stood when she saw Henry returning to the house from the barn. He stopped at the wagon he and Lottie had arrived in to retrieve a thin leather pouch, one Nell recognized as something he only used to transport important documents.

He stepped onto the porch. "Nell, if you and the doctor are finished, we need to talk—in private."

"All right," Nell agreed. She had learned long ago to gather her facts before making a decision. Lottie's gossip had been upsetting, but perhaps she had misunderstood. Henry might not always make the best choices for her welfare, but she had little doubt that he took his responsibilities as her protector seriously.

She turned to Addie. "Thank you for everything. I'll see you tomorrow."

Addie stood and hugged her, then set about the task of putting away her stethoscope and closing her black medical bag. At the same time, Lottie seemed inclined to join her husband and Nell in the house.

Nell had no intention of discussing the business of the ranch in front of her sister-in-law. "Lottie, would you be so kind as to make sure Joshua has what he needs and hurry him along so we don't delay Doc Addie further?"

Lottie pursed her lips and looked up at her husband.

"Well, go on," he grumbled. "We all need to get home before dark."

While Lottie went upstairs to Joshua's bedroom, Nell led the way to the dining room, where she pulled out a chair, sat, and folded her hands in her lap. "What is this about, Henry?"

He cleared his throat, laid out several official-looking documents, and took the chair opposite hers. "As you know, Nell, I have only your best interests at heart."

"I am grateful for that. What is all this?"

The last item he pulled from the pouch was a fountain pen. He twisted the cap off and handed it to her as he slid one of the papers toward her. "I need you to sign here." He pointed to a blank line toward the bottom of the page.

Nell ignored the proffered pen and picked up the paper. "You haven't answered my question. What is this?" She began to read, and while the language was English, the words made little sense to her.

Henry snatched the document away and laid it back on the table. "Simply put, it appoints me as guardian for you and Joshua."

"And for this ranch?"

"I'm not trying to steal your land, Nell."

"But you would be in charge? You would be the final word in any decisions to be made?"

"Nell, you need someone to take control of this place. If you marry Ernest, then the problem is solved, but I know you've got a problem with him, so this is the next best thing."

"And what if I choose to marry someone else?"

Henry actually laughed. "If that day ever comes, little sister, I will gladly relinquish my position to your new husband. But face facts. If you turn Ernest down, there aren't many other options, and for the near future, you need protection. With me in charge, we can share the hired help and combine the flocks. You and Joshua can go on living here or go someplace else—move into town if you like."

She could see that in his way, Henry was truly concerned for her welfare. This was not about taking her land or livestock. But if she gave him control of the ranch, she gave him control of her life—her future.

Gathering the papers and stacking them, she stood and reached for the leather pouch. "Give me a few days to read through these and try to understand them, perhaps review them with Reverend Moore and seek his counsel," she said.

Henry stood as well. He was not happy, but he agreed with a curt nod. "Don't put this off, Nell. Right now, you've got two options—marry Ernest or sign the papers. Make your choice, and let's get on with it." He slapped on his hat and headed for the porch. "Lottie, let's go," he shouted as he went.

Three options, Nell thought. If she was going to marry anyone, at the moment, her choice would be Trey Porterfield. She slid the papers back inside the pouch and carried them to the desk dominating one corner of the sitting room. She had always thought of it as Calvin's desk, but these days, this was where she sat to study reports related to the flock and to work through the tight budget that kept the ranch in operation.

After placing the satchel on the desk, she thrust her hands into the pockets of her skirt and felt the crumpled edges of the envelope. She took it out, opened it, and pulled a single sheet of paper free.

I am counting on the fact that Addie has persuaded you to let Joshua stay the weekend. Reverend Moore has given us his blessing. Come to the falls at sundown…alone. If you have changed your mind, I understand, but I will wait there.

The message was signed simply: *Trey.*

No endearment, but why would there be? The union he had proposed was a business arrangement, nothing more.

&

Juanita stood in the shadows of the corridor that led from the kitchen to the bedrooms and watched. Trey stared at himself in the mirror, smoothed back his hair, then put on his Stetson, brushed off his shoulders, and softly closed the door to his room.

"Where are you off to now, Trey Porterfield?" She spoke in a normal tone, but Trey flinched, and she knew he'd been unaware of her presence. Juanita had a sixth sense when it came to the offspring, both Porterfield and her own. Jess had once accused her of being able to smell when they were up to something, and she definitely smelled something amiss now. "Well?" she pressed.

"I've got a meeting," he mumbled.

"With?"

He hesitated. "Reverend Moore," he replied.

Because his voice held a hint of triumph, she knew he was either lying or not telling her the whole truth.

"It's business," he added.

Now she was certain he was padding the facts.

"So after all these years, you've found religion?"

She watched his shoulders slump in defeat.

Slowly, he turned to face her. "I need to go, Nita. I can't tell you the whole of it until I know for sure it will all work out, okay?"

"And if it doesn't?"

He smiled. "Then we move on, right? Isn't that what you always told us when we were kids and got upset about something?"

Juanita moved into the light so she could see him better. "This isn't about the business with the herders then?"

He shrugged. "Depends on who's asking."

She punched him hard with her forefinger. "Do not be smart with me, *joven.*"

He looked down at her. "I promise you, Nita, if this works out the way I hope, then I think you will be mighty pleased."

"And no one will get hurt?"

Again, she saw his hesitation, but this time, she was pretty sure it was because he hadn't considered that idea. His smile was the one she remembered from the time he was a sick child, the one where he always tried to put a brave face on his feelings, not wanting to worry his mother—or her.

"There won't be trouble, Nita, and I'm in no danger. But I might not get back until morning, so don't sit up all night worrying."

She patted his forearm. "I see you're determined, and whatever happens, you know Eduardo and I will be here. We are as much your family as any, I guess."

Trey kissed her forehead. "You have no idea how much I count on that," he said softly. Then he straightened and tipped his fingers to the brim of his hat. "Wish me luck," he said as he turned and left the house.

"Oh, *mi'jito*," Juanita whispered to herself as she watched him ride away. "I wish you more than luck. I wish you happiness and peace. It's your turn." She mentally recited a prayer to the Blessed Virgin, crossed herself, and went back to her kitchen to await the outcome of Trey's mysterious meeting.

❧

The sun was low and the sky streaked with orange, pink, and lavender as Trey paced the uneven rocky ground that ran up to the falls. Now that spring had mostly passed, the rush of water fed by the melting snows had weakened some, but still gurgled over the rocks in a steady flow. By contrast, the countryside was dangerously arid, and unless they got rain soon, the falls—and the creek they fed—would dry up altogether. But Trey had things other than the weather on his mind.

Will she come? And even if she does, will she go through with this marriage?

Reverend Moore had met Trey at the falls and sat on a boulder, his short, stubby legs swinging idly back and forth as he studied the sky and setting sun. He pressed his Bible to his chest with one hand, and Trey suspected he was praying. And well he should. The idea that a marriage between Trey and Nell would change minds on either side was a long shot at best and downright foolhardy at worst.

Footsteps on the loose rocks of the path made both men turn. Reverend Moore got to his feet and stepped forward to offer his hand to Nell, guiding her over and around the last of the boulders that led to the apex of the path.

"I'm here," she said, slightly breathless from the climb.

Trey could not help but notice she made the declaration as if she were surprised. He also noticed she did not look at him but kept her focus on Moore. She was wearing a cotton calico dress in shades of blue. Her hair was twisted into a knot at the base of her head. She looked a good deal as she had that first day he'd called on her.

"Why don't the two of you sit here?" The minister pointed to a large, flat rock and waited for them to follow his suggestion. They sat side by side, leaving several inches between. Reverend Moore cleared his throat and opened his Bible. "I thought it might be appropriate for us to discuss this union together before we proceed."

Trey nodded, and Nell whispered, "Yes, please."

Over the next several minutes, Reverend Moore went over the pros and cons of the plan. The longer he spoke, the more Trey felt the actual presence of Nell's tension. And when the minister suggested they bow their heads in silent prayer, he did so but left his eyes open and focused on Nell's hands. He watched her fingers twisting nervously, heard her quick, shallow breathing. Instinctively, he reached over and covered her hand with his, and she grew still.

"We don't have to do this," he said softly when the prayer ended.

"No, you don't," Reverend Moore said. "If either of you need more time or is having second thoughts…"

To Trey's surprise, Nell looked up at him and turned her palms so that they were holding hands. "There is so much we have to learn about each other. In time, I pray we will come to a comfortable union—one of respect and friendship. For now, I trust you, Trey Porterfield, for your kindness to me and to Joshua. Perhaps those are reasons enough for us to move forward together."

Her hands were dry and smooth against his rougher skin, and her words had the cadence of vows—promises she was prepared to make to him and their shared future. He laced his fingers with hers and then raised their united hands to his lips and kissed them. "Once we do this, Nell, you can be sure that I will give my life to protect you and Joshua, and—"

"Shhh," she said huskily. "No more promises. Let us simply begin and see where life leads from here." Trey nodded, and she turned to Reverend Moore. "We're ready," she said.

If it had seemed an eternity while Trey was waiting and wondering if she would come at all, by contrast, it felt as if only seconds had passed before he slipped the thin silver band his father had given his mother onto her finger and they were married. He didn't quite know what to do. He wanted to seal their union with a kiss, but it would be their first, and he wasn't sure how Nell might react. The reality that their marriage was starting out as a business arrangement rather than a love match—at least on her part—made him reluctant to do anything that might upset the delicate balance between them.

But they had continued to hold hands throughout the short ceremony, and now it was Nell who raised their joined hands to her lips and kissed them. Then she turned to the minister. "Thank you, Reverend Moore."

"I'll give the two of you some privacy," Moore said, shaking hands with each of them before pocketing his Bible, retrieving his hat, and heading down the path to where he'd left his buggy and Trey had left his horse. It was then Trey realized Nell had walked all the way from her ranch to their meeting.

She turned to him and smiled. "And so we begin," she said.

But it occurred to Trey that by beginning in secret, they had not thought through what their next steps might be. Where would they live? How would they handle the logistics of managing their separate properties? Should he see her back to her home and then go back to his ranch? Should he stay the night? He had been so nervous and half certain she would not come that he had failed to consider the details. If they went back to her house, what if her nephew or brother…

"Trey, please do not worry that I have…expectations. I mean, I fully understand that this arrangement is—"

And in that moment, he cast aside any doubts he might have had. He cupped her face with his hands and kissed her. He intended for the kiss to be gentle and tender, a kiss she could easily pull away from. To his delight, she stood on tiptoe and wrapped both arms around his neck and kissed him back.

Nell Porterfield, he thought, and that made him be

the one to pull back. "Hello, Mrs. Porterfield," he said, his hands still framing her beautiful face.

"Hello, Mr. Porterfield," she replied. "We have a good deal of work to do," she reminded him.

"Tomorrow," he said and pulled her to him again for one final kiss good night.

She did not protest, and he realized it would never matter if they shared her house or his—they were already at home because they were together.

∽

Nell felt light-headed but also as if something weighing her down had been lifted. She felt happy—and a little brazen—once she realized how willingly she had accepted Trey's kiss. But the realization that he seemed as delighted as she was with their unorthodox union gave her courage. Oh, they would have more than their share of problems—especially once others learned they had married—but before all that, they had tonight. Suddenly, she wanted to share her happiness with Addie and give the news to Joshua.

"Could we go into Whitman Falls tonight?" she asked, looking up at him. "Could we go and tell Addie—and Jess?"

Trey's breath caught, and that confused her. Surely, he had never intended to keep their marriage a secret. What would be the point?

"I guess I had hoped we might be able to hold on to this moment a little longer," he said. "Come home with me tonight—to the ranch, Nell. I promise first thing tomorrow, we will tell my family—and yours."

"All right," she agreed, wondering if he intended

to sneak her into his house without others seeing them. *Trust*, she reminded herself, but she felt doubt creep back in where just a moment earlier, she had felt only joy.

He wrapped one arm around her shoulders as they started down the trail to where he had left his horse. Reverend Moore saw them coming, waved, and then drove his buggy back toward town. As he had the day he'd rescued her from the vandals, Trey mounted his mare and then pulled her up to sit in front of him. Once again, she snuggled against the warmth of him, the scent of him, the sheer force of him. But this time, it was not fear or exhaustion that drove her. This time, it was a determination that whatever might come, she and Trey would face the future together.

He held the reins loosely in one hand, his other arm wrapped around her and holding her close. Was this really happening? She felt lighter, like a young woman without all the responsibilities she'd had to face over the last several months. She stroked Trey's jaw. He smiled and, with his free hand, tucked a strand of her hair behind her ear and rested his cheek against her forehead.

"That first day when I came out to see you and you were repairing the chicken coop," he said, "I knew then—well, I didn't *know*, but there was something there. I stopped when I reached the top of the mesa and sketched your face, but I couldn't capture the essence of you. Since then, I've drawn you time and again, and each time, just when I think I've finally succeeded, I realize something is missing."

"Addie told me about your drawings—you're a little famous."

He chuckled. "I wouldn't say that. I like to draw. It calms me and helps me to think. Sketching you is how I think I came up with the idea that we might be together. There was something there that made me believe we could make a real difference, and then…"

"What?"

"Then, the more I tried to capture your image, the more I understood that I wasn't drawing someone who might help me solve a business feud. I was drawing a woman who fascinated me, whose courage and determination inspired me. A woman who drew me into the depths of sorrow and unhappiness reflected in her eyes. I was drawing a woman who needed—deserved—to be loved. I fell in love."

"With a drawing," she reminded him.

"No. With you."

"You can't know that," she protested.

"Pretty damn sure," he whispered as he kissed her temple.

He dismounted and guided the horse to a cluster of trees on the banks of the shallow creek. He kissed her, and this time, the kiss was filled with the passion of his desire for her. Now that they were married, she had a decision to make, and she was stunned to realize that she had made it already. Tonight, they would lie together as husband and wife. She would open her body to him as even now she was parting her lips to receive the depths of his kiss.

"Nell?" His question was contained in the simple

sound of her name. "What if instead of returning to the ranch, we—"

"Yes," she whispered. "Here. Now."

He touched her face, running his finger along her jaw, his thumb along her lower lip. She gasped but not in shock. It was a breath of pure longing.

Taking a step closer, he wrapped his arms around her. He pulled her to him so that her face rested against the hammering that she realized was his heart—or was it hers? It seemed only natural for her to relax into his embrace, give herself over to his warmth and strength. She tilted her face up to his and kissed the stubble on his chin.

The shudder that hurtled through him told her there would be no going back now. And the truth was, whatever might happen between them, she did not want to stop. In marrying her, Trey was offering her the opportunity to lay down the burdens of responsibility and fear and allow him to care for her—perhaps, in time, to love her the way he already claimed to.

"Yes," she whispered, even though he had not asked a question.

He took a step away, his hands cupping her face as he studied her. "I want you, Nell, in every way a man can want a woman. I want to make love to you."

"Yes," she repeated.

He brushed her hair back from her forehead and kissed her skin, dampened by the heat of the late afternoon sun, or perhaps simply by the heat that rose between them. "Be very sure that you're ready, Nellie. We can wait. I don't want you having regrets."

She barely knew this man, but what she knew of

him was that he was kind and good and caring. After everything she had been through over the last months, that was more than enough. She touched his mouth. "Kiss me, Trey."

The kiss was gentle, a brush of his lips against hers, but then he ran his tongue over her mouth, and when she opened to him, he groaned. "Nellie," he whispered as he lifted her in his arms and carried her to a spot close to the creek where soft grass grew.

He knelt next to her on the bank of the creek, pulling off his boots and setting them aside. He glanced at her, suddenly shy, something he covered by unlacing her shoes and removing them. He watched her as he unbuttoned his shirt, pulling it free of his trousers. If he saw any sign she was hesitant, he would stop, let her know they could take their time. But then she sat up and began to unbutton her dress. Trey let out a breath and covered her hands with his. "Let me," he whispered.

He shed his shirt and then sat next to her again, reaching for her buttons, opening them one by one as he allowed his fingers to brush against the chemise underneath and the swell of her breasts. He pushed the garment over her shoulders, imprisoning her in her own clothing as he bent and branded the side of her neck with his kiss.

"Trey," she said, and he knew it was a plea.

He moved away, freeing her to finish undressing—or not. With every gesture, he sent the message that the choice was hers to make. He wanted her, but he would not take without her permission. She rolled away from him and stood. She heard him sigh—a sigh of resignation as he sat with his head down, not looking at her.

Quickly, she shed the rest of her outer clothing and, clad in her chemise and pantaloons, knelt behind him. She wrapped her arms around him, running her hands against his muscled chest as she pulled him against her.

"Come here," he murmured as he turned and reached for her, laying her on the ground. He straddled her and rested his palms on his thighs. "Do you have any idea how beautiful you are?"

She wanted to deny that, but when he ran his fingers along her shoulder and throat and down between her breasts, she lost the ability to utter a sound. When he began untying the ribbons of her chemise, she felt her breath quicken, and when he spread the garment open and pressed his lips to her bare skin, she gasped and reached for him.

In a rush of combined breaths and her hands stroking his chest, he wiggled free of his trousers.

"Nellie," he whispered as he pressed the fullness of his desire against her. "My wife."

And in that moment, nothing mattered but that they seal the vows they had taken. From this moment on, they were one.

"Get the blanket," she said, and immediately, he moved away.

"I didn't think," he said, scrambling to his feet and turning to unfasten the straps that held the blanket he carried behind his saddle.

By the time he turned back to her, she had finished undressing and was holding out her hand for the blanket.

"Holy…" he muttered.

While he hurried to shed the rest of his clothing, she spread the blanket over the grass. The sun was a half

circle on the horizon as she knelt and held out her arms
to him. He came to her willingly, covering her face and
neck with kisses as he eased her back onto the blanket
and covered the length of her with his hard body.

He slid inside her easily, for she was as ready as he
was to consummate their union. There would be time
later for the kind of slow exploration she knew they
would both savor. For now, what she wanted was the
explosion—the fury of his passion and hers coming
together. She grasped his bare hips and held him to
her. She rose to meet each thrust. She thrilled to the
quickening pace of their lovemaking, and when he
cried out, she clung to him.

When he rolled to lie beside her, she assumed he
would turn away and fall asleep. Her experience with
Calvin had been that once he had satisfied his need,
he was done. But Trey rose to one elbow, brushed
her hair away from her face, and then ran his fingers
up along her inner thighs, gently stroking her with
his fingers until she could not lie still, until she was
the one to cry out and clutch Trey to her. She tried
desperately to hold onto the unfamiliar but thrilling
feeling that rocketed through her. When she could
hold it no longer, she collapsed against him.

He kissed her tenderly. "Next time, we go there
together," he promised.

A moment later, she heard the soft, even rush of his
breathing and knew he had fallen asleep.

Next time? she thought and smiled as her eyes fluttered closed and her breathing matched his.

But the dawn came, and so did the harsh reality of
all that lay ahead for them. As she came awake, Nell

shuddered to think how Henry would react. She had little doubt he would be furious. He would exact a price, although what that price might be, she did not wish to imagine. As for Trey's family, she was fairly certain Addie would be delighted, but Jess would be certain his brother had made an enormous and irrevocable mistake. And she could not even begin to fathom the reactions of their respective communities. She trembled.

Trey turned in his sleep and pulled her to his side as if he had instinctively heard her fears. She nestled close to him, noting the way she seemed to fit perfectly under the crook of his arm and shoulder. For the first time since months before Calvin was killed, she felt safe. They would find a way, together. By the time Joshua was old enough to take charge of the ranch—their ranch*es*—the land and its people would be at peace. Imagining what could be and doing so in the safe haven of Trey's embrace, she drifted back to sleep.

When she woke the second time, the sun was climbing higher, bringing the promise of a hot day. Trey was gone, and she panicked, scrambling to her feet and pulling the blanket around her to cover her nakedness. She saw his horse grazing near the creek and heard the cascade of the falls as water tumbled over the rocks. That was when she heard a blood-curdling shout. Thinking Trey had been attacked, she slipped on her chemise and pantaloons to cover herself and ran barefoot over stones and dirt to the creek's edge.

There she saw him—her husband—splashing around

in the water like a boy who had just discovered what fun playing under a waterfall could be. He radiated joy and happiness, and she could only hope, perhaps, marrying her might have something to do with that.

"Trey!" She had to shout his name repeatedly as she worked her way along the bank. But his joy was contagious, and by the time he heard her, she was laughing.

"Come on," he called, holding out his hand to her.

"It's slippery," she protested, giving little thought to the fact that if she took his hand, she was likely to end up soaked.

"I won't let you fall," he promised.

He was naked and wearing his hat, and that made her laugh out loud. She took his hand as he pulled her to the safety of his arms. They stood together under the shower of cool, clear water with the sun sparkling on the still pool below. And suddenly their laughter died, although the fire in their eyes did not.

This time, their lovemaking had a familiarity about it, as though with that first time, they had already learned how to pleasure each other. Trey took his time as they stood under the falls. He lifted her onto a flat rock to bring her almost to the point of no return and then picked her up and guided her legs around his hips as he entered her. Their bodies joined slowly at first and then with increasing urgency, and as he had promised, they came together. Their voices raised in passion as the water babbled and rushed around them, murmuring in symphony with their cries.

Afterward, they walked back to the campsite and dressed in silence, an element of shyness still lingering between them. They would glance at one another and smile, then look away.

"We should go," she said as she twisted her wet hair into a knot and anchored it with the pins she retrieved from the ground near the tree. "Addie will be worried when I don't show up for church and Joshua."

"I told Addie you would be with me," he admitted. "Just Addie."

"But she's bound to tell Jess, and he'll be upset, and what about the men at your ranch? Won't they come looking for you when they realize you haven't come home? And what about—"

He put his arms around her. "Shhh. Everything will be all right, Nell. We'll make it all right. We can do this."

And she believed him. Right up to the moment when they came riding up to Addie and Jess's house and saw the cowboy she knew worked for Trey, the man who had ridden with the others to terrorize her. Javier was standing on the porch with Jess.

"Javier." Trey spoke the man's name but said no more as he dismounted, then lifted Nell down. She saw two other horses, saddled and waiting, tied to the hitching post.

Jess stood with his arms folded across his chest. "Where have you been?" he asked without so much as a glance at Nell.

Trey ignored his brother and focused on his ranch hand and friend. "Has something happened?"

"Galway claims his sister is missing and blames you. They set the meeting," Javier replied. "If you don't show—"

"I'm ready now."

Nell started to protest, but Trey spoke first. "Go on in the house, Nellie. Joshua will be waiting, and you can tell Addie our news. I'll be back as soon as possible."

"I need to talk to Henry...before—" she said.

"I'll meet with him, and then we'll come to your ranch." He pulled her to him and kissed her full on the mouth, leaving little doubt as to their circumstances.

She heard Jess suck in his breath and saw Javier look down at his boots.

"You want the whole town talking?" Jess said.

Trey mounted his horse and looked down at his brother. "I'll kiss my wife any damn place I please," he said.

"Tell me you're joking," Jess said, his gaze darting from Trey to Nell and back again.

"Nope. Now where's the meeting?"

"Deadman's Point," Javier mumbled as he untied and mounted his horse.

Trey looked at Nell and smiled. "Seems Henry might have a sense of humor after all." He glanced at his brother. "Is Pete coming?"

"He said he'd meet us there."

Nell continued to stand at the foot of the porch steps as Trey followed Javier down the dirt street. At the far end of town, they turned a corner and galloped on into the barren landscape.

Jess hesitated before mounting his horse. "You're going to get my brother killed, Nell Stokes. And you may as well know now, I will never forgive you for that."

Nell wrapped her arms around herself to stop the shaking that had begun almost the minute Trey had lifted her to the ground. "My name is Nell Porterfield now," she replied, "and if you're so worried about your brother, then I suggest you be at this meeting where you have the best chance of seeing to his safety." She climbed the stairs to the porch of the frame house and watched as Jess rode away.

"You're married?" Joshua stood just inside the front door. "Does that mean he's my pa now?"

Nell saw Addie come to stand behind Joshua. She rested her hands lightly on the boy's shoulders. "Let your ma get in out of that hot sun. We'll have something to eat and talk about everything." Nell could see Addie's children lining the hallway. "Children, go out back and play," she said.

"But you said—" Isaac began a protest that Addie cut short.

"Joshua will bring you milk and biscuits in a few minutes," she promised. "Now scoot!"

The children scattered, and Addie held the door open for Nell to enter. Nell opened her arms to her son, but he turned and walked away, down the hall to the kitchen. By the time she and Addie followed, he was already seated at the table, his eyes downcast. His arms were folded across his thin chest in imitation of Jess, and one foot rhythmically kicked the pedestal of the round table.

"Stop that," Nell said and heard the irritation in her tone. While Addie busied herself setting up a tray with glasses and a pitcher of milk and filling a plate with biscuits, jam, and butter, Nell took the chair closest to her son. "I am sorry for not talking to you about this, Joshua, but I need you to understand. Some things are adult problems, and the solutions might not seem right to you, at your age."

Joshua sat still as a stone and continued to avoid looking at her. Nell watched Addie slice each biscuit open and fill it with butter and jam. The butter oozed down the sides, telling Nell that the bread was still warm. Her stomach growled as she tried to think of how to make things right for her son. "Mr. Porterfield and I believe that by joining together, we can begin to heal this terrible hostility between those who raise cattle and those who raise sheep."

She could tell he was listening, so she continued. "Mr. Porterfield will see to it that we never have to be afraid again. Not of night raids, or fires, or any of the things we've been through since your father died."

"How's he gonna do that?"

"I'm not sure, but I trust him. He's been good to us, Joshua. I thought you liked him."

She saw her son wrestle with that truth. "Do I have to call him 'Pa'? What about my name? Does that change?"

Nell realized that for her son, this was a question of loyalty. While he and Calvin had never been close, the boy had idolized his father and sought to please him. She placed her hands on either side of Joshua's face, gently forcing him to look at her. "You are and always will be Joshua Stokes, son of Calvin Stokes. As for what you will call Mr. Porterfield, we can work that out once he returns from his meeting and we're back home again."

She had raised yet another question for Joshua—and herself. "Where will we live?" Joshua's eyes were wide with alarm, and that's when Addie—bless her—decided enough was enough.

She brought the tray to the table, set out glasses of milk for Nell and herself, and turned to Joshua. "Seems to me like you might be making problems where none exist, young man. You have your ranch and the house and room you like there, but now, in addition to that, you will also have your own room at the Clear Springs Ranch and a whole bunch of new territory in need of exploring. And then there's that library you were going on about. All those books just waiting for you to choose them?" She shook her head in wonder at all that awaited the boy.

Joshua fought a smile with a determined frown. "I guess," he admitted grudgingly. "Can I go now?"

This was directed to Nell, who nodded, carried the tray to the door, and then handed it to Joshua as he stepped outside. Addie's children surrounded him right away, more eager for information than they were for refreshments. Nell stood for a moment watching and wondering if she had just made a huge mistake.

"No regrets," Addie said. "What's done is done." Gently, she guided Nell back to the table where they both sat. Then Addie gave her a sly grin and said, "So how was the honeymoon?"

Nell blushed.

"That good, huh?" Addie toasted her with her glass. "It's all gonna work out, Nell. Trey fell for you that first day—I knew it the minute he showed up here after. Never saw him so unsettled. Of all the Porterfields, Trey has always been the calm, quiet one. But that day, he could barely sit still."

"I think I love him," Nell whispered. "But isn't that impossible?"

"Love comes in all sorts of ways, honey. Slow for some and a thunderbolt out of the blue for others. You can fight it with all manner of rationale, but when it's right, there's no denying it. I ought to know. Jess and I tried every way we could to deny our feelings, but in the end, love won out—as it does every time."

And in that moment, Nell felt as if Addie might just be right. Everything would work out. She and Trey and Joshua would face whatever challenges came their way, and in between those challenges, their days would be filled with laughter and love and all the good times that came from being part of a family. "I'm going to work every day to make sure Trey doesn't regret his decision," she promised.

Addie laughed. "My guess is, if the glow I saw on both your faces earlier is any indication, you just need to keep on doing whatever it was that you did last night."

Once again, Nell felt her cheeks flush. "Addie!" she protested.

"Doc Addie knows of what she speaks," her friend replied with a wink. "Now drink your milk, and let's see about getting you and Joshua home."

Six

DEADMAN'S POINT WAS AN ISOLATED MESA SOME distance from town, much closer to the Galway ranch than Trey's place. The three men pushed their horses hard to make up for lost time. Trey was the one to set the pace. If they were riding at a gallop, there would be little chance for Jess to question his marriage to Nell.

"Up there." Javier pointed to the top of a flat cliff where a trio of men waited.

Instinctively, they slowed their horses to a walk, and they studied the group standing above them. "No sign of Reverend Moore," Trey noted.

"Or Pete Collins," Jess added. "That's probably not a bad thing."

"The preacher might not come," Javier said. "Old Man Thomas died this morning, and he went there instead. Me and Pete tried to set another time, but Galway insisted. Reverend Moore said he'd get here as soon as he could."

"And Pete?" Trey asked.

Javier shifted uncomfortably. "Pete changed his

mind, says the time for talk has passed. He says he wants no part of this meeting."

"I don't like this." Jess glanced around. "We're miles from town or the fort." The regiment at Fort Lowell had jurisdiction over open range at least for the time being. In spite of his badge, Jess had no authority here. Trey had had his doubts the minute he heard about the meeting place because of its proximity to Henry Galway's ranch, but he'd figured with Jess and the preacher there, it would be all right. Now he wasn't so sure.

The three of them urged their horses up the steep, rocky trail leading to the point. As they topped the rise, they saw Henry had brought one of his two sons and Ernest Stokes. Trey tipped his hat to the trio but kept his eyes on Nell's half brother. "Beautiful day," he said.

"This ain't no tea party," Ernest grumbled.

"Just making conversation," Trey replied. "And it was my understanding talking was the purpose of this get-together. How about we move over there by that juniper tree, take advantage of what shade there is?" He pointed to a lone tree at the edge of the cliff.

Galway and his party stayed where they were, their expressions and posture mirroring their suspicions. Hoping to show good faith, Trey climbed down from his horse and nodded to Javier and Jess to do the same. He faced Henry Galway. "I hope that—"

"Is it true what Ira here told me about you and my sister?" Henry interrupted, his clenched fists evidence that Trey had misread the prevailing mood.

"Well now, I reckon I'll be needing a little more

information to answer that." Trey glanced at Ira and waited. Nell's nephew took a step toward him. Javier and Jess closed in, but Trey waved them off. "What have you told your father?"

"I seen you with Aunt Nell riding away from the falls this morning just after sunup," Ira said. "Looked like the two of you was mighty cozy."

Trey heard Jess mutter an oath under his breath.

"Well?" Henry demanded.

Focusing his full attention on Nell's half brother, Trey took a deep breath. "Your boy is right, although he doesn't have all the facts. Nell and I were married yesterday. Reverend Moore performed the ceremony." He prepared for Henry to charge at him and saw Javier was ready to intervene. "I got this," he said quietly to his friend.

But Javier was not about to listen. He stepped between Trey and Henry. "Just listen to what my boss has to say," he said, placing his hand on Henry's shoulder.

That was too much for Ira, who pushed past his father to shove Javier. "Get your filthy hands off my pa." The younger Galway placed his palms flat on Javier's chest and kept pushing him.

Before anyone could stop them, the two young men had fallen to the ground, their fists flying and their legs tangled. Trey and Ernest immediately leaped into the fray to separate them while Jess pulled out his pistol and fired a warning shot in the air. Ernest jumped away while Trey took hold of Ira's shirt, but the boy jerked away and got to his feet. He brandished a knife, threatening anyone who came close.

Javier looked up at Trey, his eyes wide with shock.

He clutched at his gut as blood saturated his shirt. "Trey?" His voice was weak and disbelieving. He held up his bloody hand, staring at it as if he couldn't quite believe it.

The instant Trey saw the blood, he grabbed Ira's arm, wrestling him for the knife. The kid was strong and quick. Trey felt the pain of the knife slicing into his forearm as Henry shoved his son aside, then faced Trey with his gun drawn. The air was heavy with the odor of gun smoke and the sounds of embattled men fighting, some of them for their very lives. Behind him, Jess fired another shot, and every man froze at the sound of it.

"How about we all just calm down here," Jess said, pointing his gun at Henry. "Put that rifle down, Mr. Galway."

But Henry wasn't about to back down. "You lyin' scum," he growled, so close to Trey that his spit sprayed the air between them. "You talk about makin' peace, and then you go and trick my sister into a sham marriage so you can lay claim to her land." The gun he held wavered.

Jess edged closer, but Ernest stepped in front of him.

Behind Henry, Trey saw Javier try to get up, ready to defend him, but then he stumbled backward and collapsed. He realized only he had any idea Javier was wounded. Everybody else was focused on the rifle Henry aimed at Trey and the six-shooter Jess was pointing at Henry.

"Get out of my way, Galway. My friend needs help." Trey attempted to push past, but Henry lunged at him. Trey dodged, and Henry stumbled forward.

Trey saw that he was headed for the cliff and reached to block his fall, but he was too late. As Henry plummeted over the edge, stirring up a small avalanche of stone and rock that followed his fall, they rushed forward, shouting and shoving and trying to stop what had already happened. As Henry hit bottom, a shot from his rifle echoed against the walls of the canyon, and he lay motionless at the foot of the cliff, a dark pool of blood forming next to him.

There was an instant when Trey realized everything had gone quiet. He heard the call of an eagle flying overhead and then a different—human—cry. In a matter of minutes, everything had changed.

"You killed my pa," Ira screamed. He half ran, half slid down the rocky path, calling out to his father. Ernest followed him.

Trey knelt next to Javier, heard his breath coming in shallow gasps, and knew his friend was dying. For the first time since his father had died, he lost hope that anything could ever be done to make things right again. Something hard knotted in his gut. For the first time in his life, he understood the poisonous pain that cut deep enough to make any man want only one thing: revenge. Oblivious to the blood leaking from his forearm where Ira's knife had found its mark, he pulled Javier's limp body close. "They won't get away with this, my friend," he said softly. "That's a promise."

Javier covered Trey's bloody forearm with his hand, a hand stained with the blood of his own mortal wound. And as Trey watched his friend's blood mingle with his own, he heard Javier breathe his last.

"Trey, you'd best get going," Jess said. He rested his hand on Trey's shoulder. "Let me handle this."

"That boy killed Javier. He brought the knife. He needs to—"

"Come on now. You take Javier home," Jess said. "You'll need to explain what's happened to Juanita and Eduardo." Together, they lifted Javier's body and placed it across the back of his horse.

The mention of Javier's parents made Trey shudder. How could he ever explain? How could they ever forgive him for getting Javier mixed up in this mess he'd made? "What can I say that will ever... Come with me, Jess."

"I'll be along directly. But you know I have a duty here. I need to check on Galway, then head to the fort so Colonel Ashwood can handle this."

Jess held Trey's horse steady while he mounted and turned toward the head of the trail.

"Take the long way," Jess advised. "Galway's boy would as soon shoot you and pay the price as look at you right now."

"But I—"

Jess breathed a sigh of pure exasperation. "Trey, you've got to stop trying to fix everything and listen for once in your life. What possessed you to marry the widow? You had to know how that would play with her brother."

"Half brother," Trey muttered. "How about I love her? Is that reason enough?"

"You don't know her," Jess scoffed.

"Well enough," Trey said.

But his best friend was dead—and for what? Jess

had warned him that his ideas for peace were fool-hardy at best and downright dangerous at worst. But Jess had come with him anyway. What if it had been Jess who the boy had killed? What would Trey say to Addie? What was he going to say to Juanita and Eduardo—and Rico? And half brother or not, Henry Galway was family to Nell, and out here, family was everything. How was he going to explain to her how this had all happened?

"I just wanted to try and work this out, Jess."

Jess looked up at the sky for a moment as if trying to hold onto his temper. He lost that battle and turned on Trey. "And you thought marrying up with the widow was the way to do that? You thought bringing Javier out here, when you knew damn well he'd been part of the raiders, was a good idea? That's just it, Trey. You live in a world that simply does not exist except in those pictures you draw." He pointed to Javier's body. "This is the real world out here. Grow up and face facts." He mounted his horse. "I'm going to the fort. There's nothing I can do for those men down there except make them madder than they already are. The sooner we get the militia involved in this mess, the better. Now go home, face the music, and let me handle this."

Trey watched Jess until all he could see was a plume of dust in the distance. Below him, he heard Galway's son calling out oaths to avenge his father's death and the low murmur of Ernest trying to calm him. He picked up the reins to Javier's horse and stared for a moment at his friend's lifeless body. Choking back tears, he started down the trail.

He was halfway home when he saw Pete Collins and two of his hired hands riding toward him.

"What happened up there?" Pete stared at Javier's lifeless body.

Trey gave him a brief account, leaving out the part about marrying Nell. "Go home, Collins. The militia needs to sort this out, and the rest of us getting involved will only make things worse."

"So you say," Pete raged. "So you're gonna just stand by while some herder murders one of our own? Past time we took charge here. Past time we showed those herders who owns this land." He kicked the flanks of his horse and took off, galloping away before Trey could say anything more. His men followed.

Trey considered going after them, but his duty in that moment was to Javier's family.

Pushing back his sleeve, he saw that the bleeding had mostly stopped. His was minor, a scratch, while two good men were dead. One more down from each side, and now the war would start in earnest. Rico was a quiet man, but the death of his brother could not go unpunished, and Pete Collins was bound to tell the other ranchers how Javier had died at the hands of a sheepherder. The battle lines had been drawn, and they were marked by the twin stains of blood where his best friend and his own half brother-in-law had met their end.

Nell!

If she and Joshua headed back to her ranch, there was no telling what might happen. But his first responsibility was to Juanita and Eduardo. If he rode hard and fast, maybe he could send one of his ranch hands back to town to make sure Nell stayed away. Then once he'd done what he could for Javier's family, he would face his wife and figure out how he was going to keep the promise he'd made Javier and still honor his vows with her.

~❧~

Despite Addie's counsel that Nell spend the night or at least wait for Trey and Jess to return, Nell insisted on taking Joshua and heading home. "Trey expects me to be there," she explained. "He'll go there after the meeting."

The truth was, she wanted to use the time it would take to make the trip to talk more to Joshua and hopefully explain why her marriage to Trey was a good thing for both of them. After that, she would prepare a proper meal for her new husband. If they were going to make this marriage work, it would mean paying attention to the small, everyday things, finding a routine and rhythm for how they would pass the days—and nights. For now, she figured it would be best if they lived in her house, away from those who were sure to need some time to get used to the idea they were married.

She rented a horse and buggy at the livery and chose her words carefully as she tried to describe for Joshua the life they could have with Trey. She babbled on about horses and books and how she was sure Trey would make time to teach him the game of baseball. When they were halfway home, Joshua leaned his head against her.

"Ma, can we not talk anymore? I'm kinda sleepy."

She wrapped her arm around her son, pulling him closer. "That's fine. It's been a busy day for you—for both of us."

While Joshua slept, she relived every detail of the night she had spent with Trey and thought of all the nights to come. She was no longer going to have to face life alone—her worries and fears would be shared. And although she realized she knew little about him, somehow she believed together they could find a way to make everything come out right.

Joshua stirred and yawned.

"Almost there," she murmured as they slowly rounded the bend that led to their property. But a plume of black smoke made her urge the horse forward. When they reached the top of the rise, she tugged on the reins, and the horse stopped. Below them, flames licked at the doorways and windows of the house she and Calvin had shared. As Joshua let out a cry and buried his face in her lap, the roof caved in, a great plume of fiery ash shooting high in the sky.

"No," she whispered, and then she was shouting the word to the sky, the blue marred by black smoke. And on a far ridge, she saw three men and heard their shouts of what sounded like celebration as they fired their pistols in the air and rode away. She shuddered with a mix of fear and rage. They had not just burned down her house; they had set fire to what had remained of her husband's legacy for his son.

Henry's place. It was closest, and Joshua was terrified. "We'll go to Uncle Henry's ranch," she assured her son as, once again, she urged the horse to action, turning the buggy to retrace their path.

Half an hour later, Lottie stood on the porch as Nell pulled the buggy into the yard. "Did you pass Henry on your way?" She looked past Nell and Joshua to the hills beyond as if expecting to see her husband and son come riding over the rise at any moment. "I sent Spud to go meet them but…"

"They burned down our house, Aunt Lottie," Joshua said, unable to keep the news to himself a minute longer. "We went home, and it was on fire and—" He started to cough, gagging on his fear and excitement.

Lottie looked to Nell for confirmation, then bit her lower lip as tears welled in her pale gray eyes. "Let's get you inside, young man," she said as she led Joshua up to the house and Nell followed. "Go ahead and settle yourselves there in that front bedroom, Nell. I'll bring some broth."

Nell nodded and followed Joshua down the short hall. As she pulled back the covers on the narrow bed, she could hear Lottie preparing the soup—a spoon clinked on the crockery, a dipper scraped the metal pot—and then she heard something that did not fit the domestic preparations.

Lottie screamed, and dishes shattered.

"Stay here," Nell instructed Joshua, fearing the raiders had now come to her brother's ranch. She shut the bedroom door and hurried to the kitchen. The floor was littered with broken pieces of china, puddles of steaming soup, and a tray. She stepped around the mess and followed the sound of Lottie's continuing wails to the back door, where she stopped, her clenched fist covering her mouth.

Lottie's sons and Ernest walked slowly into the

yard. A lifeless body was slumped over a burro that Ernest was leading.

Lottie gathered her skirt and stumbled toward them. "No!"

Nell recognized Henry's worn denim jacket, and she followed her sister-in-law, letting the screen door of the house slam behind her. Her mind raced as she tried to make sense of what was unfolding before her. The men had all gone to a meeting—a meeting Henry had arranged. A meeting Trey had also attended.

"Trey," she murmured, not realizing she had spoken aloud as she reached the gathering that now included the Mexicans who worked as shepherds for the family.

Ernest fixed her with a cold, hard gaze. "He done this," he said. "Your so-called husband done killed your brother, Nell. Happy now?" He stalked away to help the others lift Henry's body.

Lottie's knees buckled, and Ira and Spud each took hold of their mother as they followed the men into the house. After a moment, the shepherds came back outside and walked toward the barn, no doubt to begin gathering supplies for building a coffin and grave marker.

Nell stood alone in the yard, her heart beating so fast and hard that she found it difficult to breathe. Not knowing what else to do, she returned to the kitchen. She could hear the others in the front parlor, consoling Lottie, moving furniture so they could lay out Henry's body. Knowing she would not be welcome, she knelt and picked up the shards of crockery. She mopped the floor and put coffee on to boil. And all the while, she thought of what Ernest had said. Trey had killed Henry. It was impossible for her to believe. It must have been an accident. Trey was a gentle, peace-loving man. He would never deliberately—

"Get out."

Lottie stood in the kitchen doorway, her face mottled with the evidence of her grief, her voice cold and bereft of any of its usual affection. "Joshua can stay, but I want you gone."

Nell was aware that the house had gone quiet. She could hear the men talking outside the window. From the barn, she heard the sound of a handsaw slicing through wood. "Lottie, I—"

Lottie slumped into a kitchen chair, the skirt of her apron knotted in one hand. "Did you not hear me, Nell? That man killed your brother, my husband, the father of my children. And Ira says you married him?" She gave a bark of a mirthless laugh. "You married this stranger— this cowboy—when your own flesh and blood…"

Nell took the chair next to her sister-in-law. "Tell me what happened, Lottie. Please. I have to know."

Lottie looked directly at her for a long, uncomfortable moment. "Why couldn't you let Henry help you? Why couldn't you see that if not Ernest, you needed to marry one of your own kind? You don't know the first thing about this man, what he's capable of. Why do you think he chose you? For your looks? He wants your land. He wants all our land."

"No. He's not like that. He wants to find a way we can all live in peace. He wants to—"

"Wake up, Nell. As your husband, does he not now hold control over your property?"

"Yes, but—"

"And where is he? Has he come to you, come to find you and explain what happened out there today? No, he's gone home to his ranch, no doubt to celebrate his victory. He's got your place now, and he's murdered the one man who might have stood against him and his friends. There's no one to stop him now from running us all off."

"He's not like that. You don't know him."

"Neither do you." Lottie's voice softened, and she placed her hand on Nell's. From the front of the house, they heard Joshua coughing. Lottie released a long weary sigh. "Stay. We'll work through this and get a lawyer to get you out of this marriage."

"But, Lottie—"

Her sister-in-law covered her face with both hands and shook her head as if to forestall anything Nell might try to say. "My boys are upset, Nell, so go be with Joshua in that front bedroom. Close the door, and don't come out. I'll see you get something to eat when the time comes."

"Lottie, if Ernest and the boys think Trey is responsible—"

"He is." She now looked directly at Nell, daring her to question what she had been told.

"Then what are they planning to do?" Nell's heart thundered with fear for what might happen.

Lottie stood and placed both hands on the table, her tenderness now replaced by her rekindled rage. "I don't know what they plan to do, Nell. I plan to bury my husband—your brother. What happens after that is out of my hands and yours. But this I know for sure—you're going to have to choose a side. Because this is war." She swept past Nell and out the back door.

Nell walked to the stove where the kettle of soup still simmered. She filled a cup, set the nearly empty kettle away from the heat, and carried the cup down the hall. Joshua was sleeping, curled on one side, his knees drawn protectively up to his chest.

If what Ernest had reported was true, where had Trey gone? By now, he should have reached her ranch, seen the burned-out remains, and known she must have headed to the closest haven. Why didn't he come? She scanned the horizon for any sign of a lone rider but saw nothing but the stark landscape pocked by cacti and clusters of sheep.

Lottie had said there would be a range war for sure now. More senseless killing on both sides. She saw her nephews leaning against the fence that enclosed the kitchen garden. Ira pounded the fence post with his fist. Spud said something that seemed to rally his brother, and they both stalked off to the barn. Everything about the way they walked screamed *revenge*.

Could she blame them? Their father was dead.

Her brother—the only kin she had out here—was dead.

She thought of how Henry had left his flock the minute he heard of Calvin's death, how he had come to her and in his way tried to make sure she and Joshua were all right. It was Henry who had seen to the details of a funeral for her husband. It was Henry who had sent Lottie to prepare the house for the wake that followed. In every way, Henry had tried to do his brotherly duty. Even that business with Ernest had been his attempt to get things settled for her.

For the first time since she and Trey had secretly married, she felt as if somehow she had betrayed her family, her community. But there were always two sides to every story. She could not bring herself to believe that Trey would ever be provoked to commit cold-blooded murder. There had to be more! She moved from the chair to the bed and gently shook Joshua's shoulder.

"I have to go away for a bit," she said when he opened his eyes and stared up at her, still half asleep. "Stay here. Aunt Lottie will bring you something to eat when it's time, but promise me you will stay right here in this room."

Joshua rubbed his eyes with his fists as he pushed himself up against the headboard. "Is Uncle Henry really dead?"

Nell nodded, her throat closing, choking off her tears. "Yes. There was…an accident."

"Are we gonna live here now?"

"For the time being, this will be home," she said. "Now promise me you'll stay right here."

Joshua nodded. "Promise," he said.

Nell kissed his forehead, tousled his hair, and then slipped out the door.

She paused a moment, listening for the others. Sure that everyone was otherwise occupied in the yard, she hurried out the front door and across the yard to a far pasture where the horse she'd rented was busy grazing. A bridle and bit were looped over a fence post where one of the shepherds had no doubt left them. She didn't need a saddle. She led the horse farther from the house and outbuildings, down a path shadowed by a large cottonwood, before mounting up and riding off toward town. She would take the route that ran close to her ranch, in case Trey had come there after all.

But Jess had also been at the meeting, and if Trey had in fact somehow been involved in Henry's death, wouldn't Jess take him into custody? Either way, by now, Addie would know what happened. Addie would tell her the whole story, not just pieces of it. She paused briefly on the rise that overlooked her property, a ruined place she barely recognized now. Seeing no signs of anyone there, she pressed on.

⤚∽⤙

Trey rode into the yard of the ranch his father had built and where his family—and Javier's—had spent their whole lives. Juanita was hanging wash on a line stretched between two posts near the kitchen. He saw Javier's brother, Rico, sitting on a banco, whittling a stick. He saw Eduardo light his pipe as Rico said something that made both his parents laugh.

And then as if they sensed something had shifted, all three of them turned to look. First at him and then at the horse carrying Javier's body.

Juanita dropped the wet shirt in her hands. It hit the dirt with a splat, and she stumbled awkwardly toward him. Rico stood and tossed the stick aside. He threw the knife at the banco, where it stuck. Eduardo was the one who cried out, in a voice that was loud enough to bring a cowhand from the barn and at the same time the gurgle of a man strangling on his own bile.

Trey kept moving toward them, not knowing what else to do, the reins to Javier's horse loose in his hands. Rico caught up to his father and held him as Eduardo struggled to reach for Javier's limp body.

Trey slid from the saddle, pulling off his hat as he faced them. "I'm so sorry," he managed as Juanita collapsed against him.

"No," she whispered. "Please, God, no."

"What happened?" Rico demanded.

"Let's get him inside," Trey replied, ignoring the question. By now, the cowboy from the barn had alerted others, and several of the men surrounded the horse. Together, they lifted the body and carried it inside. "The dining room," Trey directed, his voice hoarse with pent-up emotion. It was where his parents had lain in state, and as far as he was concerned, it was where any family member would lie.

Once the men had followed his instructions and he'd sent them back to work, Trey knew he could no longer avoid the question. He led Juanita to the intricately carved armchair his mother had always occupied, eased her to a sitting position, and knelt next to her. He held her hand between his. Eduardo stood, staring at his dead son, and Rico gazed out the window. Trey told them how the Galway boy had provoked Javier and how the two had wrestled, how Henry had tried to pull his son away. That's when they saw the knife. "But it was already too late, Nita."

Rico glanced over his shoulder and stared at Trey. "There's more, isn't there? That can't be the whole of it." He pointed to the wound on Trey's forearm.

Trey let out a breath he hadn't realized he'd been

holding. "There's more," he said softly and tightened his grip on Juanita's hand. He told them how he and Ira had fought for the knife and how Henry pulled his gun. He told how he had stepped away to avoid Henry's enraged charge and Henry had fallen, shooting himself in the process.

"So two good men are dead, one from each side," he finished. "And it has to stop here." This last he directed at Rico.

Without a word, Javier's older brother left the room. Minutes later, Trey heard hoofbeats and saw Rico riding away. At least he was headed toward town, not in the direction of the sheep ranches. Trey hoped Rico had left to tell his wife, Louisa, the news and bring her out to the ranch to be with Juanita. It occurred to him that he needed to get word to his siblings—Chet and Maria in California, Amanda and Seth in Tucson. Jess would tell Addie; if she was thinking straight, maybe she'd send telegrams. He needed her to come to his ranch as soon as possible and with the priest. And maybe Nell and Joshua as well.

But then he remembered what Nell had said about needing to get back to her ranch. There was no way she could have known about the trouble up on Deadman's Point. No way she could know the danger had taken a turn for the worse.

"You married that woman?" Juanita said, her eyes meeting his for the first time since they'd entered the house.

"Yes."

"And her brother is also dead?"

Trey nodded.

"Does she know this?"

"I don't think she knows about any of this," he admitted. "I need to find her, Nita, before…"

Juanita looked at her dead son and then bowed her head. "Go," she whispered.

"Nita, I—"

"Go!" And this time, the single command was a growl. Juanita looked up at him, her face ravaged by loss and tears. "There is nothing you can do here, Trey. You made your choice. Go find your wife before there is more killing."

The sun was low in the sky as he approached Nell's place. He saw the wisp of smoke before he was in sight of the house and outbuildings. The chimney—Nell had returned, then, and was waiting for him! He spurred his horse, anxious to see her. How would she take the news of Henry's death? Topping the mesa, he drew in his breath, and his heart hammered. There was nothing but devastation below—the house had caved in on itself and was still smoldering, livestock wandering aimlessly around the yard, and no sign of human life anywhere.

He rode full-out down the rocky trail and up to the house, shouting his wife's name as he came closer. The stench of the burned-out house reached him. "Nell! Nellie!" And with every repetition of her name, he prayed that the silence meant she wasn't there, not that she was unable to answer.

He explored the ruins, satisfying himself that Nell and Joshua were not there, and his mind raced with the possibilities in the aftermath of the day's events. Two men dead and a ranch destroyed. All-out war would be impossible to avoid now.

Nell.

Looking around, he searched the horizon as if she might appear. Where would she go? Back to town? No. Too far. Her brother's place was closer.

He hesitated. How would her family react if he showed up there now that Henry was dead? They no doubt blamed him. And what were they telling Nell? He had to see her, make sure she understood the last thing he'd wanted from this meeting was violence. Henry's death had been a horrible accident.

Even so, would Nell want anything to do with him now? Would she regret her decision to marry him? Would she turn away?

All these questions and more raced through his mind as he traveled cross-country. He refused to believe he and Nell had made a mistake in marrying. The timing might not have been right, but he was more convinced than ever that this woman was the one he'd waited his whole life to find. Still, he could not deny that neither of them had really thought about the reactions of others beyond the general idea that their union would upset some, but in time… So preoccupied was he with his fears that he almost missed seeing the lone rider galloping along the trail that ran on top of a ridge. A woman. She wore a sunbonnet, and as he came closer, he realized she rode bareback.

"Nellie!" He continued to shout her name as he pushed his own mount to top speed. He doubted she could hear anything more than the thunder of her horse's hooves, so he stopped calling out to her and focused instead on gaining on her.

The two riders rode on a course that would have

them intersect eventually, leaving dual trails of thick dust in their wake. The only sounds were the beat of the hooves and the combined breaths of horse and rider, each pushed to the full limits of their abilities.

When Trey started to gain ground, he saw Nell glance back over her shoulder and urge her horse to greater speed. Had she seen him—recognized him—and now was trying her best to outrun him? No matter. She might not believe him, but she had to hear him out.

"Nell! Hold up," he shouted as he finally overcame the distance between them. He reached for the bridle even as she pulled on the reins. He could not read her expression but saw her face was streaked with dirt and tears. "Please." He wasn't sure what it was he was pleading for, but their horses slowed and then stopped, and suddenly, the world was silent except for the bellows of their mounts and their own rapid breathing.

"I'm so sorry." They spoke in unison.

He dismounted and held out his arms to her. Without hesitation, she slid from her horse into his embrace. Holding her now felt very different. There was no hesitation, no shyness. Instead, there was raw need on both sides, and there was comfort.

"What are we going to do?" she murmured, her voice muffled by his shirt.

"Is Joshua still with Addie?"

She shook her head and pulled free of his hold. "They burned our house, Trey. I saw the men, three of them, riding away. I was afraid, so I took Joshua and went to Henry's and then…"

"I know. How's your sister-in-law holding up?"

"She's devastated. The boys are telling everyone you murdered Henry."

"It was an accident, Nell." He explained what had happened—about Javier and the knife and then Henry and the gun. "He tripped and went over the edge, Nell, and it was his gun that went off. I swear. You have to believe me. Jess was there. He saw it all. You can ask him."

She caressed his cheek. "Shhh," she whispered. "I believe you."

Relief raced through him with such force that he pulled her to him again, this time to draw on the strength he felt radiating from this incredible woman, this woman who was his wife. Together, they would make this right—the deaths of her brother and his friend would be the end of it.

"Come home with me," he said. "We'll send one of my men for Joshua."

"Joshua will be fine with Lottie, but Trey, we can't go back to your ranch."

"Why on earth not?"

"My nephew killed Javier. His parents will never—"

"Juanita knows I came to find you. She will not welcome you with open arms, but she—and Eduardo—will understand that, as my wife, the ranch is where you belong."

"And Javier's brother?"

"That'll take more time," he admitted.

"And those men who burned down my house?"

"Those men don't work for me."

"Javier did," she replied softly.

She had him there. Javier had fallen under the

influence of Pete Collins, a man on a mission. The death of Javier at the hands of the herders would give Collins all the reason he needed to seek revenge and persuade others to join him. Trey had no doubt Pete had some hand in the burning of Nell's home, and that was evidence enough of Collins's determination to declare open warfare.

"I need you by my side, Nell. I need to know you and Joshua are safe at the ranch."

She chewed on her lower lip. "I don't know, Trey. Perhaps one night," she bargained.

"My home is your home, Nellie—yours and Joshua's. Tomorrow, we'll bring him from your brother's place and get settled in. It will help Juanita to have a kid she can fuss over."

"Or it could remind her of her loss and be far more painful than you could ever imagine, Trey. I'll stay tonight but make no promises beyond that."

⟞⟝

It was dusk when they reached the Porterfield ranch. Addie and Jess had arrived, along with a couple of neighbor women Nell had seen in church. Javier's brother, Rico, was there with his wife, Louisa, and their toddler. Everyone was seated in the courtyard, except for the women who bustled in and out of the house, bringing tea and a shawl for Juanita. From the barn came the sounds of hammering and a plane smoothing wood—no doubt for Javier's coffin. Only Juanita looked up as Trey rode to the corral and handed his horse and Nell's over to one of his hired hands.

Nell was glad when Trey took a firm hold of her

hand as they walked back to the gathering. Rico took one look at her and walked away, ignoring the way his wife reached out to stop him. Nell could see a couple of Trey's hired hands scowling from their vantage point just outside the barn.

But Javier's mother scooted to one side of the bench and patted the seat next to her. "Come sit with me, child." She stretched out her hand to Nell, the simple—and generous—act making it clear to all that this matriarch expected others to mind their manners.

Nell sat. "I am so very—"

Juanita stopped her condolences with a wave of one calloused hand. "There is grief enough on both sides."

Nell nodded and bowed her head, respecting the silence but aware that Trey had taken his brother aside. There was a heated exchange between them, and Nell tried to catch Addie's eye, but the woman she had counted as a friend would not look at her. And when the neighbors emerged from the kitchen bearing a tray filled with mugs of steaming tea, they stopped dead in their tracks at the sight of her.

"We'll be needing two more cups," Juanita said. "Trey and his wife are here."

"I'll get them," Louisa offered. She relieved the women of the tray, passed it to Addie, and then ushered the neighbors back inside the house. Nell was touched by Louisa's kindness. She realized this young woman must have faced her fair share of whispers and scowls after marrying Rico—she, the daughter of a wealthy white rancher, and he, the son of Mexican hired help.

Nell imagined a similar gathering at her brother's

place. By now, others would have gotten word and come to offer support and comfort. And would the men gather as Rico did now with the ranch hands near the barn, their planes and hammers silenced as they talked, gestured, and cast furtive looks in her direction?

So lost in thought was she that she was unaware of the mug of tea being offered until Addie said, "Where's your son, Nell?"

The inquiry garnered the attention of the others.

"It's been a confusing time for him."

"You left him alone at your ranch?" Addie's disapproval was palpable.

"No. He's with family."

Suddenly, Trey was at her side, his hand resting lightly on her shoulder. "Nell's house was set afire. She and Joshua took refuge at her brother's place. I persuaded her to come here, but she thought it best to let Joshua stay there. We'll send for him tomorrow."

"It's a total loss, the house?" Addie studied Trey closely.

"Not that it matters if it was partial or total, Addie," he replied, an edge to his voice, "but Nell has lost everything."

"I'm so very sorry." Addie's sympathy seemed genuine; maybe there was some measure of hope that at least their friendship could survive this madness.

"It's been a day of sorrow for everyone," Trey said. "If you'll excuse us, I want to get Nell settled."

He offered her his hand, and she grasped it as the lifeline it was. Together, they walked to the portico that covered the front entrance of the house and on inside. Nell felt immediately calmed by the surroundings—thick adobe walls, beamed ceilings, tile floors covered here and there with colorful handwoven rugs, furniture lovingly carved by the hands of craftsmen who took pride in their work. Through an open arched door, she caught a glimpse of the library Trey had mentioned to Joshua and found herself imagining her son there, his appetite for learning sated at last.

She followed Trey down a hall lined with framed portraits. She recognized one of Jess, another of Addie, and assumed the others were of his sisters and parents. There were even drawings of Javier and his family. "There's none of you," she said as she paused to look at the portrait he'd done of Juanita.

"Never tried a self-portrait," he replied as he opened a door at the far end of the hall and waited for her to enter. "Welcome home, Nellie."

A large four-poster bed dominated the room. More handwoven rugs covered parts of the dark wood of the wide-planked floor. There was a large wardrobe, a matching bureau, and dressing table. Across from the bed was a small arched fireplace with two worn leather chairs facing it and a shelf filled with books set into the wall. The windows were fitted with intricate ironwork that filtered the waning light. It was the most beautiful room Nell had ever seen.

She walked around looking at everything as she allowed her fingers to brush over the inviting bedding, the intricate carving on the furnishings, and the details of the filigreed shutters.

"Say something," Trey pleaded.

"I can't find words. 'It's lovely' hardly seems enough."

"It's yours—ours. Joshua will be right down the hall there in my old room." He glanced around as if seeing his surroundings for the first time. "I know it's not what you had, what you may have liked better, but—"

"Trey, how will your family feel about this? This is the room your parents shared, is it not? And now to have it…to have someone like me here?"

He crossed to her in three determined strides and wrapped his arms around her. "You are my wife, Nellie Porterfield, and as such, you have every right to be in this house, this room, and my life, okay?"

She diverted his fierce determination to make everything seem normal by turning away and pushing loose pins back into her hair. "Well, I'm sure your mother was never so coated with dirt and grime when she was here. I need a place to wash my hands and face at least, and perhaps you could leave me to undress and brush the dust from my clothes so I might be a bit more presentable." She bent to see her reflection in a pedestal mirror on the dressing table. "I look a fright."

Trey stepped around her to open a narrow door and reveal a copper bathtub serviced by a pump. Then he opened the doors to the wardrobe. It was filled with women's clothing.

"I couldn't," Nell protested, guessing that these were clothes his mother or sisters had worn.

"You can and you will," Trey said softly. "Ma would insist." He backed away toward the door open to the hall. "Shall I send Addie or Louisa to help you?" Suddenly shy, he was actually blushing. "I mean—"

"I can manage," she assured him, and then she rushed to him and pressed her cheek to his chest as she wrapped her arms around him. "*We* will manage, Trey. Together, we can see this through." And for the first time since that morning, she felt a kernel of truth in that statement.

They held each other for a long moment, both aware of the quiet voices in the courtyard, the hand tools at work once again in the barn, and the heaviness of sorrow that covered everything like the desert dust of Arizona.

~

After making sure Nell was settled, Trey went in search of Javier's parents. There was much still to be explained, and yet he had no words. He heard Louisa singing a lullaby to her child as he passed the library. When he reached the kitchen, he was surprised to see the neighbor ladies gone and Juanita going about her routine. "I'll get someone in to handle things for a while, Nita. You and Eduardo take some time."

She paused in the task of washing dishes but did not turn to him. "And what's the point of that? Will it bring Javier back to us? Will it make one damn bit of difference what we do?"

Her shoulders slumped and then began to shake, and he realized she was crying again. He couldn't recall a time when Juanita had ever shown such emotion. Her strength in the face of adversity and tragedy had been the glue that held the family together. Now that she was the one in need of comforting, Trey did not know what to do.

"Nita?" He attempted to place his hand on her shoulder, but she shrugged him off. She began scrubbing a skillet, rubbing it so hard that the veins in her bare forearms stood out below the rolled-back sleeves of her dress.

"Nita, I am so sorry. I wish—"

She flicked her eyes toward him and then immediately back to the pan. "You've always been a dreamer, Trey, but when dreams buck up against reality, reality will win. Every time. Two men are dead. Your new bride's former husband is dead as well, and for what? Land? Power? Where does it end, Trey?" She clanged the wet pan down on the drain board and turned away. "I've got work to do, and so do you. We'll be burying Javier day after tomorrow—you and your wife should be here."

Drying her hands on her apron, Juanita stepped outside and began shouting orders at her husband and chastising a cowboy who was leaning on the corral fence talking to Rico. "Stop your jawing and get back to work," she shouted. "Rico, time you and Louisa headed back to town. That baby needs to be put down for the night. Jess? Go home. You look like you've been rode hard and put away wet."

"Where's Addie?" Trey asked.

"She headed over to the Galway place. One of their hired hands came by to say Lottie Galway was not doing well." She brushed past him as she headed for the library, and a minute later, he heard her talking softly to Louisa.

Trey observed it all, but his mind was stuck on Juanita's question: *Where does it end?*

Just a few days earlier, he'd thought he could answer that. He had believed talk would be a start. He had trusted his union with Nell could eventually be a bridge to peace. He'd been wrong on both counts. As the largest landowner in the region, it was up to him to step up and make sure this went no further. His goal had gone beyond simply trying to end the range war. Now what mattered most was that Javier had not died in vain. He went to his office and sat at the same desk where his father had wrestled with the challenges of his time. He started listing the names of the ranchers in three columns: those who favored Pete's way, those who were on the fence, and those who stood with him. The last column was the shortest.

He expected all his fellow ranchers to attend Javier's funeral, if for no other reason than their respect for Rico. Ever since Javier's brother had taken over the blacksmithing and livery stable in town, he had proven himself to be someone all ranchers could rely upon when they needed help. Trey understood that his biggest problem was that the others didn't trust him, and until they did, his hope to make Javier's death mean something was a lost cause.

By the time he left the office, Rico and his family had left, and so had Jess. Trey saddled his horse, aware that Juanita was watching him from the kitchen doorway. "Tell Nell I'll be back," he shouted as he rode away. He heard Juanita calling out to him but kept riding. He needed to clear his head and consider next steps, but after a while, he found himself heading to the Galway ranch.

It was fully dark by the time he reached their homestead. He guided his horse slowly through the clusters of sheep grazing on the open land outside the fence surrounding the house and outbuildings. Once again, he was struck by how often he had visited this ranch as a boy, when cattle had grazed here. He could not deny the difference between cattle and sheep when it came to the land. The grass he crossed had been chewed down to the root, and there were gouges in the earth that he never saw in cattle land. But there were also shoots of new growth, something he realized he would not see where cattle grazed.

He reined in his horse when he came in sight of the house and yard and took stock of who was around. Lottie Galway was no doubt inside the house, its windows glowing with the light. He had no idea what he'd hoped to accomplish by coming here, especially at this hour. He was prepared to head back when he saw Addie's buggy tied up outside the house. He knew she'd come for Galway's wife, but what if Joshua had taken a turn for the worse? Nell would never forgive him if she learned he'd ridden all this way and had failed to check on the boy.

As he approached the house, one of the Galway boys emerged from the barn, then immediately ducked back inside. He reappeared with his brother and Ernest Stokes. Ernest carried a lantern, but Trey saw they were unarmed as they watched him dismount and head up the porch steps. Trey nodded to the trio but kept walking. The front door was open, barred by a screen door, beyond which he could hear the clink of crockery from the kitchen and the low murmur of female voices. He knocked.

A woman he recognized from the church social came down the hall, wiping her hands on a towel.

She stopped and stared when she saw him, her mouth open, before hurrying back to the kitchen where the chatter increased in both volume and intensity.

"Oh, for heaven's sake," he heard Addie say, and seconds later, she was striding toward him. "Not your best idea," she muttered as she pushed the screen door open and stepped out onto the porch.

"I thought I should check on Joshua," he said, ignoring her reprimand.

"Joshua is fine. Lottie Galway, on the other hand, is anything but fine. Seeing you might just undo the little I've been able to do to calm her. You should leave—now."

She glanced beyond him, and Trey turned. He saw that the Galway boys and Ernest had moved closer to the house. They now stood just outside the front gate. "Maybe I should take Joshua back to my place," he said.

"The boy is in no danger here. I would think you'd be more worried about Nell."

"Nobody is going to hurt my wife," he said.

Addie sighed. "A group of 'nobodies' burned her house to the ground, in case you forgot."

Trey drew in a long breath. "Have they set a time for Galway's funeral?"

"The day after tomorrow, and please do not tell me you plan to attend." Addie actually grasped his arm.

"I'm thinking of Nell. He was her brother after all."

Addie rolled her eyes. "You are determined to go looking for trouble, Trey Porterfield. Tell Nell she should stay put. She can pay her respects once the dust has settled. Feelings are running pretty hot right now, and there's no reason to stir that pot."

"Can I at least see Joshua so I can assure her that he's all right?"

"Take my word for it, Trey. The boy is fine. He misses his mother, of course, but he's best off here. As you said, this is family."

The way Addie placed her emphasis on the word *family* left no doubt that he was intruding.

"I'll be going then," he said.

"Good plan." Addie folded her arms and waited, and he understood she would not go back inside the house until she was sure he was gone.

The Galway boys stepped closer as he opened the gate. Ira glared at him, but it was Spud who spat at him, landing a glob of saliva squarely on his cheek. Trey wiped it away with the back of his hand, then mounted his horse and left.

As he covered the distance he'd traveled so many times before, Trey tried to work out what he might say to the other ranchers. Pete Collins would be all fired up and no doubt refuse to even listen. The truth was, Trey was fairly certain Collins had been behind the burning of Nell's home. Until he had proof, though, he would treat Pete the same as any other neighbor. The man had a following of those who believed the only answer was "them or us."

Maybe if he could get Jess to talk to the cattlemen. After all, the ranch belonged to his siblings as much as it did to him. But while Jess might not go along with Pete on most things, the two men were in total agreement when it came to thinking Trey had made a real mess.

Still…

Crack!

A shot! Close—too close.

Trey headed for the shelter of a cluster of trees. He hunched low, making himself as close to being part of the horse as he could.

A second shot whizzed past.

He reached the trees and slid from the saddle, pulling his rifle from its sheath as he did. Slapping the horse's rump to send it on its way to a safer place, he took up his position behind the thick trunk of a Gambel oak. The cover of night worked both for and against him. In the trees, he would be harder to see, but the inky night also made it impossible to mark the position of whoever might be stalking him.

He waited.

All was quiet.

The cry of a night bird startled him, and he tightened his grip on the weapon. But then he loosened it. What was he going to do? Kill whoever was shooting at him? What would that solve?

Trey waited.

Finally convinced his attacker had given up or perhaps only meant to warn him, he gave a low whistle, and his horse ambled over to the trees. Using the horse as shield between him and anyone who might still be waiting to take a shot at him, he put away his rifle. Following the nearly dry creek, he headed home.

Nell was in the yard when Trey got back. The night air was chilly, and he saw she wore no wrap. "Go inside, Nellie. I'll be right there."

Ignoring his instruction, she walked alongside as he rode to the corral. "Where were you?"

"I went over to your brother's place," he admitted.

"Oh, Trey, what did you think to accomplish?"

He finished removing the saddle from his horse before answering. "I thought…" He stared at the ground and shook his head. "I don't know what I thought. Addie was there. I don't think your sister-in-law is doing too well."

"Joshua?"

"I asked after him. Addie said he's fine—sleeping." He opened the gate to the corral, slapped the horse on the rump to send him inside, then closed and fastened the gate. One of the cowhands would see to brushing the animal down. "I've made a mess of everything, Nellie."

"You couldn't have known things would turn out this way," she protested. "Ira has always had a temper, and from what you've told me, Henry's death was a horrible accident."

"An accident I had a hand in causing." He put his arm around her and walked back toward the house. "How are Nita and Eduardo doing?" Nell did not speak for a moment, so he pressed. "Nellie?"

"They are devastated, Trey. How do you think they're doing? They have been cordial to me, but who can blame them for keeping their distance? Their child is dead, and yet they soldier on. I don't know how they can do it."

"You did it," he reminded her. "When your husband died, you must have wanted to…I don't know… leave everything to others."

"And how do you know I didn't?" They had reached the courtyard, and she turned to face him.

He cupped her face with his hands. "Because I think I know enough of you to know that in such a time, you would think first of others—especially Joshua."

"He needed me, and that saved me." They had reached the front door, and when Trey reached for the knob, she put her hand on his to stop him. "Rico is inside. He left Louisa and the baby in town and came back."

"I'm not surprised. He would want to be here for his folks."

She tightened her grip on his hand. "He's very angry, Trey."

He hesitated. "He's also part of my family," he said as he opened the door and waited for her to go ahead of him.

❧

Nell was relieved to see the large front room was empty except for Javier's body lying on the dining room table. Candles burned throughout the room, casting eerie shadows on the adobe walls and the beamed ceiling. The heavy draperies had been pulled shut, and a fire in the arched fireplace gave off the scent of juniper and piñon. She could hear the low murmur of voices coming from the kitchen.

Trey walked to the table and stood next to his friend's body with his hat in his hands and his head bowed. Nell waited in the doorway, unsure of what to do. She saw Trey's shoulders slump and realized he must be as exhausted as she was. They'd gotten little sleep the night before, and the new day had drained them both of their strength and any ability to understand what had happened.

Moving to stand next to her husband, she gently took his hand. "Come," she said softly.

He did not resist. With a glance back at Javier, he followed her down the hall to their room. "I should let Nita know I'm back," he said. "She'll worry and—"

"I'll tell her. You need to lie down, Trey."

He sat on the edge of the bed, and she pulled his boots off. She set them by the door and hung his hat on a hook nearby. By the time she turned around, he had collapsed onto the bed and was staring at the ceiling.

Nell opened the door. "I'll be back in a minute," she said softly.

When she entered the kitchen, three sets of dark anguished eyes looked up. Javier's parents both immediately lowered their gaze to the cups of warm milk before them. Rico continued to stare at her, his scrutiny unnerving in its silent intensity.

"Trey is home," she reported. She prepared to return to the room she would share with Trey, but something made her hesitate. "I love Trey," she said quietly as if someone had raised the question. She turned back to face them and found her voice. "And because I love him, I will do whatever is necessary to see that he—and you—are safe and—"

"Even leave him?" Rico's voice was raspy, and he continued to glare at her.

She met his look, going so far as to take a step forward to be sure he noticed. "Even that," she replied. She turned her attention to Juanita, a mother like she was. "I'll say good night now."

She had barely turned to go when she heard a chair scrape on the tiles of the kitchen floor. Fearing Rico was about to come after her, his fury and grief too much for him to bear, she glanced back and saw it was Juanita who had risen. Nell hesitated.

"Take Trey a cup of this warm cinnamon milk," Juanita said as she filled a mug and held it out to Nell. "It's his favorite. You need to learn these things, child." The cup wobbled dangerously.

"Thank you," Nell replied, her voice barely a whisper as she accepted the offering. Fighting tears, she hurried down the hall and slipped inside the bedroom. Trey's even breathing told her he was sound asleep, so she stood at the window and drank the spiced milk, wondering if in spite of their love, they had made a terrible mistake.

Seven

THE RANCH WAS UNUSUALLY QUIET THE FOLLOWING
day as everyone went about their business with a kind
of respectful reserve. After discussing it with Trey,
Nell decided it would be best to leave Joshua with
Lottie until after the funeral. She would follow Addie's
advice and stay away until then. Trey had one of his
men deliver her note to Lottie. The only reply was
the cowboy's report that Lottie had said Joshua was
welcome to stay as long as he liked.

Nell observed the preparations for Javier's funeral
and helped wherever she could, although she felt
completely out of place. The truth was, she was torn as
to where she truly belonged. On the one hand, Henry
was her brother. They had never been close, but he
was still blood kin. On the other hand, Trey was her
husband, and his evident heartbreak over the loss of
his best friend had her worried. He blamed himself,
and on the night before the funerals for both men, she
woke to find his side of the bed empty. Terrified his
grief had found its way to anger, she hurried barefoot
down the hall that separated the bedroom wing from

the rest of the house. The front door was closed, and the only light came from the candles that Juanita had insisted remain lit in the room where Javier's body lay.

A shadow cast by the flickering light took on a human form. Nell hesitated before entering the room, not wanting to disturb Juanita or Eduardo, should they be sitting with their son. But it was Trey who stood motionless next to his friend, his hand resting gently on Javier's coffin. Relieved that her husband had not gone out seeking revenge, as in her experience, men were prone to do, she stepped back into the darkness of the hall.

"He was more than a friend, Nell," Trey said softly, inviting her into the room with his comment. "Growing up, he was my brother in every way but blood. Out there——" His voice broke, and he shook off the emotion as he ran his fingers over his forearm where the mark of his wound was still evident. "Out there, we became true brothers, his blood mingling with mine."

Nell moved closer. "I'm so sorry I will not have the chance to know him better, Trey."

"He wasn't the man who raided your place, Nellie. I mean, he was there all right, but he got caught up with a gang who believed their livelihoods—the futures of their families—were in danger. Even when Pete Collins decided against being at the meeting, Javier came. He chose to try and work this out. That says a good deal about the kind of man he truly was."

It occurred to Nell that from what Trey had told her of the meeting at Deadman's Point, none of the other herders had come with Henry—just Ira and Ernest.

There was so much bitterness, resentment blossoming into outright hatred. And now Trey would be caught in the middle. Having married her, he had alienated both sides. Her people thought he had tricked her to get her land. Trey's friends would question his loyalty to their cause.

"Trey, I—"

"Somebody took a shot at me the other night after I stopped over at your brother's place, Nell."

Nell drew in her breath and gripped his arm. "Did the boys or Ernest see you there?"

"Yeah, but it wasn't one of them. That's what whoever fired wanted me to think. I've been studying on it ever since, and I'm pretty sure it was a cowhand, maybe one of Collins's boys. Maybe Pete himself."

"But why?"

He withdrew the hand he'd used to cover his wounded forearm and pulled her close to his side. "I expect to make the point that the time has come for me to choose sides."

"But you have chosen. There's a third side in all this, Trey. The side that has us all living together in peace. That's your side."

He kissed her temple. "Pretty lonely standing on that side with just you," he said.

"Nonsense," she replied. "There are many who would like to see an end to this business—Javier's family, your family…"

"And yours?"

It was a question she couldn't answer. "Come to bed," she said softly, resting her head on his shoulder.

"You go on. I just need a few more minutes." He

kissed her gently on the lips. "Go on, now. Sun will be up before we know it."

Reluctantly, she returned to the beautiful room his parents had shared. Not for the first time, she wondered if she and Trey could find the kind of happiness and joy that Isaac and Constance Porterfield had found there. And not for the first time since learning of the carnage played out first at Deadman's Point and then at her ranch, she wondered if perhaps it might not be best for everyone—especially Trey—if she just left.

⁂

Juanita was overwhelmed by the turnout for Javier's funeral. Every cattle rancher in the area was there, each man bringing his family and what hired hands could be spared, to pay their respects and offer their support to Juanita, Eduardo, and Rico.

The day had dawned with a vivid blue sky streaked with swaths of pink and pale purple, the kind of sky Javier had once called a rainbow sky. Juanita smiled at the memory. He'd been five or so the first time he'd named it and had come running into the kitchen while she was trying to get breakfast on the table for the Porterfield family.

"Come, Mama," he'd pleaded, tugging at her skirt. "It's a rainbow sky. You have to come now, or it will go away."

The entire Porterfield clan had followed Juanita and her son to the yard where he pointed at the sky as he jumped around with excitement. "See? I told you. Trey, get your stuff. You have to paint this right now."

And because Trey and Javier were the best of

friends, in spite of the difference in age, Trey had hurried back to the house. His wheezing had echoed across the courtyard as he emerged seconds later with his sketchbook and box of pastels.

That crude drawing still hung in the room Javier had once shared with Rico. Juanita glanced across the open grave to where Trey stood with his siblings—and his new bride. The boy was as much her son as Rico and Javier were, and yet if he hadn't drawn Javier into his fight to bring the herders and cattlemen together, would they be here at Javier's grave today?

She was so stricken with grief that nothing made sense to her, least of all where her loyalties should lie. It was hard to forgive Trey for his naïveté in thinking he could even start to solve the fight between sides so simply. And to have married the herder woman without letting her family know? Juanita was well aware Trey had feelings for her, but to act so impulsively was completely out of character. It was the kind of thing she might expect of his brother, but Trey had always been so steadfast, even guarded in his actions.

As the priest droned on, she focused her gaze on Nell Stokes—Porterfield, now. Nothing to be done about that. It was hardly the young widow's fault that things had come to pass this way. On the other hand, she should have known marrying Trey would open a hornet's nest of trouble. She was a grown woman and seemed to have a good head on her shoulders, so why hadn't she refused Trey?

The herders thought Trey had tricked her so he could take over her land, but what if the shoe was on the other foot? What if she had been the one to trick him? Certainly, she had no future on her own. There was no way she could manage that sheep ranch without help—financial and otherwise—and Trey was a good catch. Any number of families in the territory knew that, and several had made their bid to have him take note of their unmarried daughters. How had Nell Stokes managed to steal his heart?

The woman was trouble, at least for Trey. Juanita frowned. She had suffered the loss of one son; she would not lose another in the bargain. Nell Stokes Porterfield had best watch herself, at least when in the presence of Juanita.

❧

Following the graveside service, Trey moved among the crowded rooms of the ranch house like a ghost. He heard friends and neighbors speaking of Javier in low, respectful terms. Occasionally, he would hear a burst of laughter as someone told a story of Javier's antics out on the range. Once or twice, he stepped up to the circle of men and tried to share in the memories, but it was evident his presence made them uncomfortable, so he moved away. They blamed him, and why not?

His sister Amanda carried a tray loaded with food from the kitchen to the tables set up in the courtyard. Trey wondered at the need for people to express their condolences through food. Something to do with sustenance, he thought, although he couldn't quite grasp the connection.

He saw Pete Collins's wife and looked around for Pete. He was the only rancher who had not shown up for the funeral. Trey crossed the yard, and as he approached Bess Collins, she looked around as if seeking an escape.

"Thank you for coming, Bess. I know the turnout gives Juanita and Eduardo some comfort. Where's Pete? I'd like to thank him as well."

Bess twisted a handkerchief and did not meet Trey's gaze. "Pete? Well, he…that is, there was… I expect he'll be along directly."

One of Pete's hired hands stepped forward. "We had some trouble at the ranch," he told Trey. "The boss sends his deepest sympathies and said he'd stop by as soon as he can." He took hold of Bess's arm and steered her away.

Trey didn't believe a word of it, but his suspicions about Pete could wait. Javier's family—and his— should be the focus now.

Juanita sat in the shade, graciously accepting the brief condolences a line of guests offered in turn. Rico stood just behind her, a sentry on guard lest anyone upset his beloved mother. Eduardo shifted nervously from one foot to the other, his head bowed, his hands clasped behind his back.

Trey looked around for Jess and saw his brother talking to their brother-in-law Seth Grover, both of them men of the law. Jess was marshal in Whitman Falls while Seth had been elected and reelected to serve as sheriff of the region with headquarters in Tucson. The two of them kept glancing his way. Something was up, and he intended to be full party to whatever decisions they were making.

"What's going on?" he asked when he reached them.

They abruptly ended their conversation.

Seth glanced at Jess and nodded.

Jess sighed. "You need to turn yourself in, Trey."

Trey was astounded that they were focused on his part in what had happened at Deadman's Point rather than what they might do to prevent all-out war. "There's no cause," he said. "It was an accident. Galway tripped while he was holding the gun and—"

"Ernest Stokes insists it was deliberate," Seth said. He placed a comforting hand on Trey's shoulder. "Just do it, Trey. We'll get this all worked out, but right now, the less fuss you make…"

Seth had been an undercover detective for Wells Fargo before taking the job of sheriff for the region. If anyone knew how these things worked, he did. Still, Trey had his doubts. "But won't that make it look like I'm guilty of something?"

"You're not saying that," Jess explained. "You're just trying to do what you can to get this whole business settled. After all, Stokes and Galway's son will tell a different version of things."

"We just buried one of those witnesses," Trey reminded his brother. "That leaves you."

"And my position as marshal ought to count for something, but still."

Trey was well aware that Jess didn't like it when others contradicted what he thought best, especially when that challenge came from his siblings.

"You're also my brother," Trey reminded him.

"Lower your voices," Addie said, coming alongside her husband.

Trey looked around and saw that the mourners were casting furtive glances in their direction. Did everyone assume he was guilty? He could understand if the Galways and other herders believed that, but his own neighbors?

He wound his way through the cluster of people that stood between him and the kitchen door. "Excuse me," he murmured to those he passed. A few nodded sympathetically and stepped aside while others turned away.

Once inside, Trey walked straight through the house to the front door. And having put the house between him and the mourners, he stood on the veranda and took in a couple of deep breaths to calm himself. He stared up at the sky, overcast now. They would have that much-needed rain before dawn. He walked over to the small fenced cemetery that held the graves of his parents and now held Javier. The mound of sandy dirt that covered the newest grave was covered with flowers. He knelt and picked up a red rose someone had left and remembered the blood, so much blood, that day.

Newly determined, he placed the rose back on Javier's grave. As he returned to the house, he heard the thunder of hoofbeats in the distance and saw half a dozen soldiers riding in his direction. Expecting this signaled trouble, Trey strode around the side of the house to the yard where all conversation had dwindled to whispers as everyone turned their attention to the approaching soldiers.

Trey joined Jess and Seth, and Nell worked her way through the crowd until she was standing next to him. Once there, she entwined her fingers in his as if she had no intention of ever letting go. "What's happening?" she asked, her voice shaky with fear. "Why are those soldiers coming here?"

The officer in charge dismounted and strode across the courtyard until he was standing nearly toe to toe with Trey. "Trey Porterfield, you are charged with the murder of Henry Galway and are to be held in custody until such time as arrangements can be made for your trial."

Seth and Jess both stepped forward. Jess cleared his throat. "Come on, Captain. Galway's death was accidental," he said.

"Not according to the witness who came to the fort this morning to report what he observed." The captain nodded to two of his men, who dismounted and approached Trey.

Nell tightened her grip on his hand and edged close to him.

"Now, ma'am," the captain said, his voice gentle and soft as if speaking to a child. "I need to ask you to let us do our duty here."

"Henry Galway is…was my brother," Nell replied. "Your witnesses are my nephew and my late husband's cousin. Both of them have reason to want to make trouble for my husband."

Trey saw a flicker of surprise pass over the captain's features. "Look, Captain," he said, "this entire business is tied to the conflict between cattlemen and sheepherders. I had hoped the meeting that day might be a first step toward finding a path through all that, a way we might share the land and get along better. Things got out of hand when Mr. Galway learned that his sister and I had married. I have nothing but respect for the Galway family, and indeed all the herders in the region, but you have to understand they might see things different."

He was tempted to ask why the soldiers weren't over at the sheep ranch arresting Ira for killing Javier in cold blood. But one step at a time. "You mentioned a new witness, Captain. May we know who that is?" If Spud was the witness in question, then that was easy to dismiss, since he'd been nowhere near the meeting.

"Peter Collins," the captain replied curtly. He nodded to his soldiers, who took hold of Trey's arms, gently prying Nell away in the bargain. The men tied his hands in front and led him from the yard to where the rest of their party waited with a riderless horse. They helped him mount before tying his hands to the horn of the saddle.

"Collins wasn't even there," Jess protested. "He was supposed to be, but he never showed."

"He says he was late, and as he started up the trail, he saw your brother push Galway—"

Any further information the soldier might offer was cut short by Juanita's feral cry as she fought her way through the throng of people and faced the captain. "This is my boy," she said, her voice coming in gasps as she pointed to Trey. Then she pointed in the direction of the freshly covered grave in the family cemetery. "And that *was* my boy," she continued, jabbing at the captain's chest to place emphasis on every word. "You speak of cold-blooded murder? What about my son, Javier? What about his killer?"

"Already in custody, ma'am. Now please"—he raised his eyes to include everyone—"let us do our job."

Eduardo stepped forward and gently led his wife back to the house. No one spoke or moved as the captain strode back to his horse, mounted, and then ordered his men to move out. When Trey looked back, he saw Nell holding Juanita as the older woman sobbed uncontrollably.

Pete Collins hadn't come to Javier's funeral, and Trey had thought that strange, but there were all sorts of reasons why a rancher might not be able to get away from his work. After all, Pete had made sure his wife and kids were there to pay their respects. But now he also recalled how nervous Pete's wife had been when he asked after her husband.

Why hadn't Trey realized Pete's wife was lying or at least covering for the man? And what could Pete hope to gain by accusing Trey?

Control.

The answer was as clear as the Arizona sky. Pete wanted—needed—Trey out of the way.

❧

Nell wanted nothing so much as to go running after the departing soldiers, scream at them to stop and let Trey go. But Juanita collapsed against her, and until Addie and Amanda came rushing to her aid, it was all Nell could do to keep Javier's mother from sinking to the ground.

As soon as Addie and Amanda led Juanita away, Nell sought out Jess and Seth. "What are we going to do?" she asked.

Both men looked down as if surprised to see her still there. Seth's gaze was kind, but Jess glared at her with the same fury he'd directed at her after Trey had announced their marriage. "Haven't you done enough?" he asked and strode away, back toward the house.

Nell watched him go. Behind her, Seth said, "The best thing you can do, Nell, is stay out of it. You have your son to worry about. We'll take care of Trey."

She understood Seth was trying to offer comfort and sympathy, but his words set off a fury within her, a fury she realized she'd been holding in ever since the day of the ill-fated meeting. She turned slowly and looked up at this man who was now her brother-in-law, and it struck her for the first time she had inherited Trey's family. His sisters and brother were hers now, his in-laws hers as well—and she theirs.

"Trey is my husband," she said calmly. "He is in trouble, and I will not stand by and do or say nothing as others decide his fate."

She thought she saw a hint of a smile before Seth said, "How can I help?"

"If you would be so kind as to arrange for a horse and buggy that I can use starting first thing tomorrow, I would be much obliged."

"And just where do you plan to go?"

"I will go to the fort to be sure my husband is being fairly treated, and then—"

"And if he is not being fairly treated?"

That had not occurred to Nell. "Surely—"

"Just making sure you think this thing through, Nell. So you go to the fort. Then what?"

"I need to pay a condolence call on my brother's wife and his sons, if they'll see me. At any rate, I need to bring Joshua back here, try to explain to him

what is happening, and get him settled. If Juanita and
the rest of the family are all right with the two of us
staying on here. If not, then I really don't have any
other—" Her eyes welled with tears, and she swiped
at them with the back of one hand. She was so very
tired—and more frightened than she had ever been in
her life.

Seth pulled a clean handkerchief from the pocket of
the coat he had worn for the funeral and pressed it into
her hands. "Come on, Nell Porterfield. Let's get some
supper, and you leave that horse and buggy to me."

⁂

The accommodations at the fort were anything but
luxurious. The soldiers walked Trey across the parade
grounds, past Colonel Ashwood's headquarters where
he had met on several occasions with other ranchers
and the colonel, and on to a squat adobe building at
the far end of the compound. Now that the native
population had been moved to reservations and towns
and settlements that dotted the area, there was no
longer a need for soldiers to be on hand to protect set-
tlers. The fort was scheduled to close later that spring,
and already the number of soldiers stationed there had
noticeably declined.

"Watch your head," the captain instructed as he
ducked through an open doorway into a narrow and
shadowy passage lined with barred doors on either
side. "In here," the soldier added as he pushed open a
rusted iron door.

Trey paused at the entrance. "May I see the colonel?"

"In time. For now, welcome to your new home."

He made a grand gesture mocking the sordid conditions, and Trey stepped past him.

He could stand in the center of the small space and touch the adobe walls with the flat of his palms. He saw a cot—the sort soldiers used when out on patrol, canvas worn thin on the edges and sagging in the middle. In the corner was a battered tin bucket. "Well, at least there's a toilet," he joked as he tossed his hat on the cot and walked to the barred window, no more than a slit really. Other than the little sunlight that made its way down the passage where the soldiers waited, it was the cell's single source of light.

The metal door clanged shut behind him, and he heard the retreating footsteps of the captain and his men. From outside came the chants of soldiers drilling on the yard, along with the familiar noises of someone shoeing a horse and the soft conversation of two military wives as they passed beneath the small window of his cell. He sat on the edge of the cot, his boots scuffing the loose dirt that made up the floor until he unearthed a small rock. He dug it out and used it to mark a single scratch on the cell wall, followed by other marks as, from memory, he drew an outline of his home.

He stopped when he heard a noise from the other side of the wall. Someone was crying and trying hard not to be heard. "Hello?" he called, moving to the bars of the cell so his voice would carry. "Who's there?"

"Ernest?" The male voice cracked with the high-low of adolescence. "They got you too?"

"It's not Ernest. It's Trey Porterfield."

Silence from the other cell.

Trey recalled the captain's answer that Javier's killer was already in custody. "You're one of the Galway boys, right?"

More silence.

"Ira, right?"

"Stop talking to me. You killed my pa in cold blood."

Trey felt his frustration build at the boy's determination to see things the way he wanted and not the way they had really happened. That, along with his rage over the senseless death of his best friend, made him want to lash out at the kid. He forced himself to take a deep breath. If his fight was to prevent more violence, then he needed to start by subduing his own urge to beat the stuffing out of Ira Galway.

"Now come on. You know he tripped and fell. It was an accident."

"So you say." The boy choked back a fresh sob. "Didn't even let me stay past the funeral. I guess you and your cowboys had something to do with that, right? I mean, what chance does my kind have with all of you lined up against us?"

Trey swallowed the bile of his rage. Did the kid have no remorse for killing Javier? "If I had any kind of influence in this business, do you think I'd be locked up next to you?" he asked.

Something metal hit the wall. Trey suspected it was the boy's tin bucket. "Just stop talking to me," Ira yelled.

There was a loud thud, one Trey deciphered as the kid collapsing onto his cot. *He's a boy*, Trey thought. *He's scared*. His innate empathy gave him control over the bitterness he felt toward Ira.

"You're gonna want to take it easy on your furnishings over there," he said. "That bucket's the only toilet you're likely to see while you're in here. Wouldn't want to puncture it and have to deal with a leak, and if you crack the frame on that cot, you'll be sleeping on the dirt floor."

"Shut up," Ira shouted.

Trey imagined him sitting there with his hands over his ears. He went back to his drawing, moving his cot away to give him the full wall as his canvas.

As always when he sketched, he was oblivious to the passage of time. He worked quickly, pausing only to scour the floor for another rock when the edge on one dulled.

"You got rats over there or scorpions or what?" he heard Ira ask after some time had passed. "What's all that scratching?"

Trey grunted. "I like to draw. I'm using a rock on the wall."

More time passed.

"Kind of a sissy pastime for a full-grown man." The boy snorted with derision.

"I guess that depends on your way of seeing things. Me, I use my drawing as time to study on things that might be upsetting to me—like somebody killing my best friend."

The kid had no comment. Trey kept working on the sketch, but his strokes were more like vehement stabs at the adobe surface.

"Whatcha drawing?" Ira's voice was soft, but that did not hide his curiosity.

Trey took a step back and looked at his work. The

light was fading, and soon, he would have to stop. He set the rocks he'd been using on the deep adobe window sill. "My ranch. Ever seen it?"

"Naw."

Trey moved his cot back against the wall and stretched out, his hands behind his head, his feet crossed at the ankles. "My pa started it from nothin'," he said. "He was killed before he could see it the way it is today." He paused. "My pa was murdered," he added softly, unsure why he would share that with Ira.

"Well, so was mine," the boy blustered. "You oughta know, since you're the one who did it."

Trey grimaced as he tried to measure his words. "Ira, your pa tripped. If he hadn't been holding that gun, he might have survived the fall. If you hadn't brought that knife—and pulled it on an unarmed man—my friend might be alive, and you might not be here. You might want to start thinking about the trouble you're in."

"So I stabbed a Mexican. Who's gonna blame me for that? He was threatening me and mine."

Trey was on his feet and clutching the bars of the cell in one swift move. "Watch your mouth, kid. That man was my best friend—more than a friend. He was a brother to me, and he was worth half a dozen of you." He hardly recognized his voice. The words came out like rasps of a saw on the wood that had become Javier's coffin.

He heard footsteps from the compound coming their way.

"Chow time," a soldier called as he entered the dim corridor. A second soldier accompanied him, holding a lantern. He unlocked Trey's cell and stood aside while the first man delivered a plate of stew, a hunk of bread, and a tin cup filled with water. The two men silently repeated the action for Ira and then, checking to be sure the cell doors were secure, left.

Trey picked up the spoon on the plate and scooped the food into his mouth, sopping up the gravy with the coarse bread. It was better than he'd expected. He washed everything down with the water, then stacked his cup on the metal plate and set them by the door. He stood at the window, gazing up at what he could see of the sky, wondering how Nell was faring. He was sure his family would treat her with respect. At least Amanda and Addie would. Jess was another matter. She wasn't one of them, and although she'd had no fault in Javier's death, Jess would blame her.

He went back to the door, listened for sounds from the cell next door. "Did you eat?" he asked.

"None of your damned business," the kid growled.

"You should eat. Gonna be morning before anything happens for either of us. You're not likely to see more food till then either." He lay down on his cot. After a minute or two, he heard the scrape of a spoon on a metal plate.

Outside, it started to rain.

❧

After the soldiers arrested Trey and rode off, the courtyard exploded in chatter. Nell filled a plate and escaped to her room, refusing Amanda's invitation to have supper with Trey's family after the other mourners had left. Everyone was trying to be kind, but it was clear they were uncomfortable in her presence.

And would it be any different if she were at Lottie's?

She thought of her son and wondered if he understood why she couldn't be with him, why, for the moment, he was best off staying with his aunt. But was it true? What were Ernest and the boys saying about her and about Trey? How might Lottie's grief come out in words that accused and confused? And had her sister-in-law even bothered to give Joshua the note Nell had included for him when the cowhand delivered the message?

She paced the large bedroom where she had slept these last few nights with Trey, her husband and a man she knew so little about. Oh, she knew he was gentle and kind, and he cared deeply about others. She knew the death of his friend had devastated him, and yet, unlike so many of the men she had known over her lifetime, his first thought had not been revenge. Trey's concern had focused on others and on finding a way to make this right for everyone involved. He was a good man, but there would come a time when he would be forced to make hard choices. Would he choose her or see her as part of the larger problem?

At night, when they lay in bed and he made love to her, she believed everything was possible. In this room, in this bed, being with him felt so right. But in the glare of day, when she left this room and sat at meals with his family, she was not so sure. She wished she could just get Joshua and go home to her own ranch. At least there she knew who she was, where she belonged. But the only home Joshua had ever known was gone, burned to the ground by men who carried only blind hatred in their hearts.

Outside the closed door of the bedroom, she heard the others come down the hall, seeking out their rooms for the night. The house went silent, but the air hummed with the remnants of the day's events, and the underlying presence of turmoil loomed over the quiet. The sense of foreboding was so pervasive that Nell knew she would get no sleep. Seth Grover had promised a horse and buggy by morning, but that was hours away. If she left now on foot, she would reach Lottie's just before dawn, perhaps have the chance to talk to her sister-in-law without the boys and Ernest around. The need to do something—anything—was overwhelming. Nell thought if she had to spend one more hour in this house, she would go mad.

It had started to rain, but that was of little concern to her. She needed to hold her son, the one constant in this chaos. Once she had been reunited with Joshua, things would become clearer. She could move forward and find a way to help Trey. She had no doubt his siblings and in-laws had already discussed the matter, but their reluctance to include her in that discussion had been obvious.

Still, he was *her* husband. Trey and Joshua were the closest family she had in this world, and she would not shirk in her responsibility to either of them. On the other hand, Henry had been family as well, and didn't she owe some loyalty to Lottie and her boys? Drawing a cloak over her head to protect her from the steady rain, she stepped outside and set out for the long walk to her brother's ranch. With luck, she would arrive at dawn and find Lottie alone in the kitchen.

✥

Unable to sleep, Juanita sat at the kitchen table, a cup of coffee gone cold in her hand. She heard the heavy front door open and close. One of the herd dogs set to barking. Someone going out at this hour? Wearily, she pushed herself to her feet. She reached the window in time to see a small figure walking up the trail that led away from the ranch—a woman in a cloak, her hood pulled up over her head. Trey's new bride.

She watched until Nell was out of sight. She thought of waking Eduardo and sending him to get her. Wherever Nell was headed, she would be soaked by the time she got halfway there. Maybe she had finally seen the light and realized she and Trey had made a terrible mistake. Of course, Trey would never admit that. He would want Juanita to go fetch Nell home. But what did she owe this woman whose family had murdered her son?

Let her go, she thought as she drew in a dry sob, her tears long since spent. Even with Trey in the house, the woman was a distraction, a presence none of them seemed to know how to face. Now Trey was in jail at the fort thanks to that woman's family's accusations. But then Pete Collins had accused him too, a man Javier had known—even admired.

For the first time since Trey had come riding into the yard leading the horse with Javier's body, Juanita had doubts. Was it possible that Trey had not told the whole truth about the events leading up to Galway's death? Jess was the hothead in the Porterfield family, but Trey's limits had never been truly tested. Perhaps he'd finally let his anger and frustration take its natural course.

She shook off the thought. Jess might lie to her to save his skin, but never Trey. That boy was far too honest, too certain of the good in every person he met. He was probably sitting in jail right this minute, trying to find something positive in this whole mess.

And while he was in jail, he would assume that his family was taking care of his wife. Juanita sighed and let the kitchen curtain fall back into place. She walked down the hall to Trey's old room. Her eldest son's snores resonated even through the closed door. "Rico, wake up," she said as she entered the room and shook his shoulder.

"What's going on?" Louisa whispered.

"Trey's wife has run off, and I need Rico to go get her and bring her back here."

Rico rolled over and rubbed his eyes. "Where's she gone?"

"I don't know. My guess is either she's headed back to her people or else she's got some fool idea of seeing Trey over at the fort. Either way, she's out there on foot, in the rain."

Rico swung his legs over the side of the bed and reached for his trousers. "Why don't you wake Jess? He's Trey's brother and—"

"And so are you. Maybe not blood, but sometimes that's not all that counts. Now get dressed. I'll fix you some coffee and wrap up some cold biscuits for you to take along. She can't be far."

A few minutes later, Rico walked into the kitchen carrying his boots. While he sat and pulled them on, Juanita placed a cup of hot coffee and a package of biscuits wrapped in oilcloth on the table next to him.

"Take Trey's slicker there. That rain is coming harder by the minute."

Rico stood, swallowed more coffee, and grabbed Trey's yellow slicker from the hook by the door. "Ma, this woman's family killed Javier."

"I know that."

"Then why—"

"*She* didn't kill your brother. And she's Trey's wife, whether we like it or not. Trey is family, and now, so is she. We take care of family. Now get going."

But Rico stood his ground. "I just don't understand how you can be so worried about her. Why not let her go back to her people and let *them* take care of her?"

"Because that woman is suffering same as us. Did you forget somebody, probably some cowboys, burned her home to the ground? What did she ever do to deserve that? She has no place in this world right now, Rico. She doesn't fit here with us, and my guess is her brother's family won't greet her with welcoming arms. Her husband's in jail, and her brother is dead, and she had no say in any of it."

"She didn't have to marry Trey. She had a say in that," Rico reminded her. "And besides, you've suffered too—you and Papa. Javier's dead, Mama."

She spun around and faced him, taking hold of his jaw and forcing him to meet her gaze. "You think I don't know that? I know my son's lying out there in the ground. I also know I can't change that, but what I can change is how I—and my family—handle our pain. What do you want, Rico? Revenge?"

"Justice," he said, pulling away from her as he

finished his coffee and set the cup on the drain board. "An eye for an eye. Isn't that what the Bible preaches?"

"And where will that get anybody? Another mother's son in prison or hanged? Another ranch burned or the stock slaughtered and decent people suffering because they can no longer make a living?" She was shaking as she gripped Rico's arm. "Go find her, Rico, and let's start down a different trail to find our way past this."

Rico wrapped his arms around her and pulled her close. "All right, Mama. We'll try it your way. Don't upset yourself, okay? I'll go find Trey's wife and bring her back."

"Take the wagon."

Rico shrugged into the slicker, pulled his hat firmly in place, and opened the door. The wind whipped through the kitchen, bringing the rain with it. Rico held tight to his hat and slammed the door shut as he hurried toward the barn to hitch up the wagon.

Satisfied she had done what she could, Juanita turned back to the stove. The others would be up soon, and they would want breakfast. Then they'd have to continue the discussion they had begun the night before about how they were going to get their youngest brother out of jail.

Eight

TREY WAS SURPRISED TO REALIZE HE'D FINALLY SLEPT. He had been awake much of the night, staring into the darkness, thinking about Nell. He had made a mistake marrying her before the meeting with her brother. As much as he had wanted to marry her, he should have taken the time to have that meeting, perhaps to even let Henry know of their plans. After all, Galway was head of that family. But he hadn't thought about seeking approval from either side. And now with her brother dead, her nephews and sister-in-law were bound to cut her out of their lives.

And then there was his family—his sisters and brother who had loved Javier as one of their own. Would they cast blame on Nell simply because of her kin? And would Juanita, Eduardo, and Rico ever forgive him for creating this mess in the first place?

The only way he could see them all getting through this was finding a way to come together, starting with the two families. After all, that had been his intent from the beginning. His family had always jokingly called him a dreamer. Well, now the label was no joke. Now, because of his certainty that he could make peace between ranchers and herders, his family and neighbors saw him as a fool.

From out in the compound, he heard men shouting. The urgency in their voices made him go to the narrow, barred window. It was still dark, although there was a faint light of dawn on the horizon where the night sky was turning gray. The rain was coming down so hard, it was difficult to see, but he was able to make out soldiers mounting up and riding through the massive double gate others held open against the wind.

"What's going on out there?" Trey asked when the guards brought breakfast a few minutes later. From the next cell, he could see Ira Galway's hands clenching the bars, his knuckles white with the force of his grip.

"Raids overnight," one guard replied.

"Them or us?" Ira demanded.

"Both," the other guard said. "And that's all you fellas need to know." He and his partner left, hunching their shoulders against the storm as they ran for cover on the other side of the compound.

The bread was soggy and the coffee cold. Trey could hear Ira muttering to himself.

"Galway?" he called. "Seems to me with your pa gone, you and your brother are in charge of things over at your place now." During the night, he had considered the futility of his rage at what Ira had done and focused instead on the possibility that the boy might be a link to the other herders.

"What's that to you?"

"Well, I was hoping to deal with your pa. When we first met, he seemed to me a reasonable man.

A man we could work with. Now I'm wondering where you and your brother might stand on this range war situation." He was well aware it was unlikely either Ira or his brother had even considered their position now that their father was gone. Perhaps they had thought Ernest would take charge. "I haven't had the chance to meet many of the herders other than you and your pa," Trey continued, "but we have to start somewhere."

"You trying to con me, mister? That's your plan, ain't it? Same way you conned Aunt Nell into marrying you so you could take her land. Now you want my pa's place as well. I'm not stupid."

"Never said you were. And I've got plenty of land, so why would I need more?"

"'Cuz if you own us, you can drive us out."

Trey felt his temper flare. "No man owns another man, Ira. We fought a war to make sure of that."

Ira took a minute to absorb that before asking, "Did you fight then?"

Trey laughed. "How old do you think I am? I was six when that war ended. They were taking them young, but not that young."

From the other side of the wall, Trey heard a snort that sounded a lot like a laugh the kid was trying to cover. He waited.

A minute later, Ira threw the tin cup against the bars, and the weak coffee spattered on the dusty floor. "This stuff tastes like piss."

"Yeah. I was thinking about the coffee Javier's pa makes—best in the territory. When we're out on the range for days at a time, it's Eduardo's coffee keeps us going. I'd give a lot for a cup of that right now. Javier used to—"

"Are you scared, mister? Pa always said when a man can't shut his mouth, he's probably scared, and you sure do talk a lot."

Trey thought about that. "Hard not to be when you can't see what's ahead," he admitted. "It's not so much for myself. More for your Aunt Nell and her boy—wondering what's ahead for them, especially if I'm not there to make sure they're all right. Your ma's got you and your brother, but your aunt? Well, without me, she's on her own."

When there was no answer, no further comment from the cell next door, Trey figured he should just let the silence stand. He walked back to the window where the downpour still fell in a curtain that blocked out anything that might be happening in the compound. He let the lashing rain soak his skin and the whiskers that had blossomed overnight. He scrubbed at his face with both hands, drying them by wiping them over his trousers. With nothing else to do, he picked up one of the rocks he'd been using to draw and started working on the sketch again.

"Hey, mister?"

"Yeah?"

"I never meant to kill him. Just wanted to hurt him." Ira's voice trailed off, and Trey knew he was crying again.

He also knew it was as close to an expression of regret as the boy was likely ever to utter.

Nell hadn't made much progress by the time she heard the wagon behind her. The torrential rains had turned the dusty trail to mud that clung to her boots and spattered her skirt. The wind was driving the rain right at her, and she had trouble seeing where she was going. Twice she had stumbled and almost fallen, regaining her balance at the last minute. She'd thought of going back. After all, Amanda's husband had promised to get her a horse and buggy by morning, and the hint of murky gray in the distance held the promise of daylight. Still, she plodded on.

"Get in," the driver of the wagon ordered as he pulled alongside her. He held out his hand to pull her up next to him on the soaked wooden seat.

She folded her arms protectively around her chest and squinted up at him. "Is that you, Rico?" she asked, finally putting an identity to the man's features.

"Yeah," he grumbled. "Now take my hand, woman."

She stood her ground. "Will you take me to get my son?"

He let out a breath that spoke louder than words. "Look, the way this trail is, we'll be lucky to make it back to the ranch without breaking an axle. You can get your son once this rain lets up. He's not going anywhere, is he? And those are your people caring for him, right?"

Nell pulled her coat closer and started walking again. She heard Rico call the horses to a halt and then heard the splat of his boots hitting the ground behind her.

"Mrs. Stokes, stop," he shouted above the howl of

the wind. She kept walking, but he overtook her easily and stepped in front of her on the path. "Look, my ma is worried, and she doesn't need any more cause right now. She just buried one son, and now Trey's over there at the fort, but she's also worried about you. So stop being so bullheaded and let me take you back where she can see you're all right."

"First of all, my name is Nell *Porterfield*. Nell is fine with me. Second, there's another woman whose had a loss in all this—my sister-in-law. I don't want her to think I've chosen sides. She needs to know that whatever has happened or will come, we are family. I expect your mother understands that, understands why I set out in the first place."

Rico stared up at the sky. Then he took off the slicker and placed it on her shoulders. "Get in. I'll take you there and wait while you call on your sister-in-law and collect your boy."

"Thank you." Nell allowed him to help her into the wagon. Once he had picked up the reins and snapped them to get the team moving, she scooted closer to him and held the slicker above their heads so that it covered them both.

Although it was already midmorning by the time they arrived, things were quiet at her brother's place. The storm had kept away any visitors who might call on Lottie. She saw no sign of Ernest nor Spud or the Mexicans hired to shepherd the flock. The yard, pastures, and outbuildings appeared to be unoccupied. "Wait here," she said when Rico pulled the wagon to a stop some distance from the house. "No need to get anybody more upset than they already are. I'll walk down and talk to Lottie and get Joshua. When we're ready, I'll signal from the porch there."

Rico drove the team forward. "I know another way. You can cut through just past the kitchen garden. The wagon will be out of sight of the barn. That way, I'll be close enough to get you and the boy out should there be trouble."

Surely, it was ridiculous to think she might be in any real danger. These people were family—even Ernest had been her late husband's cousin. And yet she did not object when Rico found a route through a grove of trees near the creek, swollen now with the rain.

"I'll wait here," he said.

She handed him the slicker and climbed down from the wagon.

When she reached the back entrance to the house, she saw Lottie sitting alone at the kitchen table, her Bible open in front of her. Nell stepped up to the door and knocked lightly on the frame before entering the house. "Hello, Lottie," she said softly.

Lottie raised her head to reveal eyes that were hollow and red-rimmed, in a face sallow and lined. The woman appeared to have aged a decade in just a few days. Her hand trembled as she reached out to Nell. "You've come home," she whispered. "Bless you for that."

Nell bit her lower lip as she took Lottie's hand between both of hers. "Lottie, I came to see if you needed anything—if there was anything I could do for you."

Lottie's eyes hardened, and she pulled her hand away. "Do for me? You could have been at the funeral—your own flesh and blood. Where were you?"

"I thought it best…" Nell could not find the words to explain why she had chosen to stay away. "Is Joshua all right?"

"You think I wouldn't take proper care of that boy? You think I would punish him for the sins of his mother? Is that it?"

"No! Lottie, it's nothing like that. It's just that you have so much to deal with right now, and I thought if I took Joshua with me, it might relieve you some."

"You want to take that boy to that rancher's place so he can learn how to hate his own kind?"

"You've got this all wrong, Lottie. Trey wants to find a way for everyone to live in peace."

"Peace?" Lottie spat the word at Nell. "Do you know where Spud and Ernest and the others are right now?"

"I assumed they were out tending the flock," Nell replied.

"They are out all right, but there's no tending to be done. There was a raid last night. They stampeded our sheep and those of yours we'd managed to round up after the fire. Ran them up there to Deadman's Point and drove them over the edge, whooping and hollering and firing their rifles in the air."

"No." Nell covered her mouth with her fist. Would this carnage never end?

"You doubt me? Where were your husband and his family last night, Nell? Ask yourself that."

Nell found her footing with that taunt. "My husband was in jail at the fort, just like Ira. And his family was at home—all night." She looked past Lottie and saw Joshua standing in the doorway.

"Ma?"

She realized what a mess she was—her hair pulled free and sodden around her face and shoulders, her clothing soaked and pocked with mud. Even so, she held out her arms to him, and he ran to her. "Joshua, go gather your things, and be sure you make the bed and leave everything in order. Then come back here and thank Aunt Lottie for everything she's done for you these last few days."

Joshua pulled away and looked up at her. "Where are we going?"

Nell looked at Lottie. "We'll be staying at Mr. Porterfield's ranch," she said.

"Not at Doc Addie's in town?"

"No, but she and her family will be at the ranch from time to time, I'm sure. Now go get ready."

Joshua turned to go but stopped next to Lottie's chair. "Aunt Lottie, don't you worry. I'll be back to see you real soon." He gave her a hug before hurrying down the hall and did not see the tears leaking down the furrows of Lottie's worn face.

Nell knelt next to her and clasped hands with her. "Lottie, please forgive me. I should have been here, if not for Henry, then for you."

Lottie sniffed back her grief. She tightened her grip. "What are we going to do to save Ira? Those people have accused him of murder. He'll hang. I can't... I've lost..." She broke down completely then, her tears soaking their joined hands.

"I'll talk to Trey and his family. They'll know what to do," Nell promised.

And in that instant, the bond between them was shattered. Lottie pushed Nell away with such force, she nearly toppled over. "Get out of my house, Nell. Take your boy and go. And be certain of this—I will never forgive you for betraying us the way you have. And if Ira goes to the gallows, that is on your head. You brought this on us." She was standing now, her body rigid with rage.

From behind her, Nell saw Joshua close the door to the bedroom and walk toward the kitchen. "Lottie, please," she whispered.

Her sister-in-law turned away and saw Joshua. "You'll be needing a slicker, young man," she said briskly as she took one down from a hook and wrapped it around the boy's shoulders. "This was your Uncle Henry's."

"It's too big," Joshua said.

"You'll grow into it, and when you do, remember where it—and you—came from." She hugged him close, then left the room without a backward glance at Nell.

⁓

The detail of soldiers returned around noon, and shortly after that, Trey was summoned to Colonel Ashwood's office. The rain had stopped, and the sun burned so hot that everything had dried up, and it was almost as if there had been no storm at all. Only a few puddles of murky standing water pitted the compound.

As he walked between two guards, Trey did what he could to make his appearance more presentable— tucked in his shirt, brushed off his vest, and while he waited to be announced, he slid the top of each boot against his calves in an effort to remove some of the dust. The door to the colonel's office swung open, and the guards stepped aside.

"Come in, Mr. Porterfield." The colonel came around his desk to greet him.

Trey was confused. Colonel Ashwood was treating him like a welcome guest rather than a prisoner. He accepted the man's handshake and his invitation to sit in one of two wooden chairs. Instead of returning to his larger chair behind the desk, Colonel Ashwood dismissed the guards, closed the office door, and sat next to Trey.

"How are you holding up?" he asked.

"I'm fine, sir. I appreciate you asking."

"As you are aware, Peter Collins has brought some disturbing charges against you. I must say I never thought I would see the day when that particular cattleman took the side of a sheepherder's family."

"He wasn't there," Trey said.

"Yes, so he has said. He claims to have witnessed the altercation from a distance."

"Then what he saw was Henry Galway pull a gun on me. I was moving to attend to Javier Mendez when Galway came at me, tripped, fell, and shot himself as he tumbled down the cliff. Jess was there. As was the boy you've got locked up for killing Javier."

"Still, I know you appreciate the need for me to follow protocol here."

"Yes, sir."

The colonel glanced toward the closed door and lowered his voice. "I had another reason for having my soldiers take you into custody, Trey. That young man in the cell next to you was near to hysteria his first night here. No one from his side of this business has been here, and that worries me."

"Herders tend to walk, and from the Galway place to here is quite a journey—more than half a day on foot. The boy is frightened. He realizes what he did. He does seem to have settled down some," he added.

"You've spoken to him then?"

"We talked some, last night and this morning."

"Excellent. That was part of my plan." The colonel stood and took a cigar from a humidor on his desk. He offered one to Trey, who declined.

"I don't understand, sir. It sounds like you wanted the boy and me to spend time together."

"Exactly. I don't believe what Collins is saying about you. He wants you out of his way so he can wage war on the herders. I can't allow him to do that, but the truth is, I don't have the manpower to stop him."

"And you think that boy over there can?"

"Not exactly. I am seeking some way we might remind reasonable men on both sides that this business can't be solved by stampeding sheep or slaughtering cattle. Right now, Collins has got them all fired up. He's convinced them this is a matter of all or nothing." Colonel Ashwood squinted at him through a ring of cigar smoke. "I understand you married Galway's sister. Can't imagine that helped your cause—or hers."

Trey felt a flush flow up the back of his neck and around to his cheeks. "My wife is—"

The colonel waved off his explanation. "None of my business. Just reminding you that it was you who put a stick of dynamite in the middle of this barrel of kerosene. It was you who jeopardized the very peace council you hoped to create."

Trey could not deny the truth of that, so he changed the thrust of the conversation back to his arrest. "If you believe Collins is lying about what he saw, can I go home?"

"Now, how would that look? We let you go scot-free, and that boy over there has no chance to give his side of things?"

"He killed my friend—that was no accident. He brought the knife, concealed it, and used it. I believe him when he says he didn't mean to, but the facts speak for themselves." The grief he'd had little time to dwell on made Trey's stomach lurch with fury. Javier was dead. Did no one care? Or was it the old story of racial differences—the death of a white man carrying far more weight than that of someone with brown skin? He forced himself to remain calm. "Colonel, if you want my help, I need to get out of here. I need to talk to the other ranchers, settle them down. I need to—"

"And I need you to get that boy to coming around to your way of seeing things."

"He's a kid. What good will it do if he decides to say his pa's death was an accident? And why would he when he truly believes it was my fault?"

The colonel smiled and moved to his official chair. He sat down heavily, rested his elbows on the desk, and pressed his fingertips together. "My guess is one more night spent in that dark cell will bring him around. He'll agree to pretty much anything, even saying he saw the whole thing up close and you had no fault in his father's tragic death."

"In exchange for?"

"His right to go home until his trial comes up."

"Now, hold on. He murdered my friend— intentional or not. You're willing to let him get away with that? Whatever happened to justice? I mean, I understand the boy acting rashly, but even out here on the frontier, there has to be some consequence."

The colonel stubbed out his cigar in a large brass ashtray. "I said he'll go home—nothing about going free. He'll stand trial for Mendez's death, but we have to give the herders something, Trey. They're bearing the brunt of this fight. Your own wife had her place burned to the ground. As of last night, the Galways have lost most of their sheep. If we let the boy go home to his mama until the circuit court can hear his case, we tip the balance—maybe not till it's even, but enough for now."

"I still think—"

The colonel ran his fingers through his thin hair. "I'm trying to prevent a range war, son. Your idea didn't work, so let's try mine."

"I don't understand yours," Trey grumbled.

"It buys us some time. If a herder stands up for a cattleman, then other ranchers—on both sides—have to think twice about their next moves. I'm convinced most of the mischief that's been done, even slaughtering cattle and cutting fences, has been at the hands of Collins and his cowhands. I just can't prove it."

"Mischief?" Trey stood for the first time since entering the office. He leaned across the colonel's desk so they were eye to eye. He kept his voice low and calm. "You call destroying a family's livelihood and burning my wife's home to the ground 'mischief'?"

"Compared to what's gone on up in Kansas and Nebraska? Yes, I do. And my job is to make sure it doesn't get any worse. Three men have died, Porterfield. How many more do we need to bury before we get this thing under control?"

Trey moved away from the desk. "And what if the kid agrees to your plan, goes home, and goes out looking for revenge with his brother and Ernest Stokes?"

"That's why you're gonna spend the rest of today and tonight trying to bring him around. You have a way about you, Trey. People like you. They trust you. Hell, you got that herder's widow to marry you." The colonel chuckled as he walked to the door and signaled for the guards to come in.

On the walk back to his cell, Trey saw the meeting for what it had truly been. Ashwood wasn't interested in justice. He wasn't especially interested in what had or had not happened at Deadman's Point. Fort Lowell was about to be shut down, the presence of a militia having run its course as the territory became more settled. If the colonel let the range war catch fire, that would be his final legacy in the area. He clearly had no intention of letting that happen. No, Ashwood would do whatever it took to prevent that stain on his record, no matter who paid the price. Trey could not understand why everyone in this battle seemed to be in it for his personal interests rather than the greater good.

Back in his cell, he added details to the drawing on the wall for a while, then lay on his cot and stared out the window. As he sketched, he thought about the mess created by what he had naively thought would be a peaceful meeting. Now Javier was dead, and so was Ira's father. There was grief enough to share. His own father had been killed when Trey was about Ira's age. The years that followed had been hard on everyone, but Trey had missed out on more than his older siblings. Now Ira and his brother would have to find their way to manhood without the strong hand of Henry Galway guiding them. They would need a friend—somebody older and more experienced.

"Galway," he said after a while. "You over there?"

"Where do you think I got to with them bars between me and freedom?"

"You're pretty quiet."

"I'm thinkin'."

Trey smiled. The boy's voice hit both a high and a low note on those two words. "Me too. Care to share?"

"No. Leave me be."

Trey sat up. "Come on, Ira. If we've got to be here, we might as well get better acquainted. Tell me what you want from this world."

The silence could either mean the kid was considering his offer or shutting down again.

"Right now, I want to get the hell out of here. Beyond that, I wouldn't say no to a big helping of my aunt's bread pudding."

"Your Aunt Nell?"

"Yeah. She's a really good cook—better than Ma."

Trey thought about the cake from the church social. It had practically melted in his mouth. "Are you and your brother close to your aunt?"

"We were. But with her and you... That really made Pa upset when I told him I'd seen the two of you. I never saw him that mad."

"No need for your relationship with your aunt to change all that much," Trey said.

Ira snorted. "Then you're dumber than I thought, mister."

"Maybe. But if you think about it, we're not only neighbors. We're family now. I guess marrying your aunt makes me your uncle."

"You ain't never gonna be my kin, mister. You got that? Now stop your jawin' and let me think."

"Never say never, Ira. More often than not, you end up having to eat those words."

Ira's cot scraped against the wall, most likely because the boy had kicked it there. "Just shut up," he bellowed.

Trey decided to oblige.

⁂

Nell could see how curious Joshua was about Rico as the three of them sat on the wagon seat on their way back to the Porterfield ranch.

"Do you work for the Porterfield ranch?" he asked.

Rico kept his eyes on some point in the far distance. "Nope."

"Rico owns the livery stable in town," Nell explained when it became obvious Rico had no intention of adding to his one-word reply.

"You and Trey are friends then?" Joshua was clearly trying to make sense of everything he'd witnessed over the last weeks and months among the grown-ups in his life. They had agreed that Joshua would simply call Trey by his given name—at least for the time being.

Rico grunted.

"I've been sick a lot," Joshua said. "But Doc Addie told me Trey was sick just like me when he was a kid. Did you know him then?"

"Rico's parents live on the ranch," Nell explained. "He grew up there. Now he and his wife and little boy live in town behind the livery."

Joshua nodded. "Ma says Trey is gonna teach me to ride and play baseball and all sorts of stuff. Is he any good?"

For the first time since they'd set out from Lottie's, Rico looked at Joshua. "You talk a lot for such a *niño*," he observed. He glanced at Nell, then back at her son. "Trey's about as good at those things as any man around."

Joshua nodded. "That's good to know. Doc Addie said he likes to draw pictures of people and read books, so I was thinkin' maybe he was better at something like that."

This time, Rico kept his gaze focused on Nell. "Trey Porterfield is one of the best men I know. Some say he's too good. Some say he'll need somebody who can rein him in a bit when he goes off thinking the world is better and kinder than it is—and thinking if it ain't, he can change it."

The way Joshua smiled and leaned his head against her, Nell had the feeling he had heard Rico's words as reassurance that Trey would be everything Joshua hoped for. She heard the words for what they were—a challenge to her, now that she was Trey's wife. And once again, she realized that this man, the one who could make her body hum with anticipation and desire, was a complete stranger in so many other ways.

"We'll be fine," she murmured and met Rico's stare without wavering.

Once they reached the ranch house, Rico collected his family and headed back to town. The horse and buggy Seth had promised waited near the barn. Juanita and Amanda stood in the doorway, and as Nell approached, Juanita held out her arms to Joshua.

"Can this be the boy Addie's been telling us about, Amanda?" She held Joshua by his shoulders as she took stock of him. "Why you're nearly grown, young man. Now you come with me, and let's get you settled in your room."

Joshua grinned and ducked his head, and Nell silently blessed the older woman for making her son feel at home. She watched as Juanita and Joshua disappeared down the corridor that led to the bedrooms and prepared to follow them. "I should get cleaned up," she said as she slipped past Amanda.

Trey's youngest sister had yet to show anything more than a polite wariness toward Nell. She stepped aside to allow Nell to pass but followed her to the large bedroom. "Nita is heating water for your bath. You go ahead and get out of those wet clothes, and I'll get the water," she said.

By the time she returned, Nell had undressed and wrapped herself in a robe.

Amanda eased past her, balancing two large pails of steaming water that she dumped in the copper tub. "I used to do this for Mama when she…after Papa died," she said. "Mama loved her bath." She stood in the doorway between the bath and bedroom and surveyed the room.

Nell removed the pins from her hair. "It must be difficult for you—and Jess—to think of me in this room."

Roused from her reverie, Amanda held out a towel to Nell. "It was always going to be the place Trey brought his bride," she said. "With the rest of us settled elsewhere, this was always going to be Trey's home." She returned to the bathroom and picked up a bottle of bath salts. She poured some into the steaming water before once again stepping aside to allow Nell to pass. But when they were side by side, she placed her hand on Nell's forearm. "Don't hurt my brother, Nell," she said. "He's the best of all of us, and he's had enough heartbreak in his life."

"I would never—"

"No, I don't believe you would—not intentionally. But it's plain to see he has given you his heart. What's unclear to us is if that was mutual. No one would blame you if you saw Trey's offer as a safe haven for you and your son. Certainly, you've had your share of heartache as well. But if you don't love him, then at least..."

Nell was not ready to discuss her feelings for Trey with anyone. They were too new to allow others the opportunity to comment or criticize.

"Trey and I are fully aware of the obstacles we may face. We will find our way. And now if you'll excuse me, I would like to bathe and dress so I can go to the fort to see my husband." She edged past Amanda and gently closed the door to the bathroom.

When she had washed away the grime of her morning

trek and combed out and braided her hair, she opened the connecting door. Amanda was gone, but on the bed was an outfit Trey's sister had selected for her from the wardrobe. Her boots sat on the floor next to the bed, cleaned of the mud that had coated them on her arrival.

She dressed and hurried down the hall to Trey's old room. The door stood open, but Joshua was not inside. She heard his laughter from the library. She slid back the pocket doors to find Amanda and Joshua sitting around a large wooden table.

"Hey, Ma, Aunt Amanda is teaching me to read this map. She used to be a teacher in Tucson."

Nell heard little of her son's words past his use of the term *Aunt Amanda*. That was as clear a sign as any Amanda had decided to give them a chance.

But it was evident Trey's brother, Jess, would not be so easily swayed.

"You ready?" Jess barely glanced at her as he led the way to the buggy. She saw he'd tied his horse to the back.

"Yes, thank you." She prepared to climb on.

"I'll be driving," he said.

"Lottie told me about the raid. I can manage," she said, trying to keep her voice calm.

"No doubt. But you are not traveling alone, not with everything going on out there."

"Has something else happened?"

"You could say that," he grumbled and said nothing more as he waited for her to climb onto the seat, then took the reins.

After several minutes, Nell became uneasy. "This isn't the way to the fort," she said.

"It's the long way around. We'll get there. Trey's not going anywhere, and I want to show you something."

He kept the horse moving at a brisk trot for several miles, but when they reached the top of a mesa, he pulled the reins and called for the horse to stop. Below them, the land was littered with the corpses of sheep, their white and gray wool covering the red-brown dirt like snow.

Nell covered her mouth, fearful that she might actually be sick at the sight. "No," she whispered. "Why? What was the sense of this?"

Jess said nothing as he urged the horse forward once again. After a while, they came to a stretch of land where the barbed wire marking cattle land had been cut and hung in haphazard loops, the connecting posts akimbo. She knew whatever cattle had grazed inside those fences had now wandered off. But the cows could be rounded up. The sheep…

"There." Jess pointed to a spot in the distance where a group of cowhands appeared to be loading bodies onto a wagon.

"The cattle as well?" She gave voice to her disbelief.

Jess nodded. "And that, Nell, is why I can't allow you to go wandering off on your own. Whoever did this could have still been out here this morning when you decided to set out. They used the cover of the storm to do their work—both sides. These are desperate men, bent on winning at any cost. They won't think twice about killing anybody who gets in their way."

"How do we stop this?" she asked, a thought she didn't realize she'd spoken aloud.

"*You* don't. And I need you to talk Trey into standing aside as well. Let the militia handle this. It's not our fight."

Oh, but it was. These renegades had not only robbed Joshua of his inheritance, but her brother's family of their livelihood as well.

"Do you understand what I'm telling you, Nell?"

She nodded. She understood all right—but she didn't have to agree. Trey was right. This had to stop, and if the two of them could do anything to bring that about, she was more than willing to take whatever risk it entailed.

❧

Shortly after finishing his lunch, Trey had started another drawing on the opposite wall of his cell when he heard voices outside the jail, among them, a woman's voice he recognized.

Nellie.

He rushed to the window, straining to see around the corner of the jail. He could hear Jess talking to the colonel and just barely caught a glimpse of a green dress he remembered his mother wearing. What could Jess have been thinking of, bringing her here? He didn't want her to see him like this—unbathed, unshaven, his clothes covered with the dust that blew through the bars of the window through the day and night.

"Ira, your Aunt Nell is here," he said as he combed his fingers through his hair. "Remember, she is blameless in all of this."

Ira snorted. "She married you, didn't she?"

"Just give her a chance."

Jess, Ashwood, and Nell stepped into the shadows of the narrow corridor that ran along the cells. He saw Nell look around, her eyes adjusting to the sudden shift in light. And then she saw him, and she hurried forward, her arms outstretched, reaching through the bars to touch him.

"Are you all right?"

He cupped her face with both hands and kissed her, the metallic odor of the bars a reminder of the barrier between them. "What are you doing here?"

"Jess will explain. Where's Ira?" Again, she looked around, her eyes settling finally on the neighboring cell. "Ira?"

"Go away."

"Oh, Ira, look at me, please. There are things you are far too young to—"

Trey heard the boy leave the cot and rush at the bars. "Don't say that," he bellowed. "I know my pa is dead. What's to become of Ma and Spud and me now? If you'd just stayed out of this...but no! Ernest is always saying you think you're better than us. You had no right to make decisions without talking to Pa first. He'd be alive right now if only—"

"Settle down, son," Colonel Ashwood said as he moved between Nell and Ira. "You're hardly in a position to go throwing blame at others. A man died at your hand. You need to concentrate on that and what it will mean for your future."

"What future?" Ira scoffed. "There'll be a trial, and I'll probably hang, even though that Mexican came at me, and I was just defending myself as any man would. But no doubt these cattlemen have the judge on their side, so what chance do I have?" The pitch of his voice continued to rise until he sounded like the child he was. "I don't want to die, Aunt Nell," he said weakly.

Trey saw her step around the colonel and reach through the bars to console her nephew. "Shhh," she whispered. "Calm yourself, Ira. We'll find a way."

"Guards!" the colonel shouted.

Two soldiers came running.

"Stand over there and listen carefully," Ashwood ordered. "You may be called upon to repeat what you are about to hear in court." He turned his attention back to Ira. "Now, young man, I am going to ask you some questions before these witnesses, and I need you to answer truthfully. And if I am satisfied with the information you provide, there is every possibility that you will be released to your mother's care this very afternoon."

Ira sniffed back his tears. "I never meant to kill him," he blubbered.

Jess sighed. "Just shut up, boy, and answer the questions when asked. Not before, understood?"

The colonel cleared his throat. "That day at Deadman's Point, did your father have a gun?"

"Yessir, but—"

"And did he aim that weapon at anyone?"

"Yeah, but—"

"Who?"

"That guy."

Trey guessed Ira had pointed to his cell.

"Did Mr. Porterfield also have a weapon?"

Ira hesitated. "He wore a gun belt, so yeah, he carried a weapon."

"Did he aim his weapon at your father or anyone else?"

"No, but—"

"And at the time your father aimed his weapon at Mr. Porterfield, had you and Javier Mendez fought?"

"Yes, sir."

"And was Mr. Mendez wounded?"

"I didn't mean to… I just wanted it to stop, and I thought—"

"Yes or no, Ira," Jess coached.

"He was bleeding pretty bad." Ira's voice was barely a whisper.

"Mr. Porterfield has claimed that he saw his friend attempt to stand and that it was his intention to offer aid. Now that you have had time to consider the events of that day, is that possible?"

Ira was quiet for a long moment. "I guess maybe, but—"

"But your father, in the heat of the fracas, misread Mr. Porterfield's intent and took his move forward as an attack. Is that possible?"

"Maybe. But that doesn't change anything," Ira added, his voice having regained some of its strength. "Pa is dead all the same."

Ashwood ignored this. "And when your father moved forward, did Mr. Porterfield engage with him in any way? Did he touch him or push him or—"

Ira scoffed. "He did what any man would do if you was facing the barrel of a gun. He ducked, stepped back, and raised his hands."

"Raised his hands or his fists?" the colonel pressed.

"Hands, fists, what's the difference? And how is this

supposed to help me? Sounds like the only man you're interested in helping here is him."

Jess leaned in close. "Wise up, kid. Helping Trey is helping you. Now tell the truth."

"Did Mr. Porterfield push your father off that cliff, Mr. Galway?"

There was a long pause before Ira answered. "Not exactly, but Pa would never have slipped if—"

"And as he fell, was your father still in possession of his weapon?" Ashwood persisted.

Ira must have nodded, because Trey heard Jess say, "We need a verbal answer, Ira."

"Yeah."

"Just one more question, Ira," the colonel said, his voice gentle. "At any time in the events we have just discussed, did Mr. Trey Porterfield take out his gun?"

"No, but—"

"Thank you, son." Colonel Ashwood turned to the two guards. "You are dismissed. Go find Peter Collins and bring him to my office, and send someone here to release Mr. Porterfield—"

"You tricked me," Ira shouted as he charged the bars. "This was not about helping me at all. This was just—"

"If you would let me finish," the colonel said. "Mr. Porterfield is free to go. Mr. Galway is to be released to the custody of his family until such time as the circuit court can hear his case. Marshal Porterfield and a detail of soldiers will see that he gets home safely."

The guards left, and Ashwood moved to Ira's cell. "Now listen to me, young man. You have just received a gift. You step out of line even a little bit, and you will be back here to stay for however long it takes. Do we understand each other?"

"I won't stand by while those cowboys destroy our herd and land and burn our house and—"

"You let me and my soldiers worry about that. Your mother has gone through a terrible loss. Do not add to her distress by acting on your anger. And tell your brother and Ernest Stokes that goes for them as well." Without giving time for Ira to respond, the colonel turned on his heel and left the jail.

A few minutes later, a soldier came to open the cells—first Ira's and then Trey's. Jess and the guard escorted Ira to the yard. Nell followed them to the exit, wringing her hands and assuring Ira that he would be all right now.

Trey waited just outside his cell, respecting her need to tend to her nephew but longing for her to attend to him as well. He walked outside and stood next to her as she watched Ira climb onto a wagon driven by two soldiers.

"Mister?"

Trey was surprised to see Ira watching him, his mouth working as if he had something to say but couldn't find the words. Trey moved closer to the wagon and offered the boy a handshake.

Ira stared at his outstretched hand for a moment and then clasped it tightly, his eyes brimming with tears. "I never meant—" he blubbered.

"You need to put that behind you and put your mind to helping your ma and brother," Trey advised.

Ira nodded, and as he withdrew his hand, he murmured, "Thanks."

Jess mounted his horse. "Let's head out," he instructed.

Nell followed the wagon a little way as it moved through the gates of the fort. She waved and watched.

"Nellie?" Trey said softly.

Her shoulders slumped, whether with relief of defeat, he could not tell. He covered the distance between them and wrapped his arms around her, pulling her against him.

She twisted to face him, cupped his face with her hands, and kissed him. "I was so very afraid for you—for us," she whispered.

"I'm right here, Nell," he said, kissing her back. "It's over, okay?"

But it was not that simple. They walked arm in arm to the buggy, and he helped her in before climbing onto the driver's seat and unwrapping the reins. Until herders and ranchers could find a way to coexist, none of this would ever truly be over.

Nine

OVER THE SUMMER, TREY WAS GONE MORE THAN HE was home, and Nell was forced to adjust to life on the ranch without him. Following Javier's funeral, her husband took on Javier's role as foreman and rode with the hired hands as they prepared to take their stock to market and all that entailed. In addition, newborns needed to be branded and counted, strays rounded up, and the Porterfield stock moved to higher, cooler pastures with the rest. Trey and his men had managed to round up a couple hundred sheep that had survived the stampede, but that was not enough to assure Lottie's ranch would survive.

Amanda and Seth had returned to Tucson, and while Addie continued to stop by as she made her rounds, she rarely stayed to visit with Nell as she had before. Javier's parents were cordial, but Nell understood. Every time they looked at her, she reminded them of their son's death. She spent much of her day with Joshua in the library and evenings alone in the room she shared with Trey.

Increased patrols from the fort and the arrest of

two cowhands who had been caught rustling sheep from a herder's flock—men who worked for Peter Collins—kept incidents of vandalism and harassment to a minimum. By early October, an uneasy truce had settled over the region. In addition to his work with the herd, Trey had begun visiting his neighbors. This time, he did not call on them to tell them what he thought. Rather, he went to listen while each rancher laid out his reasons for believing a truce between herders and cattlemen was unlikely. Nell could always tell how a particular meeting had gone by Trey's posture as he unsaddled his horse and walked to the house. More often than not, his step was slow and his body hunched with exhaustion. And yet once he saw her and Juanita waiting for him, he always grinned and teased them about having better things to do than keep a lookout for him. He would kiss each of them on the cheek and announce he was hungry enough to eat a horse. Nell understood that he was still trying to earn Juanita's forgiveness. Not only did he blame himself for Javier's death, but he was convinced that the housekeeper would never fully absolve him.

But when he and Nell were alone, standing at Javier's graveside as was Trey's nightly habit, she saw the weariness that bordered on defeat as he told her about his meeting and worried that he was failing at giving Javier's death some meaning. Later when he peeled off his shirt and sat on the bed to pull off his boots, she would kneel behind him and massage his bare back and shoulders. Finally, the knots of tension she felt under his skin would unravel, and in time, he would lie back on the pillows and pull her into his arms.

"Ah, Nellie, it's so hard to make a man who thinks he's in the right see another possibility." He was frustrated by the way the same old arguments spooled out every time. "I just can't seem to break through that."

She would let him talk until his exhaustion overcame him and he fell asleep. After that, she would lie next to him, wide awake, wondering what she might do to help.

Night after night, this became their routine. In the predawn hours, usually just after she had returned from checking on Joshua, Trey would hold out his arms to her, and she would snuggle against him. They kissed, and the kisses grew in passion. They would find release from the troubles that stalked them during the day in the tenderness they lavished on each other in the night. In his embrace, Nell felt safe and cherished. With each passing day, and in spite of everything that had happened, Nell refused to believe that marrying Trey had been a mistake. The timing perhaps, but not the union.

And in that certainty, she found renewed strength and self-confidence, so much so that one morning early in October as she dressed after Trey had left for the day, Nell came to a decision. There were two sides in this fight. There would be no point, even if Trey convinced the other cattle ranchers to see things his way, unless the herders came to the same conclusion. But no one was visiting them or listening to them. And the truth was, with Henry gone, she couldn't think of anyone among them who would take on that task.

"Well, I am still a landowner," she muttered as she dressed. "And so is Lottie. What if the women…"

But was she? What proof did she have? And what about Lottie? Were there documents to prove her ownership—or Lottie's? The last time she and her sister-in-law had been together, the parting had been anything but cordial, at least on Lottie's part. Of course, they would have to prove they held owner-ship, and that might be difficult given that the lawyer who had drawn up the deed had closed his office in Whitman Falls and moved farther west.

"Ma?"

Joshua stood at the open door to her bedroom. He was dressed in canvas trousers, a chambray shirt, a vest Trey had given him, and the narrow-brimmed straw hat his father had always worn.

"Don't you look a picture?" she said as she hugged him.

"Could we go out today? I'm really doing good and—"

"You're doing well," she corrected. "That's true, but—"

"Ah, Ma, please don't say I need to watch myself. I'm tired of always being cooped up here. Please can we just go someplace else today?"

And suddenly, Nell knew how she would approach Lottie. Her sister-in-law's hard feelings had not extended to Joshua, and it had been a challenge explaining to her son why he never saw his aunt or cousins these days.

"How would you like to go visit Aunt Lottie?"

His smile told her everything she needed to know. In spite of feelings they might harbor toward Nell, Trey's family had treated her son with kindness, but

Joshua missed the family he'd grown up with. In better times, he had idolized Ira and Spud, trailing after them like a puppy whenever he was allowed to visit. And for their part, the boys had made sure he was included in whatever they were doing, taking great care to see he didn't overdo.

Her brother's family had accused her of choosing sides, and she understood that. But while she loved Trey and found his family as warm and welcoming as could be expected given the circumstances, she could not simply forget the history and times she had shared with Calvin's family and hers. No, she would not choose. Where Trey saw bringing the two sides together as the only possible solution for ending the range war, Nell's purpose was far more personal. For Nell, reconciling the two sides was all about building a future for her son—one where he would not need to choose.

"Ma, can we go right after breakfast?"

"We can," she agreed.

Joshua beamed. "I'll go tell Nita," he announced, already halfway to the kitchen.

Nell had tried without success to have Joshua address Juanita and Eduardo more formally, but Trey had insisted that giving them titles like Mr. and Mrs. Mendez would make them uncomfortable. When Nell had raised the topic with Juanita, she had agreed with Trey.

"I have always been Nita to the children in this house. There's no reason for that to change."

"But—"

"If it's a lack of respect you see in that, stop your

worrying. Joshua will not need to use a fancy title for me to know when he's crossed a line. Isn't that right, Trey?"

Trey's cheeks had flared an embarrassed red, and he'd laughed. "Yes, ma'am."

So Nita and Eduardo it was, and by the time Nell finished straightening the covers on Joshua's bed and reached the kitchen, Juanita was already instructing her husband to go hitch up a buggy while she made a picnic lunch for the journey.

"The soldiers have been vigilant, and things are certainly quieter with everybody busy getting ready to take the stock to market, so you should be all right, but be sure you start back well before sundown. No reason to court trouble," she instructed Nell.

"We'll be fine," Nell assured her, mostly because Joshua was listening closely to the conversation, and his expression told her he had questions. "Finish up, Joshua, and let's get going."

Juanita handed her the picnic basket and surprised Nell by leaning in to kiss her cheek. "Take care, *mi'ja*," she said softly. "When Trey gets back, I'll send him to meet you."

Nell wasn't sure that was the best idea. But she was fairly certain that Trey would not be back for hours, so the chances were that if he came to meet them, they would be well on their way back by then. "Thank you, Nita—for everything."

Along the way, Joshua kept up a constant stream of chatter about all the things he was planning to tell Ira and Spud about life on Trey's ranch. He was fascinated by the cowboys and the way their work differed from that of the herders. Trey had given him a pinto pony of his own, and the hired hands had taken turns teaching Joshua how to handle it. At first, Nell had been afraid to allow the cowhands to have much interaction with her son. After all, how did she know one or more of these men weren't responsible for the raids that had terrified them or the burning of their home? But so far, not one of them had given her cause to be concerned.

"Ma, is Ira going to jail again?"

Nell hesitated. "He has to stand before the judge first, and then the judge will decide his punishment." A date for Ira's trial had not been set—something about the circuit judge being too ill to travel. It had been months, and Trey saw that as a good sign.

"I been thinkin'," Joshua said. "It seems to me like some of the ways the cowboys work might just work for herdin' sheep. I mean to talk to Ira and Spud about that. If Ira has to go away for a while, Spud's gonna have a lot to do all on his own. Maybe I could help."

"You'll want to temper any ideas like that with the understanding that you've seen those ways, Joshua. Your cousins have not, and for them, the way their father handled the flock is right. Go easy. Nobody likes to be told they're doing something wrong."

Joshua laughed. "I know that. The other day, I told Uncle Jess he ought to let Isaac help Rico over at the livery like he's been wantin' to. I said Isaac would make a fine blacksmith."

"And what did your Uncle Jess say to that?"

"He got all red in the face the way he does some-times when Aunt Addie fusses at him. 'Boy, you need to mind your own business,' he said in that way he talks when he's being the marshal."

"And what did you say to that?"

"I said 'yessir' just like you taught me."

Nell smiled and hugged him to her. "Your pa would be so proud of you," she said softly.

They were nearing the fork in the trail that would either take them on to Lottie's or to their former home. "We've made good time," Nell said. "How about we make a stop at our old place before going on to see Lottie and the boys?"

"Really?" His eyes told her he'd wanted to do just that but had been afraid to ask.

"Let's go," she said as she snapped the reins and took the trail to the right.

❧

Trey had avoided calling on Pete Collins for as long as he could, hoping pressure from the other ranchers would bring him around. Earlier that spring, Colonel Ashwood had questioned Pete about the differences between his version of that day at Deadman's Point and the testimony of the dead man's son. Jess had told the family how Collins had hemmed and hawed about maybe being farther away than he'd first thought and how things could look different from a distance. In the end, he had retracted his accusations against Trey and apologized profusely to the colonel.

He had yet to apologize to Trey.

But Trey wasn't after an apology. What he wanted was to assure himself that Pete intended to observe the uneasy peace. There had not been a single incident since the militia had stepped up patrols, and Trey wanted to keep things that way.

When he rode under the arches announcing the Collins spread, he saw the rancher talking to two of his hired hands. The three of them were so intent on their conversation, Trey was nearly upon them before they noticed. "Gentlemen," he said, tipping his fingers to the brim of his hat before dismounting.

"Trey Porterfield, you're a ways from home." Pete stepped forward, his hand extended. The two cowboys nodded in Trey's direction before returning to the bunkhouse.

Trey accepted the handshake. As he'd met with the other ranchers, he had become aware that the only rancher who had suffered loss of livestock or damage to property was Pete Collins. That seemed odd to Trey. "I was hoping we might talk, Pete."

"Well, sure. I reckon that's overdue, come to think of it. Guess we've both been busy. I mean, I'm hoping there's no hard feelings between us, Trey. Your family and mine? Why, your brother and me were best friends once upon a time."

His voice was too loud and his manner too overtly friendly. Trey decided to come to the point. "I've called on every cattle man in these parts, Pete, and most have come around to at least agreeing that we need to be of one mind in this business."

Collins spit a stream of chewing tobacco on the ground and squinted at Trey. "I guess I don't rightly catch your meaning."

"Pete, we have got to find a compromise to living side by side with herders. They aren't going away, and neither are we, so let's work this out once and for all."

Collins's smile was at odds with the pure hatred Trey

saw in the man's eyes. "Look, everybody appreciates that you kind of inherited this job of managing the ranch once your sister and her husband took off for California. Truth is, our hearts went out to you. Like throwing you in the water and expecting you to swim."

Trey returned the man's tight smile. "Well now, I reckon I learned to swim almost before I could walk. That was something my pa made sure of. And if I understand what you're trying to say under that pretty wrapping paper, most people around these parts are well aware that I've been herdin' and roundin' up cows since I was fourteen."

"No doubt, my boy. But working a ranch and managing a business are different, and—"

Trey slapped Pete on the shoulder to take the edge off his reply. "Who you callin' 'boy'? You can't be but maybe a year older than Jess, which makes neither one of you old enough to be my pa. Although I'll grant you, Jess does try from time to time."

All trace of a smile or hint of camaraderie vanished. Pete scowled at him. "What is it you want, Porterfield?"

"I already told you. I want you to sit down with me and the other ranchers and agree to get this thing worked out."

"And what of the herders? What happens when they slaughter our cattle, cut our fences, poison our wells?"

"Then we deal with that—when it happens."

"It already has. I lost half a dozen—"

"See now, Pete, that's the thing. I was talking to the other ranchers, and they haven't lost a single calf or steer. For that matter, neither have I. Only you. How come?"

"Ask your wife," Pete said and sneered.

Every muscle in Trey's body stiffened, and he clenched his fists so tight, they felt like rocks. "My wife is not part of this discussion, Collins," he said quietly.

"The hell she isn't. Don't get me wrong. I get why you chased after her. She's a real looker with a body that would give any man ideas. But if you'd used your noggin to do your thinkin' instead of your—"

He didn't finish his thought, because Trey smashed his fist into the man's leering face. The two cowboys came running and grabbed Trey as he stood over Collins.

"Let him go, boys," Pete said as he staggered to his feet and wiped the blood running from his nose with the back of one hand. He stepped forward so close that Trey could smell the onions he'd eaten earlier. "Now you listen to me, Porterfield. Your pa ran this territory like he owned it all, but that's changed. I'm the one running things now, and I say the herders have to go. You got that?"

"Or what? You and your boys here will burn them out?"

"It's worked before. Now git off my land." He stepped back and accepted a bandana from one of his men, pressing it against his swollen nose. The man wasn't even trying to deny his role in burning down Nell's house.

Trey paused before climbing into the saddle. "You know, that house and land once belonged to a friend of yours."

"Yeah, and George Johnson must be rollin' over in his grave knowin' his wife sold out to a bunch of

herders. They was the ones defiled the place, not…
whoever set it on fire."

Trey started to ride away.

"Hey, Porterfield," one of the hired hands shouted
when he had almost reached the arched gate that
marked Collins's land. "Watch yourself out there. It's
comin' on dark, and you never know about snipers
and such."

He heard the other hand howl with laughter as he
rode on.

Pete and his men were so sure of themselves, they
had just pretty much owned up to committing most
of the damage done, up to and including taking shots
at him and burning down Nell's house. Trey was also
more certain than ever that Pete had ordered some
of his own stock slaughtered and fences cut to make
it look like the work of sheep ranchers. This was no
widespread range war. This was a war between Pete
Collins and anyone who dared oppose his will.

༺༅ོ

Instead of pulling the buggy under the shade of a
cluster of trees on the rise overlooking her property,
Nell drove all the way down to where, if the house
were there, guests would have stopped outside the
fenced yard. The gate was half off its hinges and hung
lopsided and open.

"Come on," she said quietly as she climbed down
and slowly walked up the path to the pile of rubble she
and Joshua had once called home.

The fire had long ago gone out, but the stench of
it clung to the charred furnishings. The fireplace and

chimney stood exposed, their clay casings black with smoke. A layer of soot covered everything. Pieces of broken crockery that had fallen when the roof caved in crunched underfoot as Nell picked her way through the wreckage. She rescued a silver framed photo of Calvin and clutched it to her chest as she continued surveying her property. *Her* property, she thought. Hers to do with as she pleased. She had signed no papers before Henry's untimely death, so this land belonged to her and to Joshua.

But if someone challenged her right to the property, she would have to prove it. Remembering an iron box Calvin always kept under their bed, she quickened her step. She should not have waited so long to return, but her focus had been on her new life—the one she was building with Trey.

"Stay there," she instructed as Joshua started to follow her over fallen beams and past charred walls. She saw evidence others had been there ahead of her, scavenging for whatever they might salvage. She hoped they had not taken the small metal box. When she reached the bedroom, she saw the iron frame of the bed had partially melted in the heat of the fire and collapsed so that it rested on the floor.

Setting aside the photograph of Calvin, she tried pushing on the headboard. The bed moved an inch but no more. She put all her weight into pushing it again, and this time, she saw a corner of the box. It was still there. She stood back and assessed the situation. If she could pull the charred remainder of the mattress free, she could reach through the opening and retrieve the box.

"Ma? Somebody's up there watching us."

Joshua pointed to a mesa where she saw a man on horseback scanning the land through a spyglass—a spyglass that seemed to settle on Nell and Joshua. She recognized neither horse nor rider. "Joshua, go get in the buggy. I'll be right there."

She wrestled the mattress, the batting made heavier by being soaked in the rain. The box was stuck under the weight of the frame. She tugged and jimmied the box until finally it came free.

"Ma? He's coming."

The lock was broken, and her heart sank. But when she lifted the lid, she found what she was looking for—the deed to her property. It was charred at the edges, but it was there. She clutched the box to her chest, then picked up the silver frame and went to meet the man riding toward her son.

"Can I help you?" she called out as she worked her way over broken furniture and remnants of draperies.

"Ma'am." The man tipped his fingers to his hat, and she saw that it was Pete Collins. "What are you doing here?"

"This is my property," she replied, having reached the buggy. "I might ask you the same question, sir."

"Just passing by, Miz Stokes. Being a good neighbor and keeping an eye on things."

She noticed he had failed to introduce himself. "It's Mrs. Porterfield now, and I appreciate your concern, Mr. Collins, but I'm sure my husband keeps a check on the place."

"Still can't be too careful in these times, a woman and boy out alone." He was smiling, but his words signaled a threat.

"We're on our way to see my Aunt Lottie," Joshua announced.

"Is that right?" He kept his eyes on Nell. "Well, you give Miz Galway my deepest sympathies, won't you? A real shame what happened."

Nell got into the buggy and picked up the reins. "Yes, this whole business is a horror, one my husband is trying hard to remedy."

Pete Collins chuckled. "Your husband is a bit of an optimist, ma'am. He has little idea of how things go in this business, and he's playing with people's livelihood."

Nell handed Joshua the picture of his father. "Better than playing with people lives," she muttered as she clicked her tongue and urged the horse forward. "Good day, Mr. Collins."

To her relief, Collins made no attempt to follow them. After a few minutes, Joshua looked back and reported, "He's leavin'. Is that man a friend of Trey's?"

"He and Trey are both in the cattle business," she replied carefully.

"I don't care for him," Joshua said after taking a moment to digest Nell's explanation.

She laughed. "Neither do I."

Lottie was sitting on the wide covered porch when Nell and Joshua rolled up to the hitching post.

"Aunt Lottie!" Joshua jumped down from the buggy almost before it came to a full stop and ran to the porch. "We brought a picnic. We stopped at our ranch just to look around, and we were gonna eat there, but this man showed up, so Mama said we should come on here, and maybe you'd like to eat with us."

Lottie hugged Joshua while Nell tied up the horse and retrieved the picnic basket.

"Hello, Lottie. I hope it's all right we stopped by," Nell said, gauging her sister-in-law's mood as she approached the porch.

Lottie kept her focus on Joshua. "A picnic, you say. Well now, that does sound fine. We can have it right here on the porch." She led the way to a table and took the basket from Nell. "Let's just see what we have here," she said. She still had not once looked at Nell.

"There's even a jug of lemonade," Joshua announced as he and Lottie began removing things from the basket. "Nita thinks of everything."

Nell saw Lottie stiffen at that, but then she looked sideways at Nell and asked, "How are Mr. and Mrs. Mendez doing?"

Given this opening, Nell joined her son and Lottie in setting up the picnic. "They're grieving, like you," she said softly.

"It don't get any easier," Lottie replied. "That business about time healing all wounds? It's a lie, at least for me and my boys." After a moment, she added, "I expect it's no different for the Mendez family. The days and weeks and months come and go, but…" Her eyes welled with tears, and she wiped them away and cleared her throat. "You seem to be doing all right."

The way her sister-in-law looked at her, Nell knew the underlying message was that while Lottie was still mourning Henry, Nell seemed to have totally recovered from Calvin's death. "Cal's been gone for nearly a year. The wounds do heal, Lottie. The scars never will."

The two women ate in silence, occasionally

acknowledging Joshua's monologue with a nod or smile. When he saw his cousins coming in from tending the sheep, he hurried off to meet them. Nell watched, mostly to make sure her son was warmly received by Ira and Spud in spite of their feelings for her. She was not disappointed. Ira wrapped his arm around Joshua's shoulders and led him off to a pen where several lambs were being held. Satisfied, she turned her attention back to Lottie. She cast about for a safe topic of conversation.

"I see Ernest separated those lambs from their mothers. I wonder—"

"They have no mothers," Lottie interrupted, bitterness dripping from each word. "Their mothers were slaughtered, as were any number of yours. If you cared. But then, why should you? You've set yourself and Joshua up with that rancher. What's it to you if everything Calvin ever did for you gets destroyed?"

"That's unfair, Lottie. Trey is trying to—"

"Trey this and Trey that." Lottie spat the words. "If I never hear that man's name again, I just might be able to mourn in peace."

Nell was at a loss. Anything she might say, it seemed, would be met with the venom of Lottie's anger. She understood some of what Lottie must be feeling. After all, the woman refused to believe Trey hadn't caused Henry's death. For several long uncomfortable minutes, they sat side by side looking out over the land, watching their boys play marbles in a circle they'd scraped out in the dirt. When Lottie stood and began gathering the remains of their picnic, Nell started to help.

"Leave it," Lottie snarled.

Nell sat down again. She shifted her gaze to the buggy where she'd left the precious documents that were her security—with or without Trey.

"Lottie? Earlier when Joshua and I stopped by the old house, I was able to retrieve the deed and other important papers. I should have done that months ago, but I didn't think of it. It would have been the first thing Henry would have thought to do." She paused and saw that Lottie was listening. "Do you have papers to show ownership of this property?"

Her sister-in-law looked up from clearing the picnic, her eyes wide with panic. "Papers? I don't know. I mean Henry handled all of that and——" She glanced toward the windows that led to the front parlor. "I never thought to have to prove anything. This is our place. We own it. Well, us and the bank, I guess."

"And have you thought about how you might keep going? I mean, the boys are a big help, I'm sure, but maybe Ernest will want to return to Nebraska. After all, he stayed to watch over me and Joshua. He's Calvin's kin, not mine and Henry's."

She was surprised to see Lottie blush scarlet.

"Well now, Nell, the thing is, Ernest has been… Ernest has offered…" Lottie bit her lower lip. "Ernest is pressing me about getting married. It's like Henry tried to tell you—a woman out here alone, even without all the trouble the cattle ranchers are causing… Well, it's the best idea, don't you think?"

Nell chose her words with care. "What do you think, Lottie? Keeping this place going carries a lot of responsibility, that's true. But if you married Ernest, then——"

"Oh, I see where you're headed with this. Well, be sure this ranch belongs to those boys and nobody else."

"And do you have papers to that effect?"

"I know what Henry would want."

"Still, maybe you and I should both see a lawyer just to make sure everything is in order."

Lottie laughed. "Look at you. Madam High and Mighty married to a Porterfield can afford a lawyer. Some of us aren't married to money, Nell. Some of us decided to stay true to our own kind rather than cross over—for *any* reason."

Nell was so tired of being accused of marrying Trey for security. "Maybe that was a piece of it—at first. But I love him, Lottie. Love him so much that he could be penniless for all I care, and I believe he loves me in return. I know he cares deeply for me—and for Joshua."

Lottie stared at her for a long moment, tears welling in her eyes. "Do you know how blessed you are, Nell? To have not one but two men care for you so much in a single lifetime? I only had Henry, and I'll never have that again."

"You can't know that, Lottie. Don't settle just because you're frightened. I'm here, and so is Trey—if you'll let him. He's been calling on all the cattle ranchers and tells me at least some of them are starting coming around to accepting that we have to learn to live together and—"

"What about that Collins fella? I seen him in town a few days ago, strutting around like he owned everything and everybody."

"He recanted his accusations against Trey, and they didn't have the evidence they needed to hold him for other things," Nell admitted, "but—"

"But nothing. They can find the evidence they need to accuse my boy of cold-blooded murder for accidentally stabbing that Mexican boy, but they can't seem to find anything allowing them to lock up a rich white cattleman."

Nell was not going to debate Ira's crime with her sister-in-law. "Come inside, Lottie, and let's look for your deed and any other documents you may want to put in a safe place. Hopefully Henry left a will?"

With obvious reluctance, Lottie led the way inside where she sat down at her late husband's desk and began opening drawers. "I don't know what it is I'm looking for," she grumbled, pulling out scraps of paper, a ledger, and finally an iron box not unlike the one Calvin had used to store important papers.

"That might be it."

Lottie set the box on top of the desk and sat back. "You open it," she said softly.

When they couldn't find a key, with Lottie's permission, Nell used a letter opener to pry the lid open. Inside were several legal-looking papers. "This is the deed," she said, handing that to Lottie. "And this looks like a will."

"Read it," Lottie whispered.

"It's a lot of legal talk," Nell replied as she quickly scanned the document, seeking the information she hoped was there. "Here," she said, pointing excitedly to a section where Lottie's name and those of her two sons were listed.

Lottie's lips moved as she read the section. "What does it mean?"

"It means the same as what Calvin wrote in his will—the land and livestock are left to your boys, but until they are of age, you, as their guardian and surviving parent, are in control. And whatever the boys decide once they are of age, you are always to be provided with a home—this house or some other bought for you if they sell the land. It's almost identical to what was in Calvin's will, Lottie. My guess is Henry and Calvin had these drawn up at the same time by the same lawyer." She turned back to the document's cover and found the name of the attorney. "See? It's the same man as on Cal's will."

Lottie ran her fingers over the paper as if it were a fine piece of fabric, precious and cherished. "Henry was always thinking of me and the boys," she said softly. "We used to argue about it, the way he was always so serious about putting things in order just in case. I used to tell him he was the only man I'd ever met who was always thinking about dying."

"He was just making sure you and the boys would be provided for, Lottie. He loved you so much."

Lottie refolded the will and placed it with the deed back inside the metal box. After closing the lid, she laid her hand on the box and stared out the window.

Nell heard the boys playing in the yard and the clock on the mantel ticking off the seconds. "Lottie, can we not join forces and work together to secure a future for our sons?"

After what seemed like a very long time, Lottie handed the box to Nell. "You keep this for me, Nell. Just in case." Her lower lip quivered as she pressed the box into Nell's hands.

"Oh, Lottie, if that means you trust me to do what's right for you and the boys, I'd be honored."

Swiping at tears, Lottie stood and cleared her

throat. "Well, the way I see it, you and me are now in charge of the two biggest sheep farms in the territory, at least when it comes to how much land we own."

"We can rebuild the flock, Lottie. It will take time, but—"

"Perhaps."

"And we can talk to the others—our neighbors and fellow herders. We can work together."

"Oh sure. We should be right up there in front at the next herders' cooperative meeting. I expect that would set them back on their heels a bit."

And for the first time since Henry's death, Nell saw her sister-in-law smile.

Nell covered a smile of her own as she imagined Lottie standing her ground with a bunch of male herders. Her sister-in-law was a little like Juanita in the way she could make others see things her way—if she felt comfortable speaking out. Of course, when Lottie felt threatened, she withdrew, became fearful and wary, and kept her thoughts to herself, looking to others to take charge. Finding the papers had given her a new sense of confidence.

The boys had finished their game and were climbing the front porch steps, helping themselves to lemonade. Through the open window, Nell heard Joshua telling his cousins about how Trey had promised to teach him how to pitch and hit better when it came to baseball.

"Is he any good?" Spud asked at the same time as Ira said, "Maybe he would let us play."

"Sure. Trey likes everybody, and he's really good— hits the ball a mile most every time. Rico says he's a lot better than his brother, even if Jess is the marshal."

Nell realized Lottie was hearing this same conversation. Did she dare suggest perhaps Trey could stop by to work with the boys? "Maybe next time we come for a visit, Trey could—" she began, but Lottie cut her off.

"Probably better if the boys come to you. Not sure how Ernest would take it if—"

"Lottie, about Ernest."

"I expect Ernest will be heading back home after all once I tell him about the papers I gave you for safekeeping. No reason for him to marry me when there's nothing to be gained now, is there?"

"And you?"

"We'll see what happens with Ira, but Nell, with the greater part of both our flocks slaughtered, I'd have to rebuild. Not sure I'm up to that."

"You wouldn't have to do it alone, Lottie. I may have married a cattleman, but I was raised by herders, and that's part of who I am—and it's what I want for Joshua."

The two women walked out to the porch. Nell held the metal box, so Lottie picked up the picnic basket and carried it to the buggy. Joshua continued chattering away to his cousins as he climbed onto the seat. Nell hugged Lottie, a hug her sister-in-law returned with the whispered words, "Thanks for coming, Nell. I've missed you."

"You bring the boys and come visit any time," Nell replied. "Trey is a good businessman, and he can advise you on how best to rebuild—if that's what you decide."

As she drove away, Nell saw Ernest standing in the shadow of the barn, watching her go.

Ten

TREY WAS IN HIS OFFICE LATER THAT EVENING WHEN Nell tapped lightly on the door and walked in.

"It's late," she said. "You should get some rest."

He glanced at his father's pocket watch lying open on the desk. It showed after midnight. He'd lost all track of time. Running both hands through his hair, he leaned the swivel chair back and let out a long breath of exhaustion. "So much to do that time gets away from me, Nellie." He stood and indicated the sofa that ran the length of one wall in the small space. "Come sit with me, and tell me about your day."

At supper, she had told him that her visit with Lottie had been far better than she had hoped, but because Joshua was there, she had not elaborated.

"So exactly what does 'better than you'd hoped for' entail when it comes to Lottie?"

"Oh, Trey, I think she has forgiven me. Maybe the boys have as well."

"That's nice, especially since you've done nothing to require forgiveness."

"I married you," she reminded him.

He grinned and pulled her close so that she was snuggled into the curve of his body. "Well, yeah, there is that. So what makes you think you're back in Lottie's good graces after all this time?"

He listened as she poured out the details of her day. She told him how Ernest was pushing for marriage with Lottie and how she had urged her sister-in-law to think carefully. And he saw how her features softened as she spoke of when the two of them had realized that Henry and Calvin must have drawn up similar wills to protect their wives and sons. "Lottie says the two of us should show up at the next herders' co-op meeting and speak our minds, since between us, we hold more land than the others put together."

"Lottie said that?" Henry Galway's wife had always struck Trey as the mousy sort.

"She's stronger than you might think," Nell replied.

"I guess so." He kissed her hair, and she twisted to run her fingertips over the creases lining his forehead. "What are you working on?"

"I've been thinking on it, Nellie. The key to this whole thing is Pete Collins, so I went to see him today. Sorry to say my meeting didn't go half as well as yours with Lottie."

"What happened?"

He hesitated. He shouldn't say anything until he had proof of his suspicions, but he was more and more convinced Pete and his men were behind all the trouble that had plagued the area for these last months.

She sat up and faced him. "Trey, I am your wife. Please don't try to shield me from whatever is going on. I assure you my imagination is far more frightening than reality could ever be."

"Don't be too sure."

She frowned, and he knew she wouldn't rest until she had drawn out the whole truth. So he told her. He told her how Collins's cowhand had as good as admitted taking shots at him. "And I have little doubt that it was him and his men who slaughtered not only your stock and Henry's, but his own as well to make it look like there was vengeance on both sides."

"What about my house? Did he set it on fire?"

"Pretty sure that was either him or his men. He sure was all riled up that day after I told him what happened at Deadman's Point. Trouble is, there's no real evidence for a trial. Ashwood didn't have enough to hold him, and right now, I can't come up with anything either." He stifled a yawn. "Got to get back to these ledgers, Nellie."

"Come to bed, Trey. You can't keep driving yourself this way." She stood and held out her hands to him.

He chuckled as he took hold of her hands and let her pull him to his feet. "Now that's an invitation I wouldn't turn down under any circumstances."

"To sleep," she said, the color on her cheeks turning a most becoming pink.

"Ah, Nellie, you know I always sleep better after." He made sure she didn't have to ask "after what?" as he pulled her close and kissed her full on the mouth. When she wrapped her arms around his neck, urging him closer, he knew he'd won. He prepared to lead her from the outbuilding that served as his office across the courtyard to the house, to their bed, but Nell stayed where she was.

"Juanita is still up," she said. "Something about needing to make tortillas for the men to take on the roundup tomorrow."

Trey groaned. He loved having his surrogate family so close, but there were times… "What about Joshua?"

"Nita said she would look in on him." She stepped closer and ran her palms over his shirtfront, tracing the muscles of his chest and edging nearer and nearer to the waistband of his trousers. "We could make love right here," she whispered as she started to unfasten his belt.

Trey started opening the row of tiny buttons on her shirtwaist. "Here?" he whispered as he kissed her with a passion that left them both staggering toward the sofa. He collapsed onto the soft cushions, taking her with him.

"Why not?" She straddled him, raising her skirt above her knees so that she felt his fullness pressing against her.

He pushed the opening of her dress aside, revealing her chemise. She fumbled to open his shirt. He cupped her breasts, feeling the roundness of them, the heat of their tips. She massaged his bare skin, pushing the shirt over his shoulders as she leaned in to kiss his throat, his jaw, and finally his mouth.

And then she eased away. He opened his eyes, ready to protest, but when he saw her intent was to undress, he relaxed and prepared to enjoy the moment. After she had stripped down to her chemise and pantaloons, she knelt and pulled off his boots, then unbuttoned his fly, and removed his trousers. He made sure she took his long johns with them.

In the flickering light of the single lamp on his desk, he saw her hesitate. They had only made love in the dark before, feeling their way to find ways of pleasuring the other.

"Nellie, blow out the light if you want to. It's all right."

She shook her head as she reached up and removed the pins holding her hair and bent forward. Her warm wet lips on him sent him spiraling, and he reached for her to pull her onto him before he lost all control. She pushed him away, and as her hair fanned over his lower body, she kissed him there again.

"You like that," she said, her voice filled with delight at her discovery.

"I love that, Nellie, but darlin', you are playing with fire. Now come here." He sat up enough to lift her to a standing position and then slipped her pantaloons over her slim hips, letting them pool around her bare feet. "You have to be the most beautiful woman God ever thought of making."

She laughed and tossed her hair back as she straddled him again and leaned in to kiss his mouth. "Liar," she whispered just before her lips met his.

And that was all it took. He moved only slightly and found the exact place where they fit so perfectly together. He slid into her and filled her. She settled into the rhythm they had perfected night after night as they lay together in that big double bed. *Man and wife*, Trey thought. *My wife. My love.*

Afterward, they lay side by side, nestled together

on the sofa. "Trey?" she whispered just before he dosed off.

"Hmmm?"

"I sort of promised Ira and Spud and Joshua you would work with them all on their baseball skills."

He groaned but then chuckled. "And just where do you see this happening?"

"I think they might come here if you asked them."

Trey was wide awake now. "Lottie as well?"

"I think so."

Trey and Colonel Ashwood had been working on an idea, a way they might give Pete Collins a false sense of confidence. If Pete thought he and his men could make a move, then they might try again, and the militia could make sure they were caught red-handed. Colonel Ashwood's concern was that the plan could put others in danger. But if Collins thought Lottie and her boys were away from their ranch, might he not use that opportunity to strike?

"Well, any time next week should be fine," he said. "But only if Lottie agrees to come. I don't want this to be just about finding common ground among the boys."

"I'll ask her at church on Sunday." Nell curled her hand so that it rested at the base of his throat. Her hair was spread over his bare chest, and he was stroking it with his fingers. "Trey? Maybe we ought to go back to the house?"

"I thought you'd never ask." He rolled over her and stood. He hopped on one foot to pull on his trousers without bothering with his undergarments, while she tied the ribbons on her chemise and pulled on her pantaloons. As they dressed, he studied her—the fullness of her breasts and the roundness of her tummy that he'd failed to notice before.

"Nellie, is there any chance… I mean, could you be with child?"

She hesitated before facing him. "I didn't want to get your hopes up. After all the times I—" She shook her head, banishing the past. "If I have things figured out right, I'm already in the fifth month. Trey, this morning, I felt the baby move." She cradled her stomach. "In the past, if something went wrong, it was earlier on, but still—"

He lifted her off her feet and swung her around as he kissed her repeatedly on her nose, her cheeks, her lips. "Finally, some good news," he crowed so loud, the dogs barked.

"Shhh," she whispered, covering his mouth with her fingers. "You'll wake everyone." But she was grinning the same way he was, though worry still lingered. *What if?*

He scooped her fully into his arms and carried her to the door.

"Trey Porterfield, put me down," she demanded, but she was laughing.

"I may never let you walk a step again until this baby gets born," he told her, and while he was smiling, he was only half kidding.

❧

They made love again once they reached their bedroom, and afterward, Nell lay curled against her sleeping husband. She stayed there, her eyes open, and savored the pure joy of being loved by this remarkable man. It had been such a wonderful day, and if she carried this child to term, that would make it just about perfect. She cradled her stomach with her hands and recalled the wonder of being pregnant with Joshua. But then she remembered the three times she had been so certain there would be more children, and none of those had come to pass.

"Oh please," she whispered. "Please let me have this child."

Trey tightened his hold on her, almost as if to reassure her, but she could tell by his breathing that he was still sleeping. She eased herself out of bed and walked barefoot down the hall to Joshua's room.

Her son had kicked off the covers and slept on his stomach, his face turned to one side. She paused in the doorway and realized she was listening for his ragged breathing, the catch that so often came as if he could not quite get enough air in or out. But tonight, there was no such sound. He slept peacefully, and it occurred to her he had made steady improvement ever since Addie had begun giving him regular steam treatments. Those had continued here on Trey's ranch; Addie's father had done something similar for Trey when he was younger, at least according to Juanita.

In some ways, my son, you are more like Trey than you were your own father, she thought. She pulled the covers over his thin body and kissed his forehead, smoothing his hair back from his eyes. "Sleep well," she whispered.

When she climbed back into bed, Trey stirred.

"Is Josh all right?" he asked sleepily. He had taken to calling the boy *Josh*—a name her son seemed to favor.

"Yes," she whispered. "Go back to sleep."

He pulled her close, his lips close to her ear as he whispered, "We're going to be fine, Nellie. I'm not going to let anything bad happen to you or Josh or this baby," he promised, his hand flat on her stomach.

"I know." But she also knew it was a promise he might not always be able to keep. With men like Pete Collins in the world—men who placed their own wants ahead of the greater good—staying safe wasn't always an option.

∽≪

The following morning, Trey could not seem to stop grinning. They sat at breakfast, with Juanita bustling around as usual. Joshua had bolted down his meal, eager to get outside where one of the cowboys had promised to give him a lesson in throwing a lasso.

"Don't you look like the cat that swallowed the canary," Juanita said as she poured Trey a second cup of coffee. She turned her attention to Nell. "The two of you were out there in the office for some time last night. Is everything all right?"

Nell felt a telltale blush rise up her neck and stain her cheeks.

"Fine and dandy," Trey replied. He reached across the table and held her hand.

"You told him then?" Juanita asked, her attention still on Nell.

"About Lottie? Yes, I—"

"About the baby," Juanita interrupted. "No other

reason I can think of why this man here is grinning like he just struck gold. I was wondering when he might get around to noticing."

Nell was incredulous. "How did you know? I mean, it's early yet, and I haven't even—"

Juanita rolled her eyes. "It's *claro*—plain as the nose on your face, Nell." She ticked off the signs on the fingers of one hand. "You pick at whatever is set before you at breakfast, then push it away. You claim no appetite, but I bet the truth is, just looking at the food makes your stomach turn over. Then there's the way your clothes have started to be just a little too tight. And that doesn't even begin to include how many times a day I've seen you pat your belly and smile."

"So you knew?" Trey asked.

"The way I see things, come winter, there will be something besides not being able to keep your hands off each other keeping the two of you up at night."

"Nita!" Nell knew the woman was direct, but really, this was too much.

But then Juanita touched Trey's face and said softly, "You are going to be a wonderful father, Trey. Your mama and me always used to talk about that." She looked at Nell, studying her for a long moment as if trying to come to a decision. And then she smiled. "But it takes two, and you've found yourself a good woman here."

And in that moment, Nell realized Juanita might just be ready to embrace her as a member of this family she had helped raise. She would still struggle with the knowledge that Nell's kin had killed Javier, but hopefully, she no longer held Nell responsible. "Thank you, Nita," Nell said softly and felt tears well.

"Ha!" Juanita shouted triumphantly. "There's another sign—getting all teary-eyed when there's no cause."

They laughed until tears of happiness rolled down their cheeks and Juanita had to sit down to catch her breath. They were still laughing when they heard shouts from outside and the thud of horses' hooves coming right up to the kitchen door.

"What the—" Trey grabbed his hat and headed for the yard. "Stay here," he said when Nell and Juanita followed him.

"Joshua's out there," Nell reminded him, her heart hammering for, from the sounds of things, whoever was outside had not come on a casual visit.

"I know. Just wait here."

She and Juanita stood side by side in the doorway, their arms around each other's waists.

"Josh, go inside," Nell heard Trey call out as he strode across the courtyard toward the cluster of riders—one of them Pete Collins—but Nell realized Juanita was more concerned about others riding with the firebrand rancher.

"This is not good," she murmured. "Those men are other ranchers, neighbors Trey was counting on to stand with him. If they are riding with Pete Collins, then…"

When Joshua reached the doorway and Nell pulled him inside, Juanita edged past her and reached behind the door. When she emerged, she was holding a rifle. "Just in case," she muttered and took up her vigil at the open window, resting the barrel of the rifle on the broad sill.

"Ma?" Joshua's voice shook a little as he stared first at the rifle and then at her.

"It's all right, Son." She turned him away from Juanita so that he was once again facing the scene outside. "See? Trey is talking to those men. They're our neighbors, and I'm sure—"

Suddenly, Pete Collins leaped from his horse straight onto Trey, and both men fell to the ground, raising a cloud of dust as they wrestled. Nell knew Trey was unarmed, but she doubted Collins would go anywhere without his gun. Instead of dismounting to help, the other men backed their horses away from the fracas. Pete landed a punch on Trey's face.

"Joshua, go stay in your room until this is over," she said, giving her son a push toward the bedrooms. Then she turned to Juanita. "Give me that," she said, motioning toward the rifle.

Neither Joshua nor Juanita argued.

Carefully, she took hold of the rifle and stepped into the courtyard. She aimed it away from everyone and everything and pulled the trigger. The recoil almost made her lose her balance, but she got the attention she sought—even Collins looked up. Steadying her grip on the weapon once again, she walked slowly toward the men. Trey pushed Pete away and got to his feet.

"Mr. Collins, whatever your grievance with my husband, it will not be resolved rolling around in the dirt like schoolboys. As for the rest of you, for shame that you would sit idly by."

A couple of men dismounted. One picked up Trey's hat and dusted it off.

Pete Collins got to his feet and moved a step toward her. "Now, ma'am, what say you put down that gun. This is—"

"Do not say this is not my business. Lottie Galway and I own property in this territory, and that gives us a stake in this so-called war you seem determined to perpetuate. If you've come to make demands or discuss terms, then herders have every right to be a part of that discussion. I intend to have my say both as a landowner and as Mr. Porterfield's wife."

She realized the men still on horseback were murmuring among themselves. A couple of others dismounted and went to stand with Trey. Her husband moved toward her, ignoring the bruise forming over one eye and the blood leaking down his chin from a cut on his lip.

Nell resisted the urge to attend to his injuries. This was her fight as much as it was his, and she would make them hear her, even if she had to do it by holding a loaded rifle on them. "My home, my son's legacy from his murdered father, was burned to the ground in broad daylight. That was months ago. Have any one of you tried to find out who did that? Or do you already know? Perhaps it was some of you? How would you have reacted had it been one of your homes destroyed? One of your fellow *ranchers* murdered?"

All of the rage she had kept at bay for months now seemed to roil to the surface and demand release. Perhaps it was seeing Trey attacked. Perhaps it was having these horrid men spoil something so innocent as the joy and laughter she and Trey and Juanita had been sharing when they rode up. Whatever the cause, she had had her fill of their need to be in control, to always believe they knew what was best.

She turned back to Collins and leveled the gun at

him, even as Trey took a step closer. She expected her husband to ease the rifle from her hands, but instead, he stood next to her, tall and solid, his hand resting protectively on her back.

Pete held up his hands and tried to smile. "Now, come on, ma'am. Trey. We just wanted to—"

"Talking doesn't seem to be something you're too good at, Pete," Trey said. He looked past Collins to the others. "Gentlemen, if you've come to sit down and discuss things calmly, you're welcome to stay. But if it's a fight you want, I won't join you. It's your choice—a truce with both sides negotiating, or surrender to all-out war."

Nell lowered the rifle as Collins returned to his horse, held for him by one of the other ranchers. He mounted and grumbled, "Let's go, boys."

But when he spurred his horse and rode away, no one followed.

"Maybe I could take that now?" Trey said as he relieved Nell of the rifle.

Was he smiling? She was in no mood to be taken lightly. "I mean what I say, Trey. I will not bring another child into a world where grown men act like children. What kind of example is that setting?"

"I'm doing my best, Nellie. Folks are afraid of what they don't fully understand."

She saw the weariness in his eyes, and her heart melted. "Pay no attention to my ranting," she said, smoothing a lock of his hair back from his forehead. "I guess I've said my piece, so go on and meet with the others."

"Come with me," he said, lowering his voice so

that he was speaking only to her. "Maybe with you there telling them what you and Lottie have been through, they'll come to a better understanding of just how out of hand things have gotten."

"I don't know. It might just make things worse." While most of the men waiting to meet with Trey had attended Javier's funeral and been civil—if not exactly cordial—to her, Pete Collins seemed to have brought them around to his way of thinking far too easily.

"Like you said, you've got as much stake in this as any one of them."

Trey handed the rifle back to Juanita, and when Nell walked with him to his office, the other ranchers followed, a few snatching off their hats in deference to her presence among them. Some sat on the sofa and a couple of straight-backed, carved wooden chairs, while others stood. The murmur of conversation she had heard as she and Trey passed them ceased the minute Trey stood at his desk and cleared his throat.

"Gentlemen, I've asked my wife to speak to you as a representative of the other side of this disagreement."

Nell scanned the room and saw a mix of rolled eyes, men muttering to each other, and a general uncomfortable shifting of feet. But one by one, the men gave her their attention—grudgingly, in some cases.

Trey sat down in his desk chair and nodded encouragingly.

She steadied her shaking knees by gripping the edge of the desk. "I can't think what else I might add to what I said outside there," she began.

"What'd she say?" bellowed old Jasper Perkins, a rancher who was notoriously hard of hearing.

Nell cleared her throat and raised her voice. "Like many of you, my first husband, Calvin Stokes, and I moved to this territory seeking a better life for ourselves and our son. We had also been told the drier climate here might be better for Joshua's health. Thankfully, that seems to be the case."

She paused, searching for words.

"For as far back as either Calvin or I knew, our families had raised sheep—first in Scotland, and then a generation ago, our parents came here. Like many others, they came for a better life and settled in Kansas and Nebraska. That's where Calvin and I grew up, met, married, and started our family. I expect many of you have a similar history, of parents or grandparents who emigrated here from other shores."

A couple of nods gave her the courage to continue in spite of a few of the men continuing to scowl at her, their arms folded firmly over their chests.

"Your neighbor, Mrs. Johnson, agreed to sell us her property. Sadly, we were only here for a short time before Calvin was killed along with our two shepherds. And as we all know, the troubles did not stop there."

A rumble of muttered comments spread across the room.

"Hear her out," Trey said.

"Also, as many of you are aware, raising sheep is a good deal different from raising cattle. An entire flock of sheep can be tended by two or three men—men on foot mostly. With cattle, you need many men—men on horseback. Of course, one thing we share in common is that we both depend on our herding dogs to help."

A man standing near the door actually smiled at that.

"There has been harm on both sides, I do not dispute that. But I would ask you to consider what it took to deliver some of that harm. Your fences were cut—in some cases, miles from the nearest sheep ranch. How did a herder get there to do such damage? When your cattle were raided and stampeded, if we don't own horses, who were those riders?"

"Next you'll be excusing your own nephew from killing Javier Mendez in cold blood," a man shouted, and others around him hardened their gaze at her.

"My nephew will stand trial for that," she said, raising her voice again to speak over the general rumble of dissent. "He will face a judge and jury, as should anyone who has broken the law in this territory. I am not denying all blame. Certainly some acts were the work of my fellow herders. But I would remind you that the murder of my first husband, the rimrocking of the majority of my brother's flock and my own, the burning of my home, and the raids my son and I endured were all the work of men who had no respect for the law. Perhaps that kind of vigilante justice was acceptable years ago when this part of the country was first being settled, but we are coming to a new century, gentlemen. Our children will inherit the ways we teach them."

"I didn't come here to hear a lecture from no woman," one man said and stormed out.

"Yeah, he gets enough of that from his wife at home," Jasper bellowed, and several men laughed. "Go on, Miz Porterfield. You're making more sense than I've heard in a good while."

Nell's heart swelled at this sign of support. "All I want to say is that everything Trey and I do is for the good of my son and the baby we are expecting come fall."

That news brought a chorus of hoots and whistles that left Trey blushing and grinning. He stood and placed his hand around Nell's waist. "Gentlemen, thank you for your kind consideration." He guided Nell to the office door, and as the men parted to let them pass, at least some of them nodded or tipped their hats to her.

Once they were outside, Trey kissed her. "Thank you, Nellie. I know that wasn't easy."

"Do you think I made things worse? I mean, that man who left—"

"Ralph Sutter is another hothead like Pete. The point is the others stayed. Now go inside out of this hot sun and get off your feet."

"You are going to be impossible about spoiling me and this baby, aren't you?"

He grinned. "That's the plan."

She touched the dried blood on the cut where Pete Collins had hit him. "We should get some ointment on that."

"It's nothin'. Worth every drop of blood if it made those men in there start to distance themselves from Collins. Now scoot." He gave her a gentle push in the direction of the house. "I'll be in directly."

❧

When Trey returned to his office, the others were deep in conversation.

"She had a point," one man said. "That business about who rides and who doesn't makes me start thinkin' on just how some of this business might have been carried out."

"The herders aren't completely without blame," another man argued.

"She never said they were, but it wasn't herders that killed Calvin Stokes or burned down her place. What would be the point?"

"The house burning could have been revenge by herders because she married Trey," another rancher said.

"That makes no sense. It'd just drive her closer to our side, so Trey ends up with her property."

"Maybe that's why he married her in the first place."

Trey cleared his throat, and the men turned their attention to him. "Let's make one thing crystal clear, gentlemen," he said, his throat tight with the fury he refused to put on display. "That woman and her family have had to endure the senseless loss of the men they depended upon. Nell's house has been destroyed, her flock stampeded. She and her son have nothing left of the life they came here to build. Take a walk in her shoes, my friends, and then tell me you want to keep fighting."

"She ain't lost everything yet, Trey. She has her boy, and the two of you are having a baby, aren't you?" Jasper might be close to deaf, but the man had a way of hearing what he needed to hear. "That's a pretty good sign things are going your way."

Everyone laughed, and Trey realized—not for the first time—that these were good men who only wanted the best for their families. There would always be men like Collins who could sway their thinking, but Trey trusted that in the end, reason would win out. Still, Pete and his cowboys would continue to cause trouble, and the angrier he got, the more vicious his attacks were likely to become. Trey wondered if he dared share the plan to set a trap for Pete, one that would unmask him as the brains behind much of the trouble.

He looked around the room. There were men he knew he could trust, but there were others who would side with whoever they thought stood the best chance of preserving their financial security. No, he would rely on the militia and his family—Jess, Seth, Rico. For now, he would simply elicit an agreement from those in the room that neither they nor any of their cow hands would be a party to any attack on herders or their property.

The others were barely aware of him as they debated the best way to move forward. Trey realized Nell had gotten to them. They were actually talking about the sheepherders as if they might share some of the same challenges. For the first time since the whole conflict had begun, Trey realized there was no talk of "those people." For the first time, his neighbors were thinking of both sides.

"I have a suggestion." He shouted to be heard above the fray. "What if we all sign a pact?" He pulled out a piece of paper from the desk drawer and wrote out the pledge. He put his own signature to the page first and then handed the pen to Jasper.

One by one, the other men took their turn and signed the paper, then shook hands to further seal the contract.

As he watched them ride off back to their ranches, Trey felt for the first time in weeks as if progress had been made. And it was at least in part because of Nell.

Eleven

JUANITA DID NOT LIKE THE WAY TREY WAS ACTING IN the days that followed the meeting with the other ranchers. He kept things to himself, was distracted during meals, and she had heard him arguing with Nell. He was a grown man—and technically her employer—and yet she felt the need to keep him close to home, especially now that Javier had been killed.

She saw her chance one October morning while Trey was finishing his breakfast. Nell had gone to lie down, and Joshua was out doing his assigned chores. She poured herself a cup of coffee and pulled a chair close to the table. "What's going on with you?"

He stared out the window, although from his expression, he was lost in thought rather than admiring the scenery. He turned his attention to her and smiled. "Just trying to figure something out." His expression sobered, and he covered her hand with his. "How are you doing these days?"

She pulled her hand free. "Don't go changing the subject, young man. You are up to something, and everything I know tells me it's going to put you in harm's way. You want to know how I'm doing? I'm worried I could lose another son—you." She cradled her cup with both hands, mostly to hide her shaking.

"Now, Nita, you've no cause to—"

"Do not lie to me, Trey. Your wife is worried, and so am I. The difference is that she knows the cause, and I don't."

She watched him wrestle with how much to reveal. "All right," he said finally. "Tomorrow at church, Nell is going to invite her sister-in-law and nephews to come here for the afternoon."

"You're saying that boy that killed my son will be here? Staying here?"

Trey ran his hand through his thick hair. "I know it's asking a lot, but it's the only way, Nita. Nell will make sure he stays out of your way."

Juanita lowered her head and studied her knobby, arthritic fingers. She felt old and tired, and she just wanted to live out her days in peace. She released a long sigh and looked up at Trey. "And you think they'll accept after everything that's passed between them and us?"

"Eventually, but that's not the point. First, we have to stop the attacks, and those point directly to Collins. So Nell's going to make sure that Pete hears her extend the invitation. It's a trap we're setting, Nita, to try and prove once and for all that it's Pete and his men behind all the trouble."

"I don't understand."

"Pete was pretty upset with what happened here that day last month, especially when the others chose to stay rather than follow him. When the boys took the stock to market, they overheard Pete make comments—veiled threats."

"He's feeling outnumbered, Trey, and Pete Collins does not like to lose."

"He's definitely ripe to try something. I suspect that if he thinks there's nobody home at the Galway place, Pete will see his chance to stir things up again."

"What about Ernest Stokes?"

"He left. Headed back to Nebraska once Lottie made it clear she has no intention of marrying again."

"So all the other ranchers are in on this?"

Trey hesitated. "Not exactly. It's hard to know who can be trusted."

"You're doing this on your own? No wonder Nell is upset. You alone against Collins and his men?" Juanita shook her head.

"Jess will be there, and Seth as well. Plus, Colonel Ashwood has agreed to have half a dozen of his men standing by. If Pete and his men show up and start to do anything, Seth can arrest them. Ashwood's men will take them into custody and hold them at the fort."

"And then you think this mess will end?" Juanita took her cup and his breakfast dishes to the sink and began washing them. "You forget there are two sides. You think the herders will thank you and do whatever you ask once you prove Collins is at fault?"

"I'm not naive, Nita. True reconciliation will take time, but if we can stop the destruction, we can make a start. Pete is desperate to be right—that's become all he cares about. Sheep people are bad, and cattle people are good. For him, it's black and white. That's how he sees it." He rubbed his hands over the stubble of beard on his face and leaned back. "There's a middle ground here, Nita. I don't have all the answers, but that I know for sure."

She studied him for a long moment, noticing how much he reminded her of his father—another man who had sought to bring people together. "Nell is expecting your child," she reminded him. "She's already lost one husband and had to fend for herself and her boy. Now you would risk putting her through that again?"

Trey's sigh told her she had hit on the nerve that was at the center of those hushed but angry exchanges. She pressed her point. "She's afraid, Trey, and that can't be good for her or that baby. Let Seth and Jess handle this. It's a good plan on the face of things, but you need to stay out of it."

She wiped her hands on a towel and crossed the room so she was standing next to his chair. "You need to stay here. Didn't you promise Joshua you would play ball with him and his cousins when they came over?"

"Yeah, I did, but—"

"Then keep your promise. Let the others deal with Pete." She held his gaze as she added, "I have asked nothing of you, Trey, but I am asking for this."

Trey stood, and as always, she wondered at how this tall, broad-shouldered man could ever have been a sickly child so frail that she'd had doubts about him even making it to adulthood. He hugged her.

"Between you and Nell, a guy doesn't have a chance," he said, but he was smiling when he released her. "I'll think about it, okay?"

It was as much as she was likely to get, so she agreed.

"Good. Now let me make up a cup of my special tea for your wife. She'll be feeling better in no time."

Trey laughed. "Your special tea has a way of curing most ills, Nita, but it's not what you put in it. It's the threat that if it doesn't work, you'll come up with something even more foul."

"Never you mind," Juanita fumed, but as she turned away, she smiled. Trey would stay away from the danger—she was sure of that. He loved that woman too much to cause her any undue worry.

❧

On Sunday, Trey and Nell arrived at the church and saw their opportunity at once. Lottie and the boys were just approaching while Pete Collins stood outside the double doors in his role as church deacon, greeting people—or at least the ranchers and their families. Nell called out to her sister-in-law.

"Lottie! I'm so glad to see you. Trey and I would like for you and the boys to come home with us after services. Juanita is preparing a feast, and Trey promises to play ball with the boys while you and I have a good long visit."

"You'd all be welcome to spend the night," Trey added. "We've plenty of room."

While she was not privy to the true reason for the invitation, Lottie played her unwitting part to perfection. "What do you say, boys?" she asked.

Ira and Spud gave their grudging approval, and the two families entered the church together—passing Pete Collins on their way.

Later, as the service progressed, Jess elbowed Trey

and nodded toward a door at the side of the church. Collins was leaving.

When the service ended, Jess kissed Addie and rode off. He would meet up with Seth and the soldiers and get into position to see if Collins and his men showed up at Lottie's place. Trey suggested Josh ride with Lottie and her sons to be sure they found their way to his ranch. At least that was the excuse. The truth was, he wanted time alone with Nell.

"With any luck at all, this thing will be over by sundown," he said.

"Did you see Addie? She's more worried than she lets on, and I imagine Amanda is beside herself thinking about Seth. We should have invited them to be at the ranch while we wait."

"Jess and Seth are lawmen, Nellie. Addie and Amanda know that. They know the risks."

"Still, you said it yourself—Pete Collins is a desperate man. And that makes him especially dangerous. If he feels cornered, no telling what he might do."

He knew she was right. He also knew the plan was in motion and there was nothing to be done but wait. He let the silence simmer between them.

Nell was the one to break it. "If this all works out the way you plan, Trey, what then?"

"Either way, we get back to our original idea—combining your property and mine and raising both sheep and cattle, proving that they can coexist."

"Maybe we should take in Lottie's sheep as well. After all, her land and mine combined aren't a quarter of your ranch, so it wouldn't be that much more to deal with. And with Ernest gone…"

"We'll see what Lottie wants to do. I'll offer, but it's her choice—hers and the boys'."

"Even if she refuses and insists on going it alone, we'll still help out, won't we?"

Trey grinned and shook his head. "Woman, you do have this way of wanting to take care of the whole world, don't you?" He wrapped his arm around her as he drove their wagon with the other hand. "Lottie and her boys are family, Nell, and we are always there for family."

As promised, Juanita had a spread waiting for them the likes of which even Trey had never seen. Sopapillas, empanadas, crusty bolillos, a pot of hominy posole covered with chocolate-infused mole, along with a pot of simmering frijoles, plenty of fresh tortillas, and buñuelos for dessert. Locally produced wine and sarsaparilla for the boys rounded out the feast.

Afterward, while Nell and Lottie insisted on helping Juanita clear and clean up, Trey took the boys out to the yard, called for a couple of his cowhands to join them, and laid out bases and a pitcher's mound. Trey put any remaining anger he was holding toward Ira aside. What was happening today was too important. He tossed Ira the ball. "You pitch," he said.

Ira nodded and strode to the makeshift pitcher's mound.

It didn't take long for everyone to get into the game, whooping at hits and runs, sliding into the makeshift bases, and recording the score of each inning by scraping out the numbers in the sandy dirt with a stick.

All the while, he kept watching for Jess. When he hadn't come by late afternoon as the sun sank lower in the sky, he began to worry that something had gone wrong. If Collins had not shown up at all, Jess would have returned, signaled, and gone on back to town. But this late in the day, something had happened. To Trey's way of thinking, it shouldn't have taken this long for the soldiers to step in and take charge.

Several times, he saw Juanita come to the door of the kitchen and study the horizon and trail that led down from the hills to their property. Trey had gotten Nell and Lottie involved in the ballgame to keep their minds off the passing of time. Still, there was no sign of Jess.

"*Cómelo!* Supper!" Juanita shouted as she rang the bell hanging outside the kitchen.

With most of his cow hands out on the range, Trey had handpicked the men who would stick around to play ball and share a meal with the Galway boys. He was gratified to see Ira and Spud talking easily to his men. Of course, they were replaying the game and not debating livestock, but still, it was progress.

Because it would be dark before Lottie and the boys could make it home, Nell persuaded her it was too dangerous to make the trip at such a late hour. "Stay," she pleaded.

Joshua turned to his cousins. "If you stay the night, Ma sometimes lets me sleep down in the bunkhouse. We play cards and stuff, and the men even let me brush down the horses." He turned to Nell. "We can spend the night in the bunkhouse, right?"

Nell hesitated, glancing at the cowhands before answering.

"It would be all right, ma'am," one of them said.

"Clearly, I'm outnumbered here," she said with a smile. "Lottie? Is this all right with you?"

"I suppose." She hesitated and looked at her sons for confirmation.

"Do you play cards for money?" Ira asked.

"Matchsticks," the cowboy replied.

Ira shrugged. "Sure. I guess." As always, Spud followed his lead.

Once the boys had headed off to the bunkhouse and Nell and Lottie had gone to make up the guest room, Trey sought out Juanita. "I'm worried, Nita. Jess should have come back by now—that was the plan. No matter how this thing went down, he would have come here to let us know what happened."

She didn't argue with what they both knew he needed to do. "Take one of the hands with you," she said.

"I'll pick up a couple of men from the range as I go." He strapped on his gun belt and pulled his hat tight over his forehead.

Juanita handed him the medical kit they kept supplied in the event of a scorpion bite, broken bone, or worse. "Just in case," she said.

"Tell Nell I'll be back as soon as possible, and keep Lottie and her boys here, no matter how long it takes me to get back." He kissed Juanita's forehead and left. He wanted to say goodbye to Nell, but she was in the library with Lottie, and Lottie would have questions he wasn't ready to answer.

As he saddled a horse from the corral, he could hear laughter from the bunkhouse and knew the card game had begun. The way his cowhands had done their part in including the Galway boys gave him hope that he was not being unrealistic in believing it was indeed possible for herders and ranchers to get along. Cowboys had a live-and-let-live philosophy that allowed them to fit into most any situation. They were a transient group, following the work as the seasons changed. But most were loyal to the man paying them—at least while they worked for him.

He galloped toward the Galway ranch. His plan was to pick up a couple of his cowboys on the way, but as he rode, he saw that they were too far away. They were moving the herd to higher ground, headed in the opposite direction. If he made the detour necessary to reach them, he would lose valuable time, and his gut told him something had gone terribly wrong. There was no time to waste, so he chose to ride cross-country, taking the shortest route possible to reach his destination.

Taking care not to be seen, Trey slid from his horse and crawled on his belly to a place among the boulders that would give him a clear view.

Everything below was as it should be—no fire or damage visible. The property appeared deserted. If Collins had been there, he'd either left or been apprehended by Jess, Seth, and the militia. But if that were the case, why hadn't Jess come to let him know it was over?

He mounted his horse and rode slowly toward the deserted yard. A few sheep grazed unattended in a field behind the house. With all the times the flock had been raided, it had dwindled in numbers to a few hundred instead of thousands. He wondered if the flock he saw in the distance also included Nell's sheep. If so, she and Lottie didn't have much more than the land. It would take years to rebuild the livestock to the point where either woman would see any profit.

He reined in at the barn and, hand resting on the butt of his gun, he slowly approached the open double doors and looked around inside. In the middle of the barn floor, someone had piled up kindling and bales of hay. He smelled the fumes of kerosene and saw the cast-off can that had held it. Then he went to the house, checked the doors, and found them locked, and he saw no sign of occupancy—or intrusion. The only signs anyone had been there recently came in the form of a jumble of hoofprints in the yard and the mud and dirt on the porch that he suspected Lottie would have insisted on sweeping up before coming to town for church that morning. All was quiet, and for once, he found no comfort in the silence. He sat down on the front step and tried to figure out his next move. That's when he saw the drops of blood. They ran from the lower step of the porch across the yard to the tangle of hoofprints.

The way he figured it, someone had been shot and had made it to a horse and taken off. With the sun nearly set and all the different prints mingled together and obliterating each other, he was having trouble following the trail.

Then he heard gunfire. One shot. Another.

He didn't wait for the third but ran for his horse, mounted, and took off toward the sound.

◈

Nell could barely sit still, much less listen to Lottie going on about how Henry used to always say this or that. She had hoped her sister-in-law would plead exhaustion and settle into her room, but instead, she seemed to be prepared to talk through the night. Nell took her cues from Lottie's facial expressions and certain phrases such as "remember that time." She limited her reactions to a smile, a shrug, or a sympathetic murmur. Not wanting to raise questions from Lottie about where he might be going at this late hour, Trey had waved to Nell from the kitchen as he kissed Nita's cheek and left. And as the minutes and then hours ticked by, all she could think of was when her husband might return.

Of course, Lottie knew nothing of the real reasons she and the boys had been invited to come to the ranch and stay over, but Nell was well aware of why Trey had wanted to bring her brother's family to the safety of his ranch. What she didn't know was where her husband had gone, why Jess had never come to tell them the results of the day, and whether either man was somewhere out of danger.

The night Calvin died, she had been at home, not suspecting she would never see him again. These days, every time Trey left her at the ranch, she felt a tightening in her chest and a constant chant of *what if* drumming in her head.

"Henry used to say—"

"Lottie, what are we going to do about rebuilding the flock? So many of our breeding ewes have been slaughtered. Lambs are without their mothers, and what stock we do have to take to market in fall is pitiful." She hoped the change in topic would give Lottie pause, providing Nell a respite from her sister-in-law's chatter.

Finally, her sister-in-law stopped chattering, bowed her head, and folded her hands in her lap. "I don't know," she whispered. "I don't know what to do, Nell. I've thought of selling out to that cattleman, Mr. Collins. He's stopped by once or twice since Ernest left. Seems like a decent sort, and he made a good case for how the money he would give me for the land would set me and the boys up for some time—long enough for Ira and Spud to find work and get settled on their own."

"That's not what Henry wanted for you or his sons, Lottie."

"I know." She sniffed back tears, but then her head snapped up, and she glared at Nell. "But Henry's not here, is he? And I don't have some man with his own fortune wanting to marry me and take on my boys, do I?"

"We're family, Lottie. Nothing has changed about that."

Lottie stood and pressed the flats of her hands over her skirt. "*Everything* has changed, Nell, whether you want to admit it or not. I'm tired, and with Ernest gone, me and the boys need to get back to our place first thing tomorrow. The shepherds can handle things tonight, especially since there's so little stock to watch. Thank you for your hospitality."

She walked stiff-backed down the hall, and a minute later, Nell heard the soft click of the guest room door. Relieved, she practically ran to the front door, tearing it open as she hurried into the courtyard and scanned the dark night for any sign of Trey.

Where are you, my love?

⁓

There were two more shots as Trey rode hard toward the sound that ricocheted off the rocky terrain. And then silence. He pulled up, trying to decide which way to go. He studied the outline of the landscape silhouetted against the night sky. *There!* He saw a man move behind a cluster of boulders. It was his brother—and Jess was hurt.

Trey slid from his horse, grabbed the medical kit, and followed the ledge until he was able to easily jump a narrow chasm and reach the other side. "Jess?" he hissed as he edged his way along the narrow path.

Nothing.

He moved higher. "Jess!" he said more loudly.

This time, he heard a low moan—and it was close. He stepped carefully around a large rock that jutted out over the chasm below. His brother was on the other side, propped up against the rock and clutching his blood-soaked shoulder.

"You want to stop that caterwauling and give me a hand here?" Jess grumbled. His voice was weak, and his head lolled to one side as if it were too much for him to hold it straight.

Trey immediately opened the kit and took out a roll of bandages. Then he unbuttoned his shirt and shrugged out of it. He wadded it up and pressed it against his brother's shoulder like he'd seen Addie do once or twice. "Got to stop that bleeding," he muttered. "Stay with me, Jess. I'll get you to Addie, and she'll fix you right up. You know how good she is with—"

"She's gonna be madder than all get-out," Jess muttered. "She told me not to come. Maybe shoulda listened."

"Stop talkin' and lean on me so I can get you bandaged up here," Trey said.

Jess chuckled. "Well, listen to you, little brother, ordering me around like you're in charge."

"I am in charge, at least for now." He tied off the ends of the bandages. "Okay, wrap your good arm around me, and let's get you on your feet. Where's your horse?"

"Collins shot it—and me. His own horse slid on the path and threw him, so he shot it as well. That man's got no respect for man or beast."

Typical Jess, Trey thought. *Making light of something serious.*

Together, they hobbled away from the ledge, back toward the chasm Trey knew he could easily span, even carrying the weight of his brother. Finally, they reached the flat of a mesa on the other side, and Trey eased his brother down. "Wait here while I round up my horse."

"Horse can't take both of us," Jess called out as Trey walked away.

"He's only takin' you. He knows the way back to the ranch, and once he gets there, Nita will take over. You tell a couple of our cowhands where to find me and Collins and send them back. I'll wait."

Trey could hear Jess still muttering his objections once he led his horse to the spot where he'd left his brother.

"This is a bad idea," Jess argued. "You against Collins? He'll kill you, Trey. Wait for the militia. They took off to round up Collins's men."

"I can get the jump on him," Trey said as he hoisted his brother into the saddle and used the reins to anchor him. "Just in case you pass out along the way," he explained. "Don't want you falling and breaking that hard head of yours." Then he gave a whoop and slapped the horse's hindquarters, and it took off, headed hell-bent for home.

He could hear Jess yelling at him as he watched to be sure his brother was well on his way. Then he followed the ledge, protected by a wall of boulders, back to where he'd found Jess, knowing Pete had to be nearby.

He pulled his gun from its holster. Trey was not a man of violence. The truth was, he understood guns and rifles only as necessary evils for living on the range, but surely those days of men taking the law into their own hands were coming to their end. And yet out there somewhere was a desperate man who had nothing to lose.

Above him, he heard a trickle of loose gravel and waited. He inched himself to a place between two boulders where he could see the path that led to the top of the cliff. Pete Collins was dragging himself along the edge of the cliff. The man was clearly wounded, his one leg useless.

Trey crept closer, saw that Pete was focused intently on the spot across the narrow gap where Trey had found Jess.

"You're a dead man, Jess Porterfield," Pete shouted as he steadied a rifle on a flat rock and took aim.

Knowing he had the drop on Pete, Trey holstered his gun and moved quickly to the top of a large boulder. He leaped and landed on the rancher's wounded leg, twisting it hard as he came down. As he had hoped, Pete lost control of his rifle. Better yet, the rifle went clattering over the cliff. In seconds, he had Pete on his stomach and pinned to the ground. "Shut up," he ordered when the rancher kept whining about his leg.

Trey stood, pulled out his gun, and aimed it at Pete. "Don't move." From his back pocket, he pulled the piggin' strings every cowhand carried when out on the range. He straddled Pete, set the gun out of reach, and prepared to hog-tie the rancher.

But Pete was strong, and in spite of his injured leg, he used both hands to push Trey off balance and grab the pistol. "Back off, Porterfield, or I'll blow your face clean off." He scooted himself into a sitting position and leveled the gun with both hands.

Trey did as the man instructed. "Come on, Pete. Give up. It's over. The soldiers will be here any time now and—"

"Just shut up. For once in your miserable life, stop talkin'."

The gun wavered, and Trey saw Pete was sweating and having trouble keeping his eyes open. The earth around them was soft and sandy. Slowly, subtly, Trey scraped dirt into a small pile with the toe of his boot. "Shoot me, Pete, and you'll spend the rest of your life in jail—if they don't hang you first."

Pete struggled to his feet, keeping his one leg stiff and grimacing in pain as he propped himself against a tree trunk. Trey saw his chance. He picked up a handful of loose dirt and flung it at Pete, hoping the wind would carry it into Pete's eyes and he could overpower the man. But the wind shifted, and the dirt hit Pete in the mouth, infuriating him further.

He charged at Trey, and the two of them fell to the ground, the loaded gun between them. Trey focused on getting the gun, pinning Pete with his weight as he forced the man's arm up and away. Grabbing a large rock, he slammed it down on Pete's hand. Pete let go of the gun, but his other hand came up and grabbed Trey by the throat. His hand spanned the width of Trey's neck, and he began to squeeze, his eyes wild with rage and revulsion.

Trey could feel himself losing consciousness as he fought for breath. *Hit him*, his brain, already foggy, ordered. He realized he was still clutching the rock. He raised his arm. Pete tightened his grip, and in an effort to break the man's hold, Trey let go of the rock. They rolled so that now Pete was on top of Trey. With one hand, Trey tried to pry Pete's fingers free of their grip while with the heel of the other, he swung wildly.

He could feel himself losing the battle, but he had too much to live for to die on this dusty mesa at the hands of a man who had tried to destroy everything his family stood for. This time, Trey wouldn't miss. He closed his hand around loose sand and flung it directly into Pete's eyes. The rancher screamed and cursed and let go of Trey's throat.

In seconds, Trey had rolled away. He was gasping for air as he located the pistol and threw it a good distance away from Pete. Then, still choking and coughing but determined to put an end to this man's reign of terror once and for all, he grabbed the piggin' strings, rolled Pete roughly to his stomach, and straddled him again.

"My leg!" Pete raged. "You're gonna break it."

"I reckon you already took care of that before I ever got here. Stop struggling and lie still, and it won't hurt so much." After he finished with Pete, he retrieved his gun, shoved it in the holster, and started down the trail.

"Wait! You can't leave me here. The coyotes—"

"We're gonna be here a while, assuming Jess makes it back to the ranch, which you'd best hope he does. Best hope he's conscious enough to send help, or that leg's gonna be a lot worse by daylight. I'm gonna gather some kindling for a fire."

Trey gathered some dried cactus and wood. Keeping his distance from Pete, he set to building a fire. "Hopefully whoever Jess sends to find us will see the smoke and get here quicker."

"Why don't you just shoot me and be done with it?" Collins snarled.

"Too easy. I want to be sure you have lots of time to consider the error of your ways."

The fire crackled and popped and cast a circle of light around them. Trey settled himself on a chair-sized rock, leaned against a boulder, and lowered his hat over his eyes. "Could be a while," he said. "Best get some rest."

"You expect me to sleep trussed up like some heifer? Show me a little of that compassion you're so famous for, Trey. I'm hurtin' here, and if my leg gets infected—"

Trey ignored him. "Why'd you do all those things, Pete? What did those folks ever do to you?"

"Them woolies was ruining the land and the water. And them herders just aren't our kind, Trey. Even somebody like you has to know that. They don't fit in. I'll wager you that no matter what you do, you'll never see cattle ranchers and herders come together. They might tolerate each other, but they ain't never gonna *like* each other. It's like the Mexicans—we tolerate them, sure, but—"

"Just stop talkin', Pete. The stuff that comes out of your mouth makes me sick to my stomach. People are people, and more and more of those 'Mexicans' you like to talk about are born right here in this country. That makes them as American as you or me. Everybody came from someplace else, Pete, so where do you get off tacking on labels that brand others?"

Pete snorted. "Next you're gonna be tellin' me you married that herder's widow because you *loved* her." He put an insulting singsong tone to the word *loved*.

"We are not discussing my wife," Trey said through gritted teeth.

Pete ignored his warning. "Can't say as I blame you wanting a piece of that. Looks to me like under her skirt lies a pair of legs that would fit just right around a man's hips, pull him in real tight."

Trey knew what the man was trying to do. He held his tongue—and his temper—but Pete didn't know when to quit pushing.

"And she's still got a firm bosom—can't hide that.

You ever suckle at those breasts, Trey? Bet she's got enough fullness there to fill a man's hands and then some."

Trey felt his hand close around an extra piece of wood he'd saved to add to the fire as needed. Slowly, he sat up, knowing Pete couldn't see him from his facedown position.

"Yep, I've studied on it, and my guess is that little lady must be a regular hellion in bed. You're one lucky bastard, Trey. Course she's used goods, but better leavings like that than fresh meat that has to be trained." He snickered and then froze as he realized Trey was standing over him, the club in one hand. "Whatcha planning to do with that stick?" he whined, struggling to roll to his back.

"If ever I hear you say one more disrespectful word about my wife or any of her kin, Collins, I will not only kill you, I'll enjoy it and feel no remorse."

"Ah, Trey, where's your sense of humor? You know I don't mean half of what I say and—"

Trey squatted beside the man and let the club come down hard within an inch of the man's face.

Pete flinched, and his eyes bulged with a mix of pain and terror. "You're plum loco," he managed.

"Maybe so, but you and I both know after what you've put this community through these last months, no one would blame me." He pulled out his knife and cut a couple of the ropes so he could grab Collins by his shirtfront and stand him upright. It surprised Trey to realize the rancher was shorter and punier than he seemed. Trey dragged him to a tree and used the rope to anchor him there.

"Look, Trey, we can work this out."

"Stop talkin', Collins. All I'm planning to do at the moment is splint that leg of yours so maybe we can both get some shut-eye before dawn."

He cut open Pete's pants leg and, as he'd done to his shirt for Jess, tore the fabric into strips. Then he laid down the stick he'd been using to threaten Pete and took hold of the man's ankle. "This is gonna hurt," he muttered, then stood and put his weight behind pulling hard on the leg to straighten it.

Pete yelled and then passed out, making the rest of the work easy. Trey tied the splint into place. Although the night was cold, he was sweating hard by the time he finished. He hoped he'd done the right thing and, realizing his concern for the man was his first thought, he laughed and shook his head. Maybe he *was* too soft for his own good. But then he recalled the emotions he'd struggled with as Collins taunted him with his filthy comments about Nell. In that moment, he'd come closer to killing another man than he'd ever been before.

He went back to his position on the rock near the fire. Maybe he wasn't cut out for this life. How many times had some other cowboy made crude comments about Trey's love for sketching and painting? He knew the only reason he held the position he did within the cattlemen's cooperative was because of their respect for his family name. If his father—or even Jess—had been leading the push for peace, it would be done by now. Hell, his eldest sister, Maria, had commanded more respect during the years she ran the ranch than Trey did.

He slept fitfully, waking frequently to tend the

fire and check on Pete. As the sky lightened in the east, he noticed Pete's leg was badly swollen. The man moaned and mumbled in his sleep, crying out from time to time. He was feverish, so Trey soaked his bandana with water from his canteen and bathed Pete's face and neck.

"They'll be here soon," he promised, hoping he was right. He untied the ropes and tried his best to make Pete more comfortable.

His stomach grumbled, and he pulled a piece of jerky from his pocket and chewed on it while he kept watch for any sign of rescue.

"Porterfield?" Pete's voice was weak.

"Yeah?"

"I didn't mean them things I said before...about your wife."

"Then why say them?"

Pete coughed. "Just trying to get at you. I don't understand you."

Trey untwisted the cap from his canteen and passed it to Pete, who seemed surprised to realize he was no longer tied up. He took a swallow and spit half of it out as he choked.

"Take it easy," Trey instructed. "That's it for water, so let's don't waste it, just in case."

Pete returned the canteen and lay down again. "This business with the herders—you're convinced our side can't win, aren't you?"

"It's not about winning, Pete. Unless we can find a way to make our peace, everybody loses." He noticed the sweat beading Pete's forehead and soaking his shirt. "Stop talking, Pete. Save your strength."

The other man struggled to raise himself onto one elbow. He grasped Trey's forearm. "Can't go to prison. Family would never—"

"You shoulda thought about them before you started down this road," Trey said, wrenching his arm away.

"What if them woolies ain't all dead?" Pete muttered, slurring his words as he fought to stay conscious. "Some…sure…had to make a point." The man rambled on for a moment about "throwing away good money" and something about "market" before he finally passed out again.

Trey went back to his post, watching for any sign of help as the sun rose and the shadows that had covered the land evaporated. He saw the cloud of dust first and then the riders—three soldiers, one of them driving a wagon with a spare horse tied to the back. Trey climbed to the highest point and stood with his arms in the air. He fired a single shot, saw the convoy hesitate and then turn in his direction.

It was over, finally. But it wasn't—not really. Pete would go to trial, and with his men singing like choir boys, there was certainly enough to convict him. But the man had done a great deal of damage. Nell would be all right, but others like Lottie Galway and her boys were unlikely to be able to recover from their losses. So to Trey's way of thinking, it would never be over until both sides could find their way back to the kind of life they'd come here to build in the first place.

❧

When the horse carrying Jess came trotting into the yard, Nell was standing outside the kitchen. She'd been waiting for Trey, determined to be there when he returned, no matter the hour.

"Nita!" she shouted. "Somebody help now!"

Two cowhands came running from the bunkhouse along with Juanita and Eduardo from the house, and Nell began loosening the ties holding Jess on the horse. The man was half out of his head as the two cowboys lifted him and carried him inside. Nell kept pace while Juanita gave orders.

"One of you ride into town and bring Addie. Eduardo, get me that bar of soap and a pan of clean water from the kitchen. Nell—"

But Nell had leaned in to speak to Jess. "Jess, have you seen Trey? Is he—"

Jess opened his eyes and squinted at her, then he gave her a loopy grin. "Hello, Nellie. You doing okay?"

She knew then that he was not in his right mind, because never in all the time she had known the man had he asked after her well-being.

"Jess, what happened?" She resisted the urge to shake him hard and bring him to his senses. "That's Trey's horse out there. Where is my husband?"

Jess frowned, and it was evident he was trying hard to focus. He settled his gaze on Eduardo. "Deadman's Point," he mumbled. "Trey's there with Collins. Tell Ashwood and—" His eyelids fluttered and closed.

"He's out," Juanita announced as she pulled off Jess's boots and then covered him with an afghan. "Well, go on," she barked when she saw her husband and the other cowboy standing by the door. "God willing, you'll cross path with some of the soldiers mixed up in this, and they can help. Meanwhile, Trey's up there with that mad man."

The two men hurried away, and a moment later, Nell heard them ride off.

"What can I do?" Nell asked.

"Nothing to be done but wait for Addie to get here." Juanita collapsed onto a straight chair next to the sofa, clearly settling in to keep a vigil until Jess's wife arrived.

"I'll fix breakfast for Lottie and the boys," Nell said. She needed to be busy, or surely her fear for Trey would overcome her. She hurried off to the kitchen. She set Juanita's favorite iron skillet on the stove, spread lard in the bottom, and chopped an onion. At first, she blamed the fumes for making her eyes water, but after a moment, she realized she was crying for real. Her hands trembled. She set down the knife and the onion and gripped the edge of the sink, Juanita's words echoing in her head—*mad man*. What if Pete had attacked Trey? Killed him?

"What's going on, Ma?" Joshua rubbed sleep from his eyes as he entered the kitchen. "How come you're cooking? Where is everybody?"

"Shhh. Jess is resting. He had a little accident, so Juanita is taking care of him while I make breakfast. Are your cousins awake?"

"No. We stayed up pretty late last night," he admitted with a sheepish grin. "Where's Trey?"

"He had to go out for a while." She sniffed back her tears, dumped the chopped onion into the sizzling pan, and sliced a large sweet potato into the mix. After adding some water and dried red chilies before covering the pan to let the vegetables simmer, she reached for eggs and saw there were only two. "Josh, go down to the coop and collect the eggs for me, please." She handed him the basket. "And while you're out there, wake Ira and Spud and tell them to get dressed and come up to the house for breakfast."

Her son took the basket and grinned. "Ma, you called me 'Josh' like Trey does. I like that." He raced out the door, shouting for his cousins to wake up as he went.

Nell heard the door to Lottie's room open. Her sister-in-law had no idea of the real reason Trey had wanted her and her boys to stay the night at his ranch. "Good morning," she said when she heard Lottie's step approaching.

"Was there trouble?" Lottie asked. "I heard shouting, and I looked out the window, and it seemed like someone was hurt and…" She took one look at Nell's tear-stained face and reached out to her. "Oh, Nell, it isn't…I mean Trey is not…"

"I don't know," Nell admitted. She poured two mugs of coffee. "Let's sit for a minute, Lottie. I've got something to tell you."

Twelve

THE MORNING SEEMED TO STRETCH ON FOR HOURS AND hours. Lottie set the boys to doing the morning chores usually handled by Eduardo and the cowhands. Addie arrived and removed the bullet from Jess's shoulder, all the while lecturing her husband on the risks he took that were driving her to an early grave.

"It's a minor wound. You'll live," she said as she fitted him with a sling to support his arm. "Not sure about the rest of us. Now, tell us what happened." She motioned for Juanita, Nell, and Lottie to sit in the chairs closest to the sofa. She stood.

Jess skimmed over the details. He, Seth, and the militia had stationed themselves around the Galway ranch, and sure enough, not long after, Collins and a gang of his men arrived. They gathered kindling in the barn, intent on setting it afire. "Collins was just about to give the order to start the fire when we surrounded them. He made a run for it, and one of the soldiers shot him, but he still managed to ride off. I took off after him."

"Of course you did," Addie muttered, rolling her eyes. "Where was Seth? He's the sheriff."

"He'd moved in on the men in the barn, wanted to be sure they didn't light that fire."

"Did Trey—"

Jess looked at her. "He wasn't there, Nell. He came on me and Pete later after Collins shot me and my horse. We were at a standoff when Trey came upon us. Found me and tricked me into coming back here while he went after Collins himself. He saved my life," he added as if he couldn't quite believe it.

"He's been there all night with that man?" Juanita's dismay was evident in the way she twisted her hands and moved to a window as if doing so would bring Trey back.

Nell's throat closed, and for a moment, she thought she might not be able to breathe. At the same time, fear gripped her heart. She willed herself to listen as Jess continued.

"Collins likely broke his leg when his horse went down, and I think one of the soldiers got a shot off as he fled the scene. Trey's in no danger from him."

"So you say," Juanita muttered.

"I thought before I passed out…I thought… You sent some men to get Trey, didn't you?" Jess's voice shook as if he was uncertain he'd actually given them the information they needed to find his brother.

"We did," Juanita said, "but even riding full out, it's over an hour to Deadman's Point from here." She glanced at Nell and crossed the room to stand with her. "Now you listen to me, Nell Porterfield. Trey is smart and strong. He'll find his way back to us. May take some time, but he'll be here."

Nell noticed how the older woman's voice

quivered her and her eyes shone with unshed tears. She knew Juanita was every bit as scared as she was. Wrapping her arms around the woman who loved Trey as much as her own sons, she murmured, "We'll wait together." She knew by the way Juanita nodded and returned her embrace that the chasm that had separated them ever since Javier's death had been bridged. They were two women who loved Trey, and they would stand together no matter what came.

Trey helped the soldiers put Pete on the wagon bed. "Pete, you said something earlier about the sheep, about there being more saved from the stampede. What did you mean?"

Collins squinted at him as if trying to decide how much to tell him. "Maybe we can make a deal," he said, his voice raspy.

"What kind of a deal?" Trey didn't trust the man, but if there was a chance some more of Nell's and Lottie's sheep were still alive, that would be the best possible news—especially for Lottie and her boys.

"Talk to your brother-in-law about having the court go easy on me, and maybe…" His words were slurred, and he passed out before he could complete the sentence.

"Gotta get going," a soldier said.

Trey nodded and watched the wagon rumble away before heading for home. Along the way, he thought of nothing but where Pete might have stashed those sheep. Or maybe he'd been lying to use hope as a bargaining chip. Tomorrow, he would ride over to Pete's place, have a look around, and find out if any sheep were there.

❧

Nell was the first to spot Trey. She hurried across the courtyard to meet him, her heart racing as she prayed he was not injured. To her relief, he grinned when he saw her and ran to meet her. He caught her in his arms and lifted her so that she rested against him. They kissed, and she pulled back to study him, tracing his features as if that would tell her what she needed to know.

"Are you hurt?" she asked. "Because Jess said—"

"I'm fine, Nellie, just fine." He set her down and wrapped his arm around her as they walked back to the house. A ranch hand took charge of Trey's horse, and, hands on hips, Juanita watched from the doorway.

"Have you had anything to eat?" she asked when Trey and Nell reached the house.

"A piece of jerky," he replied. "I was countin' on you saving me something." He grinned at the housekeeper.

"You know I did. You smell like a wool blanket that's been left out in the rain, and you need a shave." She touched his cheek on the pretense of examining his whiskers, but Nell wasn't fooled. Like her, Juanita needed to assure herself he was safe and home. "Go get yourself cleaned up, and see that your wife takes a rest. She's been worried sick."

"I'll help," Lottie said as she followed Juanita into the kitchen.

Trey looked at Nell. "I'm sorry, Nellie. I thought

Jess would assure you I was in no danger." His eyes widened with concern. "Jess made it back, didn't he?"

"I'm in here, little brother," Jess shouted from the front of the house. "No thanks to you. Did they arrest Collins?"

Trey crossed the hall so he could speak face-to-face with his brother. "Yeah. They also have several of his cowhands in custody."

"It's over then," Jess said, and he squeezed Addie's hand.

"Not quite," Trey replied. "Pete hinted at the possibility that not all the sheep were stampeded over that cliff. I think he saw an opportunity and took some to a place where he could go back for them later and sell them at market. If there are more than the ones we were able to round up, that could be good news for Lottie."

Nell drew in a breath. "You mean Lottie and the boys are not ruined?"

"Now, don't get your hopes up too high, darlin'," Trey said. "Pete could have been bluffing, hoping to make a deal."

"Or he could just be the meanest son of a gun in these parts," Jess added. "Could be he wanted to raise hopes and then when there were no sheep, he'd have the last laugh."

Addie shushed him and turned to Nell. "It would probably be best not to mention the possibility to Lottie until we're sure," she said. "Your sister-in-law is still in a pretty fragile place, and the closer she gets to seeing her son in court, the worse it will get for her."

"I won't say anything, but we have to know." She

turned to Trey. "Not right away, of course. You need your rest."

"I'll go first thing tomorrow," he assured her.

"Take our shepherds with you. They know how to track, and if anyone can find those sheep, they can."

Behind them, Nell heard Juanita let out an exasperated huff. None of them had heard her enter the room, but now they gave her their full attention. "If the four of you are done solving the problems of the world, maybe Trey could have his bath and a hot meal?"

"Yes, ma'am," Trey said, and as he passed her on his way to the bedroom, he leaned down and kissed her cheek.

"Get away from me. You smell to high heaven." But she was smiling as she returned to the kitchen.

Nell followed Trey down the hall. While he undressed, Eduardo brought pails of hot water and filled the tub for him. Once he had sunk into the steaming bath with a sigh of pure exhaustion, Nell washed his hair and sat on the edge of the copper tub to shave him. With each pass of the straight razor, she revealed more of his handsome face and thought how blessed she was to have married him.

"How's the baby?" he asked, pressing his wet hand to her stomach.

"Fine." She hesitated, afraid to jinx their good fortune.

Trey pushed himself to a sitting position in the tub. "Fine, but?"

"No, truly. We are both doing well. I'm just a little superstitious. I mean, with Calvin—"

"I'm not Calvin," Trey said softly.

"I know." She hated upsetting him, so she changed the subject as she finished shaving him. "Joshua noticed all the family portraits you've done and is curious when you might do one of him—and me."

Trey chuckled. "How do you know I haven't already started?"

"Truly? When can we see them?"

"Go get my sketchbook while I dry off and put on some clean clothes. It's in the library."

Nell had seen the sketchbook, had even seen Trey working on a sketch when he left their bed late at night and needed to think. But on the rare occasions when she'd wandered into the library, she noticed he closed the sketchbook and set it aside before turning to her and holding out his arms to her. So she had never asked to see the work. But now with permission granted, she laid the thick pad on the table and opened it. Inside were pages of drawings of her, of Joshua, of her with Joshua. She spread them out on the long library table and studied each one. In every portrait, she was looking directly out of the page—presumably at the artist—and smiling. Sometimes, the smile was tender, a lifting of the corners of her mouth, and other times, she was almost laughing. He'd made one drawing of her reading with Joshua and another of the two of them sitting outside in the courtyard while he sketched them through the window.

"Got a favorite?" Trey asked, buckling his belt as he padded barefoot into the room.

"I love them all. Oh, Trey, when did you do these? I don't remember posing for them."

"Did most of them from memory at night after you

were asleep." He pointed to one. "This was that day we spent collecting piñon nuts."

"You have such a gift."

He fingered a drawing of her alone. "Yeah, I do at that." He dropped the sketch and took her in his arms. "I have you."

She rested her cheek against his chest and closed her eyes. He was home safe, and the danger they had all been in had passed. They were going to be all right.

And then she thought of Lottie—her husband dead and one son possibly on his way to prison. "Trey, we have to find those sheep," she said softly. "Lottie's future depends on it."

"I'll start hunting for them first thing tomorrow," he promised as he kissed the top of her head. "But tonight, I don't want to think about anyone but my family—you, Josh, and that baby."

She wrapped her arms around his neck and drew him closer. They were kissing when Nell heard Addie clear her throat.

"Sorry to barge in, but if you two don't come eat something, I'm afraid Nita might explode."

Trey laughed and took Nell's hand as they headed for the kitchen. "Can't have that now, can we?"

As they passed in the corridor, Addie whispered, "Remember not to overdo." It was a warning, but it was also the first time since Javier's death that Addie had reached out to her.

Nell paused and squeezed her friend's hand. "I'll be careful," she said. "Besides, as long as you're there, this baby is going to be just fine, right?"

Addie grinned, and it was the smile Nell had come

to cherish—a smile shared between two women who could count on each other to be there through anything that might come.

"Try keeping me away," Addie said. She glanced at Trey. "Seems to me this baby might be in need of a godmother. I'd like to apply for the job if it's open."

"You're hired," Trey replied. "Pay's not much but—"

The rest of his words were drowned out as Nell hugged Addie and the two women squealed with joy.

❧

Juanita sat up late that night, and for once, it was not because she was worried. She simply wanted to drink in the relief of knowing Trey and Jess were both safe. Hopefully with the arrest of Pete Collins and his men, the troubles that had plagued them all for months now were finally over. *Us versus them…those people…* Was it just possible that the two sides had finally come to their senses and realized people were people, regardless of how they made their living? Was it too much to hope that maybe someday people would not judge each other by the color of their skin or where their ancestors had come from? Maybe someday. Not in her lifetime, but maybe in Trey's or his child's.

"That baby will be here before we know it," she said as Eduardo joined her. When they were alone like this, they spoke in their native language. Trey and Nell's baby—a child to be raised right here on the ranch.

"And you'll be spoiling it and then fussing because the kid doesn't listen." He patted her hand as he sat in the rocking chair next to hers.

"Keeps me young," she replied with a smile. "I think Nell will be a fine mother. The way Joshua has turned out is a good omen."

Eduardo lit his pipe, drew on it, and blew out the smoke. "I know you were worried when Trey married her, Nita, but she does seem to be working out just fine."

Juanita snorted. "You make her sound like hired help, a cowhand you might have doubted who has proved himself worthy."

"She's strong, I'll give her that. Not many I know could have come through what she's had to endure without bending—or more likely, breaking."

"She's got one more test ahead—this baby. She lost three before."

"She seems all right."

Juanita shrugged. "Still, Addie's worried. I can tell."

"And you?"

She released a heavy sigh. "We need children on this ranch, Eduardo. Life—we need life and liveliness and laughter. Things are changing so fast, and I don't like it. I want it to be the way it was."

"And we both know that isn't possible." He took hold of her hand and continued to smoke his pipe as he gazed out into the darkness. "You know Nell being here means that boy will be coming around as well."

Juanita didn't have to ask who he meant. Neither of them had been able to look at Ira Galway during the time he'd been at the ranch. They were polite as was their duty, but this was the boy who had killed Javier, and Juanita knew it would take a minor miracle for her to ever be able to look directly at him without showing the anger she felt toward him.

"I know he and his brother and mother will likely be coming around. I don't have to like it, but we must find our way to peace, or this never ends." She heard the front door open and close and saw Trey walk away from the house to the cemetery. It was a walk Juanita had watched him take every night he was home in the months that had passed since Javier's funeral, sometimes with Nell, more often alone. The low wrought-iron gate squealed in protest when he opened it. He touched the markers for his parents' graves and then knelt next to Javier's tombstone.

"There's Trey," Eduardo murmured as if she wouldn't have noticed.

"He still blames himself," she said. "He shouldn't, but he does."

"Maybe it just gives him some peace to be there," Eduardo suggested.

"I hope so," she whispered. "He reminds me of his father more and more every day." She stood. "You should go with him tomorrow to look for those sheep."

"Already planned on it," Eduardo said as he tamped out his pipe. "Got a good feeling about that."

～

The following morning, Trey packed his saddlebags with jerky and other provisions he, Eduardo, and the shepherds were likely to need as they began the search for the missing sheep. He refused to consider that there might not be any sheep at all, but even so, the search would be long and tedious.

"The shepherds suggest we start at the Galway

ranch," Eduardo said. "We can start where the sheep
were grazing that night, and since we know where
some of them died, that might give us a direction."

Trey nodded.

But when they reached the Galway ranch, they saw
a detail of soldiers escorting Ira to a wagon. Lottie and
Spud were standing on the porch.

"What's going on?" Trey asked as he came alongside the wagon and soldiers.

"Judge Ellis is holding court at the fort," one of
the men said. "This one's case comes up first thing
tomorrow."

Trey shifted his attention to Ira. "How are you
holding up?"

The boy was scared, but he put on a brave face.
"I'm all right, but Ma—"

"Eduardo, go send word to Seth and Jess to meet
us at the fort as soon as possible. Then bring Nell
and Juanita here—and Josh as well. We'll be staying
here until the trial is over." He calculated the distance
between the fort and the Galway property and figured
they could make the trip back and forth in just over
an hour. When Eduardo rode away, Trey reached
down and covered Ira's shackled hand with his. "Stay
strong," he said softly.

Ira nodded, but he was shaking with fear. As the
wagon surrounded by soldiers on horseback pulled
away, Ira looked back at his mother and brother and
tried to wave.

"Lottie?" Trey dismounted and approached the
porch. "I've sent for Nell."

Lottie kept her gaze fixed on the wagon carrying

her son. She was dry-eyed, and it occurred to Trey that with everything she'd been through, there were no more tears.

"Spud, you think you can handle the chores on your own for the time being?" he asked.

"Yes, sir." He glanced at his mother and then strode toward the barn, a boy who moved like he knew it was time to be a man.

Trey climbed the steps to the porch. "What did the soldiers tell you, Lottie?"

She shrugged. "Just that the judge had arrived and the trial would start tomorrow." She continued to stare at the now deserted trail. "I didn't give him anything to eat. He's had nothing since breakfast."

"They'll see he's fed at the fort," Trey assured her. Gently, he led her inside. He was out of his element, not knowing what to do. "Can I get you anything?"

"I'll make us some coffee," Lottie said, leading the way to the kitchen. "We can wait for Nell together." She pumped water for the coffee before adding, "And then we can all go to the fort."

The way she said it, Trey knew there was no point arguing.

❧

Juanita was unusually quiet as they made the trip to Lottie's place. Nell noticed that any comment Eduardo made to her was answered with a shrug or a noncommittal grunt. While Juanita sat on the wagon seat next to her husband, Nell sat in back with Joshua. Her son lay on the bare boards of the wagon bed, his head in her lap, his hat covering his face.

"Lottie must be beside herself," Nell observed.

"Hmm," was Juanita's reply.

Nell couldn't stand the silence, so she spoke the thoughts that crowded her mind. "Ira is so young."

"*Sí*," Juanita agreed.

"I can't help thinking if that were Joshua, how would I feel?"

No response. Nell dropped her attempts at conversation and stroked Joshua's hair. She had almost dozed off herself when Juanita made an announcement that brought her wide awake.

"I would like to speak at the trial," she said. She turned so that she could look back at Nell. "Do you think they would allow that?"

Nell was speechless with surprise. "I…what would… You weren't there," she finally managed.

"It was my son who died that day, my son who was there but cannot speak for himself."

Fear grabbed Nell by the throat and held her paralyzed. If Juanita spoke out, would that not makes matters worse for Ira? Nell struggled between her respect and admiration for Javier's parents and her need to do what she could to protect her nephew.

Juanita was still staring at her, still awaiting some form of agreement—or disagreement.

"We'll see what Trey says," Nell said, her voice barely a whisper.

Juanita snorted and waved a dismissive hand. "We'll see what the *judge* says."

When they arrived at Lottie's house, Nell was surprised to see her sister-in-law standing on the porch, wearing her best dress and hat and clutching a carpetbag that was clearly filled and heavy. Trey was outside the barn, speaking with Spud and the shepherds.

"Refresh yourselves if need be," Lottie said the minute they were close enough to hear. "You're welcome to stay in the house, or you can come with me, but I am going to the fort."

Trey walked toward them, his eyes on Nell. "You and Josh should stay here with Nita and Eduardo. Spud is going to need help managing things and—"

"I'm going to the fort," Juanita interrupted.

Trey glanced from Lottie on the porch to Nita in the wagon. He removed his hat as he approached the wagon. "Nita, it would be best if—"

"Don't try and stop me, Trey. This trial is as much our business as anybody's."

Nell took Trey's arm. "She wants to speak at the trial."

"I don't think that would be allowed," Trey replied, clearly every bit as taken aback as Nell had been.

"We'll see," Juanita grumbled through lips she had drawn into a determined line. She settled herself more firmly on the wagon seat. "Nothin' to be lost by asking."

"I'll stay and look after the ranch and the boys," Eduardo said as he climbed down and faced Trey. "She needs to be there, Son."

"We'll all go," Nell suggested, seeing no way out of the impasse. In spite of her outward appearance of strength and determination, to someone who knew her, Lottie looked to be close to a complete breakdown. "All except Eduardo, Spud, and Josh. As you said, they can manage things here." She gripped Trey's arm more firmly, entreating him to accept the plan.

"You need to rest," he insisted.

Nell turned from the others and lowered her voice. "I'm fine. Lottie needs me right now. Please don't fight me, Trey. We'll ride in back while you drive and try to talk sense into Juanita."

Outnumbered, Trey helped Lottie and Nell into the wagon and climbed up to take the reins. Juanita sat next to him but kept her focus straight ahead, as if they were already on their way. Nell saw him glance first at Juanita and then back at her.

"Let's go," she said softly.

❧

Ira's trial was held in a small, barren room next to Colonel Ashwood's office. Even though the fort was technically shut down, it seemed the most logical place to hold the proceedings. The colonel's aide had set up a wooden table at one end of the room and two chairs—one for the judge and the other for the soldier who would record the proceedings. Under the high, narrow windows that lined both sides of the room were two more tables—one where Seth sat next to Colonel Ashwood and across from that, a smaller table where Ira sat alone.

Trey, Nell, Lottie, and Juanita sat in chairs hastily crowded into the room when they'd made their intention to attend the proceedings known. The heat was oppressive with so many people in such close quarters.

Juanita stared at the boy—a child really. Of course, she had seen him before when he and his brother had come to the ranch, but she had kept her distance. Oh, she had done her job—prepared and served food—but she had refused to speak to him or indeed to look at him if she could help it.

Now she had little choice. She saw that he was afraid—and ashamed. The way he had reacted when he saw his mother the night before told Juanita that he had begun to come to terms with how his rash act had affected others. She recalled a time when Javier had exhibited similar humiliation. He had been caught with two other boys harassing an old miner who worked a claim not far from the Porterfield ranch.

Of course, her son hadn't killed anyone. Or had he? Had he been party to the murder of Nell's first husband? Had her son gotten so caught up in Pete Collins's vile hatred of anything that struck him as different that he'd ridden with Collins that night?

"I wish to sit with my son," Lottie said to no one in particular.

Judge Ellis glanced up from the papers he was reading. "Ma'am?"

"That is my son. I would like to sit with him."

The judge looked a bit mystified. "Well, I suppose it would be all right."

Juanita watched Trey move Lottie's chair to the table where Ira sat. Once she was settled, the judge went back to reading the papers, then cleared his throat. "Colonel Ashwood, if you are ready…"

Juanita was vaguely aware that the trial had begun. Colonel Ashwood was standing before the judge reading from a paper that outlined the charges. Jess spoke next, describing the events of the day. Then the judge asked Ira a series of questions. The boy stuttered his way through his answers, his body twitching nervously, his voice barely audible.

It was all going so quickly, and Juanita felt a panic rise in her chest. Everything she'd heard told her the boy would be found guilty and sent away. She had come here to remind the judge that Javier had been brutally murdered, to add to the weight of the evidence against her son's killer. But in Lottie, she saw a mother who was helpless to save her child—and she understood that feeling. So when the judge instructed Ira to stand and was clearly about to pronounce sentence, she knew she had to speak. There was nothing to be gained from vengeance.

Juanita leaped to her feet. "I have something to say, if it please Your Honor," she announced. Her voice echoed off the stone walls in the mostly deserted room.

From the corner of her eyes, she saw Jess half rise from his chair. She fixed him with the look that had brooked no argument when he was a boy, and he sat down again.

"Who are you?" Judge Ellis asked.

"My name is Juanita Mendez. It was my son, Javier, who died that day."

"Mrs. Mendez, the court has heard the information it needs to come to a decision. I know this must be upsetting for you, but I assure you justice will be—"

"May I speak?"

"This is most unusual," Judge Ellis commented more to the colonel than to Juanita, but she stood her ground. The judge looked around the room. "Are there any objections?"

No one spoke. Every eye was fixed on Juanita.

"Very well, Mrs. Mendez, but I would entreat you to be brief."

Juanita stepped away from her chair and walked to the table where Ira stood next to his mother. She gave the boy her full attention, commanding his in return. "On my way here yesterday, I was filled with a fresh dose of all the anger and grief I felt that day they brought my son's body home to me. I wanted to be sure that someone would speak for Javier Mendez, who cannot speak for himself."

Tears rolled down Ira's cheeks, but to his credit, he did not look away.

She looked at Lottie. "But now I think what good will it do to destroy the life of another mother's son? To cast her into that pit of loss?" She moved a step closer and squeezed Lottie's hand before turning to face the judge.

"We do not know your decision, sir, but we can guess based on what we have heard today. As the mother of the victim, as someone who has watched as my neighbors have suffered the loss of life and property, I say it is enough. I am pleading with you to forgive this boy as my husband and I must. Surely in these difficult times, it would be more charitable to forgive than to dole out a punishment, one that will not bring back my son and will destroy not only this boy's life, but that of his mother and brother as well."

Her knees were shaking as she returned to her chair between Trey and Nell, and the only sounds in the room were Lottie Galway's soft sobbing, the rustling of papers, and Trey's long exhaled breath. She took hold of his hand and Nell's and held on as they waited together for the judge to read his decision.

∽

Nell squeezed Juanita's hand, overwhelmed by the woman's benevolence. Ira sat on the edge of his chair, nervously cracking his knuckles while they waited to see what Judge Ellis would do. Lottie was looking at Juanita, her mouth open in disbelief.

When Judge Ellis cleared his throat, every eye turned to him.

"Ira Galway, please approach," the judge intoned.

Ira glanced at his mother, who urged him forward. "Yes, sir," he said.

"Do you have anything to say?"

Ira's chin dropped to his chest as he muttered something.

"Speak up!"

Ira looked at the judge. "May I say something to Mrs. Mendez?"

Nell heard Juanita draw in a breath. Without waiting for the judge to give permission, she walked to Ira's side. "Yes," she said firmly. "Speak to me."

Judge Ellis threw up his hands in a gesture of surrender and leaned back in his chair.

"I never meant... After Uncle Calvin was killed, I always carried the knife. My pa never knew I had it, but I thought one day, I might need it. That day when..." He hesitated.

"Javier," Juanita said softly.

"When Javier and me was fighting, I realized he was stronger and bigger, and I thought..." Tears rolled down his cheeks, and he shook his head, signaling he had no more words.

Juanita wrapped her arms around him. "Shhh,"

she whispered. Then she turned with him to face the judge.

Judge Ellis spoke. "Ira Galway, you have admitted bringing a weapon with you that day. You have admitted using it. You have acknowledged that while your intent was to wound, you did in fact kill Javier Mendez. Therefore, I find you guilty as charged."

"No!" Lottie screamed.

"No," Nell whispered.

Trey shifted onto the chair Juanita had left vacant between them and wrapped his arms around her.

Judge Ellis banged his gavel on the wooden table. "As for your sentence, that has given me pause. I find I must take into consideration the forgiveness tendered to you by your victim's mother." He drew in a breath and slowly let it out as Nell held hers.

"I see nothing to be gained in putting someone so young away for the rest of his life. I will admit that I felt I had no choice, for the fact is that if I were lenient with you, others would feel that it was because you are white and your victim was not. Others would say that if the situation had been reversed and you had died in that fight, there would be no question regarding the appropriate sentence."

Trey tightened his hold on Nell while Juanita took a firm hold of Ira's hand.

"This has been a most unusual proceeding, and therefore, I feel inclined to offer an unusual sentence. Ira Galway, I sentence you to return with your mother to your home, with the provision that at least three times each week, you spend time at the Porterfield ranch. There, you will work under the guidance of

Mr. Trey Porterfield, completing the chores your victim would have done had he lived. You will not move away or leave the area for any reason until such time as this court agrees. If you do, you will be arrested and imprisoned. Do you understand?"

Nell stared at Trey. Had she heard the judge's words correctly? Was he saying Ira was free to go home with Lottie? To live his life without serving prison time? Trey was smiling, so it must be so.

"Well, speak up, Mr. Galway," the judge demanded. "Do we have an understanding of the terms of your release?"

"I think so… Yes, sir."

"In that case, court is adjourned." Ellis banged down his gavel and stood.

Lottie ran to Ira and hugged him, then turned to Juanita and clasped hands with her, thanking her repeatedly.

Nell smiled. She could not remember a time when Juanita had ever seemed quite so embarrassed. "We should have a party," she told Trey.

He kissed her forehead. "No. We have to get you home. It's high time you took care of yourself and that baby, Nellie."

"We still need to find those missing sheep," she reminded him.

"*We* do not. I'll take care of it."

And she knew he would.

Thirteen

NELL SAW THE FIRST SPOT OF BRIGHT-RED BLOOD ON Thanksgiving Day.

It was the day they had decided would be perfect for the Porterfield ranch's annual party, a party that included neighbors and friends, and that Trey's sister Maria and her husband, Chet, had made the trip from California to attend.

After Ira's trial, Trey had taken Lottie's boys with him to search for the missing sheep. As Trey had suspected, the sheep had been put to pasture deep inside Pete Collins's property, and the man would pay the price for his misdeeds—years in prison and the loss of everything he'd worked so hard to build. The discovery was cause enough for celebration. Lottie and the boys had livestock to take to market, plus the stock they needed to rebuild the flock over the coming year. And because Lottie and her sons knew little of the business end of things, Trey helped out there as well. The melding of the Porterfield ranch with that of the Galways was accomplished, and other ranchers and herders paid attention.

Juanita had argued for postponing the party until after the baby arrived. "Nell Porterfield, you seem determined to tempt fate with this child. There are only weeks to go. We can have a party then."

"But the tradition is to have the party now, in November, before the cowboys scatter for the winter. The tradition is to show appreciation for their hard work, to allow everyone to take a moment to be thankful for a good season."

Trey looked at Juanita. "We are not going to win this, Nita. What if I put Amanda and Addie in charge instead of Nell?"

Nell had grabbed at the compromise he suggested. "Yes, that's perfect. And I promise I will stay out of the way and take a nap every afternoon."

Juanita had given in. Amanda had moved back to the house for the weeks leading up to the party, and Addie came twice a week and stayed over. Everything was going splendidly—invitations had been sent to every cattle and sheep rancher in the area. Several had accepted, although Nell was aware that among the sheepherders, only Lottie had responded. But the telegram announcing Maria's intent to be there assured a successful day no matter who else chose to stay away.

Nell could hear Amanda chattering on to Juanita. She heard Trey laughing at his sister's wild ideas for the party, and that was all she needed to decide she would keep her discovery to herself. For the rest of the day, she watched for any more signs, and when there were none, she breathed easier and told herself it was the result of overdoing things, nothing more.

Maria and her family arrived midafternoon, having

taken the train to Tucson and come the rest of the way with Amanda's husband and children. The cousins were loud and lively, and Nell worried that Joshua might feel left out in the boisterous crowd. But her fears were unfounded. Addie's son, Isaac, took charge and announced that because he and Josh were older, they would take care of "the little ones" as he called them. "Come on, Josh, let's round up these kids and get them out to the barn," he said.

Josh grinned, picking up Amanda's youngest—a girl who had just started to walk—and carrying her outside.

"Well, that's a relief," Maria said, facing Nell and smiling. "So you and my baby brother are about to make me an auntie, I see."

Nell blushed, but she couldn't help liking this new sister-in-law. Maria was direct, like Addie, but there was a softness to her that Nell found very appealing.

"How are you feeling?" Maria glanced around at the chaos Amanda had created with decorations and such. "I hope this isn't too much for you."

"I think it's wonderful," Nell assured her. "A house filled with laughter and love—what could be better?"

Later, she overheard Maria talking to Trey. "She reminds me so much of Mama," she said. Then she poked her brother with her elbow and added, "And the way you look at her reminds me of the way Papa couldn't take his eyes off Mama, even after all those years."

Trey blushed. "That's the plan," he replied. "Years and years of trying to figure out how I got so lucky."

Guests started arriving shortly after noon, and soon, the area between the house and the barn was filled with an assortment of wagons and buggies. Although the herders continued to keep their distance from the ranchers, the courtyard resonated with laughter and squeals of recognition as friends who had not seen each other during the long summer season hugged and found a place to sit while they caught up. The kitchen was a hothouse of activity, with Juanita firmly in charge. Where the women gathered to carry out the tasks of giving a party, there seemed to be no room for making a distinction between those who raised sheep and those who herded cattle. Inside the barn, Rico and some of the cowboys provided the music while Jess called the square dances. Even the herders joined in the dancing.

Just before Juanita and her helpers were about to bring out the food, Trey wove his way toward Nell through the clusters of guests. "Come with me. I've got a surprise for you."

Nell had been standing at the edge of the courtyard, tapping her toe in time to the lively music, trying to decide if dancing with Trey would be tempting fate. She so wanted to share a waltz with him. "What kind of surprise?"

"You'll see. Come on." He held her hand and led her to the house. Every room glowed with candlelight and kerosene lamps, and because the temperature dropped once the sun set, there was a fire in every fireplace. The front rooms were crowded with guests who all seemed to be talking at once, but Trey bypassed those rooms and instead led her down the corridor that connected the front of the house to the bedrooms—the corridor lined with the portraits he had made of family members.

Maria and Chet, Jess and Addie, and Amanda and

Seth stood crowded next to each other at the far end of the hall. They were smiling—even Jess.

"What on earth?" Nell could not imagine what Trey had done.

"Jess, will you do the honors?" Trey asked.

Jess pulled a small hammer from his back pocket and a nail from between his lips and pounded it into the wall.

Then Maria stepped forward holding something covered by a cloth. With Jess's help, she hung the object on the nail.

Finally, Amanda—wonderful, dramatic Amanda—took hold of a corner of the cloth and pulled it free. "Ta-da!"

Trey urged Nell forward as Addie held high a lantern, illuminating the addition to the gallery—a drawing of Nell. "It's official, Nell," Addie said. "Like it or not, you are one of us."

They all burst into applause, and the women pressed forward to kiss her cheeks.

"Do you like it?" Trey asked shyly.

Nell ran her finger over the portrait. Trey had drawn her seated under a tree near a creek, and the sun was setting, the sky behind her alive with lavender and orange. She wore the dress she had worn the day they were married, the night they had sealed their vows. He had recalled every detail down to the slim silver band she wore on her finger. "I love it," she whispered, unable to find her voice. "Thank you." She turned to the others. "Thank all of you. I really don't know what to say."

"It's we who thank you, Nell," Jess said. He

grinned at Trey. "There was a time there when me and Addie thought we might end up having to take care of this guy forever. You've done us all a big favor, taking him off our hands."

"Yeah, Trey," Amanda added. "We're relieved you had the good sense to marry a woman with her feet firmly on the ground. Now when you go off thinking how you're going to change the world, somebody besides us and Nita will be there to set you straight."

"Look who's talking," Trey said. "You were the one driving Mama and Nita loco long before I came of age."

The bell in the yard clanged, announcing the meal was served.

"Let's eat," Jess said as he herded the siblings and their spouses back down the hall, leaving Trey and Nell alone.

Trey stood behind her and wrapped his arms around her as he rested his chin on top of her head. "I'll do one of Josh and one of the baby this winter. I'll have the time, but I wanted you to know how much I love you, Nell. And I wanted you to know that my family is now your family. It was their idea to present it to you this way."

"You made me so beautiful, Trey."

"I draw what I see, Nellie."

Outside, the band was playing a waltz, and they swayed slowly to the rhythm of the music. "Come dance with me," Trey said.

Nell felt a twinge and then a wave of dizziness. Not wanting to alarm Trey, she turned to face him. "I have a better idea," she said. "Go dance with Nita."

He grinned. "She won't do it."

"Don't take no for an answer."

"All right, but I intend to dance with my best girl before this party's over."

They returned to the kitchen where Nell sought the fresh air blowing through the open door while Trey invited Juanita to dance.

"Don't be foolish," Juanita grumbled.

Trey ignored her protests, humming along with the music as he pulled the housekeeper away from the dishes she was filling and led her out the door. Nita was smiling as she passed Nell and laughing out loud as Trey led her to the center of the courtyard. The other guests stood aside, giving them an open space for the waltz. Everyone was smiling—herder and rancher standing side by side, watching the man who had brought them to this time of peace and cooperation.

And as she watched, Nell felt her stomach cramp and a rush of fluid that three times before had signaled the end of a pregnancy.

∽

As he and Juanita waltzed, Trey saw what he had wanted for this community: people with their differences celebrating the things they shared in common—family, children, the beauty of the land. And in that moment, Trey had an image of the future—his children living in a community where differences no longer mattered. All were neighbors. He grinned and looked toward the kitchen where he'd left Nell. She was standing as if intending to come to him, but he saw her grip her stomach and then lean heavily against the adobe wall.

"Nellie!" He ran through the crowded courtyard to reach her.

She was sobbing when he caught her in his arms, and he eased her to sit in a straight chair just outside the kitchen. She clung to his hands as he knelt in front of her. "Tell me what's wrong, Nellie," he pleaded.

"I...the baby...please..." She was incoherent, but Trey thought he understood.

"Addie!" he bellowed.

All conversation and music stopped.

"Addie, come quick," he called, his voice catching with fear. "Shhh," he whispered as he stroked Nell's face and wiped away her tears. "It's going to be all right."

"You can't know that," she managed.

"Here's what I know, Nellie. We—you and me—we're going to be fine. Whatever life throws at us, we're going to get through it. Look what we've survived already—you especially."

"But a child—*our* child," she whispered. "It's too soon, too much, Trey. I can't do this."

"You can't do this *alone*, but you have so many people who love you, Nellie, people who will see us through this, whatever the outcome may be." He was mouthing the words he thought necessary to calm her, but the truth was that he was terrified. All he had thought about these last weeks as her time came closer was the baby—their child—and all the children that might yet come. He wanted to be a father. More to the point, he wanted to be a family with Nell and Josh—and the baby.

He felt a firm hand on his shoulder and heard his brother say, "Let's get her inside, Trey."

"I can walk," Nell insisted as she grabbed hold of each man's arm.

"No." Trey lifted her. When they reached the bedroom, Juanita, Addie, and Maria were already there. The three women bustled around, draping the bed in a canvas sheet, barking out orders to anyone within earshot, and sending the general message that this was not good, even as they tried to soothe Nell.

When Trey laid her on the bed, tears filled his eyes as he brushed her hair away from her cheeks and tried to smile.

"Trey," Maria said, placing her hand on his shoulder. "You should let us attend to Nell. Go wait with Jess and the others."

"I'm staying."

He was aware of the glances that passed among the three women attending his wife, but he was not to be denied. He heard a chair dragged to the head of the bed and Addie's voice. "Well, at least sit down before you fall down, and stay right here, no matter what happens. Agreed?"

He was about to argue, but Juanita fixed him with the glare she had used on every Porterfield child when she expected an order to be obeyed without question. Trey nodded.

Juanita set a pan of water and a stack of cloths on the bedside table. "May as well make yourself useful," she grumbled. "Use these to—"

Suddenly, Nell clutched his hand so hard, he thought his fingers might snap. She let out a guttural sound that rose to a high-pitched scream as her body went rigid.

"What's happening?" Trey demanded, on his feet at once.

"Sit!" All three women chorused the command as they rushed to attend to Nell. Addie climbed onto the bed and knelt so that she was positioned between Nell's bent legs. Maria stood opposite Trey and gripped Nell's other hand while Nita dipped a cloth into the cool water, rolled it, and handed it to Trey.

"Let her bite on this when the pain comes," she said.

"Nita, it's too soon," Nell murmured, her voice weak, her face and neck dripping with sweat.

"Many a child has come into this world earlier than planned," Nita replied, leaning in to brush Nell's hair off her forehead, "including your husband here."

The contraction passed, and Nell closed her eyes, trying to steady her breathing. Trey stroked her hand and looked at Addie.

"I expect it's gonna take some time," Addie said.

Nell bolted upright, gripped Trey's fingers, and looked as if she might explode from the pain.

"Do something," Trey demanded.

"This is the way it goes," Juanita said. "Now you can either be here or wait out in the hall with the others. Either way, you need to understand you are not in charge here."

"I'm not going anywhere." He rinsed a cloth in the water and wiped Nell's cheeks and forehead. "Shhh," he whispered. "Rest now."

"Trey," she whispered, "I'm so very tired and afraid. What if it's like before and—"

"That won't happen." Trey leaned close. "It's

going to be all right, Nellie. No matter what happens. *We're* going to be just fine. Do you hear me?"

He saw tears leak from beneath her closed eyes and wiped them away with his finger. He kissed her temple, smoothed back her hair soaked with sweat, and whispered, "All I will ever need is you, Nell Porterfield."

Once again, she tightened her grip on his hand and Maria's and cried out as another contraction built.

"I see the head," Addie announced. "One big push, Nell. Come on. You can do this."

Trey saw Nell preparing to endure the pain. He placed the cloth between her teeth as instructed, then held tight to her hand as he kept his focus on Addie.

A moment later, he saw Addie smile. "That's it, Nell. Push. Head and shoulders are out."

Nell collapsed back onto the pillows, spent from her efforts, and Addie held a bundle of slime and blood. Trey heard a weak cough and then a mewing cry coming from that bundle.

"Nell, you have a beautiful baby girl," Addie announced as she cut the cord and laid the child in the blanket Maria held to receive her.

"Just let me get her cleaned up a bit," Maria said.

Minutes later, Trey and Nell were marveling at their newborn daughter when Nell went rigid once again, and Addie muttered, "Hold on."

"There's another one," Addie said, bending to her work.

Trey felt a wave of dizziness pass through him, even as Nell released a long, keening cry of pain.

"Push, Nell," Addie instructed. "Come on. Almost there."

Moments later, Addie held up a second bundle whose cry was a good deal stronger than the first child's had been. "A girl *and* a boy," she announced.

Juanita received their son, and after she and Maria washed the second baby, Nita handed the boy to Trey. "Best hope the children favor their mother," she teased.

"Are they…" They were so tiny that Trey was afraid to speak the question uppermost in his mind aloud. But how could anything so small survive?

"They are perfect," Nell whispered, cupping his cheek with her hand as tears of exhaustion and joy ran down her cheeks. "Go find Joshua," she said. "He needs to meet his sister and brother."

Reluctantly, Trey did as she asked. As soon as he stepped into the hall, he was surrounded by his family. "It's twins," he managed and then felt a loopy grin spread across his face. Jess pounded his back while Amanda leaped up and down, squealing like a ten-year-old. Seth and Chet pumped his hand and congratulated him as he moved toward the front door. Outside, he could see their guests all gathered in the yard, their voices hushed as they waited for news.

"It's a boy," Trey announced when he reached the courtyard. The crowd started to cheer, and he raised his hands to silence them. "A boy *and* a girl!" He chuckled and shook his head, because the truth was, he couldn't quite believe what had just happened. Somebody tried to hand him a glass of hard cider, but he passed that by on his way to the corral where another guest had told him the children were playing, oblivious to the drama that had played out in the house over the last hour.

When he reached the gate, he saw Joshua demonstrating the rope tricks one of the cowboys had taught him. "Josh," he called. He motioned for Nell's son—*his* son—to come closer. "Come up to the house with me. Got a couple of people you need to meet."

⁂

The following Sunday, Nell sat in the yard, savoring the cooler days and the sun on her face. Juanita had finally agreed she was recovered enough to leave her bed. "As long as you don't overdo." Between Trey and Nita, Nell feared she might never again be allowed to do anything close to her normal routine.

Josh was feeding the chickens while Trey sat nearby. Trey was always nearby these days, ready to spring into action at a moment's notice should either baby Joe or his sister, Hannah, need anything.

"You know one of these days, you're going to have to get back to work," she told him.

"There's time. Let's get through Christmas and the New Year." He rocked the double cradle Eduardo and the cowhands had made for the twins. "Can't get over how little they are."

"They don't stay that way for long," Nita said as she joined them and pointed to the horizon. "Company coming."

Three wagons followed by half a dozen men on horseback approached the ranch. Nell felt her heart quicken and instinctively moved closer to her babies.

"Hello!" Reverend Moore drove one of the wagons right up to the house. "Hope this isn't an inconvenience," he said when Trey went to greet him and help a group of ladies from the wagon.

"Not at all," Nell heard her husband reply, but she could see he was as mystified as she was as to why so many people had shown up at once.

Lottie climbed down from the wagon and retrieved a large wicker basket before entering the courtyard with the minister's wife. Others crowded around to admire the babies, while the men stood a little apart, talking to Trey. That's when Nell realized that the group included both ranchers and herders, mingling freely as if they were friends.

"Nell?" Mrs. Moore was opening the wicker basket. "Remember when you and I spoke about possibly starting a ladies' guild, a place where the women of the church might gather to knit using local yarn?"

Nell nodded.

"Well, the night your lovely babies were born, I was talking to your sister-in-law."

Lottie stepped forward. "That night, the women got talking, and we thought maybe we might make a few things for the twins, just to see how things went."

Reverend Moore's wife set the basket on the ground and pulled out booties and blankets and caps—some expertly constructed, others endearing because they were so crudely done. A few pieces had even been dyed with dyes from local plants to make them more colorful. Suddenly, the women were talking over one another, laughing as they told the story of each item.

"That blanket Lottie made for her boys years ago,"

a rancher's wife explained when Nell held one lacy piece, the color of sand, up to her cheek to feel its softness. "She promises that with practice, we'll all be able to do something so lovely one day, but somehow I doubt we can ever come up to her talent."

"And here's a shawl for you, Nell." A herder's wife stepped forward and draped the pale-blue wrap around Nell's shoulders.

"I don't know what to say. Trey, Nita, come see," she called.

Trey admired the handiwork, teasing the women about his need for a new winter scarf to wear on the range as he draped Nell's shawl around his shoulders and struck a pose.

"You look like an old codger," Nita told him, and everyone laughed. "I'll get some coffee started," she said, heading for the house.

"Oh, no, Juanita, stay," Lottie said. "We brought refreshments for everyone, and we promise not to stay long."

Trey invited everyone inside. The women exchanged ideas for projects the ladies' guild might take on, while the men gathered in the library to talk and smoke their pipes and cigars.

Nell observed it all from her rocking chair near the fire, her babies sleeping peacefully in their cradle, apparently undisturbed by the conversation and laughter. She could see Trey standing near the fireplace in the library. He had his arm around Josh's shoulders, and whatever the men were discussing made his eyes shine with interest.

After an hour had passed, Reverend Moore led the

men across the hall to join the ladies. "Could we have a word of prayer before we head back?"

Everyone bowed his or her head as the minister thanked God for the many blessings the community had received over the last weeks. He asked for a special blessing for the babies and for Nell, Trey, and Joshua. "Amen."

The word was repeated by every person in the room. Once again, there was an explosion of chatter and pleas from the men to get going before dark set in as the women insisted on clearing away the remains of their refreshments and having one more look at "those sweet babies."

"I'm going down to the bunkhouse to stay the night, if that's okay," Josh announced.

"See to your chores first, Josh," Trey instructed.

"Yes, sir." Josh grabbed his hat and took off at a run.

Trey sat on the footstool next to Nell's chair. "You must be exhausted, Nellie. Why don't I have Nita fix us some tea and a bowl of soup while you get ready for bed."

Nell smiled and brushed his hair away from his forehead. "It's not even five o'clock, Trey, and I have to feed your children."

Trey frowned. "How long before they eat on their own…I mean before they don't need you to…"

The darling man was blushing, and Nell loved that on the one hand, he was shy with her, while on the other, he could barely let an hour pass without touching her cheek or letting his hands linger on her shoulders, his desire written clearly in the furrows of his brow.

"It'll be a while." She opened the front of her dress and camisole before lifting little Joe to her breast.

When Hannah squirmed and protested, Trey picked her up and paced the length of the room and back. "Now, just stop your fussing, Hannah," he told her as he rocked her in his arms. "You'll have your turn."

Later after they had gotten the babies settled and retired for the night, Nell heard Trey rise and pull on his trousers and boots. His habit of visiting Javier's grave each night had worried her at first, but now she understood his need to share his life with his friend. What surprised her was when she saw him pick up one of the babies before leaving.

Mystified, she rose, put on her robe and slippers, wrapped herself and Joe in the shawl the women had brought, and followed Trey.

He was standing inside the fenced cemetery and had positioned himself so that he was standing in a circle made up of the markers of his parents and Javier. He had wrapped the baby in his jacket.

"Trey?" She walked toward him.

He smiled sheepishly. "Didn't mean to wake you, Nellie. Just thought Javier and my folks might want to know how things have turned out."

Nell watched him holding their daughter and realized he had kept his promise to his friend—and to her. For their children, there would be no "us" versus "them." For their children, it would be one world where neighbors worked together to face the challenges and celebrate the joys for generations to come.

Nell rested her head on her husband's broad shoulder.

"We should go in," he said. "You're cold. I'll make you some warm cinnamon milk—it will help you sleep."

"Nita left a pot warming on the stove before she went to bed."

Trey laughed as he wrapped his free arm around his wife and they walked together back to the house. "I really thought once these babies were born, she'd turn to mothering them. I doubt that woman will ever see me as anything other than that sickly boy she fussed over for so many years."

"And you love it," Nell teased.

Trey ducked his head and grinned. "Yeah, I do." Then he stopped walking and turned to face her, his expression sober. "Nellie, we did it. There's work to come, but I want you to know, without you and Lottie and Juanita... Well, men are stubborn, and we're taught from early on that we need to win, but you ladies—"

"We did it together, Trey. Everyone did their part—eventually."

He placed his finger under her chin and lifted her face to meet his kiss. "I love you, Nellie Porterfield."

Nell ran her finger along the outline of his jaw. "And you, Trey Porterfield, are my beloved."

Later, as they lay in bed together, the twins asleep in their cradle and a full moon casting its light on the portrait of Trey's parents that hung over the fireplace, Nell stared at Constance and Isaac Porterfield. And as she drifted off to sleep, for the first time, she felt worthy of her place in this house, this room. This perfect life.

About the Author

Award-winning author Anna Schmidt resides in Wisconsin. She delights in creating stories where her characters must wrestle with the challenges of their times. Critics have consistently praised Schmidt for her ability to seamlessly integrate actual events with her fictional characters to produce strong tales of hope and love in the face of seemingly insurmountable obstacles. Visit her at annaschmidtauthor.com.

THE LAST OUTLAW

Fourth in the epic Outlaw Hearts series from *USA Today* bestseller Rosanne Bittner

The old West is changing—not that rugged outlaw Jake Harkner would let that stop him. Setting out on his most dangerous journey yet, he takes the law into his own hands as he rides into Mexico to rescue a young girl from a fate worse than death. This time, Jake's family and his wife, Miranda, worry that Jake's end will come the same way he's lived his life—by the gun.

"Powerful, beautiful, harsh, and tender stories that take readers' breaths away with their emotional depth."
—RT Book Reviews, 4.5 Stars, Top Pick, for *Love's Sweet Revenge*

For more Rosanne Bittner, visit:
sourcebooks.com

THE HEART OF A TEXAS COWBOY

Meet the Men of Legend

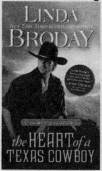

It only takes one bullet to shatter Houston Legend's world. He swore he'd never love again, but with his ranch's future on the line, he finds himself at the altar promising to love and cherish a stranger whose vulnerable beauty touches his heart.

All Lara Boone wants is a name for her baby. She never expected to fall in love with her own husband. Yet when her troubled past catches up with them, Houston will do anything to protect his bride...

> "Fans of classic Western tales will delight in the rough-and-tumble world Broday creates."
> **—RT Book Reviews** for *To Love a Texas Ranger*

For more Linda Broday, visit:
sourcebooks.com

A MATCH MADE IN TEXAS

Welcome to Two-Time, Texas: Where tempers burn hot, love runs deep, and a single woman can change the course of history.

As Two-Time, Texas's first female sheriff, Amanda Lockwood is anxious to prove herself. She takes down wanted man Rick Barrett, but there's something special about the charming outlaw. Common sense says he's guilty...but her heart tells her otherwise.

"A great story by a wonderful author."
—#1 *New York Times* bestselling author Debbie Macomber for *Left at the Altar*

For more Margaret Brownley, visit:
sourcebooks.com

TEXAS BRIDE

Love blooms in unlikely places in this tale by *USA Today* bestselling author Leigh Greenwood

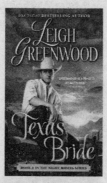

The war has left Owen Wheeler a changed man. Now on the trail of a fellow Night Rider turned traitor, he will stop at nothing to ensure that justice is done.

There's nothing about fiercely independent Hetta Gwynne that should make Owen long to trade his vendetta for peace, but something about her makes him feel like the man he always wanted to be…if only he could convince her to trust in the passion neither of them can deny.

"A joy to read."
—Long and Short Reviews for *No One But You*

For more Leigh Greenwood, visit:
sourcebooks.com

RUNAWAY BRIDES: THE GUNSLINGER'S VOW

An exciting new historical Western series about rugged cowboys and the runaway brides who steal their hearts by *USA Today* bestselling author Amy Sandas

Alexandra Brighton spent the last five years in Boston, erasing all evidence of the wild frontier girl she used to be. Before she marries the man her aunt is pressuring her to wed, she's determined to visit her childhood home one final time. But when she finds herself stranded far from civilization, she has no choice but to trust her safety to the tall, dark, and decidedly dangerous bounty hunter Malcolm Kincaid.

"Pure perfection."
—Romancing the Book for *The Untouchable Earl*

For more Amy Sandas, visit:
sourcebooks.com

CHRISTMAS IN A COWBOY'S ARMS

Stay toasty this holiday season with heartwarming tales from bestselling authors Leigh Greenwood, Rosanne Bittner, Linda Broday, Margaret Brownley, Anna Schmidt, and Amy Sandas.

Whether it's a lonely spinster finding passion, an infamous outlaw-turned-lawman reaffirming the love that keeps him whole, a broken drifter discovering family in unlikely places, a Texas Ranger risking it all for one remarkable woman, two lovers bringing together a family ripped apart by prejudice, or reunited lovers given a second chance…a Christmas spent in a cowboy's arms is full of hope, laughter, and—most of all—love.

"Everyone will be uplifted and believe in the joy and wonder of the season through these wonderful novellas."
—RT Book Reviews

For more from these authors, visit:
sourcebooks.com

Also by Anna Schmidt

The Drifter

The Lawman

The Outlaw

The Rancher